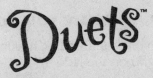

**Two brand-new stories in every volume...
twice a month!**

Duets Vol. #91

Talented Dawn Atkins serves up not one but two
delightful stories in a special Double Duets.
Wedding for One and *Tattoo for Two* are about
two bad girls—and buddies—who come home
again. Mariah hooks up with the sexy Mr. Right
she left at the altar eight years before. Meantime
Nikki shows up with a fake fiancé whose kisses
are a little too real at times! Chaos ensues as
these two girls set things right.

Duets Vol. #92

Versatile Natalie Bishop returns to the series
this month with the quirky *Love on Line One!*
"Ms. Bishop writes with a sizzling intensity...
spirit and depth," says *Romantic Times*.
Completing the volume is popular Holly Jacobs
and *Not Precisely Pregnant*. Bestselling author
Lori Foster notes that "every Holly Jacobs book
will leave you with a laugh and a happy sigh."
Enjoy!

Be sure to pick up both Duets volumes today!

"Mariah, what are you doing?"

Nathan's voice startled her, making her almost lose her grip on the ladder. "I'm...fixing...this valve."

"Don't do that!" He grabbed the ladder, making it wobble. Then she did lose her grip, and suddenly she plopped into a pool of red jelly.

"Are you okay?" He looked down at her.

"I'm fine. Sticky, but fine."

"Give me your hand and I'll get you out."

She reached up to grasp his hand, but the jelly made her hand slip out of his and pulled him partially over the edge of the drum.

Hmm. Not a bad idea. This could be fun.

She reached up, looking innocent. "Let's try again. Lean over and give me both hands." Mariah gripped his hands, and levered as hard as she could....

Nathan teetered for a second, then slid down and thumped into the gelatinous pool.

"Come on in, the jelly's fine." She laughed and met his gaze. But instead of seeing anger there, she saw attraction, heat...desire.

A sexy smile spread across his face. "So, Mariah, you up for some jelly wrestling?"

For more, turn to page 9

"Hollis, I have to tell you a couple of things."

Nikki had to say this fast, because they were almost there and he needed to know the secret.

"Like what, Nikki?"

You're my husband and your name's Warren. No, too abrupt. "I ran away from home."

"Okay." He sounded puzzled.

"My parents and I were a mismatch. They're serious people. Conservative...I caused them some grief."

"But you've grown up."

"Not the way they think I have. See, that's why you're here.... I told them I'd be bringing someone...special."

"Someone special? I'm just your date, right?"

"Well, yes...truth is, I'm hoping you could pretend to be, um, more." Oops, out of time! She'd just pulled up in front of her parents' house and could see the family coming out to greet them.

He blew out a sigh. "Okay. I'll do it. But—"

"Great!" Then, because everyone was watching, she leaned over and kissed him. Instant sparks ignited between them, and suddenly she knew she'd *never* be able to keep her hands to herself!

For more, turn to page 197

HARLEQUIN DUETS

ISBN 0-373-44157-6

Copyright in the collection:
Copyright © 2003 by Harlequin Books S.A.

The publisher acknowledges the copyright holder of the individual works as follows:

WEDDING FOR ONE
Copyright © 2003 by Daphne Atkeson

TATTOO FOR TWO
Copyright © 2003 by Daphne Atkeson

Dawn Atkins

Wedding for One

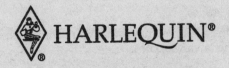

HARLEQUIN®

TORONTO • NEW YORK • LONDON
AMSTERDAM • PARIS • SYDNEY • HAMBURG
STOCKHOLM • ATHENS • TOKYO • MILAN • MADRID
PRAGUE • WARSAW • BUDAPEST • AUCKLAND

Dear Reader,

Exploring the theme of these two comedies—
bad girls go home—was both fun and emotionally
satisfying for me. Rebellion and conformity, success
and self-acceptance, and the importance of friendship
are threads that run through both stories.

Mariah and Nikki go for it—heading off to live
authentic lives. Two girls against the world. Of course,
no one is truly "free to be" in life, and both girls have
regrets and doubts. As their stories unfold and they
fall in love, they both see themselves with new pride
and self-acceptance.

Wedding for One is a story about the one who got
away. It's heartbreaking when Mr. Right slips through
our fingers. That's why it was such a delight to help
Nathan and Mariah fall in love all over again eight
years after their disastrous almost-wedding.

The operation of Cactus Confections is based on
information I obtained from two Arizona-based
candy companies—Ceretta's Chocolate Factory in
Glendale and Cheri's in Tucson, which produces
prickly pear cactus candies, jellies and even a prickly
pear margarita mix like the one Mariah dreams up
and her father invents.

I hope you enjoy Mariah's and Nikki's stories.

Best,

Dawn Atkins

P.S. Please let me know what you think. Write me at
daphnedawn@aol.com.

Books by Dawn Atkins

HARLEQUIN DUETS	HARLEQUIN TEMPTATION
77—ANCHOR THAT MAN!	871—THE COWBOY FLING
	895—LIPSTICK ON HIS COLLAR

To Wanda, my remarkable editor,
who knew this story before I told it

Prologue

Eight years ago

"OUCH. JEEZ. When I said, 'Somebody pinch me,' I didn't mean to really do it," Mariah Monroe said.

"I'm just trying to do whatever you want on your special day," her mother Meredith said, fluffing the frothy wedding veil. "There! Perfect." She surveyed Mariah in the full-length mirror. "Now, aren't you glad we didn't go with that terrible fuchsia minidress?"

"It had *lace*," she said in her own defense.

"And fishnet. Please."

"Whatever." For once, though, Mariah agreed with her mother. This was better. She looked like she'd floated off the cover of *Today's Bride,* and she felt like a princess. Teardrop pearls extended on slender wires from her headpiece, exquisite sequin-dotted lace scallops made a graceful beeline to her cleavage, and yards and yards and yards of satin billowed to the toes of her white satin pumps.

She'd considered hand-painting the dress and creating a papier-mâché flower bouquet, but decided to go traditional for Nathan, who was such a straight-arrow guy. She still couldn't believe he'd chosen her. For the first time in her seventeen years, she felt like she fit in, instead of being kooky and contrary and just plain weird.

At the same time, she felt uneasy, as if she'd disappeared, been replaced by an actress—*I'm not a bride, but I play one on TV*—or a store mannequin, or a collectible doll ready for a display case. She ignored the feeling. This would all be worth it because in the end she'd have Nathan Goodman, who loved her, and they'd live happily ever after.

Abruptly, her mother stopped fussing with Mariah's curls, which she'd pomaded into submission a few minutes before, placed a hand on each of her daughter's temples and looked Mariah straight in her reflected eye. This was serious.

"You have nothing to be ashamed of, sweetie. Some of the best marriages start out with a Pop Tart already in the toaster."

"A what?"

"I'm your mother. You can tell me." Her hands dropped to squeeze Mariah's shoulders in sympathy.

A chill raced down Mariah's satin-bound spine all the way to her pink-polished toes. "What is it you think I have to tell you?"

The answer began to trickle into Mariah's brain at the same time the color drained from her face beneath the chichi makeup her mother had insisted on. In the mirror she looked like a ghost bride.

"Nathan will make a wonderful father. And he thinks you hung the sun."

Hung the moon, she wanted to correct. Instead she stuck to the terrible thing her mother was saying. "What are you talking about?"

"Honey," her mother said in a tone that said Mariah was stretching a joke past credulity, "I know you're pregnant."

"Where did you get that idea?" Mariah realized the answer before her mother gave it.

"That blue box on your dresser. I wasn't snooping—I know you hate me going in your room—but it said 'pregnancy test' really big, so I couldn't help but be curious."

"That was a joke I bought for Rhonda to freak out her boyfriend."

"Pregnancy is nothing to joke about, Mariah," her mother chided. Then she frowned. "Wait. You mean you're not pregnant?"

"No!"

"Oh, dear." Meredith's brows lifted in alarm, then lowered. "Well, it'll still be okay."

Suddenly, Mariah realized a terrible possibility. "Did you tell Nathan?"

"Not exactly. He overheard me talking to your father in the factory, so—"

"Nathan thinks I'm pregnant? But we haven't even... Why would he want to marry me? Oh, God." She covered her face with her hands, stricken with shock and humiliation. "*That's* why he said 'what's past is past. You don't have to explain a thing.' I thought he meant being with other guys, not *that!*"

"Honey, Nathan worships you. And he'll be good for you. He'll help you settle down and stop flitting from thing to thing."

Mariah jerked her face up to confront her mother, hating being reminded that this was how her mother saw her. "I'm not flitting. I'm being me." And Nathan had seemed okay with that, though she'd tried to act more mature around him. They'd only been dating a month when he'd told her he loved her and wanted to marry her—saying the words in a rush, as if they'd been wrenched from him. She'd believed him and said yes without pausing for air. Because she loved him, too. Desperately.

It had amazed her that Nathan had even wanted to *date* a crazy girl like her, let alone marry her. He'd come to Copper Corners with a brand-new business degree from the University of Arizona to take a job helping her father run Cactus Confections. He was serious, stable and responsible. The exact opposite of her. The fact that he loved her had seemed like a miracle.

But it hadn't been a miracle. It had been an act of mercy. He'd thought she was pregnant with another guy's baby—since they hadn't even slept together yet—and he was going to make an honest woman of her. He felt *sorry* for her. Oh, ick.

With that, her Cinderella story burst in her face like a six-piece bubble of Bazooka, leaving a sticky mess.

Well, she knew what she had to do. She couldn't go through with this sham and she couldn't let Nathan ruin his life just to be a hero.

"Tell Nathan to forget it," she told her mother. She lifted her thick skirt and ran for the door, fighting tears.

"What are you doing?" Meredith asked.

"The wedding's off, Mom. Tell everyone." She galloped down the stairs, then stopped at the landing and looked up. "Tell Nathan...." What? That she wouldn't settle for a mercy marriage? That she couldn't bear to be the only one desperately in love? "That I changed my mind. I need my own life, not his."

"Don't run away, Mariah," her mother called to her from the landing. "For once in your life, stick to something."

With the deadly words ringing in her ears, Mariah lunged out the door, desperate to escape. Luckily, at that moment her best friend Nikki pulled up in her battered red Miata with the top down. Relief flooded her. Nikki would understand. They were soul sisters.

Mariah hiked up her dress and climbed into the convertible, not bothering with the door. Satin and lace puffed up to her chin, and flapped over Nikki.

"Phht!" Nikki spit out fluff. "What are you doing? I thought we were going to the church in your parents' car."

"Just drive, okay?" she said, as fat tears rolled through the Honey Luster powder her mother thought brought out the peach in her skin.

"Where to?"

"Anywhere." Then she corrected herself. "Anywhere but the church."

Nikki shot her a puzzled look, then accelerated, throwing them both back in the seats.

At the stoplight, Mariah looked at Nikki in the maid-of-honor dress her mother had urged her to choose. Lavender satin with puffy organdy sleeves and a huge satin bow over the left shoulder. It looked ridiculous on her wild friend, who was more comfortable in black leather and boots than frou-frou girlie clothes. The only thing that looked normal was the funky ceramic butterfly pin Mariah had made for her. "What was I thinking making you wear that dress? You look like Glenda the Good Witch."

"More like Skipper does Dallas," Nikki said with a shrug. "It's not too late to dye my hair purple and wear my mauve snakeskin boots."

Mariah laughed through her tears.

"We're buds, Mariah, you know that. Thick and thin. Anything you want, I'm down for it."

"I know. And I couldn't stand it without you." She leaned over to hug Nikki, organdy crackling.

"Watch out!" Nikki said, as the car swerved. "Hard to see through satin." Still, she grinned. "So, what's up?"

"I'm not getting married."

Nikki slammed on the brakes. "What?!"

A car behind her honked.

"Keep driving," Mariah said. "I don't know what came over me. It's like I thought I was a Bridal Barbie doll marrying Ken and moving into the Dream House. That's nuts. So *not* me."

"But you love Nathan."

"I do." It hurt to say that. "But I'm only seventeen. I haven't even graduated."

"Abso-flippin'-lutely!" Nikki said, pure relief in her voice. "I mean, I was on your side, if marriage was your gig, but, hell, you've got your whole life ahead of you."

"Exactly. What was I thinking? Too *Twilight Zone*."

"What happened to change your mind?"

Mariah told her friend the sad tale of the false pregnancy and the pity proposal. As she talked, an ache began to spread from her chest to every part of her body. An ache that came from losing Nathan and all that she'd believed he felt about her. The zapped wedding fantasy was nothing compared to that.

She felt herself slipping into self-pity, so she grasped at indignation. "He probably thought it was like a duty, now that he's working for my dad. You know, manage the factory, marry the kooky daughter. God. It's so hu*mil*iating."

"At least you found out before you said *I do*," Nikki said, patting her knee through the cloud of satin and netting. "Now you can put it behind you."

"Right. Behind me." But it felt like it was all around her—a big ball of agony she couldn't escape. She knew breaking it off was best—a quick, sharp pain, a bit of bruising, and then the healing would happen. But right now, it hurt like hell.

They drove in silence for a bit. Since Copper Corners only had five streetlights, they were soon speeding along the highway. Mariah surveyed the passing desert landscape—tall, crazy-armed saguaro, clumps of cholla and prickly pear in bloom, chaparral bushes and mesquite trees. They were headed north toward Phoenix on a wide-open highway. Wide open. Like her life had suddenly become. The thought made her feel empty and scared.

As if she'd read her mind, Nikki pressed the brakes, whipped the car into a doughnut, fishtailed in the shoulder gravel and jerked to stop, turned toward the town. "What now?"

"I don't want to go back there and face that," Mariah said fiercely.

"I don't blame you. I don't want to go back, either, and all I have to face is telling my parents I don't have enough credits to graduate next semester."

The best friends sat in glum silence for a few seconds, the cicada hum filling the air, buzzing along with their brains, which were busy sifting options.

Finally, Nikki spoke, her words coming slowly, excitement building as she talked. "I know what we should do...."

"What?" Mariah said, hope rising. Nikki had the best ideas.

"Let's blow this pop stand."

"What?"

"Let's leave. Move to Phoenix. I was going anyway, this summer, unless my parents kicked me out early for ruining their image." Nikki had her own problems, with her father the principal and her mother a teacher at the high school, and both the biggest worrywarts on the planet. Yet one more bond Mariah and Nikki shared—disappointed parents.

"So let's leave now," Nikki concluded.

"Now?"

"There is life beyond Copper Corners, Arizona. You want to mix cactus jelly in your dad's factory all your life?"

"Absolutely not."

"We can stay with my cousin in Phoenix. She can get us jobs at the restaurant where she works. We'll save our money and get an apartment together. We can do our art, theater, all that—just experience what life has to offer—keep it real."

"What about school?"

"Real life will be our school. If you want to get constipated about it, we'll get GEDs."

"Wow." The idea had possibilities. She'd be away from Copper Corners, where she didn't fit in, away from her mother who couldn't help interfering with her every breath, and, most of all, away from Nathan and his mercy marriage.

Maybe it was time to declare her independence. Like in the books. The young rebel makes her way in the world....

Besides, right now she'd do anything to escape the humiliation of going back to town to face the looks—exasperation and worry from her parents, pity from the people in town, and, worst of all, relief from Nathan at being off the hook.

"Okay," she said. "Let's do it." What did she have to lose?

"Killer! We'll pack bags and take off."

Mariah, of course, already had her bags packed—for a honeymoon trip to Hawaii. Her heart throbbed at the thought. She'd been dying to see Hawaii. Even more, she'd been dying to tantalize Nathan with a black lace peignoir she'd picked out for their first time of going all the way.

Forget it. She and Nikki would start a new life in the big city. This was the right thing for her. This tiny town grayed all her colors, clipped her wings. She looked into her friend's fierce, brave eyes and wondered why there weren't more girl buddy movies. Of course there'd been *Thelma and Louise,* but they'd *died,* for Pete's sake.

"No looking back." Mariah held out her hand, her elbow bent, in ready position for their rebel-girls-forever handshake.

"No looking back," Nikki echoed. The girls clasped hands, slid to a fingertip grip, twisted palms, then kissed the air beside each other's cheeks.

Mariah's heart began to race. Her future was wide open now. She could be anything she wanted. How exciting! She tried to stick with that feeling, and ignore the way she throbbed with pain over losing Nathan, like one giant, all-body toothache.

They raced back the way they'd come, stopping first at Nikki's so she could throw clothes in a bag. It took only a sec to get Mariah's stuff, since she was already packed. She tossed out her wad of sexy lingerie, piled in more clothes and shoes, and they were off.

As they drove through town, Nikki caught sight of the church. Dozens of her parents' friends were waiting inside in hushed anticipation for the wedding to start. Nathan was probably standing at the altar waiting for his pregnant bride to waddle down the aisle. Mariah's heart clutched. She grabbed her friend's arm.

"Stop here. I want to look in for a second." She just wanted to see Nathan's face once more. Beyond her humiliation was a deep sadness. She would miss him so much—even if he only felt sorry for her.

They stopped on the hill overlooking the church. Mariah scanned the parking lot. Where was Nathan's gold Volvo? She hitched up her voluminous skirt and hurried down the hill, her satin heels sinking into the soft soil. Reaching the building, she saw through a side window that her mother was talking to the assembled group. To her amazement, she saw there was no groom.

Nathan was not there. She couldn't believe it. Responsible, mature Nathan Goodman had skated on his own wedding? God. She took a backward step. She still couldn't believe it. He'd lost his nerve probably. Realized what a flake she was and hightailed it out of there. The coward. The jerk. The ass.

Anger flooded her. Good. Anger was better than sadness or heartache. She owed Nathan nothing. Not one thing. Except maybe hate mail from her apartment when she got one. As she ran back up the hill, one shoe snagged in the ground and she just left it there, like Cinderella, without a prince who cared to find her.

"COULD YOU PLEASE step on it, sir," Nathan asked the ancient gentleman who'd been the first driver to stop for his frantic wave. "I'm...late...for...my... wedding." He spoke each word distinctly. It was his bad luck to get the one guy who not only drove like he was on a tractor, but who was nearly deaf.

Damn. Nathan looked at his watch. At this rate he'd be half an hour late. He knew he shouldn't have let his college buddies talk him into a bachelor party in Tucson last night. They'd plied him with drinks and exotic dancers. He'd ignored the dancers—all he could think about was making love to Mariah—but to appease his friends, he'd had the drinks. It had been weird. He hadn't been in a bar like that since he'd stopped hanging where his mother's band performed. He'd had enough of constant travel, new addresses every six months. He couldn't wait for a normal life in a nice house in a quiet neighborhood with regular mail delivery and the woman he loved.

Too buzzed to drive home, he'd gone to sleep at one of his friends' houses. When he'd headed home that morning, the rocks his buddies had affectionately loaded into his hubcaps had somehow messed with the axle, and his rear assembly had frozen, leaving him stranded on the highway on a stretch of nothing between Tucson and Copper Corners.

He'd called from a pay phone at a rest stop, but gotten the machine at Mariah's house and no one on the church phone, so they'd just kept driving.

They finally pulled into town—a half hour late as he'd predicted. Surely all of the guests would still be waiting at the church. Mariah had probably been late anyway. She operated on ''whenever'' time. That made him smile, thinking of her sweet face under all that fierce eye makeup and wild hair. He couldn't wait to make her his. She was so amazing. When he was with her he felt stunned with joy at his good fortune.

Doubt flickered through him. She was so young. Maybe too young to know her own mind. Afraid she'd get away somehow, he'd been pretty insistent about getting married. She'd said yes, though— eagerly, too, he reminded himself.

As they passed the 7-Eleven at Cholla and Main, a red convertible bearing a cloud of white caught his eye. He turned to look more closely as it drove away, and saw, to his shock, that it was Mariah in her wedding dress in her friend Nikki's car. Mariah was leaving town? Wait a minute. She must have thought he'd chickened out. Oh, no.

''I...have...to...drive!'' he shouted to the kindly old man.

''Hmm. What's that?''

''Could...you...turn...around?'' He made a circling motion.

''Turn around? Did we miss the turn there?''

The speeding Miata would soon be just a red dot in the distance. ''Never mind,'' he told the old man.

He'd get to the church, explain to the waiting well-wishers, borrow a car and chase her down. The poor girl. She thought she'd been jilted. She was so young, so insecure. She must be devastated. His heart squeezed with the desire to rescue her, tell her it was all a mistake, kiss away the pain....

He was charging up the steps to the church when a stunning thought hit him. Mariah hadn't looked like a bride who'd been jilted. She'd been laughing, gesturing wildly. Even worse, two suitcases had jutted up from the space behind the seats. She'd packed bags. She was running away.

From him.

He was the one who'd been jilted. *Flighty as a butterfly.* That's what Mariah's mother had told him about her. But she was pregnant, for God's sake. Terrible as it seemed, he'd thought that was the one thing that would make her want to settle down with someone like him. Someone stable, who would be a good father.

For a moment he considered chasing after her, demanding she give him a chance. But if she was willing to go off on her own *pregnant,* what hope did he have of stopping her with his love?

"Where have you been?!" Mariah's mother bustled out of the church, flustered, her whole body vibrating with distress.

"Car trouble," he said heavily. "I saw Mariah drive off with Nikki." Laughing...happy...looking free.

"Oh, dear. I was afraid of that," she said. "I made a boo-boo, Nathan. She's not pregnant, it turns out. She canceled the wedding in a huff. You go get her.

I'll tell everyone to just talk amongst themselves for a bit.'' She turned toward the church.

"What exactly did she say, Meredith? About me."

"Oh, I don't know. Something about changing her mind. But that means nothing. Mariah's one big mind change. Also, she said some nonsense about needing her own life. It's just jitters."

He wanted to believe Meredith. With his whole heart. *She needed her own life.* He couldn't forget the air of joy surrounding the two girls he'd picked up as he watched them roar away.

She was only seventeen, hadn't even graduated, wasn't even pregnant. Why *would* she want to settle down? She'd probably come to her senses and figured out she didn't want a dull guy like him. Not now, not ever.

He'd wanted her so much he'd let himself think that would be enough for both of them. He'd just gotten carried away with his dream of settling down safe and sound forever.

"No. I think Mariah knows what she's doing, Meredith.'' His heart aching, he headed inside to let everyone know his butterfly bride had fluttered away.

1
___

Present Day

MARIAH RIPPED off her rainbow wig and clomped up the stairs to the apartment she shared with Nikki, careful to point her flappy feet outward so she wouldn't trip. If she never in her life had to make another Pokémon animal balloon at a kiddie party it would be too soon.

As she unlocked the door, she heard the phone ring. Maybe it was the temp agency with a new job adventure for her. She'd had enough of Party Time Characters, the company she'd created with four friends from her acting class. She was near her six-month mark—her max for sticking with a job—so she'd sell Leon the costume inventory and he could take over.

She lunged for the phone, tripped over her flappy feet and crashed against the table, catching the phone as it fell.

"Hello?" she managed on a gasp of air.

"Hello, sweetie. This is your mother." She always said that, as if Mariah wouldn't instantly know the honey bubbly voice of Meredith Monroe.

"Hi, Mom," Mariah said on a sigh, rolling onto her back. "Thanks for the package. The paint-by-number set was nice, except in my painting class we work freehand.'' Even long-distance, Meredith continued to try to nudge Mariah's life into a shape she recognized. She'd been doing it for the eight years since Mariah had left Copper Corners.

"The saguaro blossom taffy hardly melted at all.'' She hated saguaro blossom taffy.

Sensing the apartment was empty, Mariah unzipped the clown suit and slid out of it, holding the phone against her ear. Cool air washed over her sweaty body. Ahhh. She unhooked her bra and tossed it to the side, then lay back to rub her back on the carpet. No wonder the Disney costume characters went on strike over their working conditions. These costumes were deadly hot.

"Your father will be glad. He knows how much you love his taffy. I'm not calling about the package, though. This is urgent. It's about Nathan.''

"Nathan? What about him?'' Her heart took the same hop it always did when she heard his name. She hadn't seen him since before they'd jilted each other on their wedding day, but she still had that maddening reaction to him. It was like a superstition or a tired habit.

"It's so terrible. We're fit to be tied beside ourselves.''

"What happened?'' Was he sick? Dead? *Married?*

"He's leaving us. We can't believe it.''

"Why is Nathan leaving?''

"It's insane, I know. He's perfect here. Personally, I think he's having a midlife crisis.''

"Mom, the man is only twenty-nine. He can't have a midlife crisis. Why does *he* say he's going?''

"Oh, some nonsense about figuring out what he

really wants. He sounds like you, with your self-actual-whatzit, and live-for-the-moment hooey. Have you been talking to him?"

"Of course not." She never talked to Nathan. She made sure of that. An arrangement she was positive he preferred. She'd been home five times in the past eight years—visits she kept short to minimize her mother's meddling—and though Nathan was always invited for a dinner, he begged off, saying it was a family time.

Which made no sense because Nathan was like a son to her parents. A fact on which she depended, since it took the pressure off her. She counted on Nathan to be the good kid she could never be.

"This just ruins everything for us," Meredith said. "Now your father won't retire."

"What?"

"I've been talking to your father about retiring until I'm green in the face. Finally, he agrees, but *only* if *Nathan* takes over," she said in her dramatic way. "Now Nathan's leaving, so your father won't retire."

"That's ridiculous."

"I know. You have to talk some sense into him."

"You can put him on, but I doubt Daddy will listen to me."

"Not Daddy. Nathan. You have to talk to Nathan. Convince him to stay. It's the only way. You know your father. He won't budge. The Monroe Doctrine—never give an inch. Come and talk to Nathan, please. Otherwise, I don't know what we're going to do." The catch in her mother's voice didn't even sound theatrical. She really was upset.

"Why would Nathan listen to me?"

"Because you're you. I know you don't want to hear this, but he still cares about you."

"Mom, stop it."

"I know, I know. You're past all that. But my point is he'll listen to you."

"I doubt it."

"Wait until you see him. He gets more handsome every year."

"Mother."

"I know, I know. You have a full life. A new boyfriend every time I turn around. Someone like Nathan couldn't possibly appeal to you. He owns his own boring custom-built home, has a dull management job and lives in an annoying little town where everyone supports each other through the good times and the bad."

"Okay, Mother."

"What? I'm agreeing with you. So, just talk to him. Come for a visit. We haven't seen you in a year. You've probably changed your hair color three times since then."

"I don't see the point."

"We miss you. Who knows how long we'll last? You know Fred Nostrad had a stroke and died at sixty-five, not one week after his retirement dinner at the bank."

"Are either of you sick?" Her heart clutched for a second.

"Not so *far*. Though your father's cholesterol…through the roof."

Mariah blew out a breath. It was just Meredith playing the life-hangs-by-a-thread card.

"So, come out. You can see us and remind Nathan

that Cactus Confections is his home. What more could anyone want than to run a candy factory?"

"Maybe something more meaningful?" Though Nathan was pretty much a nose-to-the-grindstone guy. Work was work.

"What's more meaningful than candy?"

"Millions of dentists agree, I guess."

"Your father has been happy here for thirty years. You could have been happy here, too, you know."

"I'm happy *here*, Mom," she said. Absently, she rubbed the callus on her thumb from making Pikachu balloon animals. Well, she *would* be happy as soon as she found another job.

"Well, hel-*lo*…"

The male voice made her look up. Raul, Nikki's latest boyfriend, grinned down at her from the door of Nikki's bedroom.

"Whoops!" Mariah yanked the puddle of clown suit over her bare breasts.

"Don't do that on my account," Raul drawled. He wore tattered jeans and a leather vest that revealed three of Nikki's original tattoos. By the way his eyes took a slow trip along her body, she knew he'd be interested in her when Nikki was through with him.

Raul was sweet, for a biker. But Mariah wasn't interested in him. She'd been taking a break from boyfriends, spending some alone time with the VCR and, lately, she'd felt like painting again. That seemed more fun than dealing with casual boyfriends. She could never quite be herself. She had to stay on guard for when they got serious. Keeping it easy in a relationship was hard work. Right now, the only thing she wanted to change was her job.

She gave Raul a neutral smile. He got the message,

shrugged, then stepped over her on his way into the kitchen.

"Mariah? Hello?" Meredith said.

"I'm here, Mom."

"You don't want Nathan to make a mistake, do you? You want the best for him, don't you?"

"Sure I do," she said on a sigh. She owed him a lot. In a way he'd helped her make her own life. Her parents had lavished their concern, affection and appreciation on him, and that reduced the hassle they gave her and the amount of worrying they did about her. He was the son her father never had and the business partner he would have wanted Mariah to be.

Nathan was probably just having the identity crisis her mother had guessed at. Or maybe he didn't think he could handle the factory on his own when her father retired. Maybe she could talk him through it, get him back on track. Maybe her mother was exaggerating.

"How about if I give him a call?" The thought of seeing him in person made her pulse race and her head pound. Maintaining the two-hundred-mile distance between them seemed the safest bet. She'd call and straighten this all out. Easy.

"Punkin!" Mariah's dad said, meeting her at the door when she arrived two days later. He tugged her into a hug against his portly frame.

"Hi, Daddy." After three failed attempts to call Nathan—she kept panicking and hanging up—Mariah had decided she'd have to talk to him in person. After eight years of silence, how could disembodied voices ever connect about something so important? Face-to-face would be the only way. She was much more convincing in person. Plus, if this was just a Meredith maneuver to get her out for a visit, she might as well get it over with, before her mother faked a heart attack or something.

So here she was home again, for better or worse. She felt the familiar mix of nostalgia, homesickness and being smothered with a pillow. She loved her parents, but she loved her own life more. And her freedom most of all.

After her mother had almost bulldozed her into that false marriage to Nathan, she'd promised herself she'd never depend on them—or anyone else—to make her choices. She'd make her own way, her own decisions. She was a butterfly, light on her feet. There was nothing wrong with that. Butterflies brought beauty into the world. They didn't stay long, but they dazzled you while they were here, and left you breathless with memories when they flew on.

She so much liked thinking of herself as a butterfly, she'd asked Nikki to sketch one she'd had made into a tattoo on her left shoulder. Nikki'd gotten a tattoo, too. And that experience had made Nikki decide to become a tattoo artist. As soon as she got together some bucks, she'd have her own shop.

"You're skin and bones," her mother said, swooping down on her from the kitchen, smelling of rosemary, onion and fresh-baked dinner rolls. "What are you eating? Soda crackers and ketchup soup? Do you have enough money?"

"I'm fine, Mom," she said, leaning down to kiss her mother's powdery cheek. She caught her mother's hand before she could slip a wad of bills into Mariah's jeans pocket. "Really, I mean it."

Before long, her father would do the same, she

knew. It was a point of pride that Mariah hadn't spent the money her parents were forever mailing her or slipping into her pockets or luggage or handbag when she visited. She'd opened a mutual funds account with the money and planned to use it as a retirement gift to them.

She gave up thumb-wrestling her mother. "Thanks," she said on a sigh, and tucked the wad into her pocket. Her eyes scanned the room. "What's all this?" She walked to the dining room table, which held a laptop computer, a globe and stacks of travel brochures. A half-dozen maps were tacked to the walls.

"The nerve center of our retirement campaign," her mother said, joining her. "Your father's finally got the travel bug and we're just itching to get going. We're thinking Barbados." She handed Mariah a thick brochure about the place.

"But now and then I do this." Meredith spun the globe, closed her eyes, then touched a spot. She studied where her finger had landed. "Tierra del Fuego. Hmm. That's a new one. Then I go to the Internet and read about the country."

"That's great," she said, then turned to her father. "I'm glad to see you're finally going to give yourself a break."

"What am I saving all this money for?" he said, though he didn't seem quite as enthusiastic as her mother.

"Now, all we need is someone to entrust with the business," Meredith said.

Her father looked at her lovingly. "You going to help out your old dad, Punkin?"

"M-me. Oh, no, not me, Daddy." She took a step

backward. "I'm just here to talk to Nathan. Didn't Mom tell you?"

"Sure, sure," he said, a shadow of disappointment crossing his face. "Nathan's stubborn about this, though."

She'd been afraid of that. She both dreaded her visit to Nathan and couldn't wait to see him. The whole thing made her feel schizoid. As soon as she got settled she planned to head right over to his house. Drop in unannounced, get it over with.

"This all you brought?" her father asked, hefting her suitcase.

"I'm not staying long, Daddy," she said, trying not to see how sad that made him. "I can carry it upstairs just fine."

"Nonsense. When I'm too old to carry my daughter's bag, they'll have to pry my cold dead fingers from the handle."

Her heart ached at his words. She loved him so much. Maybe she should try to visit more....

"I made a special batch of saguaro blossom taffy for you."

Ick. She'd made the mistake once of telling him she liked the stuff, just to be polite, and now he thought it was her favorite. "Great," she said, swallowing hard. "I can't wait to taste it."

Once in her bedroom, bittersweet memories bloomed, as they had each time she'd returned. The walls were the way Mariah had left them eight years ago, each a bright color—cranberry, purple, lime green, orange. It almost hurt to look. Every inch of wall space was filled with Mariah's artwork. Abstract oils and watercolors in garish ceramic frames, charcoal sketches, etched prints, collages, even some weavings.

She'd been so intense about everything back then. Only Nikki had understood her passion—because she shared that fascination with the mystery in ordinary objects, the magic of creating something, saying something with paint or clay or paper.

Nikki was a great artist. Mariah was only good. Her biggest problem. She had an artistic *streak,* not a path or a yellow brick road to a career.

Over the years, she'd accepted the fact that she didn't really excel at anything. She contributed where she could for as long as she could, then moved on.

Her bureau was filled with jewelry—much of it she'd designed herself. Scarves dangled from the mirror along with a program she'd taped there from the one-woman play she'd performed on talent night her junior year—*Dishwater March.*

She usually didn't unpack, but this trip would be longer than usual, so she opened her bureau drawer. Right on top was the black negligee she'd gotten for the honeymoon trip to Hawaii. She'd tossed it out of her bag when she and Nikki packed to leave. And now here it was in all its sex-kitten glory. Her heart squeezed tight and she shut the drawer with a bang that knocked over a ceramic picture frame.

She picked it up. The frame, which she'd made herself, held the photo of her and Nathan that Nikki had taken just after they'd gotten engaged. In the photo, Mariah leaned into Nathan's chest as if he were a windbreak protecting her from a storm. She looked timid and sad, with flyaway hair and frightened eyes. Her heart pinched at the sight of how insecure she looked.

She was just lucky she'd realized her mistake in time and not married Nathan. What a disaster that would have been. She would have tried to be a suburban wife and failed miserably. Suburbia was not her, though at the time, she'd have done anything to please Nathan. Now she knew she had to be true to herself.

The photo got suddenly blurry and she realized her eyes had filled with tears. The past always made people sad. She'd been too young to be in love. She'd simply had a crush. She'd been infatuated with Nathan's college degree, his four years as a man on his own, his maturity and his confidence about his future.

And the way he'd looked at her. That had been the kicker. Seeing herself reflected in his eyes, she'd felt not goofy and ditzy, but beautiful and artistic. And loved. So loved. But Nathan had probably just wanted to rescue her.

Now he was having some identity crisis and might be about to make a terrible mistake. Maybe, this time, she could rescue him.

2

NATHAN'S TWO-STORY ranch home—just a block away from her parents'—was gracious and classy and very Nathan. The only thing wrong was the garish for-sale sign stuck in the middle of the perfectly trimmed rose bed. The sight made her stomach sink. His house was already for sale. If he'd gotten this far with his plan, convincing him to stay might not be easy.

She followed the curving flagstone path to the huge door, on either side of which was a stained-glass panel featuring a hummingbird on a prickly pear cactus. Before she rang the doorbell, she became aware of an awful honking that at first she thought was a goose in great distress. After a few seconds, she realized it was a musical instrument being played badly.

She rang the bell and the tortured fowl fell silent.

In a second, Nathan stood in the doorway wielding the saxophone he must have been abusing. The instant he saw her, his face lit with amazement, then joy, and he gave her a smile as big as the one he'd delivered when she'd agreed to marry him.

"Mariah? What are you...?" Abruptly, the light switched off and the smile faded. "Your mother sent you."

She didn't answer. She was busy storing the memory of the joy on his face when he'd seen her.

"My mind's made up, but come in," he said.

She stepped into the entryway, which was tiled in whitewashed saltillo, with a high ceiling and a bright airy feeling. It opened into a spacious step-down living room at the far end of which a floor-to-ceiling window invited her into the backyard with its glittering pool, lacy palms and Mexican bird of paradise bushes, iridescent with feathery orange blossoms.

"Your home is beautiful," she said. "It's so…" *you*, but that would sound silly.

"So predictable, so yuppie," he said with a tired sigh. "I know. Come in and sit down." He laid his saxophone on the marble entry table.

She stepped down into the living room and went to sit on the white leather sofa, soft and yielding as a gloved hand. Seeing Nathan again made her heart pound so hard she was afraid he might hear it. She concentrated on the bad art on the wall—completely dead couch paintings, probably chosen because they matched the decor, not for their power. She wished she could have advised him. "I didn't know you played the saxophone," she said.

"My mom was a musician, so I thought it might be in the blood. I think maybe the talent skipped a generation."

"Practice makes perfect," she said.

"Maybe," he said. His eyes flicked over her. "It's a little early for cocktails, but something tells me I'll need a drink for this." He must have caught the hurt look on her face because he quickly added, "Because of why you came." He headed for the wet bar in a glassed-in alcove. "Would you join me in a glass? I've got a nice cabernet here."

"Sure," she said. Wine might calm her nerves, but she wished it weren't red, in case she spilled some onto his elegant white carpet.

He did look good. Her mother had been right about that. More handsome and more masculine than he'd been eight years ago. At twenty-one, he'd been wiry. Now his shoulders and chest were broader and more defined. What she could see of his arms beyond the short-sleeved shirt were tanned and muscled. He must work out. Maybe in that fabulous pool.

His hair, cut fashionably short, was thick and dark. His face looked older, too—more experienced. There were crinkles at the edges of his eyes, and his smile was more relaxed than she remembered. Though he wore a button-down, well-pressed oxford shirt and crisp khakis, he'd be equally at home on a golf course, in a corporate boardroom or a smoky biker bar. In fact, he'd look great in black leather.

With practiced moves, Nathan took two goblets from the rack overhead, opened the bottle and filled the glasses. She realized he probably did this on all his dates. As much as Mariah tried to avoid it, her mother had kept her apprised of the details of Nathan's love life. In fact, she was pretty sure he had a girlfriend right now. A math teacher, if she wasn't mistaken.

Nathan came toward her carrying the wineglasses. Now that he knew why she'd come, his smile seemed flat, and she could tell he was being careful not to touch her fingers as he handed her the goblet.

"So, how have you been?" he asked, sitting at the

farthest end of the sofa, like he thought she might pounce on him.

"Fine. Good, actually."

"Your mother tells me you own a condominium now?"

"Hardly. I *rent* an *apartment*. Nikki's my roommate."

"Oh, yes. Your wild friend." He shook his head in wonder. Nikki bewildered lots of people. "Living in an apartment is probably fun."

"Oh, yeah. Gallons of giggles." She thought of the funky building with its erratic air-conditioning and thin walls, on which they had to pound to get the rock band next door to stop practicing after midnight. Not to mention the deals she and Nikki had to make to keep the phone and gas hooked up.

"It's nothing like this, that's for sure," she said, waving out the window. "I bet you come home every night from a hard day at the candy factory and dive into that crystal cool pool, huh?"

He shrugged as if it were nothing. "How about work? Your mother says you're acting. Community theater? A play you wrote?"

Oh, for God's sake. She'd written the skits for most of the costume characters they took out to kiddie parties, but that was hardly theater. "Meredith tends to embellish," she said. "Actually, I'm between jobs right now."

She just couldn't bring herself to explain that she'd turned over her clown suit, Barney costume and Power-puff Girl tights the day she'd left, and told the temp agency to put a hold on her job application until she settled this family situation. "Enough about me,'' she said, uncomfortable with the way his blue eyes seemed to dig down inside her. ''Let's talk about you.''

Nathan gave a weary smile. ''That's why you're here, right? Guess we might as well get to it.''

Very cool, Nathan congratulated himself. He couldn't believe how relaxed he'd sounded, considering the fact that the woman who'd flitted through his dreams for the past eight years had suddenly lighted on his sofa. He wanted to move very slowly so she wouldn't zip away. That was stupid, though. Mariah had come here with her own agenda, not to restart their abandoned relationship.

She was prettier than the photo her father'd let him have. The camera deadened her electric blue-green eyes, doused the life in her face, dulled the gleam in her golden brown curls. She'd done something to the ends—bleached them blond. An interesting effect that made her look exotic. Though he'd left plenty of distance between them on the sofa, Mariah's intensity seemed to fill the room all the way to the predictably high ceiling.

He thought about the last time he'd seen her, zooming down the highway, in a sea of white satin laughing her way away from him with Nikki, her partner in crime. He often wondered how things would have turned out if he'd gone with his first impulse and grabbed a car, chased her down and dragged her back. But those were just late-night thoughts with one too many scotches in his bloodstream. They were past all that now. It was about time he realized it and moved on.

"So, I hear you're blowin' town," Mariah said. "What's the deal?"

The *deal* was that he'd finally figured out why no relationship seemed to work, why he could be surrounded by people, busy with work he enjoyed, and still feel dead bored and lonely as hell. He'd been holding a torch for Mariah since she drove away from him eight years ago. He was a complete idiot. "I just think my life should be more…"

"Meaningful?"

"Exactly."

"As my mother says, what's more meaningful than candy?"

He laughed. "Your mother's something else."

"I know. And, Nathan…" She looked down, then up at him. "I really appreciate all you've done for my parents—looking out for them, working with my dad these past years."

Mariah's words made Nathan realize how much more mature she'd become. She'd seemed so scared and uncertain at seventeen, he'd wanted to protect her from everything. Now, besides being more beautiful, she'd become more confident, more sure of her place in the world.

"It's been a pleasure," he said, pushing away his observations. "They're great people. Like family. But I think it's time for me to move on."

His words seemed to worry her. For a second, he had the insane hope she didn't want to lose him. "What are you thinking of doing?" she asked.

"I'm not sure. I signed up for a conference to explore my options. It's a retreat for business people tired of business."

She was trying not to laugh, he could see. Her face had always revealed every feeling. "A retreat for businessmen? Isn't that an oxymoron—like jumbo shrimp or military intelligence?"

"Not at all." He'd explain it in its best light. "They have career counselors there. Motivational speakers. Aptitude tests, résumé analysis and, I don't know, discussions. Speakers who've broken off and done different work. It's a place to start."

"Mom thinks you're just having an early midlife crisis."

He barely managed a smile. "She may be right. I just know I can't stay here."

"My parents are completely freaked about you leaving."

"We've got good staff. The floor manager, Dave Woods, could probably take over. He's not as passionate about the product as your dad, but he'd do fine. As far as that goes, we could hire a headhunter to find someone your dad likes."

"That would take a while, wouldn't it? Maybe you just need a breather. A vacation or something?"

"A vacation won't do it. I've decided."

"What does your girlfriend think about you leaving?"

His eyes shot to her. "How did you know...?"

"How else? Meredith, who knows all and tells all."

He smiled. "She doesn't know all, I guess, since Beth and I broke up a couple of weeks ago."

So that was why he was leaving. "I'm sorry, Nathan, but you might be able to work this out. Sometimes things seem bad—"

"Beth's not the reason I'm leaving." Except that his very lack of feeling for her had proved he had to get away. "I just need to go," he said firmly.

"You've got your house up for sale." Mariah worried her lip.

"Yeah. I figure I'll find a place in southern California when I'm out there for the conference."

"You're moving to California without a job? With housing prices the way they are? That's not very sensible."

He shrugged. "I'll play it by ear."

"This doesn't sound like you. Are you sure you're feeling okay?" She pretended to check his forehead for a fever.

He braced himself against the sweet brush of her fingers and managed a smile. It was out of character, but if he didn't break out, do something different, he'd never stop clinging to the impossible.

"The kind of life you're thinking about is not as romantic as it sounds. It's uncertain and kind of scary." She slid closer to him on the couch. "Believe me. I'm living it."

Her lips were so red, so inviting.... After that first kiss eight years ago at the dry creek make-out spot, he'd have done anything for more of that mouth.

"Definitely not you," she concluded, shaking her head.

"That's the point. I've had enough of being me." He wasn't about to explain that *she* was the reason he needed to escape. "And how is it you know what's me anyway? We haven't seen each other for eight years, when you ran away from me." He gulped. He hadn't meant to go there.

"I wasn't running *from you.* I was running *for me,*" she said. "Besides, at the time I thought you were doing the same thing, remember?" She smiled wistfully, laughed a little.

"Of course I wasn't doing that. I—"

"I know, Nathan," she interrupted. "Drunken bachelor party, rocks in the wheel, slow ride with Farmer Jim, everything. It's fine. We were just lucky my mom made that remark about my Pop Tart in the toaster."

"Your what?" What was she talking about?

"Never mind. I just mean my mom did us a favor by telling me you thought I was pregnant." She seemed troubled by what she'd said, so she glanced away from him, out the window. "Oh, look, there are some baby quail under that mesquite." She rushed to the window carrying her wine, clearly wanting to change the subject.

"They were born in the yard a couple weeks ago," he said, following her to the window. "You should hear their parents squawk them into line."

She was silent for a moment, watching the birds. She spoke, still looking out the window. "You were marrying me under false pretenses, Nathan."

He had the insane desire to take her by the shoulders, turn her and tell her the truth. *I wanted you no matter what. Pregnant and all. I loved you. I still do.*

As if she'd read his mind, she turned to face him. Maybe she felt the same.

His heart stopped and he held his breath, waiting for her to say it.

"We would have made each other miserable," she said with a short laugh.

His heart started up its slow, sad rhythm and he released his breath. "Yeah," he said, swallowing hard. "Miserable."

"Thank God we're past all that." She lifted her glass to clink against his. "It was for the best."

He clinked back and managed a smile, but he couldn't echo her toast. "So, now I'm taking a page from your book. Hitting the road, being free. You should be happy for me."

"Freedom's not good for some people."

"Thanks a lot."

"No offense, but how could you give up all this?" She indicated his living room.

"Would *you* want to live here?" he asked.

"Not me!" She stopped. "Sorry, I just mean, this is you."

Maybe, but he figured turning his life upside down would keep him too busy to mope about her.

"It looks like you're serious about leaving." Mariah sighed as she headed back to the couch. "So, what should we do about my parents?"

"They'll be fine," he said, but guilt tightened his gut. He did hate hurting Abe and Meredith. They'd been like parents to him—or at least the way he thought parents were supposed to be. His mom had been more like an older sister, way too relaxed about her motherly duties. Abe and Meredith counted on him and now he was letting them down. He wished he could fix that.

And then, looking into Mariah's face, the solution came to him. It was a long shot, but it would give him a way to keep Mariah too busy to poke around in his motivation for leaving. "If you're really worried about them, why don't you stay?'' he said. ''You could take over for me.''

''Are you out of your mind?'' Her glass sloshed.

He caught it before anything spilled. ''Not at all. You've had business experience. You managed a restaurant and a boutique, didn't you?'' The idea was sounding better and better, except for the horrified look on her face, which made him want to grin. He hadn't wanted to grin in a long time.

''I was a waitress and sold jewelry on consignment. Like I said, Mom tends to exaggerate.''

''You learn a business from the ground up anyway. If you're smart and motivated, the sky's the limit.''

''Tell that to the Caravan Travel Agency. I motivated them right into a three-month slump with a couple of my out-of-the-way trip ideas. Turns out there are reasons some places are out of the way— like ankle-eating fleas and no flush toilets.''

He shrugged. ''I could teach you all you need to know before I leave. You said you're between jobs. Maybe you need to try stability on for size—changing jobs can be a rut, too.''

''I could never stay here. My mom's probably already picking out paint to redo my room and signing me up to sing in the church choir. It would be crazy.''

''No more crazy than asking me to stay.''

She gave him a long look. ''I suppose so.'' She paused. ''When do you leave?''

''In two months, when I go to the conference. How about you? How long will you be in town?'' He hope he didn't sound too interested.

She didn't answer immediately, and he could practically see her mental gears whirring through their calculations. "I'll stay until I figure out what to do about my parents. And you." She gave him a Cheshire cat grin he'd never seen before. Eight years ago, she'd been too uncertain to act mischievous around him. What the hell was she cooking up? The prospect of finding out made him happier than he'd been in a long, long time.

"So how was Nate?" Nikki asked Mariah the next day when she called home.

"Great," she said.

"Nate the Great. Poetry. How did he look?"

"Great."

"If you don't give me details right now I'll go moshing in your Madonna bustier and get it all sweat-stained."

"Okay, okay. He looked the same. Better. More built, more masculine, more confident. I don't know."

"Does he still act like he's got a stick up his—"

"Nikki!"

"Well, really. He's definitely a *Wall-Street-Journal*-with-breakfast-martini-after-work guy."

"He's different now. He wants to discover himself. It's kind of cute, really." She explained Nathan's desire to search for meaning in his life. "He kind of reminds me of me."

Her friend paused. "Jeez Louise, Mariah. You're still hot for the guy, aren't you?"

"No more than any woman would be. He's still a babe, and I'm only human."

"So, sleep with him. That'll clear the cobwebs from his psyche. Talk about *finding* himself. Whoo, baby."

"That would be manipulative. Besides, I doubt he wants to sleep with me." Not true. She'd definitely felt vibes. That was gratifying, but unsettling, too. "It would just complicate things."

"For who? Two months and out, remember? How deep can it get in two months?"

That was the rebel girls' philosophy on relationships. In two months, the sex was still fresh, both of you were on your best behavior, solicitous and eager to see each other. After two months, you started taking each other for granted, stopped doing the dishes at each other's place. Soon, the guy was scratching his belly and belching in front of you, and you stopped wearing makeup and lace teddies.

On the other hand, Mariah had begun to weary of the constant change. That's why she'd taken a time-out on dating. That way she didn't have to be on guard against leading someone on. It was lonely, but at least no one got hurt.

"He might get too attached," she said.

"Right," Nikki said. "*He* might."

"There's no point to it, Nikki. If I convince him to stick around here, which is where he belongs, I certainly won't be staying. The best thing I ever did for Nathan Goodman was to climb in your car and drive away from that stupid wedding."

"Take a breath, girlfriend. I'm not the one who needs convincing."

"Anyway, what I have to do is get him through

this career crisis, so he can realize he's happy where he is. I've got two months."

"Two months, huh?"

"Yeah, until he goes on some kind of self-discovery retreat in California."

"Nathan Goodman at a retreat? You're kidding!"

"Crazy, huh? Hell, I could probably teach the thing. If you can take a class in it, join a club about it or buy a self-help book for it, I've taken it, joined it or bought it."

Nikki paused. "You could, you know."

"What?"

"Teach him. Give him his own private retreat. The Mariah Monroe Institute of Self-Discovery."

"Hmm. Not bad…" Actually, it was a great idea. And it could be a shortcut to keeping him at Copper Corners. "I could. I could teach him to meditate, do yoga. I could even do a little Gestalt therapy with him."

"Absolutely."

"And you know the best part?"

"What?"

"He'll hate it. Left-brain guys like Nathan hate meditation and energy flow, exploring their emotions, any of that stuff. The yoga postures will make him feel silly."

"And when you ask him to get in touch with his inner child?"

"He'll run screaming from the room, forget all about that stupid retreat and realize the grass is greener right here in Copper Corners."

"Sounds like a plan."

"It couldn't be better." She gave Nikki a list of

self-help books, manuals and materials to send to her, and hung up.

It would work out great. In a few weeks, her father could safely retire, leaving his factory in the hands of the newly contented Nathan, and Mariah would be back on track to whatever the future brought. Whatever it was, it had to be better than Copper Corners and the church choir.

3

TWO DAYS LATER, Mariah rang Nathan's doorbell. He opened the door, then stared at her, blinking sleepily. "What the...?"

"Help me," she said, tilting some books and the yoga mats from her arms into his.

He backed up under the load. "It's six-thirty in the morning. What are you doing here?"

"The early bird catches the self-awareness worm," she said, pushing past him and loping into the living room, where she dropped her folded easel, collection of CDs, candles and more books on the cocktail table. The truth was, she hadn't been able to sleep for planning her approach, so she'd rushed over.

"What are you talking about?" He followed her, looking dazed.

"It's simple. I'm going to give you your own personal retreat," she said. "You don't need to spend a fortune to sit around and whine with a bunch of corporate clods in California. I can get you straightened out right here—a customized self-awareness experience in your own home."

"What?" He looked completely stunned. Maybe she should have given him a few minutes to wake up.

"Sure. I've got all the experience you need," she said patiently. She proceeded to recite her self-actualization curriculum vitae while he stood blinking at her, holding the books and yoga mats.

As she talked, she noticed how great he looked right out of bed. There was a charming pillow crease on his cheek and dark, sexy stubble that made him look born-to-raise-hell-ish—an effect completely ruined by the monogram on his robe and the crisp seams at the shoulders and sides. The thing had been steam-pressed. Sheesh. This guy was so far from free-to-be she couldn't imagine where he got the idea that was what he wanted. It should be a cakewalk making him long for his uptight way of life.

"So what do you say?" she asked when she finished with her credentials.

Nathan blinked. "I need coffee." He dropped the armload of stuff beside hers on the table and turned toward the kitchen.

"Oh, no coffee," she said, rushing to stand in front of him. "Caffeine is a stimulant. It confuses the body's natural wake-up mechanism."

"The body's what?"

"Look, Nathan. I'm going to save you a ton of money and wasted time. We should get started right. No coffee."

He looked at her for a long moment. "I need a shower," he said.

"Dress comfortably," she called to him as he dazedly lumbered off, mumbling to himself. "We'll start with meditation and yoga."

While he was gone, Mariah decided to create the ambience she needed. She closed the wooden shutters so the room's light dimmed and laid out the yoga mats so they would face each other. She lit a cluster of scented candles and two cones of patchouli-vanilla incense. Considering the size of the room and the high ceiling, she lit three more for good measure.

Then she put on a soothing CD that featured bird songs, wood flutes and soft percussion. Perfectly serene. The light filtered in through the cracks in the shutter slats, cozy and dim. She sat for a moment and took a few calming breaths. She had to be very convincing, so he would trust her to help him.

Hearing footsteps, she opened her eyes. Nathan stood a foot away. He was naked to the waist, wearing only black jersey shorts. Short shorts that showed legs that definitely got regular workouts. His hair gleamed with water and his pectoral muscles were perfect. A light dusting of dark hair filled the middle of his chest and arrowed to his waistband. He looked like he'd stepped out of an ad for Calvin Klein underwear.

"Aren't you a little chilled?" she asked, finding it hard to swallow. She wished desperately she'd brought one of those long-legged East Indian coverall robes for him to wear.

"It's a hundred and five outside." He coughed and waved the incense smoke away. "Where are the marshmallows? Smells like you started a campfire in here."

"That's incense," she said, trying to focus on her task. "Scents are mental cues, bringing direct sensation to the brain. Just breathe it in like this." She took a deep breath, then burst out coughing. Okay, maybe she'd lit a couple too many cones. Her eyes watered.

Nathan picked up three of the smoking cones, moistened his finger and extinguished them. "Before the fire department gets here, okay?"

"If you insist." Cough, cough. "Now sit on the mat, and we can get started."

He obeyed her, sitting across from her, his legs crossed in a decent imitation of her lotus position. Great definition on those legs.

"So, what did you decide? You going to let me help you?"

He gave her a look that made her nervous. He had something up his sleeve. "On one condition."

Uh-oh. "What's that?"

"That you work with me at Cactus Confections."

"What?"

"Just assist me. I'll show you the business and what I do and let you get a feel for the place."

"I told you I won't stay."

"Think of it as research so you can help your dad hire my replacement."

"That's ridiculous, Nathan. We don't need your replacement because you'll be staying."

"I think you'll like it."

"No way."

"Take it or leave it. I'll do what you want if you'll do what I want. Even steven." His blue eyes crackled at her.

"Even steven? That's so high school."

"Maybe so, but that's how it's gotta be." His jaw was firm.

Okay, what would it hurt? She'd take a tour, admire the place for Nathan's benefit while she straightened out his life. "You drive a hard bargain, Nathan Goodman."

"I'm a businessman." He waved at the lingering smoke. "And you set a mean fire."

"Very funny."

"Okay, how does this go?" He closed his eyes and said, "Ommmm."

"If you're going to make fun, then forget it."

"Sorry." He grinned mischievously at her.

"We've got to tap into your intuitive sense of what you need. It's a mind-body-spirit thing. Right now, you're all up in your mind. We need to engage your spirit and your body. Get all your parts working together."

He pretended to ponder the idea. "Get my parts working together, huh?" There was a crackle of sexual interest in his eyes that she chose to ignore.

"We'll start with meditation, then yoga, which should free your energy and increase your awareness. Then, we'll...well, we'll go from there." She wouldn't mention Gestalt therapy yet. Or his inner child.

"And you'll come with me to the factory, right?"

"As long as you do what I say."

"Yes, O Mistress of the Soul Search. Your wish is my command." He pretended to salaam.

"Nathan," she warned, fighting a smile. She hadn't seen the playful side of him during their short weeks of courtship. He'd been so serious then. They both had been. He'd been just starting his career and she'd been trying not to blow it with him. Plus, they'd been so hot for each other that most of their time was spent making out, while resisting the hunger to go further. Nathan had thought they should wait because she was so young, and he wanted her to be "ready," whatever that meant. And then, after he'd proposed, he'd wanted to wait until they were married. It had been so sweet...and sexy. Very sexy.

"So, let's get meditating," Nathan said, bringing her back to the present.

"Oh. Okay." She had to stay focused. "Close your eyes and I'll lead you through a visualization. Just follow along. If a thought comes into your mind, notice it, then let it go."

"Okay."

His broad chest rose and fell, his breathing deep and even. The muscles of his chest and legs rippled a little as he swayed slightly. Even his feet looked strong....

"Now what?" he asked, opening his eyes, catching her staring.

"Oh, um, where was I? Oh, yes. Close your eyes again." The truth was, she'd never been that great at meditation, even when she wasn't staring at a gorgeous, nearly-naked man. She found it impossible to slow her mind or settle it on one idea. She loved the music, the candles and the calm, even if the serenity of the experience didn't last more than a few moments for her.

"Take a deep breath in through your nose, then blow it out slowly through your mouth, counting to seven slowly. Let your cares flow out with your breath. Slow, slow, let it flow out, disappear on the air... Going, going, gone." She watched him breath out slowly, exactly as she'd instructed. God, he was handsome. *Focus,* she told herself. "Your breath removes toxins from your body. Now you must remove toxins from your thoughts...."

NATHAN DID what Mariah told him to do—sucking in air and blowing it out. He was more aware, all right. More aware of Mariah. He could smell her, even over the smoky incense and the cloying scent of the candles, and could practically hear her breathing.

"Now, imagine yourself in a peaceful place," she said in that sexy voice of hers, velvet against his ears. "Absolutely serene. Nothing but pleasant sensations."

Pleasant sensations, huh? In his mind, he moved to his pool. Cool water, soft motion. Very pleasant. Except then Mariah appeared in a tiny bikini, looking almost edible. Mmm, even more pleasant. She dived to him, all wet and wild. Soon that perfect mouth was doing something way more interesting than whispering in his ear. Oops, he was getting an erection. Did it show? He hoped to hell Mariah had her eyes closed.

He cleared his throat, and tried to think about baseball, or burning a batch of prickly-pear jelly, or bungling his tax return. Anything to stop his body from revealing its response to his meditation on Mariah.

It was no use. "I'm not getting anywhere with this," he said, his voice raspy. "Maybe we should do something more active. Like jog a couple miles." Or ice-cold showers.

"Relax, Nathan. It takes time to develop your ability to focus. Be patient. Whatever comes up for you, release it.''

He wasn't about to ''release'' what had ''come up'' for him, that was for sure.

''Let your mind carry you to a place you'd like to be,'' Mariah purred.

Instantly he went there—in bed with Mariah, with those trim legs wrapped around his back. Oops. He jumped to his feet. ''I need water.'' *Ice water, strategically applied.*

''No coffee, now, remember?'' Mariah called to his retreating back. His retreating, *muscled* back, and his tight butt and strong thighs. At least she'd have a few seconds away from all that raw manhood. She'd hardly been able to keep words coming out of her mouth for the animal awareness she felt. Being this close to him made her whole body—scalp to soles—tingle.

On the other hand, her plan seemed to be working. Already, he was bored out of his mind, asking to do something more physical, jumping up for a drink of water.

In a moment he was back. ''So, let's move on to that yoga thing,'' he said brusquely, slopping water as he gulped it down. ''Something with movement to it.''

''Okay, but tomorrow we'll try this again and you can build up your tolerance. Meditation is key to your self-discovery.''

He muttered something that sounded like ''God help me,'' but she didn't pursue it. Things were going according to plan.

She started with an easy warm-up, then some simple postures—Rama's Easy Pose, Stretching Dog, Standing Sun Pose, Tree Pose, then the Dancer Pose. Luckily, he was a quick study and had great balance. She dreaded having to adjust his postures by touch. Putting her hands anywhere on his body would be tough to do without showing some reaction.

"Don't rush your movements," she said, watching him do the Easy Fish, which required him to arch his back and reveal the incredible line of each abdominal muscle. "It's a smooth movement and a slow stretch. That's it. Yoga is a deep muscle activity, so don't underestimate its power." Damn, he was in good shape.

She explained the Easy Bridge, which required lying on his back and thrusting his pelvic area upward. She didn't demonstrate because it was too suggestive. "Hold it, that's it, hold it...." Man, could he hold it! She was dying. She couldn't help imagining how he could use all that holding in bed with her. "Now release."

He released the position, thank God.

"This next posture is the Cobra," she said. She demonstrated for him, lying on her stomach, palms braced parallel to her chest, then pushed her upper body into a slow curve meant to resemble a cobra about to strike.

"Nice technique," he breathed. He lay on his side, propped on an elbow, his chin resting in his palm, his eyes glued to her chest. There was an edge to his voice that made her realize that all the stretching and holding and panting was having an effect on him, too. She was partly pleased, but mostly nervous.

"Now you," she said.

"Okay, but I don't think God meant me to bend that way." He rolled onto his stomach, put his hands in place and pushed up. "Ow," he said. "Is this supposed to hurt?"

"Not if you're doing it right. You don't want too much strain on your back." She checked the angle of his arms, lying on her side almost under him. At that moment, his elbow gave and he landed on her, tipping her onto her back so they were chest to chest.

"That's much better," he said, his eyes gleaming. "You're right. This yoga stuff is powerful."

The moment stilled. Nathan's terrific body was right on top of her, his face inches away, his mouth so close. How she wanted to kiss that mouth. Would it feel the same as it had eight years ago? She began to tremble. This was insane. "Nathan, we don't want... I mean this wouldn't be good." She pushed at his chest, but he stayed stubbornly in place.

"There's still something between us, Mariah," he whispered hoarsely. "I can tell you feel it, too." His eyes locked on hers and she knew if she held his gaze any longer they'd be trying some positions that were more likely to be in the *Kama Sutra* than her yoga book.

"What's between us is just...just...nostalgia." She squeezed her eyes shut.

"Nostalgia? That's a new name for it."

"You know what I mean," she said shoving him off and sitting up. She straightened her leotard and smoothed her hair. "I think that's enough yoga for today," she said primly.

"If you say so, O, Spiritual Advisor," he said, a

trace of a smile on his lips, "but I was just getting the hang of it."

"We'll do more tomorrow."

"Great." More wicked twinkling.

"But you have to behave yourself," she warned, knowing her own face was still flushed with heat.

"Oh, absolutely." He crossed his heart.

"I mean it."

"Oh, me, too."

"You're impossible," she said. "Tomorrow, we'll start fresh. I have some more ideas."

"Mmm, I can hardly wait."

"Oh, don't be so sure," she said, deciding she'd start with counselling. That would make him completely uncomfortable and put an end to this flirtation. "I'll leave a couple of these books for you to look over, and the mats and candles. You can practice the yoga positions on your own."

She picked up a few of the career counseling books to do a bit of studying, and started toward the door.

"Where do you think you're going?" Nathan asked.

She turned to him. "Home. We've finished for the day."

"Uh-uh. We had a deal. You're coming to the factory."

"Today? But I'm not dressed," she said, indicating her leotard and gauze skirt.

"Go get dressed. I'll meet you at CC in one hour."

"But—"

"No buts. We made a deal."

Damn, he was going to get technical on her. She'd definitely have to figure out a way to turn this to her advantage.

4

MARIAH PULLED INTO the parking lot of Cactus Confections precisely an hour and a half late. What better way to prove to Nathan that it was a waste of time to drag her into the business than to show him she had no sense of time? She'd never deliberately goofed up before, but she'd decided it could be fun. A new way to be creative.

The solid sandstone building with Cactus Confections in copper letters across its face brought back complicated memories—love and frustration, comfort and boredom.

She pushed through the glass door and met the delighted smile of Lenore, the receptionist who'd worked there forever.

"Mariah, honey, you're here! Your daddy said you'd be coming to work, but I didn't expect you today. Gimme some sugar."

Lenore wore the same blond beehive with a little curlicue at the top she had always worn, and her nails were as long and sharp and fire-engine red as ever. Mariah's father hated when she painted them in the office, since the fumes interfered with the candy smell he loved. "It's so good of you to help the poor man," she whispered, enveloping Mariah in her soft hug.

"I'm not here to work," she said, stepping back. "I'm just here to, um, observe, get a feel for the place."

"Oh, I see," she said, smiling a your-secret's-safe-with-me smile, a dimple in her chipmunk cheek. What the devil had Mariah's father told her?

"Louise, get your hiney in here," Lenore shouted over her shoulder into the business office. "Mariah's starting work today."

"I'm not working. I'm just...never mind."

Louise, Lenore's twin, leaned out the business office door, where she served as bookkeeper. "Hi, there," she said, with a tentative wave of a hand that she swiftly withdrew. She was as shy and thin as her sister was chatty and chubby. "You've grown up so, um, pretty," she said.

"Thanks," Mariah said, though the woman was obviously just being polite. Mariah's fingers flew to her curly hair, the tips of which she'd bleached white, and she looked down at her baggy pants, black tank-top and studded bracelet. Pretty, she wasn't. Arty, maybe. Interesting, but not pretty.

"Is that my girl I hear?" Her father's booming voice came to her and he marched down the hall toward her. He wore his big green cooking apron, so she knew he'd been in the mixing room. "About time you got here. Ole Nate's been champing at the bit to put you to work." He put his arm around her. "Come on, I'll take you to him. Isn't it great to see her?" he asked Lenore.

"Just wonderful," Lenore chirped.

"We'd better get going," Mariah said, uncomfortable in the Kodak moment of it all. She hurt inside, feeling loved and valued and dead certain she'd disappoint these people. She had the urge to run before she could actually let them down. Instead, she followed her father down the hall past his office to a frosted-glass door, stenciled with Nathan's name and title.

Nathan looked up, then glanced at his watch and frowned. He'd noted how late she was. She tried to look innocent.

"Here's your new partner," her father said to Nathan.

"Dad, I'm not a partner, I'm—"

"Observing, yeah, yeah. Anyway, Mariah, Nate here has been my right hand. He knows everything I know and does half of it better," her father said, resting a hand affectionately on Nathan's shoulders.

"I've just done what needed doing, Abe. You set up the business and now it practically runs itself."

Affection passed between the two men and Mariah felt a surprising jolt of loneliness. What would it have been like to share the workday with her father in the family business? To have him describe her as his "right hand."

Suffocating, that's what it would have been. She'd have been controlled, bossed, fussed over, and watched every minute. Thank goodness she'd escaped.

"You should be very proud, Abe," Nathan continued. "You've left a tremendous legacy."

"Hold on. I'm just retiring, not dying. I'm just handing it over to you two."

"Dad, I'm just—"

"Observing. Right. Well, I've got to get back to

the gumdrops. I'll leave you two…all on your own."
He gave Nate a wink.

A wink! Like there was going to be hanky-panky
or something. She felt herself blush and fought it
down. She was relieved to see that Nate had turned
a matching pink. She changed the subject. "I guess
I'm a little late."

"Ninety-two minutes," he said, his brow dipping.
"I thought you'd reneged on our deal."

"I just lost track of time. I tend to do that. My
mind is such a whirly-gig." Her stomach tightened
at the words. She usually fought the airhead impres-
sion she sometimes left because of the way she
dressed and how her brain spun, kaleidoscope-like.
She believed you could be professional without being
all linear and uptight. With Nathan, however, her job
was to intensify the effect. She needed to be airhead
incarnate.

The misrepresentation would be worth it to be
done with this and gone. Plus, the more irritated he
was with her, the less attractive he'd be. Men who
got annoyed with her were complete turnoffs. Which
was exactly what she needed to be around Nathan—
turned *off*. "I just can't help being a butterfly."

"Right," he said, rolling his eyes at her. Perfect.
She'd already gotten the eye roll. Soon she'd get the
heavy sigh, the head-shake, then the lecture. She'd
argue, and it would be happily downhill from there.

He looked her over. "I see you're dressing for
success."

Oooh, even better. He was already insulting her.
"So, this is your office," she said, ignoring the dig.

"It could easily become yours."

She gave an exaggerated shudder. It was so *not* her. The place looked like a museum display of an office—practically shellacked into neatness. Perfectly arranged file folders, everything at right angles. There were no stacks of paper, no open books, scattered pens or left-over fast-food meals. If Nathan was as hopelessly anal-retentive as he seemed, frustrating him would be easier than she'd thought.

"I'm just finishing up analyzing the month's receipts and the profit-loss statement," Nathan said. "It's all on computer. I'll show you if you'll step over here."

"Oh, I believe you," she said, barely glancing his way.

"I had this software customized to suit our process," he said. "With it, I can track cost per candy, and—"

He looked up as she started the steel-ball perpetual motion pendulum toy clacking on his desk. "Go on," she said innocently. "You can track…?"

With an irritated sigh, he reached out and stopped the steel balls from knocking together. "Would you come here and look at this?"

"Maybe later. I'm deadly with numbers." She grinned sweetly at him, then picked up a manipulable desk sculpture made of small metal diamonds shaped around a magnet, and changed its rectilinear shape to a helix.

He did *not* like that, she could see. This was fun. "Why don't you show me the plant?" she asked.

"All right." Nathan pushed away from his desk, stood and came toward her, wearing a long-suffering expression.

At the doorway, she paused to brush her finger on a bad painting on the wall, so that it hung slightly crooked. Then she picked up a huge geode from the top of his bookcase to examine its purple-and-white crystal interior before placing it on a lower shelf before she walked out, watching Nathan as he followed.

Sure enough, he paused to straighten the picture and replace the geode. She smiled. Things were going like clockwork.

At the end of the hall, Nathan pushed open a double door into a wide hallway where the factory began. The hum of human activity, machinery, and steam filled the air, along with the familiar smell of her childhood—candy cooking. Nathan led the way to the first archway. "The mixing room. Where we put it all together." He led her farther into the room.

"I remember," she said. "When I was a kid, everything in here seemed so huge." She'd loved to watch her daddy work with the gigantic mixing bowls with their huge mechanical stirrers.

"Almost all of our products—the jelly, jellied candies, taffy and lollipops—come from the juice of the prickly pear cactus fruit," he said, sounding like a tour guide. "Summer is prickly pear harvest time. Over just six weeks each summer, we process all the juice we'll use for a year's product. We had an exceptional harvest this year. In fact, we'll be freezing a substantial amount for next year. Here's where it starts." He indicated a huge vat where red bulbs of cactus fruit bobbed and bubbled in boiling water.

"Once the fruit is softened, we crush it with this." He indicated a wooden device.

"The wine press from Italy," she said. "Dad was always so proud of that."

"Yep. He got it straight from a vineyard. Anyway, after that, the juice is strained, then sent through these pipes," he indicated shiny brass tubes overhead, "to the separate areas to create each kind of candy."

He moved to a stainless-steel tub. "Here is where we make our most popular item—jellied candy squares. Here we add lemon, corn syrup and eventually gelatin," he said.

The juice bubbled in the drum, cranberry red, giving off a tart steam that filled her nose. She paused to identify the elements. "Lemon, lime, cranberries and cotton candy all rolled into one great smell."

Nathan took a quick, short sniff. "It's nice, I guess."

He walked over to a man who reached up with a pole to switch off a valve, then scooped out some of the red jelly, which he allowed to fall slowly back into the bowl.

"How's the consistency, Jed?" Nathan asked the man.

"Better. That new coil evened the heat like you said it would."

"Great," Nathan said, his eyes alight with satisfaction.

He was proud of his work here, she could tell, but she wouldn't mention it. Not yet. He'd just deny it.

"When I was little, Dad would let me add ingredients sometimes." She'd loved watching the corn syrup cascade into the mixture, a river of sweetness.

"It was like Willy Wonka and his chocolate factory, only for real."

"Sounds like you loved it here."

Whoops. She didn't want him to think she missed the place. "It got old, though. Imagine every day as the day after Halloween. Pretty soon if you see one more piece of candy you want to throw up."

"Exactly. Imagine eight solid years of Halloween. That's why I need to move on."

This was backfiring. She had to point out the good things about the place to encourage Nathan to stay, but not give him the idea she'd ever consider staying herself.

"The problem was me, not the factory, Nathan," she said. "When I started getting into trouble, Mom grounded me here while she did the bookkeeping and reception work."

"What did you do that was trouble? When I met you, Nikki and you were doing a lot of ditching."

"I straightened out once I met you. Nikki and I used to hitch to Tucson or Phoenix, go to art shows and underground dances. Some drinking and carousing. Meredith thought she needed to crack down."

Chained to the factory, she'd grown to hate the place and the way its false promise of sweet fun hid the sticky grip of duty and routine.

"You were a kid. Kids rebel. I'm sure your mother was just doing what she thought was best."

"She pay you to say that?"

"I just know Abe and Meredith love you."

"Yeah. They do. Too much. That's what makes it hard. I've always disappointed them." Just being who she was seemed to hurt them. Sometimes her uniqueness felt like a badge of honor. Other times, it felt like a scarlet W of weirdness.

"Maybe if you talked to them you'd find out they feel differently."

"I'm fine, Nathan. My parents are fine. You're the one on the self-improvement kick, remember?"

"Right," he said, but he held her gaze, cupped gently, the way you'd hold a fuzzy dandelion. *I'm here for you. You're okay just as you are.* There it was—that look of acceptance that had made her say yes to him when he'd proposed. She'd just melted into that look, heart and all.

But she'd grown up and accepted herself now. She didn't need Nathan *or* that look. She broke the gaze. "How about the rest of the tour?" she said and shot ahead of him so that he had to gallop to catch up with her.

He showed her where they squirted the jelly into jars, where they stretched the saguaro blossom taffy—its pale orange and green strands looped by the industrial-sized stretcher as if it were skeins of thick, silky yarn—and where they extruded the mesquite-honey meringue buttons, and slow-cooked the syrup that went into the hard candy and novelty lollipops shaped like saguaro cactus, coyotes and cowboy boots.

In the processing room, she watched the sheets of cooled jelly get cut into shapes. As a kid, she'd loved the magical way the designs appeared and the unused jelly paste peeled away to be remolded again. She loved the assembly line with its jerky machinery and geared conveyor belt that had seemed almost alive. "This place looks exactly like when I left."

"Unfortunately, it *is* the same as when you left. We need new equipment, but your father doesn't think the capital investment's worth it. Luckily, Benny Lopez, our mechanic, has a way with a steam valve you wouldn't believe. I think he puts a spell on the boilers. They practically purr when he goes by."

They glanced into the formulation and tasting kitchen, where her father experimented with new creations or brought clients to impress them. It was empty. "Abe hasn't tried anything new in a while," Nathan said.

That fact struck her as sad. On the other hand, he was about to retire, so maybe it made sense. Who would come up with new formulas after her father was gone?

"I think there was a jalapeño jelly he was working on, though," Nathan said and went to the refrigerator. He pulled out a sample jar. "Want to try it?"

"Why not?"

Nathan spread a bit of the bright jelly on a tasting biscuit. Mariah opened her mouth and he held the cracker for her to taste. The air grew tense with the intimacy of the moment. She extended her tongue to accept the cracker. Her lips closed, brushing his finger and he made a sound.

She could almost see the electricity pass through him. Then it hit her, jolting her to her toes. The jelly's tartness and the chili's burn seeped into her mouth, which filled with saliva. She wanted to taste Nathan, too.

She could see he wanted to kiss her, was about to move forward. She remembered those lips—they knew when to be rough and demanding, and when to be soft and teasing. She licked her lips, waited...

"There you two are!" Her father's deep voice bellowed out.

They jerked apart as if stung.

"Mariah, I want you to meet Dave Wood. He's the floor manager and my chief cook. He's the wizard who keeps things rolling around here."

"Miss Monroe," Wood said, bending slightly in greeting. "You should be wearing gloves and a hair net in this room. As should you, Mr. Goodman." He looked at them the way a disapproving valet would look at the profligate playboy he served.

"Dave runs a tight ship," Nathan said.

"Aye, aye, Captain," she said, saluting him as she clicked her heels together. Woods nailed her with a look. *The boss's airhead daughter.* Even though it was what she wanted him to think, she felt wounded. He hadn't even given her a chance to prove it.

"Dave could take over this place if he wanted to," Nathan said to her.

"My job is fine as is," Dave said.

"You'll want to shadow Dave," Nathan said. The idea seemed to annoy Dave, so she knew getting on his wrong side would be an easy way to make herself unwelcome around here. Hair nets, huh?

Their last stop was the packaging room, where Nathan described the shipping process. She could hear pride in his every word. Her task was to reinforce that pride, while helping him work through this strange spell of dissatisfaction.

"It's obvious you love this place," she said.

"Maybe all that's wrong is you've been taking it for granted."

"You think that's what's wrong?"

"Maybe. I just don't think Cactus Confections is what's bugging you." And a man who couldn't stand a decorative rock being moved didn't seem a likely candidate for running off to find himself. There was a sadness in his face, a disappointment almost, that she couldn't figure out. "We'll know more once we've tried a few more exercises."

"Exercises? That sounds scary." She could see he was trying to lighten the moment. "Will there be a rack involved? 'You vill work in ze vactory and you vill *like* it.'"

"I was thinking some counselling," she said.

"Counselling?" He pretended to shudder. "I'd rather have the rack."

"Relax. I'll go easy on you. We won't get to the primal screaming until the third day."

His eyebrows lifted. "What will the neighbors think?"

"That you're finally getting laid right."

"What makes you think I need that?"

"Look at you." She gripped the muscles below his neck, trying to ignore how terrific he felt. "You're tight as a coiled spring. If you were getting what you need, you'd be more loose."

"Sounds good. Maybe you could help me, um, loosen up?"

Her mouth went dry. "Sex isn't the only way, you know."

He stepped toward her, close enough to kiss. "Just the best," he murmured. Was he serious or teasing?

Why on earth had she brought up sex again? It was her traitorous subconscious that wouldn't let her forget how much better Nathan had been at making out than the frantic high school boys she'd gone all the way with. He knew how to take his time, how to give her pleasure....

"Where's the harm?" Nathan whispered. "We can start with just a kiss." His lips met hers.

The word *just* didn't belong anywhere near that kiss. She felt lit up inside. His lips were firm against hers. His tongue pushed its way in, and he shifted his mouth to reach more of her. She made a sound and her knees gave a little. His arms went around her, tight and secure.

She remembered him holding her this way all those years ago—making her feel safe, protected and *so* desired. But this was even better because this Nathan was more mature, more sure of what he wanted than the Nathan of eight years ago.

She just wanted to let go in his arms, keep kissing him and being kissed by him. She knew Nathan would never let her fall.

A fist of rational thought muscled into her dazed brain. She was letting one kiss turn her back into the needy teenager she had been once. This was absolutely *not* part of the plan. She broke off the kiss and shoved at his chest. "Enough!"

"But I don't feel loose yet," Nathan said, reaching for her.

"Then take a hot bath," she said, trying to catch her breath. "I came here to work, so let's work. Show me a spreadsheet or something."

What in the world was she saying? She made a

wobbly turn toward the corridor that led to the offices, gratified at the shocked look on Nathan's face. Good. He had no idea what she'd do next.

The problem was neither did she.

THAT KISS HAD BEEN a mistake, Nathan told himself in the shower the next morning—lighter fluid on the embers still glowing in his heart for Mariah. He was an idiot to tempt himself with the impossible. Mariah had moved on. He should, too.

He'd heard that men sometimes locked onto their first loves and stayed stuck. That was obviously his problem. Eight years was too long to hold on to someone who'd flown away.

He shoved his face in the pounding stream and promised himself no more flirting or kissing or touching. Period.

There was good news, though. There was a chance he could get Mariah hooked on the factory. She'd loved seeing the place, he could tell, and she'd stared, hardly breathing, at the spreadsheet while he'd explained it. Fascination was probably what accounted for the odd trembling he'd felt her doing. He, on the other hand, could hardly keep from grabbing her and kissing her.

She definitely liked being back at Cactus Confections. Hell, she even loved how it smelled—something he was no more aware of than the air he breathed.

She'd always been a sensitive person. That was one of the things he'd loved about her. She'd made him more aware of things—sunsets and cricket rhythms, the textures of things. Like skin and mouth… His mind locked on the kiss in the tasting kitchen.

Talk about tasting. He'd wanted to swallow her whole. *Forget it,* he told himself, toweling down roughly. If he kept himself in check and played it right, he could get Mariah to take his job. Then he could leave with a clear conscience, knowing Meredith and Abe would be fine and Mariah would have found her place in the world.

She'd be here any minute for more self-discovery baloney. She'd said therapy was the plan for today. He could only hope she wasn't as good at psychology as she was at kissing. He did not intend to confess the real reason he wanted to leave Copper Corners.

He sighed, heading into the bedroom for clothes. He had to have some coffee. Screw the body's natural wake-up mechanism. For this, he'd need fortification.

5

"I SMELL COFFEE," Mariah declared, frowning at Nathan in the entryway of his house. It was only day two of the Mariah Monroe Institute of Self-Discovery and he'd already broken a rule.

"I needed coffee. Let's just leave it at that."

"If you don't follow my instructions, we won't get anywhere." She was actually grateful for the irritation because it distracted her from how fabulous he looked in a white T-shirt and soft gray shorts.

"Want a cup?"

"Absolutely."

He turned to go and she watched the way the fabric clung to the curve of his butt like a cotton hand. She wished desperately she hadn't told him to dress comfortably. His comfort gave her considerable *dis*comfort.

Walking farther into the room, she saw that he'd set up the yoga mats, dimmed the lights, and lit candles and incense. She turned to him as he arrived with a steaming mug. "You set everything up."

"Like I said, I'm your willing disciple."

"You promised not to make fun."

He shrugged and went to sit cross-legged on his mat, looking unbearably sexy in the dimly lit room.

Mariah took a deep gulp of coffee—the last thing

she needed, since looking at Nathan already made her jittery—and took her place across from him.

"Relax your mind. Think peaceful thoughts," she said, closing her own eyes so as to avoid looking into his and thinking about yesterday's kiss. "Visualize the sun kissing your—" Kissing? What was she saying? "Um, the breeze caressing your—never mind." She broke out in a sweat. "Just do what you did yesterday."

"Yesterday? If you say so," he said with a sigh, lifting a pillow off the sofa and tucking it into his lap. For comfort, she guessed.

While they meditated, Mariah tried to focus on the upcoming counselling session, but she kept feeling this energy between them shimmering like heat above a summer sidewalk. Finally, when Nathan's gorgeous butt floated one too many times before her mind's eye, she said, "Whenever you're ready, open your eyes."

"Mmm." He slowly opened his eyes. Their gazes locked. "That was nice," he said. "Very real."

"Good. We want to make meditation real for you."

"If that were any more real, we'd both be sorry."

Her stomach flipped. Nathan was having the same kinds of thoughts she was. That was good. No, bad. Oh, hell. She didn't want to think about it.

They worked through the yoga postures avoiding each other's eyes the entire time, and when they were finished, Nathan sat up. "So, now you counsel me?"

"Right." Except she'd never be able to do it with him looking like *that*—his face flushed from exercise, his sweat-damp T-shirt clinging to his chest, and his shorts outlining *bumps* she didn't want to be aware of. "Why don't you shower and dress for work, so we can concentrate better?"

"I can concentrate just fine like this."

"It will feel more like a real appointment, okay?"

"Suit yourself."

By the time he came out, she'd opened the shutters and turned on the lights and was seated on the edge of the leather chair kitty-corner to the sofa, which she patted. "Have a seat."

He sat straight up on the edge of the sofa, then tugged at the collar of his shirt.

"Don't be nervous. This won't hurt a bit. We won't discuss anything you don't feel comfortable with, but if you're truly interested in working through what you're conflicted about, I advise you to be as open as possible."

"I *am* open," he said, folding his arms.

Impatience rose in her. *You're blocked. Defensive. In denial.* But she couldn't say that. The Gestalt therapist's job was to carefully guide the client into a deeper awareness of his feelings and thoughts, all while keeping him grounded in the here and now. The key word for the Gestalt therapist was patience.

Which was exactly why two months of training hadn't been enough to turn Mariah into one. She was too quick to draw conclusions, too eager to tell people what to do. Alarmingly like her mother, she'd been sorry to realize.

She took a breath and blew it out, trying to center herself. To do this correctly, she should focus on Nathan's face, watch his eyes, his breathing patterns, become aware of his energy, notice where in his body he carried his distress, and share that with him. The body told the story of the mind if you paid attention. Except she couldn't bear to look so closely at him. "So talk to me about what's happened to lead you to want to change your life."

He frowned. "I don't know. Since I came to Copper Corners, I've had my nose to the grindstone, I guess, and I think it's time to smell the roses, explore the world, do something different."

"Hmm," she said, putting on her most therapist-like expression. "Why don't you tell me more about wanting to leave Cactus Confections?"

"I need a challenge, I guess. You should know the answer to that. Why do *you* leave jobs?"

"Our focus is on you, Nathan."

"Yeah, but maybe your insights can help me." He looked at her steadily. *You tell me yours, I'll tell you mine.*

She sighed. "Okay. I change jobs when I get bored, or when it's obvious I don't belong there any more, or something more interesting comes up, or I feel finished."

"Exactly. I feel just like you do. Finished."

"Except I'm hard-wired for short-term jobs and you're Mr. Stable. You have a career and a degree and special expertise. You shouldn't leap from job to job like I do."

"You have expertise, too." Nathan scooted closer and leaned toward her. "Your problem is obvious. The jobs you take aren't challenging. If you had a job that used your creativity and skills, you'd want to stay."

"That has nothing to do with it. What happens is that I—"

"You just need to make a commitment to a place. If you decided to stay and work through things—"

"Hold it," she said, lifting her hand. "What you're doing is 'deflection' and it's the oldest trick in the therapy book. We're focusing on you, Nathan. Not me."

"First, tell me if I'm right."

"Nathan."

He gave her that stubborn look. Why hold out if it helped?

"I'm not saying I wouldn't like work that kept me interested for a longer time. I did enjoy the travel agency, until that problem with the tours to no-toilet land."

"So, instead of working things out, you decided you were bored." He moved even closer, holding her with his eyes.

"But I *was* bored. And it wasn't that creative."

"So what about your creative jobs—the jewelry business?"

"It started out fine, but then I had tons of orders and it was one long assembly line. Completely dull. I—damn. You're doing it again. Scoot back there." *Away from her.* "I'm the therapist. You're the client."

He moved back with reluctance.

"So, you say you're finished here," she continued. "How did you come to that conclusion?" She held his gaze and managed to keep her therapy focus, too.

He seemed to be having an internal struggle. Probably with whether or not to tell her the truth.

"What are you feeling right now?" she asked. "This minute."

He stared a moment longer and then the word just slipped out. "Empty." His shoulders sagged, signaling he'd decided to be honest. "When I come home, I'm just…there. My house is comfortable and I have everything I need here, but I still feel…"

"Empty?" But she could see in his eyes that what he meant was *lonely*.

He saw that she understood and that seemed to scare him, because he folded his arms and began to babble about being able to run Cactus Confections in his sleep and how startup companies were so challenging, and on and on. As he talked, his expression was flat, his eyes dead. This could go on for hours, with Nathan pretending he was worried about his career, when it was really his heart that hurt. She decided to cut to the chase. "What about the rest of your life?"

"The rest of my life?" His gaze shot to her.

"Yeah. Tell me what happened with your girlfriend." She wasn't being nosy. This was therapy.

"There's not much to tell. It was mutual. We got along well, but there was no fire. We were just passing time with each other." He swallowed hard, then looked past her, lost in emotion.

There was more to it than that. "And does the breakup have something to do with your decision to leave?"

His eyes shot to her, then he looked away, then back. "In a way, I guess. When I start over in California I hope I'll meet someone. I want love in my life."

"Tell me more about this someone," she said, swallowing. The question made her nervous. "What will she be like? How do you see her?"

"You really want to know?"

She nodded.

He leaned forward, his elbows on his knees, so close she leaned back. "She'll be someone with fire in her soul, who'll make me think and make me laugh. Someone I can't wait to come home to so I can see her face, hear her voice, find out how she's been while we were apart... You know what I mean?"

Yes, oh, yes. She swallowed and fought to maintain her therapist composure. She forced her words to come out calmly. "It sounds like having someone special in your life is very important to you."

"Yeah. My life feels empty without her." His eyes flared with emotion. For a second, she thought he was talking straight to her. *My life feels empty without you.* But that couldn't be. How vain of her to think he was talking about her. That had been so long ago. They'd been kids. Or at least she had been.

She felt herself redden. She had to say something therapeutic, but she couldn't come up with anything.

"Don't you feel that way?" he asked her, still leaning close.

"Of course."

"But you probably have your pick of men." His eyes dug into her.

She sighed. "Not really. I've been on my own lately. Dating gets routine."

"I know what you mean."

"It's like riding around the rotating restaurant at

the top of the Hyatt hotel—how many times can you look out at the same landmarks?"

"Exactly," he said.

She'd said the same thing to Nikki, but Nikki shrugged it off. She enjoyed the challenge of keeping things light with men more than Mariah did. "You start saying the same things," she continued, "hearing the same lines, and pretty soon you just want to—"

"Find someone special," he finished.

"I was going to say, 'rent a good movie and eat some red licorice.'"

"Oh, sorry. So, you've given up on finding that person?"

"No, I'm just not looking now, I'm…" What was she doing? Holding her breath? Waiting for Mr. Perfect? Who probably didn't exist anyway? She hadn't felt sure of her feelings about a man since Nathan. And then she'd been a kid—clueless about love.

"You're…?" Nathan prompted.

"I'm…" Nathan was the last person she should be talking about her love life with. "I'm late for work, that's what I am," she said, making a big show of looking at her watch. "I've got to go. I'm not even dressed."

"When did you start worrying about being late for work?"

"I guess you've been a good influence on me. I think we've done enough for today anyway, don't you?"

"Yes, actually. I think I've said enough." He looked relieved to be off the hook.

She didn't need more therapy time anyway. Na-

than was lonely. And he was sublimating that loneliness, claiming it was career dissatisfaction. The obvious cure was a new woman. But Mariah wasn't
about to round up eligible singles. She did not want
to be his dating service. *Sleep with him yourself.* She
knew that's what Nikki would advise her. *That'll
clear the cobwebs from his psyche.*

No way.

But you're lonely, too.

Ouch. She hated when she was honest with herself.
Turned out Nathan wasn't the only person getting
therapy here. Talking about his experience made her
realize that the empty feeling she'd been carrying
around for months—and trying to ignore—was loneliness. She wanted a special someone, too.

So, sleep with him.

Uh-uh. At best, that would be a short-term solution
and, at worst, a heartbreaking disaster. Whatever Nathan felt for her was mostly the backwash of nostalgia. Even if it was more, she never stayed in relationships, and Nathan was the kind of guy who
stayed and stayed. And stayed.

No. She had to find another way to cure Nathan's
loneliness besides sleeping with him. The sooner she
did, the sooner she could leave everything about
Copper Corners that bugged her—her parents, the
candy factory and, most of all, Nathan.

Still pondering, she went home, took a shower and
got dressed for work, choosing the most inappropriate thing she'd brought—a lime-green miniskirt and
tank top.

"Good lord, Mariah. You're not going to work in

that,'' her mother said, watching her dash from her bedroom to the bathroom to brush her teeth.

''It'll be fine, Mother.''

Her mother tsked at her from the doorway. ''Pardon me for saying this, dear, but the Salvation Army is for people who can't afford clothes. Why don't you spend some of the money I gave you on something new? Let's go to Tucson and shop.''

''My clothes are fine,'' she said, scrubbing her teeth.

Watching Mariah critically in the mirror, her mother lifted her hair off her neck. ''Sergei could really work with this.''

''My hair's fine.''

''You have split ends everywhere!''

''Didn't you know? Split ends are all the rage.'' She rinsed her mouth. When she raised up, her mother examined the size label on her blouse. ''Mom...'' she warned, but her mother patted the label in place, smiled and left.

''My clothes are fine!'' she shouted down the hall. She had a terrible feeling it was too late. Meredith, the steamroller, had begun to chug into gear.

MARIAH PUSHED through Cactus Confections' glass doors with a purpose. It was time for the next phase of her plan—getting banned from the premises. Lenore whistled at the sight of her. ''What a hot tamale,'' she said. ''Louise, get out here and see this.'' She turned back to Mariah. ''Won't Nathan be pleased?''

Oops. Maybe she should have gone with the baggy black jeans again, she thought as she headed for

Nathan's office. She'd meant to look inappropriate, not sexy.

"Late again," Nathan said, not looking up.

"Sorry," she chimed happily.

He looked up, then boggled. "You're going to make men fall into the machinery dressed like that."

"Should I go home and change?" she asked innocently.

"Forget it. You're already two hours and twelve minutes late. Take a look at this printout." He turned a bound thickness of computer paper to face the guest chair across from his desk.

She made a cross with her fingers and held it out, as if warding off the undead. "Anything but numbers."

"Look, Mariah. If we're going to do this, you've got to work with me here. Pay attention and make an effort."

"Okay," she said, "but don't think I'd even *consider* staying."

"Right," he said.

"Just so we're clear." Then she smiled. "All right. Tell me everything I need to know." *So I can mess things up.*

Nathan showed her the computer printout and explained the operations of Cactus Confections—the production calendar, hiring policies, the business plan, profit projections, equipment maintenance schedules, payroll, bookkeeping, on and on.

She did her best to act disinterested and confused, but she was annoyed to find it interesting. It wasn't because of the way Nathan explained it, either, because every time he looked at her—or her cleavage—

he lost his thought and she had to remind him what he was saying.

She was mostly pleased that it all made sense. She did have some expertise—Nathan was right about that. She'd seen the inside workings of a small ice cream store, and built her jewelry business and the kiddie party company, so she understood profit and loss and building a customer base.

She hid all that from Nathan, though, with stupid questions. She was soon delighted to see him grit his teeth whenever she interrupted him with an inane query.

"No, we don't have our own trucks, Mariah. That's why we use a distributor, remember?" He tapped the product list. "We count on our distributors to get product out fast and fresh. 'Homegrown, handmade and fresh to you from Arizona's desert,' is our slogan. Stale product means lost accounts. And every account we have is critical."

"Critical?"

"Yes. This is a specialty market."

"What's your advertising budget like?" Whoops. A sensible question.

"Good question," he said, surprised. His gaze zipped to her face—after a little side trip to her cleavage. "You've hit on a problem. Let me introduce you to our marketing man, Bernie Longfellow, and that'll explain everything."

"I remember Bernie. He used to pretend to steal my nose."

"You'll probably recognize the suit he's wearing from back then, too." Nathan led her to a tiny office next to the entrance to the factory floor. He tapped on the door, then opened it.

Bernie was in the act of peeling an invoice off his cheek. He'd apparently been napping at his desk when Nathan knocked. He looked the same, except his hair was now white, instead of streaked with gray. "Hey, there," he said, blinking rapidly.

"Bernie, Bernie," Nathan said affectionately. "You've gotta quit partying 'til dawn. Say hello to Mariah."

"Well, look at you, all grown up." He stood to shake her hand, smiling fondly.

She blushed, feeling twelve all over again.

"I heard you were coming to work for us."

She resisted the urge to explain his error and just smiled.

"Why don't you tell Mariah a little about our marketing plan, Bernie?"

"Marketing plan? Now, let me see… Where did I put that?" He pretended to pat the surface of his desk. Mariah noticed he didn't even have a computer on his desk. "Ah, here it is." He picked up an index-card box and delivered it to her like a present. "Our customers," he said, grinning broadly. "And the plan?" He tapped his skull. "All up here."

"Bernie's an old-style marketer," Nathan explained.

"Marketer, my ass. Pardon the language. I'm a salesman. I don't need no phony-baloney title. I'm in sales. Life is sales. And sales is personality. And relationships. I've got good steady customers who know me and trust me. That's how it works."

"I see," Mariah said. She flipped through the dog-eared cards and saw that in addition to order dates and amounts, the cards contained wives' birthdays and reminders to ask about how kids' weddings had gone. "Impressive," she said, handing him back the box. "Have you had any luck with the new coffee-houses and gourmet grocery stores? Seems to me I've seen some obscure products there—Australian rock candy and Native-American flat breads. I bet our candies would fit right in."

"Fads come and go," he said. "We stick with the basics, and the basics stick with us. I've been here twenty-five years and I know what works."

"I'm sure you do. I know my father counts on you."

He looked pleased at the recognition, then smiled wistfully at her. "I remember when I used to steal your nose. You remember that?"

"Sure do." She hated feeling twelve. "What ads do you run?"

"A couple in warehouse catalogues. A full-color ad in *Candy International.* Advertising isn't the answer. Relationships are the answer. My customers know me and trust me."

"I see what you mean," she said. "You're the expert."

"If you want me to show you how it all works, just stop in. End of the month I make my calls."

As soon as Nathan and she were outside his door, Nathan said, "See what I mean? Bernie's locked in the eighties. That coffeehouse and gourmet store lead sounded good. Why don't you make some contacts?"

"I was just talking."

"I mean it. You can see we could use the help." He paused. "You're fresh and new and—" He ripped his gaze from her chest—"Anyway..." A crafty look came over his face. "On the other hand, why bother? You'd never be able to get around Bernie. He's completely set in his ways."

"All you have to do is draw him into the planning. Lean on his expertise. Made sure he knows he's respected and valued."

"Good point," he said, and she could see he was fighting a grin. "But still. I think it would be virtually impossible."

"I could talk to him," she said. "Just to keep busy."

"Of course. Might as well use your time well." He couldn't hold back his smile. Okay, he'd manipulated her. But if she helped boost business, that would boost Nathan's enthusiasm.

She could always goof up later. Or in between times.

WHEN SHE GOT HOME that night, Mariah's mother met her at the door. "Tada!" she said and waved her arm to indicate the sofa on which she'd laid out three business suits with matching handbags and shoes. "Look what I got for you!"

"Mom, you shouldn't have."

"Sure I should. You're a businesswoman. A tiger has to change his spots."

"Tigers have stripes, Mom, and they don't change them. That's the point of the saying." She went to finger one of the suits—gray and tailored. It was something a funeral director might wear. "This isn't me, Mom."

Then she caught sight of her mother's crestfallen face. She hated that look. She'd caused it so many times as a teen. Since she'd been here, there had already been difficult moments. Her mother had pointed out her bad posture, bad eating habits— "you'll give yourself cancer"—her *colorful* language and how loud she played the stereo.

"All right. I'll wear them." Dressing like a flight attendant for the few weeks of her visit wouldn't kill her. She'd spice up the suits somehow. She knew her mother meant well. Mariah was her only child, after all. Why not give her this small pleasure? Clothes weren't permanent at least.

"Terrific. You can model them for the girls when they come for pinochle."

Before she could object, the doorbell rang. Her mother bustled to the door. "Why, Sergei, what brings you here?" she said, faking surprise.

"A hair emergency, you told me it was," he said, sounding gay, Russian and worried at the same time. He looked past her mother at Mariah. "And you were correct, I can see."

Before Mariah knew it, Sergei had her by the hair, tsking and huffing. She relaxed and let herself be styled to her mother's satisfaction. No matter what, though, she was *not* joining the church choir.

6

"TODAY, WE GET IN TOUCH with your inner child," Mariah announced to Nathan after they'd finished the yoga session.

"My inner child? Shouldn't we let sleeping kids lie?"

"That's dogs, Nathan, not kids. And you need to remember the simple joys of childhood, so we can identify what might make you feel that way again." She folded her legs under her on the loveseat and patted the couch for Nathan to sit. "Let's talk."

"I'm not doing anything goofy." He eased onto the edge of the sofa, looking ready to bolt at the first hint of weirdness.

"Come on. You weren't even goofy as a kid. Lean back on the couch and picture your childhood...."

Eventually, he opened up to her, sharing a touching story of a childhood spent in apartments all over the country as his mother moved from band to band, town to town, gig to gig. Nathan had had a lot of responsibility as a kid—shopping, laundry, errands—and hadn't gotten too close to friends, since a move was always around the corner. But he had loved his mother's music, and that was a perfect place to start.

Finally, she convinced him to bring out that poor abused saxophone and play it for her.

He started out with a few broad squawks, adjusted the reed so the squawks became squeaks, adjusted some more, played a halting scale, then took a few breaths before he launched into an absolutely wretched version of what she eventually recognized as "Satin Doll." When he faltered to the end, he looked at her with a sheepish smile. "Migraine kick in yet?"

"There's a learning curve. How long have you been playing?"

"Two months."

"Two months? Oh. Well, maybe you're just tense. Let's pick an easier song." She sat beside him on the sofa, and flipped through the pages of the music book he had—*Jazz Greats Made Easy*—looking for something simple. At the back of the book, she noticed a cardboard flap that held a CD. "What's this?"

"A CD of the songs. So I can compare how awful I am with how it's supposed to sound, I guess."

"Maybe if you played along with the CD, your timing would be better."

"Mariah…"

She rushed to his stereo, put the CD in place and pushed the number for "Satin Doll." A simple orchestration filled the air. "That sounds easy enough." She hit Stop. "Play along this time." She started the song.

Nathan missed the first few notes the first three times, but she put the track on repeat play, and came to sit beside him as he kept trying. By the tenth time, he was getting it.

"That's enough," he said, clicking the CD remote

so a new song played. "That did help," she said. "Thank you."

Terrific. This was working. A hobby was just what he needed to ease his loneliness. "You're starting to sound good," she said. "I bet if you get good, you could start performing—"

"Mariah, hold it. I'm better, not transformed." He grinned and nodded, though, his eyes twinkling. As he looked at her, his expression took on the eager glow it used to have when he would come to pick her up—almost as though if he didn't see her soon he'd just die.

The CD moved on to a sweet and tender torch song, and Nathan said, "I think my inner child remembers something else I used to like." He took Mariah's hand and pulled her to her feet and into his arms, leading her in a slow dance with assurance and grace.

She tried to ignore how great it felt to have his hands on her—one holding her hand, the other gripping her back. So familiar, so right. But she was delighted to have a semi-legitimate reason to be in Nathan's arms.

"So, tell me about *your* inner child," Nathan said, smiling down at her. "What does she want?" He dipped her, then swept her up.

You. Just you. "My inner child is not the issue here," she said, trying to sound stern.

"You loved to paint, I remember that. And to act. I remember that weird play you did about washing dishes."

"A metaphor for the pointlessness of existence." She blushed. "It sounds so stupid now."

"But you were so passionate about it. Art and life had to be authentic, you said."

"Are you making fun of me?"

"Of course not." He leaned back so she could see his face. "I was charmed. Amazed and in awe."

"Not really."

"Oh, yeah. You seemed so free and wild and full of surprises."

"Compared to you, yeah. You were so serious all the time." She'd liked that about him—and been scared by it, too. How could she ever meet his expectations?

"*Lighten up, Nate,* you used to tell me," he said, smiling. "*Smell the roses.* I remember watching you working on a mural with Nikki. You used your whole body with each stroke." The memory seemed to give him great pleasure.

She felt embarrassed, though, remembering what an oddball she'd been—always trying to make a statement, be different. As if she didn't already stand out with her wild hair, strange clothes and weird ideas. "I wasn't very good, you know. At art."

He shrugged. "Didn't matter. You loved it. That was the point."

She wanted to kiss him then in pure gratitude. "You were so sweet to me."

"Sweet? I remember being a lot of things to you, but *sweet* wasn't one of them." He paused and she knew he meant the way he used to kiss her—endless and slow, then rough and rushed and so hot she thought she might melt and trickle out of his arms.

She had to change the subject. "I'm sorry you're unhappy right now, Nathan. You know, just because things didn't work out with Beth, doesn't mean you shouldn't get out there and try again. You'll find your special someone."

"You think so?"

"Sure." But just then, ridiculous as it was, all she wanted was for his special someone to be her. "She'll be one lucky girl, I know that. You always made me feel special."

"That was easy. You were a wonder. You still are."

She couldn't bear feeling this way—seeing that familiar admiration in his eyes and wanting to believe it and melt into it. Wanting to step up on her tiptoes and meet his mouth. They were both lonely. He still cared for her. What would it hurt?

Against all reason, she was just about to lift her face to his and kiss him, when an earsplitting squeal filled the air. They tore apart like they'd set off the alarm themselves.

Then Mariah smelled smoke and realized the squeal was the smoke alarm. Her gaze flew around the room, finally locating the source—one of the candles for their meditation session had caught on the edge of Nathan's curtain and flames were shooting upward along its edge.

"Oh, my God!" she said, running for one of the yoga mats, which she slapped against the flame-laced fabric, succeeding only in speeding the fire's climb up the curtain.

Nathan ran to the kitchen and came back with a plastic bucket of water, which he tossed at the window, dousing the fire—and her while he was at it.

She shook her dripping arms and surveyed the

damage. The silk drape was ragged and charred, the air was gray with smoke and water dripped onto the floor from the window ledge, making the white carpet dark.

"I burned your curtain. I'm so sorry." She had to shout to be heard over the squealing alarm.

"It's okay," he yelled back. "It could have been worse." Their eyes met. "Something else was just about to burst into flame, anyway. And that would have been worse."

"You're right," she yelled back.

"All I have to say is thank God for smoke alarms."

The smoke alarm chose that instant to cut off abruptly, as if their words had been the proof that it had done its job.

THE DOG MARIAH PICKED OUT for Nathan at the pound looked like a cross between a St. Bernard and a boxer with a square face, upward-pointing ears, and droopy, rheumy eyes.

The saxophone was a start on fixing Nathan's problem, but she wanted insurance, so she'd gone to the Pima County pound to look for another thing to lick loneliness—a pet. This dog had been on death row, so even if he'd been a horrific creature, she would have felt compelled to take him out of there. Luckily, he was a dream, galumphing joyfully around her car on his too-long legs like he was on stilts.

By the time she got him inside, she was covered with mud and claw marks and every window had been streaked with dog spit. He sure seemed a lot bigger in her car than he had in that terrible chain-link-and-cement cage, but he was so full of love—with his inner puppy right there all over his face—that she knew Nathan would love him.

A dog was just the thing to cure Nathan's loneliness. A big cuddly dog he could come home to. A big cuddly dog he couldn't possibly take to California into whatever rat-infested apartment he ended up living in because he didn't have an income.

Nikki's advice on Nathan's loneliness had been absolutely not helpful—*Forget the dog, forget the sax, forget the counselling. Sleep with the man. Get it over with. You'll both feel better. Now that's therapy.* She had to stop calling Nikki. Her advice was getting dangerous.

Once she started home—a forty-five-minute drive—the beast settled down, resting its big mug on her lap, making it hard to steer, snorting and snuffling as she moved. She could feel a little drool trickle down her shin. Oh, well.

She was proud of herself. She'd scored a double coup today. On the way out to the pound, she'd stopped at Louie's Italian Restaurant and convinced the owner that a little jazz would liven up his place. Now Nathan had two weeks to work up a short set of songs. She was definitely fixing up his life for him.

When Nathan opened the door, the dog lunged forward, yanking its leash out of Mariah's hand and slamming her into Nathan's chest. Wonderful.

"Whoa," Nathan said, his gaze lingering on her as she pulled away, until he noticed he'd been invaded. "What the hell is that?" he said, indicating the dog snuffling madly around the living room.

"I think he looks like a Maynard, don't you?" she answered, as the dog dashed into the kitchen.

"What did you do?" Nathan asked her menacingly.

"I got you a dog."

"But I don't want a dog."

"Sure you want a dog. A dog will be good for you. Did you know dog owners have fewer heart problems and live longer?"

"There's nothing wrong with my heart, and I don't want a dog. I'm leaving in two months."

"Uh-uh-uh."

"Okay, I *might* be leaving in two months."

"That's better. He was on doggie death row, Nathan. His days were numbered. How could I walk away? Just give him a chance, okay? I'm sure he won't be a bit of trouble," she said as Maynard trotted toward them carrying a loaf of bread in his jaws. He dropped it at her feet.

"Oh, look at that. He's giving us a gift." She picked up the slobbery, tooth-pierced bag of mangled bread and handed it to Nathan, who accepted it with two fingers, letting it dangle like a dead rat.

The dog gave Nathan a that-wasn't-for-you look, sniffed at each of his kneecaps, then leapt onto Mariah's shoulders and gave her a big, slobbery lick before returning to the floor. Yuck.

She tried to smile. "Isn't that sweet? See how affectionate he is?"

"Right. If you're not scared of drowning."

"Anyway, I have news," she said, going to sit on the couch so she could tell Nathan about the gig at the Italian restaurant. Maynard sat at her feet, desperate longing in his eyes. "Maynard, go see your master," she said, pointing at Nathan.

Maynard evidently misunderstood the command because he leapt onto the sofa and scrambled onto her lap, his haunches spilling past her thighs and his head a foot higher than hers.

"Looks like Maynard's made his choice," Nathan said.

"He's just grateful I saved his life. Once he gets to know you, he'll be your best friend." She turned Maynard's mug so Nathan could appreciate its charms. "Just look at him. How could you send this guy away?"

"Watch the drool," he said as a big glob dripped onto the sofa. She wiped it up with the edge of her blouse. "You'd drool too if you had the chance to live in such a great house with such a great owner."

Nathan rolled his eyes. "You are too much. And I don't mean that in a good way."

Despite his grousing, Nathan agreed to keep the dog overnight. Unfortunately, the dog overshadowed her news about the gig she'd gotten him. Before she left, she gave Maynard a fierce lecture about loyalty and bonding. "Do not slobber on the hand that feeds you." But it went in one perky ear and out the other. She could still hear him whining for her when she drove away. He'd settle down, though. By morning, the two would probably be joined at the hip.

"THE DOG GOES," Nathan said the instant he opened the door to Mariah the next morning. "The damn thing sat by the door and howled for you all night."

Nathan did look haggard—his eyes had dark circles under them and his hair was adorably mussed.

Maynard bounded from behind him and leapt to her shoulders. "Hey, there, boy," she said, staggering a few steps under his weight. "He just thinks I'm his rescuer." Maynard dropped down onto all fours, then to a sit, looking adoringly up at her. Two little puddles of spit dropped onto the porch from either side of his mouth. "Plus, he's probably picking up your rejection vibe."

"Rejection, hell. About 3:00 a.m., I dragged out the Yellow Pages to search for an all-night glue factory."

"Nathan!" She put her hands over Maynard's ears. "You don't mean that. Besides, glue factories are for horses."

"Exactly."

"Come on. He's not that big. Or that bad."

"Sure. He's a perfectly fine dog." He patted him on the head. "Providing you have a ranch. Or a death wish."

"How can I help you if you won't even try?"

Maynard woofed in agreement, spraying Nathan's knees with spit.

"Let's get started," she said, wiping the slobber from Nathan's kneecaps as she moved inside. They managed their meditation session, despite the sound of Maynard's nails on the tile as he dashed around the house. When they finished, they opened their eyes to find tribute items around her, including a grapefruit, an Italian loafer—slightly chewed—and a lovely pair of red silk boxers, which she picked up. "Pretty racy."

"Give me those," he said, yanking them away. "The dog goes." He balled up the boxers, still blushing.

"He's not 'the dog.' He's Maynard. And you said you'd give him a chance."

They had to skip yoga because Maynard was such a pest, but somehow Mariah got Nathan to agree to keep him for a few more days. This time she threatened Maynard—"Love the man or you'll end up at my mother's house wearing a terrycloth bib and eating crumbs under the pinochle table on game nights."

At home, she got ready for her day shadowing Dave Woods and getting banned from the factory. She sparked up the funeral-gray suit her mother'd bought with a zebra-striped leotard, huge silver earrings and a headband fashioned from a tattered feather boa. Ignoring her mother's gasp, she set off for work. At the factory, she stopped by Bernie's office to show him the printout from the Web site of a candy warehouse dealing with novelty items she'd found last night.

By the time she left, Bernie's annoyance had turned to interest and he was busy figuring how to cover the higher overnight shipping costs. She knew enough about people to know he'd come around fine. That was a fun project, but she reminded herself that she had more important work to do—getting herself kicked out of the place.

She found Dave Woods waiting for her with an apron, hair net and gloves, which she donned under his watchful eye. She took a clipboard with her to pretend to take notes.

They walked through the juicing room, and she watched him supervise the tightening of the wine press. Every bit of mischief she could come up with in this room would cost the factory money, so, since she had nothing better to do, she asked questions.

Suspicious at first, Dave eventually warmed up. She was asking about work he loved, after all.

They stood by the fruit press, watching the juice flow into the basin below. "Why not double the output with a second press?" she asked.

"We'd need another holding container to keep up with production. And your father doesn't want the capital outlay."

"But with higher sales, the new equipment would pay for itself."

"Possibly."

"We'd be changing the scope of our operation, of course. That's something to consider. We'd have to do the math first."

He looked her over with his sharp blue eyes. She'd surprised him. And herself, too.

They moved into the processing room—where the taffy was stretched, the jellies poured, the candies cut—and Dave explained each procedure, answering her questions completely, now that he believed her to be sincere. She was. Kind of.

They stood between two giant kettles, listening to the soft humming of the machinery. The warm sweet smell of candy was a pleasant memory, cozy and familiar. She'd taken all this at face value when she was a kid. Now she saw how all the pieces of the puzzle fit together. It was exciting to think that her father had built this, had all these people working for him. The whole operation fascinated her.

Stop it. She was supposed to be causing trouble, not traveling down memory lane. In the wrapping room, she saw her opportunity.

Workers were guiding streaming cellophane packages of prickly pear jellies into shipping boxes. All she had to do was shift the delivery chute slightly and the bags would go everywhere. She'd pick them up—verrry slowly—and irritate the hell out of Dave Woods. Perfect.

"Can I help?" she asked him. "Do some work here?"

"Huh?" Dave looked at her.

"I think I should get my hands in it a little. Get a sense of how things work." She smiled at one of the workers. Her name tag said *Delilah.*

"I can show her what to do," Delilah said quickly.

Dave's walkie-talkie crackled with a demand he come to the processing room.

"Yeah, Benny. Be right there." He clicked off. "All right. Go ahead, I guess. I'll be back in a half-hour." He gave her a sideways look like he didn't quite trust her. He was right, of course.

When he returned, right on time, she'd made a successful mess of things. "What the hell?" he said, surveying the mounds of candy all around Mariah. She was putting the bags one by one inside a carton.

She looked up and tried not to smile. "I had a little accident."

"'Sall right," Delilah said, snapping her gum. "Just a little goof. She's picking it up all by herself. Wouldn't let a one of us help." Bless her heart, Delilah was defending her, even though she'd looked at her like she was nuts as she stood there letting the chute spew waves of bags onto the floor. Mariah felt a little queasy doing something so obviously dense, but it was for a good cause.

She was mixing up the styles in the boxes, too, a fact she would notice *after* they'd sealed up the cartons. Then she'd have to redo the work. "I guess I'm just all thumbs," she said.

"All thumbs, huh?" David said. *Figures.* Her stomach dropped at his tone. Even though she had good reason to act like one, it was no fun to be thought of as an idiot. "Why don't you go sit on that bench and just watch for a while, okay?" Dave said.

"No, no. I'll be more careful," she said. "I want to help."

"We don't need any help," he said. *From you.*

"Boss, we could use a hand over here," one of the workers said. He was pushing a hand truck with sacks of sugar.

"Let me," she said. "Please."

Woods rolled his eyes. "Just do what they tell you, okay? Don't improvise."

"Sure. No problem." She saluted him and headed for the man with the dollie to goof up a bit more to be certain she'd sealed her fate. She dawdled with the loads, deliberately knocked sugar bags off the cart, took things to the wrong room and generally made a pest of herself.

The trouble was that she hated annoying the workers. The whole thing gave her a heavy heart.

When she figured she'd done enough damage to her reputation, she felt safe actually being helpful for a while. Everyone broke for lunch, but she stayed in the storage area to move cases of corn syrup and lime juice from the top shelves to lower ones for easier access.

She was pretty sure she'd done enough to make Dave complain to Nathan about her. Tomorrow, if she had to, she could cause some trouble in the front office. Cook up an expensive employee incentive plan, or design some ridiculous uniforms or something.

Finished and hungry for lunch, she headed through the processing room on the way out. She heard a fizzing sound and saw that an overhead valve that looked like it was supposed to release prickly pear juice into an open holding tank was only partially open and the juice was hissing in the backed-up pipe.

No one was around to ask about it. There was a ladder right there. She could open the valve and re-lease the pressure herself. This assistance would maybe redeem her in the workers' minds anyway. She put the ladder in place and climbed up. She had to lean way out and she couldn't…quite…grip…the handle….

"Hey, Mariah," Nathan called from across the room. "What are you doing?"

"Fixing…this," she said, starting to twist the knob.

"Don't do that." She heard him run toward her.

"Relax, I've got it."

"I mean don't open the valve." He grabbed the ladder to steady it, making it wobble. At the same instant, the handle gave a little. Mariah lost her grip, then her balance and before she knew it she'd toppled over, skidded down the side of the tank and plopped into a pool of red jelly. About knee-high, she noticed when she managed to get to her feet.

"Are you okay?" Nathan looked down at her from the ladder.

"I'm fine. It feels kind of good." Warm and spongy.

"What were you trying to do?" he asked.

"The valve was stuck," she said, shaking jelly from her arms. She'd loosened it enough that the faucet now sent a thin, steady stream into the drum.

"We don't use this basin," he said. "The valve shouldn't be loose. Give me your hand and I'll get you out."

She reached up and he grasped her hand. She tried to walk up the side of the drum, but the jelly made her hand slip out of Nathan's. She wiped it on her chest and tried again. This time her feet slipped.

"Whoa," Nathan said as her weight pulled him partially over the edge of the drum.

Hmm. Not a bad idea. A chance to bring home her point about not belonging here and have some fun at the same time.

"I'll get some help," Nathan said.

"No, no. I think I can do it this time." She reached up, trying to look innocent and serious. "Lean way out and give me both hands."

He did, and she gripped his hands, climbed up partway and levered as hard as she could....

"What the—" Nathan teetered at the top for a second, then slid down, and thumped into the gelatinous pool "—hell are you doing?"

"Come on in, the jelly's fine." She scooped up

two handfuls of jelly and plastered them in the middle of his chest.

Nathan looked down at his now-goopy white shirt in dismay, then at her, then up at the faucet. "I hope you realize you've just ruined a couple hundred dollars worth of juice, not to mention my clothes—and yours."

"Sorry." She *was* sorry about the wasted juice, but not about the clothes or making the most of the disaster.

Nathan tried to look stern, but his face softened just looking at her. "At least help me shut the valve down." He held his hands in a foothold. "Hold onto me and jump up and I'll bet you can reach the knob."

She pushed off her shoes, grabbed his shoulder, put a foot in his hands and tried to climb. Her foot slipped and she slid down his body.

"Whoa," he said, and seemed to enjoy the experience as much as she did. "How about we try that again," he said huskily.

"My pleasure." She stepped up, held his shoulder and pushed slowly upward, wobbling.

This time Nathan lost his footing.

"Whoa!" She grabbed his head.

"Hang on," he said, steadying himself.

She concentrated on reaching the valve, slightly distracted by the fact that her belly was rubbing against Nathan's face. She stretched, reached, stretched. Almost. With one last stretch she got the edge of the valve. She tried to twist it, but her hand was slippery. She wiped it off on Nathan's cheek.

"Hey!" he said.

"Sorry. I just about have it." She reached up again, and this time succeeded. "Got it!" She twisted the valve fully off.

Nathan lowered the foothold, and she slid down his body, aware of him the entire time.

"Good job," he said, his face inches from hers, his cheeks streaked with the jelly she'd smeared on them. "What a disaster."

"Don't be such a stick in the mud—I mean in the jam. This is very good for your inner child." To prove it, she put her arms around him and tilted back until they rested against the curved side of the basin up to their necks in jelly.

"It's like a mud bath, except—" she ran her fingers through the jelly on his cheek and tasted it "—sweet."

"You are crazy, you know that," he said, trying to be exasperated, but he didn't look the least bit unhappy. He lay where he'd fallen, close beside her. He reached forward to push her goopy hair from her face. "Now what do we do?"

"You up for some jelly wrestling?"

"Mmm. If you only knew."

Wow. Heat sizzled through her. She could imagine how great it would be to tangle bodies in all this lovely stuff. "That would be nice, huh?" she said seductively. She was playing with fire, but just then she didn't care. He was as into it as she was. "All warm...and wet...and soft...mmm...and sweet."

"Yeah," he murmured, angling his mouth for a kiss. "Very sweet." His lips met hers.

What a kiss. Tart jelly, mint breath and hot man. Mariah wrapped her arms around Nathan and leaned back against the basin's surface, glorying in the feeling of Nathan's mouth on hers, his body weighing her down in the warm, sensuous jelly.

They were just getting into it when they heard the door bang open and worker voices echo in the room.

Nathan broke off the kiss. "God. How will we explain this?" He sat up and started brushing at his shirt. "Okay, we'll say we were trying to shut off the valve and had a little spill."

"That's what happened, isn't it?"

"You know that's not what happened," he said, low and sexy. "And they'll know it, too."

She grinned. "Then we might as well go for it, since that's what everyone will think anyway."

She caught a sizzle of interest in his eyes. "I'd like to think you're kidding, but somehow, I know you're not." He looked at her, lust-hazy but happy. "Look what you've done to me—dragged me into a vat of jelly...and made me like it!"

She splashed a big gob of jelly into the middle of his chest.

"You never quit, do you?"

"Never." She plopped some on his head.

"That does it," he said, lobbing a small blob onto her shoulder.

She returned fire. They were deeply engrossed in their jelly fight when the workers found them.

It couldn't have gone better if she'd planned it, Mariah concluded. Not only would her accidental screwup get her booted out of the factory, but she'd introduced Nathan to his inner child at the same time.

Not a bad day's work for a butterfly.

7

THE NEXT MORNING, despite Nathan's complaints about his lack of artistic ability—he'd tried painting once and was terrible—Mariah set up two easels on his back patio. Art therapy was the perfect thing to follow up with the gelatin tank experience from the day before. Nathan needed more delight in his life. Painting was not only fun, but creative.

She was busy putting acrylic paints on palettes when Maynard trotted out of the house with a rectangular object in his teeth—a canvas.

Nathan saw it, too, and blanched. "No, boy." He lunged for the painting. After a brief tug-of-war, Nathan wrenched it away from the dog.

"What is it?" she asked, reaching for it.

"Nothing. I tried a painting a while back. I told you I'm no good." He hid it against his body and loped into the house with it.

She was dying to see what he'd painted, but he came back looking so embarrassed she couldn't bring herself to pry. At least not this minute. "Okay, dig in," she said to him. "Dip your brush and paint. Feel the colors. Go with your emotions."

She watched him gently apply blue paint to the top of the canvas, his strokes more than a little erotic. "Not like that. Bigger, broader. Use more energy."

To demonstrate, she slashed a full brush of red diagonally across the white surface of her own canvas. Then she did the same with yellow. "Don't be stingy with the paint. It doesn't have to *look* like something, it has to *feel* like something."

He tried a barely energetic stroke.

"Come on, Nathan. What do you feel like painting? Show me what you feel."

She barely caught the twinkle in his eye before he made two swipes of blue paint above her lips, forming what must be Snidely Whiplash mustachios, then gave her two blue eyebrows. "There. That's what I feel like painting."

"So that's the way you want to play?" She whirled, dabbed a smaller brush with red and smooshed two blobs on his cheeks.

"Nice," he said, still grinning.

"Hold still." She used black to create exaggerated eyelashes. "Lovely," she said. "Raggedy Andy. Now your lips."

"Uh-uh, it's my turn." He took more blue paint and dabbed at her cheeks and chin.

"Oh, now I'm the bearded lady, huh?"

"Very hot," he said, admiring his work.

"Yoo-hoo. Oh, dear!"

They looked up to see her mother leaning over the fence, staring at them. "You're painting each other?"

"Mom," she said, embarrassed. "What are you doing here?"

"I just wanted to drop off some things for the dog," she said. "I had no idea..." She seemed to think they'd gone crazy.

They stopped long enough to haul in all the supplies her mother had purchased—a huge basket of chew toys, two big bags of dog food, box after box of doggie treats, a studded collar, a cedar-chip bed, even a doghouse for the patio. Mrs. Newman and Mr. Corday, the neighbors from either side, came out to watch while they unloaded.

"They're thinking about community theater," her mother said for the neighbors' benefit, pink with embarrassment. "Isn't that fun?"

After the neighbors decided nothing more bizarre was going to happen and returned to their homes and her mother left, Mariah and Nathan stood in the entryway looking at all the dog junk decorating the living room, then at each other, painted like circus clowns, and burst out laughing. It felt so nice to laugh with Nathan, to hear his low voice rumble in counterpoint to her own.

Together they headed to the bathroom to clean up. Mariah thought she looked goofy in her blue beard, brows and mustache, but Nathan looked nothing but cute as a rag doll. Being in the bathroom, watching themselves in the mirror made the intimacy of gently wiping each other's faces even more intense—as if there were four of them all touching and stroking and smoothing and studying each other.

"I hope this won't ruin your skin," Nathan said, gently sliding a cotton ball along her left cheek.

"I'm sure it will be fine," she said, rubbing the red off his nose. "Now close your eyes so I can get the eyelashes off." With his eyes closed, she was hyperaware of his face, the clean line of his jaw and nose, the strength of his mouth, the texture of his skin. She hadn't thought painting could get intimate. But with Nathan, everything ended up like that. She sighed and wiped the last of the paint off. "All done."

Nathan opened his eyes, blinked, then examined her face, cupping her jaw so he could dab at her chin. "Just a bit of blue still here." His face was so close she could see the darker flecks in his blue irises and every darling crease around his eyes. She wished he'd never stop. She thought about that cactus-jelly kiss of the day before and all she wanted was to move two inches forward and go for more.

Then he stopped dabbing and leaned back to admire his handiwork. "All better," he said.

"You're always taking care of me," she said.

"You're taking care of me with all this meditation and inner child junk. Why can't we take care of each other?"

Why can't we? She reached up and dabbed at a fleck of black paint that remained on his forehead, bracing herself with a hand on his chest. His heart was pounding like her own. *Why couldn't they?*

Because they couldn't, that's why. She had a plan. She had to stick with it. "At least I'll be out of your hair at Cactus Confections."

"What do you mean?"

"After everything I did yesterday, I'm sure no one wants me back."

"The faucet leak wasn't your fault."

"But didn't Dave tell you about the chaos in the packing room?"

"No. Actually, he said you did a good job of re-organizing the storage area. And Bernie's completely jazzed about your ideas. All you need is a little confidence in yourself. You're learning.''

''Learning? I'm a disaster.''

''You give up on yourself too soon.''

She looked at his implacable expression and realized that no matter what she tried, Nathan wouldn't let her quit. She could burn the place down and he'd say she was just catching her stride. He'd probably even let her put the workers in some outrageous uniform just to boost her confidence.

Damn. She was stuck. And she couldn't face trying any more deliberate screwups. She'd have to settle for helping Nathan to see how much he loved it there. Unfortunately, that meant spending more time with him. She tried to pretend the idea didn't thrill her to her toes.

For a moment the possibility of staying in Copper Corners flickered through her, but no, that was impossible. She knew herself. She was still a butterfly—beautiful while she was there, and a lovely memory when she left. Staying too long would spell disaster.

''AREN'T YOU DUE over at Nathan's?''

Mariah was so intent on the computer screen, she didn't even look up at her mother's question. ''Not today. I called him.'' She'd told him to proceed with yoga, meditation, sax practice and positive affirmations without her. She'd been so excited about what she'd discovered on the Internet the night before, she couldn't wait to get at it again today.

They could spend all weekend on self-discovery,

if they needed to. She planned to go through the career aptitude checklists next.

"How are things going with Nathan?" her mother asked. "You looked like you were having fun when I saw you painting each other that time."

Her mother's tone made her jerk her eyes away from the screen and face her. "Things with Nathan aren't going anywhere, Mother. Don't even think that. I'm helping him figure out that he wants to stay in Copper Corners. That's it."

"I know that, dear," she said breezily. "I just wondered how you're getting along at the factory. Don't get defensive." She wandered away, calling over her shoulders, "And wear the navy pumps with that plaid skirt. It'll look nice."

Two weeks had passed since the jelly bath with Nathan. This would be the first time in three weeks she'd missed their morning self-awareness session. She looked forward to that time, even though they seemed to get more comfortable and more intimate with each other every day. As she helped Nathan explore his feelings and goals, some of it had rubbed off on her. She'd begun to feel a bit more centered and sure of herself.

Except when it came to Nathan, of course. He threw her completely out of whack. Just the sight of him made her heart kick into overdrive. They were constantly together at the factory, which meant she was always a mess. She'd stopped calling Nikki altogether, afraid her friend would urge her to give in and go for it with Nathan, and more afraid that she would take her advice.

Nathan was in his office when she walked in. "Missed you this morning," he said.

"Um, me, too."

He cleared his throat, obviously embarrassed that he'd said too much. "The yoga didn't go well. I think I tore something doing Downward Facing Dog." He rubbed at his shoulder.

"Let me help." She squeezed where he'd indicated, all shaky inside from the sensation of massaging his upper arm and his back while he rolled his neck and made agreeable noises.

"There, all done," she said, patting him matter-of-factly to make up for the wobble in her voice. "I have something cool to show you."

She plopped into his chair and clicked into the Internet, while he stood looking over her shoulder.

"Why do you keep wearing these weird suits?" he asked.

"Meredith. It's the only way I can still hold out on the church choir. I already gave in to pinochle."

"Sorry. Meredith can be a bulldozer."

"No kidding." She found the Desert Botanical Garden Web site. "Forget that, look at this. I was looking for info about their gift shop—as a place to sell our candies and jelly—and I found this." She clicked to a news story about the health-giving properties of prickly-pear juice. "According to this research study, prickly pear juice reduces bad cholesterol. Can you believe it?"

"Interesting, I guess."

"Don't you see what this means? This opens up a whole new market—health food stores! I worked in a To-Your-Health store once and those places have terrific mark-up and tons of loyal customers who listen to the staff about health products. We could sell the candy, along with a little information sheet. Or even just package the juice for drinking, you know?''

''Hm,'' he said, skimming over the research. ''Possible.''

''Possible? It's fantastic.''

''We'd have to cost out the production. Why don't you call the health food store where you worked and see what kind of interest the manager thinks there might be. Then you can contact the corporate office.''

''Great. I'll do that.'' She rose from her chair, starting to leave.

Nathan grabbed her arm to stop her and held her gaze. ''Good job, Mariah.'' His hand was warm on hers, the fingers strong. A shudder traveled through her body. He was reacting to the moment, too, she could see in his face, except he seemed to feel more pain than pleasure. He released her arm, but didn't move.

''Terrific, then,'' she said. ''I'd better go talk to Bernie.''

''Right,'' he said, watching her.

She couldn't move.

''Go talk to Bernie.''

''Bernie? Oh, right.'' She moved away. On her way out the door, she put his geode on the wrong shelf again. Had to keep him guessing.

THE NEXT FRIDAY EVENING, Nathan looked over at Mariah from another aptitude test he'd finished filling in. The third. Complete overkill. But that was

Mariah. If a thing was worth doing, it was worth overdoing. She was hell-bent on proving he was perfectly happy at Cactus Confections.

Mariah glanced up from clicking numbers into a calculator. "You done with that one?"

He handed it to her, then watched her bend over the work, her face intent. He didn't often get a chance to look this closely at her without getting caught. Besides, she rarely held still. Her face was so active—smiling, laughing, quirking with mischief or consternation. Now, as she concentrated, he could study her thick lashes, the soft curve of her cheek, her sensual mouth and the smooth line of her neck. He longed to brush his mouth along the length of it.

Whoops. His body let him have it again. Where was that pillow? He grabbed a clipboard and covered the evidence of how much Mariah Monroe got to him downstairs. She got to him everywhere, but this was the one place he couldn't hide.

He should tell her he had to leave, start breaking things off. He had to move on soon—the retreat was next month. It was time. After spending three weeks there, Mariah was clearly attached to Cactus Confections. She'd even stopped trying to hide it.

"Another top score, Nathan. This proves it. You're doing exactly what you want to be doing. All we need to do is raise your personal satisfaction index and you'll be fine. Hmm. Give me that clipboard."

"Um, I need it."

"Oh, for heaven's sake." She picked up a book— *Rolfing Made Easy—No Pain, No Gain,* one he was grateful she'd decided not to try on him—and braced her paper on it. She tapped the pencil against her teeth. "Let's take stock. We've been working on you for three weeks. What have we done so far? Meditation and yoga... You've got that going." She made a check mark. "We had a Gestalt therapy session..." She made another mark. "We've explored your inner child.... Are you practicing the sax twice a day?" She looked up at him sternly.

"Yes, but that doesn't mean I'm ready to perform in public."

"Sure you are. You still have a week. Do you want to practice on me?"

"That depends what we're practicing." Everything she said seemed to have sexual implications to him.

She blushed. "You know what I mean."

He loved making her blush. He could tell she was having trouble resisting him. But he knew she didn't want to get serious. And he didn't want just an affair. If he made love to Mariah, he'd never want to let her go. "I can barely manage three songs. I doubt anyone wants to hear 'Satin Doll' more than a couple of times."

"So vary the synthesizer and no one will notice. Nikki's boyfriend knows lots of musicians who make a living that way. Think how much fun this will be. This is the perfect creative outlet for you."

"Okay, okay," he said, wanting to laugh at her enthusiasm.

"Good. Creative outlet..." She checked it off. She was as much of a bulldozer as her mother. Just so much more charming. She'd strong-armed him into a jazz performance at Louie's. Oh, well. Publicly humiliating himself was no big deal if it made her happy. He'd do anything to make her happy.

"We got you a pet." Another check mark.

Anything except that. "Uh-uh. I'll make a spectacle of myself at Louie's, but you're taking back that dog. I mean it. He practically sneers when I walk in the room."

"He's still hurt that you wanted him euthanized."

"I don't want him hurt. I just don't want him here."

She shrugged, studying her list. "So, what do you think, Nathan? How are you feeling these days? More together? More integrated?"

"I'm more flexible, anyway. Look at this." He did Downward Facing Dog and touched his palms flat to the floor. She was impressed, he could tell by her sharp inhale.

"Very good," she said shakily. "But I mean your attitude. Has it changed?"

"My attitude's fine. How about yours? You're enjoying Cactus Confections, aren't you?"

"I'm keeping busy," she said, pretending she didn't love it. "If I don't stay out of the house, Meredith will have me hooking rugs with her."

"Come on. You like it. I know you do."

"How about you? You've been tons more cheerful."

Of course. How could he not be cheerful seeing her every day? But he had to let her know he was going. "Mariah, I haven't changed my mind."

"What?"

"About leaving."

"But you promised to try."

"I am trying. I'm doing everything you tell me to. And I've enjoyed the yoga and meditation. I'm not too hot on the affirmations, but the counselling session was good—it got me thinking about my mother. I called her the other night and we had a nice talk, by the way. The painting was good for laughs and I'm happy to be playing the sax. Except for that damn dog, you've done a great job. I just need to start over. Somewhere else."

"But I don't understand that." She looked so sad he almost took it back. "I mean, you love it here."

I love you *here.* He almost blurted it.

Then she got that determined look on her face. She wasn't giving up yet. "You must have some fantasy of what this free life you're planning will be like. What do you think you're going to do anyway?"

"You really want to know?"

"I have to know. How else can I help you?"

"Well, I thought I might sell my car and buy a motorcycle. One of my mom's boyfriends taught me how to drive a bike and I really enjoyed it. Plus it would be cheaper, if I have to pay a fortune for a rat-infested hovel like you predicted."

"A motorcycle? A motorcycle is so *not* you. Have you ever ridden a motorcycle in the rain? It's miserable. Plus, they're deadly. Do you know what hospital workers call motorcyclists? Organ donors."

"I appreciate your concern, but I'll be fine. I need to experience new things in my life. You, of all people, should approve of that. That's your philosophy."

"It's not fair to use my life against me. Let's examine this further. So, you're tooling around on your motorcycle. Then what?"

"I won't look for a place to live right away. I'll travel around a bit, check out places, find a town I like."

"Hotels get expensive."

"So, I'll camp."

"You? Camping? Now I know you're crazy. Most campgrounds don't even have showers. You're too into grooming—hell, even your robe is starched."

"I'll adapt. I'll be fine, don't you worry." He patted her hand, wondering if he'd ever be fine without Mariah in his life. He had no choice but to try.

THE NEXT MORNING, Nathan was making himself coffee when he heard an unmuffled engine rumble to a stop outside his window. Then the doorbell rang. He opened the door to Mariah. "Grab a toothbrush and a change of clothes."

"What are you talking about?"

"I borrowed a motorcycle," she said, jabbing a thumb behind her, where he saw a bike parked in his driveway, two bedrolls tied onto it. "We're spending the weekend the way you think you want to live."

He just stood there, blinking like a fool, stunned by the sight of Mariah on his porch in extremely sexy shorts proposing, of all things, a camping trip.

"Meredith will stop by to take care of Maynard, so pack a gym bag quick, no more," she said. "No credit cards and just fifty bucks cash. We're keeping this real."

REAL. RIGHT. Real sexy. Real tempting. Real mistake, Mariah realized as soon as they'd roared off on the bike. Her job was to show him the ugly, uncertain underbelly of living without income, but all she could think about was how natural he seemed on the bike, and how good she felt wrapped around him, snug as a biker chick on a biker dude. All she wanted was to press her cheek against his back and stay that way forever.

Nikki would have said *I told you so.*

They headed north for a while. When Nathan suggested food, she made him pull into the diviest place she could find along the highway, claiming it was the only place within their budget—Jimmi's Hot Dog, whose very sign looked like a health code violation.

As they drove off, her stomach declared its objection to the cuisine. It kept it up—churning, then lunging. When it threatened to empty itself, she tapped Nathan's shoulder and indicated she wanted to stop.

The instant he parked, she jumped off the bike and ran for some bushes where she could hide and throw up. No luck, though. She just felt more queasy. She sat on a boulder, put her head between her knees, and waited for the nausea to fade. She heard Nathan approach. She looked up to see he was holding out a travel-size bottle of Pepto-Bismol.

"Good lord," she said, amazed. "How did you…?"

"I was a Boy Scout. We're prepared."

She swallowed some of the pink liquid and felt it soothe all the way down. "Boy Scout, hell. You're a saint. Want some?"

"No, I'm fine." Annoying, but true. Nathan's chili cheese dog with nachos seemed to have settled in his stomach just fine, while her simple dog had created holy havoc with her insides.

They drove off, traveling until late afternoon, when they decided to camp near Oak Creek. She could have insisted on finding some place worse, but she'd barely stopped feeling nauseated. She'd prove her point about deprivation further along the trip.

"This will be perfect," Nathan said, stopping at a fairly isolated spot with a fire pit, not far from the creek. They unloaded their bags and bedrolls. Mariah was bone-weary from being ill and trying to *not* enjoy riding behind Nathan.

"What about dinner?" she asked.

"Got it covered," Nathan said. She was amazed to watch him remove two cans of potato soup and some corn bread from his gym bag, along with a handy-dandy collapsible cook pan, a small jug of water and some cups.

"How did you…?"

"The corn bread's from my neighbor, Mrs. Newman."

"No, I mean—"

"The pan? I told you I was a Boy Scout." He grinned. "Help me find some wood and we can start a fire and heat this up."

"Okay." She was stunned. She'd only given him fifteen minutes to throw stuff in a bag and somehow he'd managed to pack dinner? He went off whistling. She took two steps and stubbed her toe on a tree stump.

Twenty minutes later, she plopped onto a boulder, swearing and in pain. She'd only managed to grab a few small pieces of wood before she lost her footing and fell forward on some rocks in a dry part of the riverbed, gouging both knees and scraping her shins.

Ouch. She slapped her forehead. Another mosquito bite. She waved away the dive-bombers getting ready to descend—she swore she could hear a teeny-tiny dinner bell—and bent to blow air on the aching sting on both knees. Her stomach was still a little queasy from the bad hot dog at Jimmi's. She would survive, though, and it would all be worth it, if this made Nathan realize this kind of life would make him miserable.

"Hey, there!" She looked up as a cheery Nathan strolled her way, his arms loaded with fat chunks of wood. He looked cool and casual and completely uninjured. Damn. So far, the only person this life was making miserable was her. Tomorrow, she'd take them to a diner for breakfast and hide the money so they'd have to wash dishes to pay the check.

He dropped the wood beside the fire, then looked at her. "What happened?"

"I fell. No big deal." She scratched the rapidly swelling bite on her forehead. "And the mosquitoes are eating me alive."

"Let me take care of that," he said.

He took a first-aid kit from that magically bottomless gym bag and produced some antiseptic, Band-Aids and a tiny bottle of calamine lotion. He dabbed the medicine on her knees and shins, his fingers soft and sure on her skin. Then he rubbed the pink lotion on the bite on her forehead.

"Any others?"

She pointed the others out on her arms, thighs and even behind her ears. He dutifully dabbed them. Finished, he looked her over. "You've got some dirt on your face." He dampened the edge of his shirt with water from the jug and started to reach for her.

"Thanks, Nathan," she said, stopping his hand. "You're doing too much for me."

"Just trying to help."

"I know." He was such a sweet man.

And entirely too cheerful about camping. She should have figured he'd be as practical and efficient about it as he was about everything else. A motorcycle camping trip had been a bad idea, which got worse when she found herself in the unbearably romantic position of sitting elbow to elbow with Nathan in the warm intimacy of campfire light roasting the marshmallows he'd had the presence of mind to bring for dessert.

"You thought of everything," she said. "You're amazing."

"I'm not amazing. I'm just prepared. Boring, but prepared."

"You're not boring. Not at all." She covered the fervent way she'd spoken by busying herself loading a marshmallow onto the stick.

"Right. I'm a wild man. I rotate my tires every three years instead of two." He finished his stick and thrust his marshmallow into the flickering flame beside hers.

As if the moment weren't already too romantic, someone nearby began playing something seductive on a guitar. They both listened, their eyes on each other.

"Too bad I don't have my sax," Nathan said. "I think I could play that one."

"Yeah," she said, wanting to kiss him so much she could hardly stand it.

"Watch it, you're burning."

No kidding. But then she realized he meant her marshmallow, which was flaming. She yanked it out of the fire and blew it out, then tentatively nibbled at the less burned side. They were always setting things on fire around each other.

She became aware that Nathan was staring at her eating her marshmallow, completely transfixed, until he finally seemed to force himself to look away. Just nibbling a marshmallow, she turned him on. That gave her a charge. What if they both gave up the struggle? Would that be so bad?

"Nice night," he said, looking studiedly upward. "The stars are bright out here."

She looked up. The sky seemed so close and thick, like a blanket of velvet with the stars as glitter twinkling in its weave.

"This was a great idea, Mariah."

"Thanks." She stopped looking at the sky and found Nathan's eyes waiting for her.

"You have a lot of good ideas. It's been nice having you around. I mean around, um, Cactus Confections. You've brightened up the place. You've brightened up...everything." He cleared his throat.

"I was between jobs in Phoenix anyway. It's been interesting work, too."

"I'm glad to hear you say that."

"But that doesn't mean I'd stay." But wouldn't it be fun if they both stayed?

"No, of course not."

"And you've been happier at Cactus Confections, too, haven't you?"

No answer.

"Come on. Admit it."

Finally, he said, "Yes, I have. Because of you." His words were low and fervent. His eyes held hers.

What was he saying? That *she* made him happy? It couldn't be. She couldn't let it be. She couldn't stay. She'd come here to help Nathan. Period. She'd stick with what mattered. "That's good. I'm glad I could help you see what you love about CC," she said, trying to sound bubbly. "The health food juice could be a coup, couldn't it?"

He paused, frowned, then sighed. "Yeah. Great idea."

"And we've already seen an increase in orders, thanks to that specialty candy warehouse. Plus, Dad's almost got a lock on the prickly-pear juice margarita mix I dreamed up."

"You've accomplished a lot in only three weeks. Just think how much more you could do if you stayed."

She wouldn't go *there*. "I'm just glad I could finally help you for a change," she said. "I mean back then you were always taking care of me. I was a mess. I guess I saw you as a father figure or something."

"A father figure? Thanks a lot. I'm only four years older than you."

"Well, a big brother, then. You were an adult, with a career and a college degree. So responsible. So different from me. You know what I mean."

"Yeah, I do." When he spoke, the words came

out so sadly they made her ache. "You were too young. I pushed you into the marriage idea. I guess I wanted that picket fence and steady address so much I didn't think about what was right for you."

"But I wanted that, too," she said. "Maybe not the picket fence, but I wanted to fit in for once." *And I wanted you. More than anything.*

And she still did, she realized. Even more, now that she was a woman and knew what love could mean. But she also knew herself. She'd never fit into Nathan's life. She wasn't the picket-fence type. That made her shiver.

"Are you cold?"

"No." She shook her head. *Just sad.*

But he'd already pulled a windbreaker out of his amazing hold-all gym bag and soon she was wrapped up in the fabric and the great smell of him. They watched the fire for a few more minutes, neither saying anything.

Finally, the intimacy became too much for her. "Shall we turn in?" she said, raising her eyes to him. If he opened his arms to her, she'd be in them in a heartbeat. She watched him read that fact in her face.

And ignore it. "I'll get the bedrolls." He got them, opened them, laying them side by side, but definitely separate. Oh, well. At least one of them had some self-control.

As soon as Mariah climbed into her bag, she remembered why she'd always hated camping. A big fat boulder was jabbing her right in the middle of her back. She wiggled around, shifted, turned, and finally found a smooth area, but now she was face to face with Nathan. He was staring at her, his eyes glittering in the moonlight.

He wanted her. She wanted him. So much.

Do it. Do it. Kiss him now, her heart and body screamed at her. *You want to. He wants to. Go for it.*

Abruptly, Nathan flipped over, turning his back to her. ''Good night,'' he said.

Good night. Right. Her plan was working, she reminded herself. Okay, the camping trip hadn't gone like she'd expected, but she'd learned something important. Nathan was happy at Cactus Confections again. He kept saying he had to move on, but what she'd done so far had gotten him more interested. All she had to do was kick in a little more business, a few more new ideas and he wouldn't be able to leave. Nikki was wrong. This was a much better way to go.

STAY WITH ME, MARIAH. The words had been on the tip of Nathan's tongue. But he'd forced himself to turn away from her. She'd been squirming and undulating in that bag until he was ready to rip it open and make love to her like a beast of the forest where they lay. But beneath that lust was the solid desire to keep her here with him. In his life.

Then he'd thought of the only thing that could cool the fire inside him. *I guess I saw you as a father figure.* Talk about cooling. More like a bucket of ice water. A father figure? Did it get any worse than that?

Get over it, he told himself for the hundredth time. He was a practical guy. He knew the past was past.

Mariah would never want a guy like him. But there was a bright spot. She'd admitted that she liked Cactus Confections. He'd given her free rein with her ideas for this very purpose. He just had to get her a little more hooked, so she wouldn't want to leave.

So maybe he'd better not draw attention to his imminent departure, or she might start resisting. He pushed the twinge of guilt out of his mind and thought about having Mariah wrapped around him on the motorcycle all the way home. Of all her ideas, he had to say the motorcycle was the best.

8

TEN DAYS AFTER the camping trip, Mariah hung up the phone and yelled, "Yes!" She did a little happy dance around the desk she'd set up in Nathan's office. One more return phone call and she'd have an entire chain of health-food stores that would buy not only Cactus Confections candies, but the juice as well. And if they said yes, they'd create promotional materials and feature it as an exclusive product line.

She had to tell Nathan. Bernie had been jazzed, her father thrilled and even Dave Woods seemed impressed, but Nathan was the person she had to tell. She had to see that look of pride on his face, watch his eyes glow with pleasure at her accomplishment.

He'd left the factory in the middle of the afternoon saying he had to meet someone at his house, so she got in her car and drove there to tell him right now.

Her plan was going smoothly. Nathan had been a hit at Louie's the previous Saturday night. Of course, she'd made certain of that. While he was in the restroom, she'd dashed from booth to table to make sure everyone would applaud wildly. He hadn't been half bad, after all.

He wasn't ready for a band, he'd insisted, but he'd been pleased and more or less committed to a continuing gig. He was happy in his work again, always smiling, and with this new project she'd scored and the challenges that went with it, he'd be locked in for good. She'd done exactly what she'd set out to do. Her only mistake had been Maynard, and her parents had been happy to welcome him in as a temporary guest.

As she pulled up to Nathan's house, she saw a man and a woman climb into the back of a BMW in his driveway. The driver pulled away and she saw the sign on the side of the car—*Realty Pro*.

A real estate agent? With two people who'd probably been looking at Nathan's house. How could Nathan be selling his house? He'd taken down the For Sale sign as part of their agreement. Why would people be looking at his house if he was happy here? She stomped up the walkway, banged on the door, then just opened it.

Nathan rose from where he was working at the kitchen table. "Mariah, what are you doing here?"

"That was the someone you had to meet?" she said. "A real-estate agent?"

"Oh, um, I decided to put the house back on the market...."

She walked closer and saw what Nathan was working on at the table. "The Retreat House at Absolon" was at the top of a form, which Nathan had obviously been filling out.

Her heart sank. "You're leaving, aren't you?"

He nodded solemnly. "I'm sorry, Mariah. I just can't stay. This is the right thing to do."

"You've been pretending all this time? About feeling better, about liking it here again?"

"No, I wasn't pretending. I have been feeling better. But that doesn't mean I should stay."

"You weren't even trying, damn it! *I'm* trying. I've kept my end of the bargain. I've been working my butt off at Cactus Confections." She started to tell him about her news, then decided not to. He wouldn't care. He wasn't even staying. He'd just been going through the motions. "You've just given up."

"No, I haven't," he said, trying to take her shoulders. "I just know what I have to do. I can't stay here any more. I appreciate all you've done to help me, but I have to go. It's the right thing to do."

"Forget it, then," she said, tears in her eyes. "I'll call a headhunter and find a replacement for you. It's for the best, anyway," she said bitterly. "This way I can quit faking it."

"Faking it?"

"Yeah. Pretending I like it here. You didn't think I meant all that, did you?" she said fiercely.

"Don't be this way, Mariah. You're doing great. You've practically got that health-food account sewn up."

"I *do* have it sewn up," she blurted. "That's what I came to tell you."

"That's great!" This time he did take her shoulders. He looked earnestly into her face. "I'm so proud of you. I knew you could do it."

"Thanks." Despite her distress, she smiled.

"Look, Mariah," he said, his eyes digging into her, his fingers squeezing her shoulders so hard it almost hurt. "I think you should take over for me."

"Forget it," she said, too wounded to let his confidence buoy her.

"You can do it. I know you can. You're upset now, but think about it. You'll see that I'm right. This would be the perfect career move for you."

But she couldn't think past her disappointment that he was leaving. All her efforts had been for nothing. "If you can quit, I can quit. And I quit." Aching inside, she turned on her heels and stomped out of his house.

EXCEPT MARIAH COULDN'T quit. Not right away. She had to work one more week to lock in the health food account, and then it would take a little time to get Nathan's replacement, even using a headhunter. Also, she'd spent the week sending out samples of the brand-new prickly-pear margarita mix to trendy restaurant chains across the country and she had to wait for nibbles.

She had to quit soon, though, so today she'd vowed to stay home. If for no other reason than to get her parents used to the idea she'd be leaving. The pair of them were in complete denial—acting as if neither she nor Nathan were going anywhere. It didn't help that she'd finally given in and joined the church choir.

This very minute, her mother had her holding up a skein of yarn while Meredith wound it into a ball, talking about how artistically free Mariah could be when she made the country cutie door knockers for that blasted bazaar.

On the other hand, all she felt capable of today was holding up strands of wool. She felt too blue to move. She didn't know why exactly—maybe the disappointment of working so hard on Nathan and failing at it. Maybe the fact that the couple had made an offer on his house and he'd be gone in three weeks. That was for the best, she realized, but somehow she wanted their little temporary partnership to go on longer.

She'd been avoiding Nathan as much as possible at Cactus Confections—wanting to adjust to losing him. She felt so sad whenever she caught sight of him at work. Another reason she was glad to stay home today.

The phone rang. She picked it up.

"Mariah Monroe, get your behind down here." It was her father.

"I'm not coming in today, Daddy. Bernie's handling the health-food store calls and there aren't any interviews for Nathan's replacement until next week."

"Well, we need you to take inventory," he said. "We've got a couple folks out sick and we can't afford to over-order. Retooling for the new accounts is already going to be high."

"Inventory?" This was the first she'd heard of that.

"Critical, my girl. We need you down here. Now."

"You need to go, sweetheart," her mother whispered. "Your father's working himself to death. I'll handle the canapés just fine."

On the other hand, she'd definitely prefer doing inventory to slicing cream-cheese-slathered salami rolls for pinochle night and listening to her mother describe Rachel Conroy's heel spur surgery in excruciating detail.

"Okay," she said, "I'll come in for the inventory." At least tucked away in the storage area of the factory, she wouldn't run into Nathan.

"I need you to stop at Nathan's house on the way in," her father continued. "The new business plan is sitting on his kitchen table."

"Can't you just print it out again there."

"We made some notes on it. Nate forgot it. He's gotten so scatterbrained lately."

"Okay, I'll stop at Nathan's." She dreaded it. Everything about him made her so sad these days.

"You're going to Nathan's?" her mother said. "Great. You can grab the other basket of toys for Maynard. He's been drooling over our shoes and chewing up travel brochures. He needs something appropriate to gnaw on."

She still hadn't told her parents that they'd have to keep Maynard until she schmoozed her and Nikki's landlord into making an exception to the no-pets rule. She doubted her mother would mind too much—she seemed to think of Maynard as her own dog already. Mariah was pretty sure Nikki would love Maynard. They were both free spirits.

She took Nathan's spare key from the hook by the door. Her mother had insisted on it for emergencies. Meredith was as overbearing with Nathan as she was with Mariah. Somehow, though, it didn't seem to bother Nathan. Maybe because his own mother had been so hands-off.

Half an hour later, Mariah opened the door to the cool airiness of Nathan's house. The living room smelled of fresh incense. Had he meditated today? She went to the cocktail table and felt the wax of one of the candles. Warm. The yoga video was in the VCR. He'd done yoga, too. At least something she'd taught him had registered.

He was still leaving, though. She'd failed. If only she could figure out a way to *make* him stay. Maybe pretend to hire someone lousy so he'd insist on staying. But she was too tired for any more games. At a certain point she had to let go.

She sighed and headed for the kitchen table. The report was spread out there. She looked it over a little. She saw that Nathan had included the health-food store account, but it looked like he'd under-estimated the profit potential in his calculations. Plus, she questioned his figures on the small candy ware-house accounts. She had fresh figures to plug in.

Stop it, stop it. You're leaving, too. She was as bad as her father. Acting like nothing would change. She'd been here a month, and only been working hard for three weeks of that. Every job got tedious. She knew that already. Six months and out. That was the way she worked. She thought about all Nathan did—hiring, dealing with insurance, quality control, handling machinery issues and suppliers. All the minutiae that took the joy out of things. She'd hate that. Especially without Nathan around. He was the real reason the place seemed fun.

She gathered up the plan, stuffed it into its folder and started to leave. Then her gaze caught on the kitchen wall. Nathan had hung the painting he'd made that day on the patio when they'd decorated each other's faces. He'd finished it off with bold strokes of brilliant color—just like she'd suggested.

It was still terrible art, but at least he'd been proud enough to hang it. She'd helped him with that, too.

Then she remembered the painting that Maynard had dragged out to the patio. The one that had embarrassed Nathan. Her curiosity got the better of her and she decided to see if she could find it. She wouldn't snoop, exactly, just wander down the hall and see if it jumped out at her.

The first place she went was his bedroom. It was torture to see the place where he slept, but she was curious, too. The bed was neatly made, of course. So Nathan. She never made her bed.

Her gaze flew around the room. Framed posters, but no canvases. There was a simple bureau, a desk with a computer, a comfortable chair. She moved closer to the bureau. It contained a man's jewelry box, a black-and-white framed photo of his mother playing the saxophone, and another photo—the one of Nathan and her that she had kept, too. And beside it, something amazing. A shoe—a white satin shoe with a grass-stained heel.

Her wedding shoe—the one she'd left stuck in the damp church lawn when she'd looked in the window and thought Nathan had abandoned her at the altar. Nathan had kept her shoe.

She picked it up and remembered how hurt she'd felt that day. How wounded by Nathan's abandonment, even though she knew she couldn't marry him. She'd been wrong about Nathan abandoning her, of course. He'd been rushing to her as fast as he could get Farmer Jim to go.

Somehow, he'd found her shoe. Had he stood there holding it, like she was doing now? And what had he thought?

Then her eye caught on a shape beyond the bureau, tucked behind it. The edge of a canvas. She lifted it up. A painting of a woman. Her. A terrible rendition—Nathan was right about his lack of artistic skill—but she recognized her dress and pose from a photograph she'd sent to her parents three years ago. Nathan had painted the photo. She glanced at the wall and saw an empty hook. The painting had hung there at one time, she guessed. When and why had he taken it down? In anger? Despair? Or had Maynard knocked it down?

Then, standing there riveted to the floor, holding her wedding shoe in one hand, the bad painting of herself in the other, Mariah felt something burst inside her—a dam or a bubble or a candy shell—and the feelings she'd been fighting since she returned to Copper Corners rushed through her. *I love Nathan.*

Still. More than ever. Tears came and she leaned over Nathan's bureau to cope with the power of the realization. She could no longer hide this truth from herself. What on earth should she do about it?

In a haze, Mariah locked up Nathan's house and headed for Cactus Confections. She couldn't stop thinking of Nathan and the shoe. Why had he held onto it? She could picture him holding it, looking out across the church lawn and beyond to the street, looking for her. Kind of like Cinderella's prince.

Except, instead of searching the kingdom for the woman who fit the shoe, he'd let her go. With relief? Disappointment? And why had he kept it? As a me-

mento? A reminder of how foolish he'd been? A warning to stay away from butterflies? That would be the sensible thing. And Nathan was a sensible guy.

She should be sensible, too, she told herself, pushing open the door to Cactus Confections. She should forget how she felt about Nathan. She should hold onto what she knew was true—that she could never make him happy. Surely, he knew that.

Except her feelings would not stay down. They were bubbling like champagne, up and up, overflowing her restraint, swamping her good sense. She had to talk to him about this. But that would only make things worse, right?

Maybe when she set eyes on Nathan, she'd know what to do. She carried the business plan down the hall toward his office, her heart beating harder.

But he wasn't there. She was both disappointed and relieved. She grabbed an adding machine from her desk, took a clipboard and the forms she needed and numbly headed out to do inventory. She walked through the factory, turned the corner into the storage area and ran smack into Nathan.

"What are you doing here?" she asked, her pulse kicking up.

"Inventory." He held up a clipboard.

"Me, too. Dad said we were shorthanded."

"That's what he told me."

Nathan looked so happy to see her she felt herself grin. "If you've got it covered, I guess I can leave." She made no move. Just kept staring into his wonderful face. The face she loved.

"It will go faster with both of us working."

"True," she said. "Very true."

"Then we'll work together," he said.

"Right. Together." What about the shoe? What about the painting? What about love? But the words froze in her throat. She couldn't talk about this surrounded by flats of cartons and giant rolls of cellophane and cases of confectioner's sugar.

So they got busy counting and writing and comparing totals and predicting supply needs. They worked seamlessly together, practically reading each other's minds. After a couple of hours they'd moved through all of the storage area and were ready for the refrigerated room. They moved past the front loader and Nathan held the heavy door for her. They worked steadily for two hours, moving quickly to overcome the chill in the room.

"Thirty-two," she called down to him. She was on the ladder counting the last cases of lime juice.

"Everyone's fired up about the new accounts," Nathan called up to her.

"That's great."

"Your dad gave me some of that margarita mix. You might want to up the lemon levels."

"I'll think about it," she said.

Their eyes met and held. "I meant what I said the other day, Mariah. You've added a lot to this place."

"I always have ideas. It's what I do best." It was implementation that hung her up. She was a butterfly who dazzled, then flew away...before she could screw up or disappoint.

"And Bernie's a different man, thanks to you. He's not even taking his midmorning naps anymore."

"He just needed something new to do."

"Nah. You've made a difference here."

"Nathan, if you're going to start that again..."

"I'm just telling you the truth."

"You think so?" she said, warmed by his words.

"Yeah."

"You may be right. Dave Woods asked my opinion the other day. He seems to think I know what I'm doing."

"You mean, once you stopped trying to get kicked out?"

She grimaced. "You knew?"

"You have many wonderful traits, Mariah, but being subtle isn't one of them."

She flushed. "Well, anyway I'm glad I could contribute."

"You have. Very much." He looked so sincere. So Nathan. She would miss him so much. How did he feel about her?

She wished they were in some dark, cozy restaurant and she was tipsy. Then maybe she could come out with it, settle this once and for all. Maybe she'd suggest dinner at Louie's when they finished with the inventory. There she could ask him about the shoe over some chianti. Lots of chianti.

They seemed to both realize they were still staring at each other at the same time and got busy again. "Where was I?" she asked him.

"Cornstarch," he called up.

"Right. Sixty-five," she called down.

"Got it. With these new accounts, we should consider buying some new equipment. Something refurbished. If we rearranged what we have on the factory floor, we maybe could squeeze a third setup in.''

"Nathan," she said, pausing to look down at him. "It's not *we* anymore. It's *they*. We're both leaving, remember?''

"Oh, right." He sounded so glum she felt sorry for him. "I hear you're interviewing people next week.''

"Yeah. We've got a couple of good prospects." She went back to counting. "Twenty cases of the Number Twenty tins," she called down to him.

He was silent, absorbing her news.

"Write it down, Nate," she gently urged. "Twenty Number Twenties.''

"Sure." He wrote it down.

"I think that's it for up here," she said, climbing back down.

He wasn't even watching her legs, as she'd caught him doing several times. He looked lost in unhappy thoughts. "There will be a lot of changes for the new person to handle," Nathan said. "I hope you hire someone flexible.''

"Absolutely.''

"Someone with vision, but grounded in reality.''

"It's right there in the job description.''

"Check out the references carefully. It's easy to puff up a résumé.''

"Why don't you sit on the interview team?''

"No. I might inhibit things. Sorry. I guess I do have a lot invested in this place.''

"You don't have to go," she said, holding his gaze.

"Neither do you." They stood there for long seconds, letting the idea sink in, letting the doubts and excuses fly and spin.

Now. Say it now. Tell him what you found. How you feel. But it was cold in the room. Some nice, warm restaurant would be better. Why was she such a coward about this? "It's getting late," she said, looking at a nonexistent watch. She grabbed his wrist to peer at his watch. "Six-thirty. How about dinner, Nathan? At Louie's?"

"Okay, sure."

She headed for the door, then pushed on the heavy latch and shoved. Nothing happened. She put her shoulder against the door and pushed again. Nothing. A chill raced down her spine, matching the cold in the air. "The door's stuck."

"What?" Nathan tried the door. "It's blocked from the outside." He looked through the crack they'd made. "Looks like the front loader's blocking the door."

"Oh, no," Mariah said, pounding on the door. "Help!" she yelled through the sliver of an opening.

"Everyone's gone," Nick said softly, searching her face.

"We're locked in?"

They stared at each other for a beat, then simultaneously threw themselves against the door.

"Ow," she said.

"We're stuck." Nathan rubbed the arm he'd slammed into the door.

"You mean, all night?" She swallowed hard. "We'll freeze."

He went to the thermostat. "Hmm. It's only fifty-four degrees. That's odd. We usually keep this colder.''

"So, then, we won't freeze to death?" she said, walking over to him, her arms wrapped tightly around herself.

"No. But it won't be very comfortable. Here." He started to unbutton his shirt.

"You can't give me your shirt." She wouldn't want to have to deal with a bare-chested Nathan on top of the cold. "I'll be okay."

"You sure? I guess there's always, um, body heat."

"Yeah," she said, a jolt of warmth shooting through her at the thought. "There's always that."

"Let's see what we can find to warm ourselves with." He rubbed his hands together briskly. "I think there were some packing pads at the back. You look around up here."

In a few moments, he'd returned with three thick protective pads and a box of red candles decorated with plastic holly. "Lenore must keep these in here so they won't melt."

"Terrific," she said. She held up what she'd found. "Something to warm us from the inside. Cooking sherry."

"Terrific. And with all the jelly and candy in here, we won't starve."

In a few minutes, they were sitting close together on one of the gray upholstered pads, a pad wrapped around each of them like a blanket, eating cactus jelly on crackers. The two red candles burned before them, not giving much warmth, but giving the room a nice glow. They could have turned on the light, but this seemed somehow nicer.

Mariah rubbed her hands together and pretended to warm them over the flickering flame. "Isn't this cozy?" she said, her teeth chattering from nervousness, not cold.

"Yeah, it is." Their eyes locked. The candle flickered in Nathan's eyes and made his face golden and shadowed.

What about the shoe? She needed some fortitude to ask. "Let's break open the sherry?"

"Exactly what I was thinking," Nathan said. He unscrewed the lid. "We'll have to swig it out of the bottle."

"No prob," she said, taking the opened bottle and tossing back a big gulp. It tasted like sweet vinegar, but it did send warmth down her throat. She scrunched up her face and handed him the bottle. "It's an acquired taste."

He took a gulp and grimaced. "At least it's warm."

"What time is it?" she asked.

Nathan held his watch within the candle's glow. "Eight-thirty."

"We've got a long night ahead of us. When will someone find us?"

"The first workers arrive about seven."

"Seven, huh? That's ten-and-a-half hours."

"You're not scared are you?"

"No. I'm fine." She was thinking of all those hours alone and close to Nathan. Not to mention the body heat possibilities. Huddling in the candlelight against the chill made the room seem as cozy and romantic as a cabin surrounded by snow. "What's to be scared of? Cavities from too much cactus candy?" She managed a smile.

"Are you cold?"

"No. Not at all."

"You can have my blanket, too." He moved to take it off.

"No. I'm fine. Really." She stopped his hand. "You're taking care of me again."

"Sorry, just habit."

"I know. You can't help the way you are. Just like I can't help the way I am." She dropped her eyes and stared at the sherry bottle. She took another swallow. This wasn't helping a bit. *Do you still love me?* Now was the time to ask. This wasn't Louie's, but they'd had dinner. And wine.

Speaking of which, she took another swallow of sherry. Maybe this stuff didn't have any alcohol in it. It sure wasn't relaxing her. She wasn't cold anymore, though. In fact, she was burning up with emotion and with everything unsaid between them. *Do you love me?*

I LOVE YOU. The words were on the tip of Nathan's tongue. The tongue that wanted to taste Mariah more and more each second. Here they were, inches apart, wrapped in blankets, staring into each other's eyes. There would never be a better time to try one last time.

But he was leaving. Moving on. Definitely. And he'd never felt worse in his life. *Look at that face. How can you leave that face?* In that hopeless painting, he'd tried to capture her energy, her spark, but it was no good. If he could just memorize it now...

Not enough. Never enough. He should just come out with it. *I love you. Stay with me.*

WHY'D YOU KEEP THE SHOE? The words screamed in Mariah's head, but still she kept quiet. They were staring into each other's eyes again for a hopelessly long minute. Like a standoff in a romantic Western movie. At the same time, they both blinked and grabbed the sherry bottle. Nathan's hand covered hers on its neck. They looked up at each other and spoke at once—"Don't go."

"Why'd you keep the shoe?"

"Huh?"

"What?"

"My wedding shoe," Mariah finished quickly. "I saw it on your bureau. Why did you keep it?"

"Why'd I keep the shoe?" He gave a humorless laugh and a wistful smile, then shook his head. "Good question."

She waited, her heart in her throat.

"You really want to know?"

"Yes," she said softly. "I do. Very much."

"I kept it for the same reason I need to leave. Because I can't let go of you." His voice was thick. "I still love you, Mariah. I never stopped." His eyes in the candlelight glimmered with an inner fire—just the way they'd looked all those years ago when he'd asked her to marry him.

Tears sprang to her eyes, making Nathan's image shimmy before her. She tried to swallow the knot in her throat.

"I know it's stupid. I know I shouldn't. You think of me as a father—"

"Oh, shut up," she said and threw herself at him so hard he practically fell over.

He recovered quickly, though, and kissed her back.

After a few glorious seconds, she dragged her mouth away long enough to say. "I love you, too, Nathan. I never stopped either."

His face lit with pure joy. The same joy that welled up inside her. And then he drew her into an embrace so tight she could barely breathe. "I want to make love to you," he said. "Are you okay with that?"

"Am I okay with that? God, don't be so civilized."

"You got it." And then he kissed her in about as uncivilized a way as she could want.

They kissed for a long time, gripping each other like they feared they might escape, hardly able catch a breath, using their lips and tongues to silently say everything they'd held back for so long.

Then Nathan's hands moved forward, slid under Mariah's shirt to hold her breasts. Thank God she wasn't wearing a bra.

"Oh," she said, breaking off the kiss at the electric charge of the contact. She'd been so intent on his mouth, she'd forgotten about how great this would feel. She pushed her breasts into his hands, wanting more and more.

"I remember this," Nathan murmured. "Holding you like this. Touching you this way." He pushed up her shirt and bent to put her nipple in his mouth. He sucked it teasingly, electrifying her, then released it. "I love how you taste," he said, then buried his face in her neck. "And the way you smell. Always the way you smell."

He kissed her neck. "And this line of your neck. So perfect." His mouth moved slowly down her throat. Meanwhile his fingers undid her buttons.

"I remember, too. I wanted you so much…oh, oh,…but you wanted to wait." She said the last in a rush, barely able to think for the sensations rushing through her. She fumbled at the buttons on his shirt, wanting his naked skin against her breasts, burning for it.

She pushed open his shirt and ran her fingers over his chest. His skin was firm and hot. Muscles glided beneath, and she could feel his heart pound like her own was doing.

Nathan pushed her blouse all the way open and off her shoulders. He paused, then touched a spot high on her left breast. "What's this?"

She glanced down. "My butterfly tattoo. Nikki designed it," she whispered.

"Your mother used to say you were like a butterfly."

"I know." *Always flitting around. Never sticking to anything.* She felt a flicker of pain. Could she stick to this? And if she couldn't, did she have any business making love with Nathan? But she wouldn't let scary thoughts ruin this moment. She placed Nathan's hands on both of her breasts.

He groaned. "God, Mariah. I've dreamed of this since the day you came back." He looked at her breasts, watched what his hands were doing, stroking her, squeezing her, making love to her sensitive nipples. She watched, too. It was so erotic she was afraid she might climax right then.

She longed to touch him. Through his pants, she felt that he was hard and ready for her. He shuddered at her touch, then stopped her hand. "I don't have anything on me."

"Oh, you have plenty on you," she said, reaching for him.

"No, I mean protection."

She chuckled, low in her throat. "I thought you Boy Scouts were always prepared."

He looked confused—so sweet, so lust-hazy.

"It's okay, Nathan," she said, kissing him softly on the mouth. "I'm on the Pill."

"Thank God. Because I want to be inside you," he said. "Where I've never been before."

She fairly melted at his words. That was true. Back then, they'd kissed, touched, brought each other to orgasm, but Nathan had never been inside her. They'd never been naked together. She couldn't wait.

"Get up," he commanded.

"Huh?" She could barely feel her legs, how could she stand?

"I want to make us a bed," he said, smiling a sexy smile. "We might be locked in a refrigerator on a cold concrete floor, but nothing says we can't be comfortable."

Together, trembling, their bodies golden and dreamlike in the candlelight, they folded the pads into a sort of mattress. In frantic wordlessness, they removed the rest of their clothing and lay down on the makeshift bed.

They were naked in a cold room, but they practically shimmered with heat as they lay in each other's arms, their legs twining, their arms around each other, reaching lower and lower.

Nathan's kiss started slow, then intensified, his tongue went deeper, his lips pressed harder. "I've wanted this so much," he breathed, holding her buttocks, pressing her against his erection.

She took him in her hands, and he groaned. "I love when you touch me."

His hand slid to her thighs. She parted them, but only a little. She was afraid direct contact might make her explode into orgasm. Reading her, Nathan barely brushed her hair, adding a tingling to the feelings she could hardly contain, but making her frantic for more of him.

Now she had to have him inside her. She shifted her body to show him what she wanted. But he already knew and gently made a space for himself and began to fill her. Slow at first, so slow, letting her feel each millimeter as he entered, joined with her. And then when her body wanted all of him, wanted to move, to thrust upward to meet him, when she couldn't wait another second, he pushed hard into her and deep.

A cry ripped from her throat. Thank God no one could hear her in this secluded place.

Again there was that sensation that Nathan was in her head, knowing her thoughts, her needs, anticipating the sensations she wanted.

"Mariah." He said her name as if being with her, inside her, was a miracle he couldn't believe was happening. He pulled away, then thrust into her, pulled away and thrust, each movement hungry and ready for more of her. And she loved it, took him in more and more, deeper and deeper, lifting her hips to catch him, to catch all of him.

She'd had good sex before—great sex—but not like this. So familiar, so deep, so in tune with her. This was so right she had no doubts at all.

He was her Nathan, her man, the man who'd wanted to protect her, wanted to wait for sex, afraid the intensity would scare her away. Now he was giving her what he'd withheld—all of it. She could feel his need for her, his love in every inch of his body, in the clutch of his hands, the way he held her trying not to hurt her even as he pleasured her and found pleasure in her. She could see it in the expression on his face, raw and hungry and adoring all in one.

She felt her orgasm coming, but she wanted to delay it. Wanted more of this moment of need and pleasure given and received. But she couldn't. She couldn't fight this feeling, any more than she could fight how Nathan felt about her.

The sensations twined and twisted and swelled and surged into a climax—a terrific jolt of joyful pleasure that made Mariah cry out and dig her fingers into Nathan's back, just to keep him close, to keep safe with him, to not fly off into oblivion. She hadn't known she could feel so much. And it scared her.

She felt Nathan tighten, his movements quicken as he, too, climaxed, his spasms intensifying her own. He made a harsh sound of need and satisfaction.

And then they lay still, quivering a little, panting. They'd made a cocoon of warmth on the cold floor. Heat radiated between them, making the space around them feel like a sauna. Nathan's lips brushed hers, then he studied her.

The expression on his face told her why he'd held

back eight years ago. Because he loved her so much. And that scared her a little. She loved him, too, but what if it wasn't enough? She was a woman now, she reminded herself, not the girl she'd been, and she could take his love and love him back.

But his love came with expectations. And hopes. And what if she failed him? What if she couldn't be the kind of person he wanted? She buried her face in his neck to hide from him.

"Please stay, Mariah," Nathan whispered so softly she wasn't sure she'd heard him at first. "Stay here in Copper Corners. Live with me. Work with me. Let's make a life together."

Oh, yes was on the tip of her tongue, and then she remembered who she was. "I don't know if I can, Nathan. I'm not good at staying. I never stay."

"But you've changed. You've grown up. We both have. And I'll help you."

Had she changed? Could she stay? The knot in her stomach tightened. Nathan was so eager and he wanted this so much. He seemed so sure. And it felt so good to be sheltered in his arms. She pulled his mouth to hers and kissed him to stop herself from thinking any more.

She would trust this, trust him, trust herself. Her arms found his broad, protective back. She closed her eyes, willing herself not to doubt, grateful to whoever had misplaced the front loader. Look what it had taken to get them to admit how they felt about each other, to take this great scary step into the unknown together. They'd had to be locked into cold storage overnight. She wasn't sure if that was a good sign or a bad one.

9

"¡DIOS MIO!"

The exclamation made Nathan open his eyes. Instantly, he realized where he was, that Mariah lay in his arms on the floor of the refrigerated room, and that Sonia Morillon and Nacho Valenzuela, two factory workers, were staring down at them in amazement from the doorway.

"We got locked in," he said, tucking the blanket protectively around Mariah.

Awaking with a jolt, she sat up and yanked the blanket around herself, completely exposing Nathan.

"Whoa," he said, retrieving a corner to cover himself. He'd intended to be dressed and waiting at the door when workers arrived, but they'd made love far into the night and only drifted off to sleep a little while ago.

"Some *idiota* left the front loader in the way," Sonia said, frowning at Nacho.

"Not me," he said, holding up his hands. "I swear."

Sonia said something doubtful in Spanish, and Nacho crossed his heart.

"Give us a minute, okay?" Nathan said.

"Oh, *sí, sí,*" Sonia said and motioned violently

for Nacho to back up, telling him in Spanish something about privacy.

"They know what happened," Nathan said, burning with embarrassment as he stumbled into his pants.

"You think?" Mariah grinned. "We were just trying to survive. All the survivalist books tell you to strip naked and combine your body heat." She stopped his frantic movements and kissed him. "I love you."

He felt like a kid at Christmas. Mariah loved him. He hadn't just dreamed it. He was so happy. And so amazed. In one cold night in a refrigerator, his entire life had straightened out. Mariah loved him. And she would stay.

At last he'd have that solid forever he'd dreamed of all those years ago. The one he'd been trying to convince himself he'd fabricated out of raw need. He didn't need a new job or a new city. The hole in his heart hadn't been from not knowing what he wanted, it had been from not having what he wanted— Mariah.

Every time he caught her eye, he saw love there. It had all worked. Impossible, but true.

When they emerged from the room every employee in the place stood in a semicircle applauding, whistling and wolf-calling. "They're probably just happy we survived the night," Mariah said.

"No, Mariah. They're just happy we're in love," he said. And then he threw out propriety and dignity and discretion and dragged her into his arms and kissed her—right there in front of God and the factory workers.

MARIAH STOPPED NATHAN outside the door to her parents' house. "Now act casual," she said. "I don't

want them going wild.'' Her father hadn't been at
Cactus Confections when they'd emerged from the
deep freeze, so she'd asked Nathan to help her break
to the news to her parents. They wouldn't make any
formal announcements about anything.

They'd just stop talking about leaving, quietly tell
the applicants for Nathan's job that the position was
no longer open, and let her parents gradually discover what they meant to each other. Nathan agreed,
though she could tell he wanted to shout the news to
the world.

She needed this to go slowly. She was happy, but
the knot in her stomach had been joined by a fist in
her chest. Things had changed so quickly, she wasn't
sure she was quite up to speed.

Nathan was right on top if it, though. Glorying in
it. So, she would try with all her might to catch up.
She took a deep breath—and Nathan's hand—and
stepped into the Monroe domain, braced for the
third-degree. "I'm home," she said.

Her mother breezed by the entryway carrying a
suitcase. "Hello, you two. I'm glad you're here so I
can tell you what to do while we're gone."

"While you're gone?" Had she missed something
here?

"Yes, your father and I are going on our first retirement trip. To Aruba. Scuba diving. For a whole
month."

"Scuba diving? Mother, Nathan and I were
trapped in the refrigerated room."

"Oh, dear," she said, fumbling with the zipper on
her bag. "But you're all right now."

"Yes, but weren't you worried?"

"Goodness no, dear. I slept like a log. Maynard was quiet as a mouse for once."

"You're going scuba diving?" she asked again, feeling like she'd been dropped into Bizarro World. "For a month?"

"One of our friends had to give up an exclusive package they'd bought. It's such a deal, we couldn't pass it up."

"Hi, there," her father's booming voice called. He, too, carried a suitcase.

"Dad. Nathan and I spent the night in the refrigerator room."

"You did? I'm glad you're okay. One pair of swim trunks or two?" he asked her mother.

Mariah had the sneaking feeling her father knew more about their ordeal than he was letting on. "You wouldn't have any idea how the front loader ended up in front of the refrigerated room, would you, Daddy?"

"Now why would your father know that?" her mother said.

It had been her father's idea that they both do the inventory. And the temperature had been set higher than normal, too. For once, though, the Monroe machinations had been on the money.

"Sweetie, this trip came up so quickly, I won't have time to take care of the baking for the high school reunion," her mother said. "I'll need you to make twelve dozen brownies. Also, don't forget to deadhead the marigolds. And it wouldn't hurt to feed the citrus trees. See if you two can get Matthew Gasteau to sing in the choir. He thinks it's a sissy thing to do, but Nathan, you're a musician. Just explain to him that music is manly, all right?''

"Sure, Meredith,'' Nathan said. He didn't seem the least disturbed by her mother's steamrolling.

"Call me Mom.''

"Mother!'' Mariah said.

"Sorry, sweetie. You two just make your own decisions about things. Take your time. But contact Imogene Simons so she can play at the wedding. She gets so busy in June.''

"Mother…''

"Anyway, can you handle those things for me?''

"I guess so.'' She felt her breathing constrict and her head start to hurt. So much was happening she didn't know if she could handle it all. If she were to stay in Copper Corners, she'd have to get her mother under control. Maybe Nathan could help her with that, too.

Her father stepped forward and put a hand on both of their shoulders. "I'm leaving Cactus Confections in your hands,'' he said soberly, looking from one to the other. "I want you to know I have complete confidence in you both.''

Her father's words felt like a lead weight on her shoulders and made her feel all wobbly. If she screwed up, she'd break her father's heart. She forced herself to smile and nod. The only thing that helped was looking at Nathan. He seemed so sure—completely serene about her father's burden. She could only hope he was right.

The next day, Mariah drove her parents to the Tucson airport, her head ringing with last-minute instructions from her mother—sign the contract with Meals-on-Wheels, make the crafts for the bazaar, weed the strawberries, get industrial freezer bags for the brownies, and on and on. She felt tense and overwhelmed. That morning, she'd woken up struggling for air with the smothered feeling she'd had as a kid. Of course, it turned out that she was holding a pillow over her face at the time, but still, the point was that she felt anxious.

LUCKILY, MARIAH WAS SO BUSY for the next week, she didn't have time for angst. She slept at Nathan's house, since her childhood bed was too cramped for them *and* Maynard, who slept at the foot of the bed. Now that Nathan and Mariah were together, he seemed to have forgiven Nathan for rejecting him, and actually went to him for an occasional scratch.

When her parents returned, Mariah could move in with Nathan and more easily evade her mother. At least she hoped she could. She tried to push away that niggling fear that she couldn't handle all this and focus on the best thing—Nathan.

Being with him was magic. They spent all their time together—locking themselves into his office to make out whenever they had a spare minute, racing home to rip each others' clothes off whenever they had a spare hour. And, each evening after work, rushing home for more, letting spaghetti burn on the stove or pizza cool on the counter as they lost track of the need for anything except each other.

Mariah couldn't stand to be away from Nathan.

Because when she wasn't in his arms, she started to think about what she'd gotten herself into.

The minute she'd stepped into Cactus Confections after her decision to stay, she'd felt it—that nervous sense of impending doom. She was in over her head. Nothing had changed except her plans, but now the new accounts seemed risky and each decision more dangerous.

Maybe it was because her father had declared he had faith in her. Or that Nathan seemed to trust her, too. Every time she told him she was nervous, he said everything was great, fine, wonderful. She was doing terrific. Her ideas were fantastic.

But she knew that he saw her through the eyes of love. To him, she could do no wrong. She was far from perfect. She had lots of flaws. What would happen when Nathan realized it?

"I DON'T THINK we can handle that kind of volume," Dave said, shouting over the hiss and rattle of the equipment in the processing room. It was two weeks after the night of love in the cold storage room, and Mariah was on the spot.

Nathan had gone to L.A. for three days to look over some refurbished machinery they might purchase, and had left Cactus Confections in her hands. "But I promised the restaurant chain the margarita mix," she said.

"The health-food juice order's due at the same time." Dave shook his head, then looked over the busy room. "We'll have to run double shifts."

"If these accounts take off, we can afford more

equipment. We just have to push it through this time.''

"Can't we wait until Nate finds some new machines?''

"I don't see how. We need the sales to pay for them. Nathan would want us to go ahead.'' She could call him again, but he'd told her she was in charge and he'd want her to act decisively.

"You sure?'' Dave asked.

Not at all. "Yes. Absolutely. You and Benny can keep the machines going. You're both magic.''

"Magic has nothing to do with it.'' He studied her a moment, while she tried to hide her doubts. "I hope you know what you're doing.''

So did she.

"Oh, and check on the containers for the juice,'' Dave added. "The shipment hasn't arrived yet.''

"Oh, right.'' She flushed with worry. Three days ago she'd realized that she'd forgotten to place the container order, so she'd had to find another supplier. The replacement jugs were cheaper, but the rush order charges made them as expensive as the ones she'd forgotten. At least they could make the juice shipment date. That was the important thing.

"What's wrong?'' Dave asked.

"Nothing. Everything's under control.'' Everything except her heart and stomach, which were pounding and aching. She hated that Nathan was gone. She needed him nearby to remind her that she could do this. He had so much faith in her.

Scared as she was, though, she did what needed to be done that afternoon. She reassured the health-food chain's marketing director that the juice shipment would go out in two days, timed to match the expensive run of ads he'd launched, and confirmed the order with the restaurant chain. Maybe everything was under control.

She got home late that evening. While Nathan was gone, she was staying at her parents' house so she could take care of some of her mother's chores. She made a note to replace the house and porch plants wilting from neglect before her parents returned. She still hadn't made the brownies for the reunion.

She opened the door and Maynard practically knocked her to the ground. "Hey, boy," she said, hugging his huge head. His unconditional affection warmed her to her toes. She didn't even care that he'd overturned the kitchen trash can so that the kitchen floor was carpeted in coffee grounds—a minor problem after the day's decisions and worries.

She couldn't wait for Nathan to get back. The message machine showed one message. Maybe he'd called.

"Hello, sweetie. This is your mother," came the familiar voice. "Don't forget the pinochle game on Friday." The line hissed with distance. "Hope things are going well. We're having a lovely time. Your father woke up a nurse shark while he was scuba diving and I'm getting a lovely tan." More crackling. "We're so happy for you and Nathan. Give him our love. Don't forget the marigolds. And choir practice tomorrow night. Is Matthew Gasteau in?"

She had that smothered feeling again. She loved her mother, but the woman was relentless. She had too much on her mind for pinochle. They could hold the game somewhere else. She deleted the message just as the phone rang.

"How's my love?"

Nathan. Thank God. "I'm so glad it's you," she said, flopping onto the sofa. She was dying to pour out her worries.

"What's the matter?"

I can't do this. I'm scared. Then she caught herself. Her anxious doubts had begun to annoy him, she knew, and there was no sense worrying him, too. "Nothing. I'm just tired."

"I know how that is. How are things going? Fine, I'm sure."

"We're getting there. I had to change the container order. And we're going to have to run back-to-back shifts to make the margarita order, too, but—"

"I miss you, Mariah," Nathan interrupted. "More than last night even." Emotion surged in his voice. The last thing he wanted to talk about right now was cheap containers and strained equipment.

"Me, too, Nathan." She closed her eyes, concentrated on the lovely longing in his voice, and blocked out her own self-doubt.

"I want my arms around you. This bed is so big and empty."

"I know. Maynard just doesn't make a good bedmate."

"I hope not. Or they'll really have something to gossip about at church."

She smiled, feeling light and happy for the first time in two days.

"I'll be thinking of you tonight," he said. "*All* night."

"I know." This was what she needed—the feeling she clung to. Of being loved, of being vital to his well-being.

By the time she hung up, Mariah felt better and more confident of herself. They'd been so busy sharing sweet intimacies, they hadn't even talked about the equipment he'd looked at.

The next morning, she went in early to see how the prickly-pear health juice was coming off the assembly line. A worried Dave was overseeing things directly. "Equipment's running hot," he said, shaking his head.

"Are we at quota?" she asked.

"Yeah," he said, his lips tight. "So far, so good."

"I'm sure it'll be fine," she said, trying to be the confident manager she should be.

Five hours later, the walkie-talkie crackled to life. "Get down here," Dave snapped.

She raced to the factory floor. The processing room had a strange echo—the machinery wasn't running—and was filled with the overpowering scent of burnt sugar and bitter juice.

"What happened?" she asked.

"The thermostats malfunctioned," Dave said tightly. "We burned a thousand gallons."

"Oh, dear." She saw Benny banging away at a valve, sweat pouring off his face.

"We'll run short," Dave said.

"We can't run short."

"If you want that margarita mix run, we'll be short."

"What about the frozen juice in storage?"

"Not enough."

"Well, just do what you can."

"You better back off the orders, Mariah. We need to shut down, oil the equipment and replace some gaskets."

"We can't. The stores are doing a promotion. I promised we'd make delivery. You've got to keep things going." Her head began to pound. She was aware of the workers watching them argue, their expressions anxious, their eyes flitting nervously from face to face.

Dave seemed to notice at the same time. "Okay, you're the boss," he said with a tight smile. Then he backed away. "Let's get to it," he said to the workers.

She watched for a while as they cleaned out the burned juice, their faces grim, conversations quiet, until she couldn't take it anymore.

She headed back to her office intending to call the health-food store to see if there was any flexibility in the schedule, but by the time she got there, she'd lost her nerve. She knew the answer already anyway. She just had to pray Benny could work his magic and Dave could stay on top of quality.

But her prayers must have gotten sidetracked because it wasn't long before one of the workers came to get her.

She found the processing room in chaos. Juice squirted from leaking pipes overhead. Workers mopped, yelled instructions to each other, and ran back and forth with tools. Dave, his face dripping with sweat and juice, worked frantically with a wrench.

"What happened?" she shouted up to him, panicking, but trying to hold it together.

"The juice got too warm and the containers warped. Some split. We shut down, but the pressure was too great and some gaskets blew."

"Oh, no," she said.

"I'm sorry," he called down to her. "I should have caught it sooner."

"You did your best. It's not your fault."

"I should have known better." He shook his head, red with heat, frustration and shame, she saw, and it broke her heart. A worker brushed past her mopping up the mess. Benny stood on a ladder, his face in a grimace, twisting a valve while a worker handed him tools. He swore and shook his hand—he'd cut himself.

And poor Dave was taking the blame. It wasn't his fault. She was the one who'd overpromised the new accounts, pushed Dave to overwork the machinery. She was the one who'd forgotten to place the container order and forced them to use the cheaper jugs.

They'd lost thousands of dollars of product and jeopardized the new accounts. And it was all her fault.

"Look out!" a worker yelled at her as another pipe cracked and juice spilled to the floor, splashing onto her clothes. The worker elbowed her aside and brought a ladder to climb up.

She couldn't stand the sight of the disaster she'd caused. She was just in the way here, anyway, so she practically ran out of the factory and back to her office. What should she do? What could she do? She felt so terrible, she just wanted to curl into a ball and cry. She should call the clients. Cancel the orders.

But maybe she should wait to be certain. Maybe they could pull this out. Maybe it would be okay. Who did she think she was, taking charge here? She was in over her head. She began to pace.

Fifteen minutes later, the door opened. "Honey, I'm hoooome." Nathan grinned at her, holding out his arms.

"Nathan!" she ran into his embrace. "I screwed up," she whispered, tears running down her cheeks.

"What's the matter?"

She told him the whole terrible story.

He stayed calm, but he went pale. "When did this happen?"

"Just now. They're cleaning up and fixing things."

"So what are you doing standing in here? You should be out there helping." He yanked off his suit coat, ripped off his tie, and started down the hall, rolling his sleeves as he went.

Mariah ran after him.

"Did you cancel the orders?" he called back to her as they ran.

"Not yet. I hoped it would work out."

He stopped and turned to her. She practically ran into him. "Are you dreaming? Go call them. Explain what happened. Then get out here and help. To boost morale if nothing else."

She felt herself redden. Right. That's what she should have done as a manager. Instead, she'd panicked and hid in her office. She nodded and ran back to make the call. The client was furious. She managed to talk him out of demanding they pay for the wasted ads and promised she'd get back to him with a revised proposal—and a deep discount. But she'd talk to Nathan about it first. She wasn't making one more decision on her own. Then she threw herself into the cleanup effort.

It was late into the night when they finished. Dave and Benny had somehow hobbled together the equipment, but only at half capacity. Grease-streaked and wet with juice, Dave wiped his forehead with his arm. "I'm sorry, Nate. It got ahead of us."

"We've got enough juice to fill most of our regular orders," Nathan said. "We'll just have to make do."

"It's my fault," Mariah said. "Dave told me the equipment couldn't handle it, but I told him to keep going, go into overtime. And I ordered the substandard containers." She swallowed, trying not to cry.

"I should have known better," Dave said.

"You both did your best," Nathan said. "That's all you can do."

Mariah followed Nathan into the office. He sank into the chair, his head in his hands.

"How bad is it?" she asked. She felt liquid with shame. They'd all trusted her and she'd failed them.

"We took a big hit."

"Can we give the health-food stores a discount? If we get more juice?"

"A discount? Are you nuts?" He looked up. She watched him try to tame his anger. "We'll have to rethink this expansion strategy. We moved too quickly.''

''You mean *I* moved too quickly.''

''No. *We*. Cactus Confections is a team effort. We'll have to buy that equipment now.'' He ran his hands through his hair, shook his head. ''I didn't think it was a good deal, but now we need it.''

She wanted to cry, but she had to behave professionally. ''I'm so sorry, Nathan.''

''Why didn't you tell me we were in trouble when I called last night?''

''I didn't want to worry you. I thought I had it handled.''

''But you didn't,'' he said tersely.

''I know that, okay? Don't yell at me.''

''I'm not yelling. I'm just...'' He dropped his hands and leaned back in the chair.

''I did the best I could.''

''I know you did. I'm just upset.''

She felt cold inside. He was trying to be nice, but he clearly thought she'd been an idiot. Irritation was written all over him. And this wouldn't be the last time. She did lots of irritating things. Right now she was on her best behavior. After a few months, when she relaxed... This was the reason for the rules—six-months-and-out for jobs, two-months-and-out for men. More panic shot through her. ''You think I was irresponsible, don't you?''

''I didn't say that.'' But it was true. ''It's over, Mariah.''

''What?'' His words startled her. For an instant, she thought he meant their relationship.

"We had a problem on the floor, but we'll just pick up the pieces and move forward from here."

What about their relationship? Would they move forward from here? Or stall out completely? She felt the tears come.

His gaze flew to hers. "Don't cry." He pushed out of his chair to hug her. But she felt the tension in his arms. He didn't have the energy to comfort her. She had no right to it anyway. She'd blown it and she had to live with that.

"Let it go, Mariah," he said. "We'll move on."

"Sure," she said. But she couldn't forget the look of anger and disappointment on his face when he'd told her she shouldn't be cowering in the office. He'd trusted her and she'd failed him. A strange feeling of doom swelled through her and a ringing started up in her ears.

She'd been so afraid she'd fail the people she loved and now she had. She hadn't even let herself think about how disappointed her father would be. He was off on a trip, swimming with sharks, blissfully confident his daughter was handling his business. Instead, she'd practically run it into the ground.

"Let's go home and get some rest," Nathan said. He put his arm around her shoulder.

But she couldn't be with him right then. She needed to be alone to think. "I'd better head to my house," she said.

He looked at her, startled. "To clean up and get Maynard. Then you'll come over. I've missed you these three days." He added the last almost as an afterthought. She could see he was still worried and very tired.

"Me, too," she mumbled. But she wouldn't come over. She already knew that. She didn't want to face him again. She didn't want to face anyone from Cactus Confections.

At the house, she found three huge cardboard boxes stacked on the porch. They were filled with ribbon and paint and pieces of carved wood she was supposed to turn into "Welcome to our Home" door decorations for the bazaar. God. The last thing she wanted to do was glue-gun baby's breath to pine boards.

She opened the door and Maynard nearly knocked her down, then loped away. She felt a rush of warmth and comfort. At least Maynard didn't think she'd failed.

She wiped at her cheek where he'd touched her in greeting. Gritty crystals. Oh, no. She followed him into the kitchen where she saw he'd somehow managed to reach the sugar canister and scatter its contents across the kitchen. His mug was snowy with sugar. No wonder he loved her. They were two of a kind. Complete screwups.

Mariah needed something to eat, but she hadn't been to the grocery store. She'd have to, soon, since she had to make all those brownies and there was a card party heading here one of these evenings. Monday, she thought.

Right now, ice cream would do the job. Cherry Garcia, to be exact. She removed a frozen turkey from the freezer and snagged the ice cream, then a spoon. Eating out of the pint container, she headed to the message machine.

The first was from her mother. "Honey, why don't

you thaw out that turkey and put it in the Showtime Rotisserie—put the prongs through it, put it on the rack, turn it on, set it and forget it. Just like the commercial says.''

She rolled her eyes. The next message was from Nikki. "Hey, girl. Check in with me. Haven't heard from you in three weeks. How's Nate the Great taking the therapy? Wait'll you hear about this great job. I make my own hours. Travel if I want. The money's terrif. I'll be able to lease my tattoo shop in a heartbeat. Call me. If things don't work out with Nate the Great, I bet I could get you on, too.''

Nikki could get Mariah a job. With "terrif" money. The idea came to her with a rush of relief. A different job. Something new that suited her. Something that wouldn't scare her.

She didn't belong at Cactus Confections. She wasn't cut out for that kind of responsibility. This was her family's company. People's livelihoods were at stake. She couldn't be in charge of that. She thought of Dave blaming himself and the bewildered, frightened looks on the workers' faces. This was not where she belonged.

It hadn't been her idea, anyway. It had been Nathan's. He'd talked her into something she wasn't ready for—just like when he'd proposed to her.

The only difference was that this time she was old enough to know what she was capable of. She was an idea person, not an implementer. And certainly not a manager. When her ideas were gone, she'd be gone. That was the way it was supposed to work. Six months and out.

She'd only been here six *weeks* and already she'd

screwed up. It would only get worse. She couldn't stand putting that look of disappointment on Nathan's face again. *What were you thinking?* he'd said to her.

What you wanted me to think. Nathan loved her and he'd seen what he wanted to see. The truth was, she was a butterfly. She stayed for a while, then she moved on. You could do self-help until the cows came home, but you were who you were.

The doorbell rang. Lost in thought, she went to answer it and found Lenore and Louise standing there, dressed in identical turquoise pantsuits. "We're a minute or two early," Lenore said.

"Early? Early for…? Oh, God. Pinochle! I thought it was Monday night. I have no food."

"Oh, dear." The twins looked at each other in alarm. They stared over her shoulder and their eyes got even bigger.

She turned and saw that Maynard had the frozen turkey gripped in his teeth. "Maynard," she said and set off after him.

When she finally wrestled the bird out of his jaws and carried it to the kitchen, nursing a bruise to her shin she'd gotten lunging over the bed, she found the beehive-coiffed ladies busily emptying cans of refried beans and grating cheese.

"What are you…?"

"We're punting, dear. Seven-layer bean dip." They set her to work whipping some cream to cover the half-gone Jell-O salad. As she whipped away, she felt tears slide down her cheeks—part gratitude to the sweet women, part despair at her own incompetence. She couldn't even handle a pinochle party.

"You're getting saltwater in the whipped cream, dear," Lenore said. "Why don't you go lie down? Today was a tough day at CC's. We'll handle things from here."

Without an argument, Mariah took Lenore's suggestion and sniffled her way back to her bedroom. She'd barely lain down when Nathan called.

"When are you coming over?" he asked.

"I'm too tired."

"You can rest over here—after we get reacquainted." He was trying to sound sexy, but she heard the weariness in his voice.

"Not tonight."

"I could come over there," he said, not really wanting to.

"The ladies are playing pinochle."

"Oh, well…if you're sure. I guess we're both pretty tired." He paused. "Listen, Mariah, I'm sorry I got on your case. It was a shock, that's all."

"You don't have to make me feel better, Nathan. I was doing too much. People have limits."

"Limits?" There was tension in the word. "What are you talking about?"

"I'm just saying…" She swallowed. "I don't think Cactus Confections is the right place for me."

There was a long, heavy silence from Nathan, and when he spoke, there was restrained anger in his voice. "Mariah, this isn't a temp job you can just quit when things get tough or you get bored."

"You saw what I did. I'm not cut out for that kind of responsibility."

"You just have to learn to ask questions when you're not certain."

"I *was* asking questions. You kept telling me to relax, that everything was fine."

"Those were little things. This was a big thing."

"It's all big to me, Nathan. I'm not the person you think I am."

"Yes, you are," he said.

"No, I'm not."

"Not that butterfly bit again. You've grown past that."

"No, I haven't. And you wanting it doesn't make it so."

"I just want you to try. Is that too much?"

"I guess so."

"What's going on, Mariah? This isn't about Cactus Confections, is it? It's about us."

"You're disappointed in me. I know you are."

"A little, maybe. I expected too much, I guess. You're new to all this. But so what? We both learned a lesson. I'll be more cautious and you'll ask more questions. That doesn't change the fact that we love each other."

"For now."

"For now? What does that mean?"

"It means feelings can change."

"Mine won't."

Sure they would. As soon as he saw the flawed, fumbling person she really was, the rosy picture he had of her would fade. She didn't speak.

"Stop it, Mariah," he said fiercely. "Don't use this as excuse to break us up."

"I've been leaning on you too much, Nathan. Counting on you for my confidence. I have to make my own way."

"So make your own way. But don't give up on what's good. Commit yourself to something. Stick it out for once."

She heard judgment in his voice. Just like her mother when she'd run from that all-wrong wedding eight years ago.

"I'm too tired to talk now." She couldn't stand hearing his voice—puzzled, irritated and hurt—any more.

"Don't do this, Mariah," Nathan said. "I love you."

"I know you do." She remembered how full of love his face had been that night in the refrigerated room when they'd first made love. He'd worshipped her. Too much. The smothered feeling she'd been having wasn't just from her mother being overbearing. It was Nathan, too. He wanted too much from her. She could never keep up. It was bad enough she'd disappointed him at work. She couldn't bear to disappoint him in love.

In spite of the tears choking her, she managed to say, "I love you, too, Nathan."

10

NATHAN FOUND THE NOTE in his mailbox, wrapped
around a house key.

Dearest Nathan: I can't be the person you want
and I can't live with disappointing you. Sometimes love's not enough. And sometimes it's too
much. Please take care of Maynard until my
folks get back.

There was more about a mutual fund she would
cash in to help cover some of the losses and that
she'd left a note for her parents, but he couldn't get
past the fact that she'd done it again. Flitted away.

And she had the nerve to sign it with a drawing
of a butterfly.

He crumpled the note in fury. She'd run away like
a teenager—picked up her wedding skirts and escaped him again. Except this time, instead of a shoe,
she'd left him a dog.

Damn it, Mariah.

He went to get poor Maynard from her parents'
house and brought him home, getting angrier and angrier every minute. How could she do this to him
again? Pain welled up in his chest.

Was he doing what she said? Trying to turn her

into something she could never be? No, he wasn't. Maybe he'd pushed her. But, damn it, she needed pushing.

He was pacing his living room when Maynard trotted into the room with something in his mouth. A shoe. He realized it was Mariah's bridal shoe. "Bring it here," he said to the dog. Subdued by his mistress's abandonment, Maynard trotted right over and dropped it at his feet.

Nathan picked it up, then tapped the grass-stained heel into the palm of his hand. Last time Mariah ran out on him, he'd stood there holding the shoe like an idiot.

Not this time. This time he'd go after her. He had her Phoenix address. Without stopping to think, he packed some clothes and set off in his car, bringing Maynard so the poor guy wouldn't think they'd both abandoned him. Damn it, he'd make her be honest with herself about what she felt and what they shared.

It hadn't been right eight years ago—she'd been too young and he'd been wishfully thinking. This time, she was a woman. And she loved him. She was just scared. He would help her face her fear. He wasn't backing down this time. For once, he was going after what he wanted.

He was an hour down the highway before he realized how stupid this was. This wasn't Hollywood, where the hero threw his love over his shoulder and whisked her back to the happy ending.

Even if he succeeded in bodily dragging Mariah back—and knowing her, that was extremely unlikely—she'd never know it was the right thing to do. She had to see that this was the life she needed—Cactus Confections and him.

She loved him, he knew that. But she had to learn a lesson about her own worth. And he knew just how to teach her.

Pulling into Tucson, he found the nearest post office and sent Mariah her wedding shoe, overnight express. She'd get the message. She'd have to come back to him on her own two feet...in her own two satin shoes.

That was Part One. Part Two, he'd implement in a few days. He'd help Dave get things under control, then head off on his motorcycle. He needed a visit with his mom—all that self-awareness crap had got him thinking about how much he owed her, and how much he'd left unsaid. He could show her his chops on the sax and get her thoughts on love while he was at it.

He'd stay away long enough for Mariah to get her head on straight, keeping in touch with Dave all the while. He'd have to make sure she knew he'd left. Maybe have Dave call and ask for her help. Mariah loved him, but she had to get her beliefs about herself in line. He was taking a chance, of course, and doing things the hard way. But he'd waited eight years for his butterfly to come back. He could wait a little while longer.

"PHONE'S FOR YOU," Nikki said to Mariah, dangling the phone over the shoulder of her boyfriend, with whom she'd been making out. "Someone named Lenore? She sounds nervous."

"Lenore? What could Lenore want?" Mariah felt

that little zing of disappointment that it wasn't Nathan. She'd been home a week and she knew better than to expect him to call. He'd sent her back her shoe. He'd given up. It was over.

Everything should be fine. She was back where she belonged, with her dear friend Nikki and a cool new job hand-selling exclusive cosmetics to boutiques. But she felt like a failure. And she missed Nathan like life itself.

"Hello?"

"So sorry to bother you," Lenore said, "but the bazaar is next week and we really need those welcome signs you were making."

"The welcome signs? Oh, right. I left them with Mary next door. She said she'd finish them."

"Well, terrific, then."

"How are things at CC?" she blurted.

"Oh, so-so. Dave's been in knots since Nathan left."

"Nathan left!?" Where had he gone?

"Oh, yes, dear. I assumed you knew that, since, well, since you both left at the same time. I was so sorry things didn't work out with you two—"

"Where did he go?" She couldn't believe Nathan had left Cactus Confections just like that.

"I wouldn't know that, sweetie, except the first day I heard Dave carrying on, swearing and muttering about why that blankety Nathan had to blankety-blank find himself on a blankety-blank-blank motorcycle. Something ear-burning like that."

Nathan had gone ahead with his plan? Left on a motorcycle? He hadn't even had a motorcycle when she left. Oh, dear. "Who's doing his work, then?" It wasn't like Nathan to just quit.

"Oh, Dave is, but he's not a happy camper about it. He keeps hollering about how he can't make all these blankety-blank-BLANK decisions. We're just hanging on by our French-tips until your father gets home next week. But don't you worry about that, sweetie. We know you were just observing and you have to dance to your drummer."

"Sure," she said. "I'm glad you understand." She told Lenore to call her back if the door hangers didn't show up, and disconnected, sick with remorse. Her parents would return to a struggling business and no Nathan. No her, either. That was terrible. Poor Dave. He didn't want to manage Cactus Confections. And her father wanted to retire. Now, he'd be stuck working until they could find a replacement for him.

"What's wrong?" Nikki asked. "You look like the world just came to an end."

"It kind of did," she said. "Nathan took off."

"Mr. Responsible cut and ran?" In her excitement, Nikki sort of knocked her boyfriend off the sofa.

"Ow," he said, but he was used to Nikki's unpredictability.

"Wow. He must have flipped out," Nikki continued.

"Yeah." Because of her.

"What are you going to do? Go after him?"

Now she and Nathan had both left a mess behind. That wasn't right. "I'm going back."

"You're what?"

"I've got to go back and fix things." Okay, she'd

screwed up. People had counted on her, and she'd let them down. She had to try to make up for it. Besides, Nathan was gone. If she didn't do it, who would? Poor Dave, blankety-blanking all the way?

"What about six-months-and-out?" Nikki asked.

"Sometimes changing jobs can be a rut, too, you know."

"Wow," Nikki said. "I'm proud of you. I'll help you pack. One thing, though. You're not taking those nasty outfits your mother bought you. Don't go corporate. Just be you."

"I will, Nikki. Thanks for reminding me. And for being my friend." The two women held each other for a long moment, wordlessly giving support.

All packed, Nikki and Mariah did a Rebel Girls Forever handshake for courage and Mariah set off. She was in a panic all the way down to Copper Corners and almost turned back twice.

The minute she pulled into the parking lot of Cactus Confections, though, a steady calm washed through her. She had work to do and she was the only one who could do it.

She went straight to the factory floor. Dave Woods caught sight of her and his eyes went wide. "How'd you get here so fast? I just left a message on your machine."

"I have my ways," she said.

"Me, too," he said, smiling as if he had a secret.

She took a deep breath. "Okay, what do you want me to do?"

"Everything," Dave said. "The place has gone to blankety-blanking hell since you've been gone."

She didn't stop to agonize or doubt or worry. She

just went to work. Maybe it was because she was needed. Maybe it was because neither Nathan nor her parents were around to be disappointed in her, but she soon found she wasn't even scared. She would do her best. If her best wasn't enough, well, at least for once she hadn't flitted away.

THREE WEEKS AFTER her return, Mariah looked up from the computer screen and saw that her office had gone dim around her. She'd stayed late again. She'd kept Nathan's office mostly the way he'd left it— adding some decent art, bringing in some plants and her satin wedding shoe, which she'd placed next to the geode. She kept it in sight as a reminder of her mistake…and her hope.

She'd been working hard. And she was careful about what she did. Double checked everything—to Dave Wood's continual annoyance. He'd become more of a partner with her, though she'd dragged him kicking and screaming into the role. And she tried not to doubt herself too much.

She hadn't changed, really. She'd just realized there was more to her than she'd thought. She wasn't worried about boredom, either. That was something else Nathan had been right about. Challenging work never got boring if you didn't scare yourself about failing.

If only Nathan could see her now. She owed him for giving her this chance to confront her fear of failure—to see what she was made of, to stick to something for once. If only she could tell him. Surely he'd call, once he figured out what he wanted to do. She could only hope what he wanted to do was come back to Cactus Confections. What if he found someone else to love? That made her heart ache.

But, surely he'd call and give her a chance to thank him, and apologize for leaving him and maybe, just maybe, to try again. Did he miss her? Or was he still angry at her? It would serve her right if he never forgave her.

The phone rang. She picked it up.

"Choir practice, dear." Her mother, in her usual bulldozer tone.

Her parents had returned a week after she had. The disappointment in her father's face over the juice fiasco had been painful to see, but her plans to recoup the loss were solid. Nathan was right. You moved on from mistakes and kept going. Disappointing people wasn't the end of the world.

Her parents had freaked out about Nathan's departure, too, until for some reason, a discussion with Dave Woods calmed them down. Mariah was grateful they'd said nothing about the love affair. She couldn't have stood their pity.

Now Mariah looked at her watch. The last thing she wanted to do tonight was sing. "Can't I skip tonight?"

"Not this practice. It's vital—v-i-t-a-l."

"Okay," she said on a sigh. She'd have to stop at the 7-Eleven for packaged donuts, since she was in charge of refreshments. She should start telling her mother "no." But strangely enough, her mother's urgings didn't seem to bother her so much any more. She just smiled away the ones that didn't fit.

Mariah flipped off the lights and locked the door. She took a look at the building's exterior and felt a deep satisfaction. Her place. Her home. She'd come into her own here. If only Nathan could see her now.

At that moment, a car whipped into the driveway, jerked to a stop beside her and Nathan jumped out.

"Oh, my God. What are you doing here?" She hadn't even wished on a star. Was there a genie around here making her every wish his command?

"We need to talk," he said, trying to sound stern with a big goofy grin on his face. "Please get in the car."

"Okay," she said, sliding into the passenger seat.

Immediately, he pushed the button locking the doors with a harsh click.

"What? You think I'm going to bolt?"

"I just want to be sure you hear me out."

She grinned, wanting to throw her arms around him, tell him everything. "Nathan, I—"

"Just let me talk first, okay? Before I lose my train of thought." He was clearly so happy to see her her heart just sang. He seemed to have a speech prepared. The least she could do was let him give it. "If you insist," she said, feigning reluctance.

He roared off, driving as fast as he began to talk. "I love you, Mariah. And you love me. I know you're afraid, but you don't need to be. You can stick it out. Just like you're sticking it out at Cactus Confections. Dave says you're doing great, by the way."

He took a corner with a squeal. "Of course there will be bumps on the way. There always are. When we hit the bumps, we'll hang on. Our love is like, um, air bags and seat belts all rolled into one. Absolutely safe and secure. I know that sounds dumb…" He glanced at her, checking her reaction.

"I know exactly what you mean. I think that I—"

"I'm not done yet. What I was saying is that I have faith in you. And by now you have faith in yourself, right? I mean Cactus Confections is out of danger, and you haven't needed me or anyone else." He jerked to a stop in the church parking lot of all places.

"How did you know I was coming to choir practice?"

He didn't answer. His eyes flickered across her face, full of love…and doubt. Doubt she'd put there, she realized.

"Is it my turn to talk?" she asked.

"It depends on what you have to say," he said, wry and worried at the same time.

"I think you'll like it."

"Well, then. Yes, it's your turn."

"Okay. You're right, Nathan. Completely. I've just been afraid you loved the idea of me, somebody I could never be, and that the real me, the screwup, would disappoint you."

"You couldn't have been more wrong, Mariah." He turned to fully face her. "Remember that special someone you asked me about during that counselling session?"

She nodded.

"I said she'd be someone with fire in her soul, who'll make me think, and make me laugh. Someone I couldn't wait to come home to just to see her face, hear her voice, find out how she's been while we were apart."

"I remember."

"That someone is you. In every way. Exactly as you are. Mariah, will you marry me?"

"You want to marry me? Again?" Her heart was pounding, her ears ringing, and she was so happy she thought she might burst.

"I know you always think of yourself as a butterfly, but even a butterfly has to rest sometime, find a mate and create baby butterflies—I mean caterpillars—to carry on the butterfly genes... Hell, I don't know what I'm saying."

"I do," she said softly. "You're saying I can stay with you and still be me."

"Exactly."

"That you'll love me even if my wings get tattered or lose their color. That however I am is good enough for you."

"I couldn't have said it better myself if I'd been able to think straight." He grinned.

"Then, yes, I will marry you."

"Thank God."

She leaned in for a kiss, but he was out of the car and over to her side tugging her to her feet before she knew what had happened.

"What are you doing?" she said as he hurried her up the sidewalk. "We need to talk. Choir practice can wait." She tried to drag her feet, but he wouldn't let her lag.

He opened the door of the church and pulled her inside. In the foyer, Mariah saw her mother standing there holding a dress. A fluffy monstrosity of a dress. Her seventeen-year-old bride's dream of a dress. It was overdone and ridiculous, but it brought tears to her eyes.

Her father stood behind her mother holding Nathan's tuxedo. Beyond them, Mariah could see that half the town of Copper Corners had assembled in the pews.

"What's happening?" she asked Nathan.

"We're getting married," he said, grinning, "Before you change your mind."

She stared at him openmouthed. "What if I'd said no?"

He cleared his throat. "I believe your father has a shotgun."

Her father lifted his thumb. "Don't forget the front loader."

"You did lock us in that cold room! I knew it!" Mariah said.

"Your father is quite a pill," her mother said. "Now you two will have to convince him he has to really retire."

"You aren't retiring?" she asked him.

"We had to do something to get you two back together," her father said. "Lord knows you didn't make it easy."

"Oh, for heaven's sake," she said, amazed and so happy she couldn't believe it. "You were all plotting against me."

"We were all plotting *for* you, sweetie," her mother said.

Mariah turned to Nathan.

"Don't look at me," he said, "The only plot I cooked up was leaving you alone to succeed at Cactus Confections and getting you here right now. And just in case you were going to be difficult, everyone's prepared for this to be the rehearsal," he said. "In case it took an overnight to convince you."

"Oh, Nathan," she said, looking into his dear face. "I love you so much." Then she kissed him, overwhelmed with emotion, filled to the brim with the feeling she'd longed for all her life—that she was solid and centered and where she belonged, sure of herself and her love for the man who'd helped her find herself. The butterfly had landed at last, safe and secure and deeply loved.

Dawn Atkins

Tattoo for Two

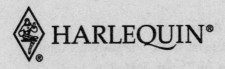

HARLEQUIN®

TORONTO • NEW YORK • LONDON
AMSTERDAM • PARIS • SYDNEY • HAMBURG
STOCKHOLM • ATHENS • TOKYO • MILAN • MADRID
PRAGUE • WARSAW • BUDAPEST • AUCKLAND

Dear Reader,

If you were shy or just plain goofy in high school, the idea of wowing them at your high school reunion is irresistible. It's so irresistible to Nikki, she's willing to fake it. This, of course, is a mistake.

I love Nikki. Her urge to protect her family from her unconventional life is so sweet and so misguided that I couldn't decide whether I wanted to shake her or hug her. With Hollis's help, Nikki learns that you have to trust your loved ones to accept you for who you are, no matter what. And Nikki teaches Hollis a thing or two about letting his hair down and doing what he wants, not what others expect of him.

I looked at tattoos while researching this book. I stopped passersby to admire their body art and to ask them how much it hurt. I even sketched out a couple of tattoos for myself. Of course, Nikki would have said my aura wasn't right—I had to put my head between my knees not to pass out when I got my ears pierced. Thousands of needle sticks would have sent me screaming into the street!

A word about friendship. Though my own best friend and I now live in different states, our relationship has grown even stronger over the years we've known each other. We may not have a "Rebel Girls Forever" handshake but just setting eyes on each other makes us laugh out loud with joy. I hope you all have love in your life and a best friend like Nikki or Mariah.

Best,

Dawn Atkins

P.S. Write me at daphnedawn@aol.com!

Books by Dawn Atkins

To my father,
whose pride in me means
more than I can say

1

"My hair is spiked with pink tips and I have four earrings in one ear," Nikki Winfield said, bracing the phone against her shoulder so she could put the last dabs of ink on a sketch. "One look at me and my mother would pass out. I'm not coming home for the reunion, Mariah. Period."

"Come on, Nikki," her best friend Mariah Goodman pleaded, perky as a cheerleader. The spirit of Copper Corners had seeped into her since she'd returned to the small town where they grew up. "It'll be fun. We can pull a stunt for old times' sake. Remember when we set up those mannequins to look like they were doing the deed in the nurse's office?"

"Like it happened yesterday. I also recall my father suspending us for a week and my mother having to leave the classroom to collect herself."

"We were kids. Our parents understand."

"Yours maybe. Mine are a little more sensitive about it—being the principal and the English teacher and all."

"Besides, you haven't been home in ten years."

"And that's for the best. My parents think I'm safe and happy."

"You are safe and happy. You have your own business."

"It's a tattoo parlor, Mariah. They'd be horrified."

"It's not like a biker hangout. It's New Age. Psychic and everything. And you're doing fabulously."

"Not on my parents' terms, or Copper Corners'. Or my landlord's right now. He didn't consider my late lease payment too fabulous."

"What happened to Rebel Girls Forever?" Mariah prodded.

"Ten years, I guess. Ten years happened." Though it had only been in the past few months that Nikki had begun to wonder if maybe the Normal Nancy Nine-to-Fivers had something. Maybe the life she'd chosen was too hard.

"You sure you don't want to come?"

"I'm sure."

"Okay, then." But her friend wasn't done with her yet, Nikki was certain.

"You know Brian Collier's getting divorced," she said.

"Really?"

"Yep. Papers filed. And he's asking about you. He came in to Cactus Confections pretending to want some cactus jam, but all he really wanted was to find out if you were coming to the reunion."

"You're kidding." The news gave her a little rush. Brian had been a popular football player and babe magnet. She'd been amazed he'd gone for her, a kooky artist, and had barely gotten used to the idea when he dumped her for Heather Haver, the head cheerleader. So cliché she would have laughed if her heart hadn't been bleeding all over the bleachers when she first saw them making out.

"So, come on down," Mariah prodded. "Give the boy another walk on the wild side."

"I don't think so."

"Copper Corners isn't the hellhole of conformity

it once was. We have a karaoke club and an art gallery now.''

''Now you're getting desperate.''

''Maybe. But I'm telling you the place has changed.''

''No, you've changed, Mariah. Found true love and a career. You're a born-again Copper Corner-ite. You've gone corporate, for God's sake.''

''We make candy, Nikki. That's hardly Fortune 500.''

''I bet you're wearing a business suit right now.''

Silence. ''Clothes aren't everything.''

''They used to be. Clothes were symbolic, remember? A reflection of the inner self. 'Conformity bites,' right?'' The idea sounded goofy now, but at the time they'd been very serious about it—dressing in wild combinations, weird fabrics and funky jewelry they'd made themselves. Everything they did made a statement about who they were.

''I dress up to meet with the accountant. So what? It's a costume, that's all. Match the costume with the performance. You do that, too, don't you?''

''Not really.'' She looked down at her leather halter top and fake leopard-skin zipper skirt. She would have worn this outfit back in high school, though she'd have had to sneak it to school in her backpack. And then been sent home to change. It had been such a drag to have both her parents at school. ''For me, going home wouldn't be the way it was for you.''

Nearly two years ago, Mariah had left the apartment they'd shared in Phoenix to return to Copper Corners to convince her former fiancé Nathan not to leave his job managing her family's candy factory. Except she'd fallen for the guy all over again, married him for real, and now ran the company with him. Instant happily ever after.

Nikki's life would never come together that smoothly.

"You never know," Mariah said.

"Believe me, I know." Her future might be a mystery, but it wouldn't be in Copper Corners.

"Brian's still a hunk. No beer gut or anything. And he got all dazed when I started telling him about you."

"You didn't tell him the truth, did you?"

"No. And when I said you were married he got so flustered that he bought an entire case of jam he didn't want. Ka-ching."

"He got flustered? That's nice. Thanks, then. You made my point for me."

The tinkling of the chimes over her shop door made Nikki look up. A young woman entered with that I-don't-care-how-much-it-hurts-I'm-getting-a-tattoo look on her face.

"I've gotta go, Mariah. Customer."

"Don't say no, say maybe."

Nikki motioned for the girl to sit in the chair across the counter from her. She turned the huge notebook of tattoo samples to face the girl. "Tattoos await," she said to Mariah.

"You can borrow my Madonna-the-early-years black-lace bustier...."

"No thanks."

"Nikki—"

"Bye."

She clicked off the phone. "Sorry," she said to the girl. "How can I help you?"

"I want a tattoo." The girl giggled. "Yeah, right.

Why else would I be here? Anyway, um, my friend Jeannie said you're really good.''

"Jeannie? Unicorn with a rainbow mane?''

"Yeah. It came out great.''

Nikki smiled in satisfaction. "When a tattoo's right, it's right.''

"Jeannie said you pick out the right tattoo for each person? Um, based on their vibes?''

"That's how it works. Shall I see what's up with you?''

The girl nodded.

"Give me your hands.'' Nikki took them— clammy and cold—and looked into the girl's face— nervous. Too nervous. "And you are…?''

"I am? You want my name? Oh…um, Le-Linda.''

Fake name. Hmm. "Okay, Le-Linda. Let's see what I can see.''

She placed the girl's hands on her palms, bounced them gently, then let them rest so she could soak up the girl's energy. She closed her eyes, inhaled deeply and exhaled slowly, her bangles jingling musically. Orange light swirled behind her eyes preparing her mental screen for the picture that would form like a fortune appearing in a novelty eight-ball.

"What is it? What do you see?'' The girl leaned forward.

Nikki held her breath…paused…the picture fuzzed, cleared, fuzzed again. She frowned.

"A yin-yang?'' the girl asked. "A sun and moon? I don't see myself as a unicorn like Jeannie, but maybe a leopard.''

"Shhh,'' she said. Fuzzy…still fuzzy…

"What I really want is Xena, Warrior Princess. I was thinking shoulder area.''

Then Nikki felt it. The no-no vibe. Clear as day.

Le-Linda was not ready for a tattoo. Probably never would be.

She'd break it to her gently. She opened her eyes, patted the girl's hands. "I felt a wobble in your vibe, Linda. You're not quite ready for a tattoo. I'm sorry."

"What do you mean? I'm definitely ready."

"Tattoos are permanent."

"That's why I want one." She locked her jaw.

Nikki studied the girl's face. She was angry and resentful about something or someone. "What's up?" she asked. "What brings you here today?"

"I want to say something, okay? About who I am."

"Because…?"

"For one thing, my boyfriend's getting all serious on me. But the big thing is my older brother. He's giving me all this attitude—straighten up, get your GPA up, your future awaits, yada, yada. I'm nineteen years old. I can live my own life without him looking over my shoulder all the time."

"I know how you feel. I had a perfect older sister who drove me nuts. I wanted to do my own thing."

"Did you get a tattoo?" she demanded.

"Yes, but it was different for me." She'd been on her own and needed the courage the tattoo represented. Le-Linda's rebellion was obviously temporary. "My best friend and I ran away from home together when we were seventeen and—"

"Really? Maybe I should do that. Drop out of college and start over somewhere else. On my own."

"You don't want that. I was too young really. It was tough. I had no diploma, had to take a bunch of bad jobs. I took the GED eventually, but—"

"And now you have this great shop."

Nikki followed the girl's gaze. She was proud of True To You Tattoo. It had a unique atmosphere. Crystals decorated the front window, art photos of her best tattoos were suspended from the ceiling. Potted herbs, exotic house plants and hanging baskets of vines gave warm life to the place, and a careful blend of scented candles and incense filled the air with spice.

"I was lucky."

"Well, my luck starts with a tattoo," Le-Linda said.

"Why don't you just talk to your boyfriend and your brother?"

The girl stubbornly tapped her own shoulder. "Xena, please."

"Look, I know a great place for henna tattoos. They last a month if you're careful. And you can see if you're really cut out for a tattoo."

"You really think I'm not ready?"

"Really." Le-Linda was wavering. Good.

"But are they as good?"

"Absolutely. And, if you decide to go permanent, I'll give you ten percent off."

"I don't know…"

"Xena will still be here."

Finally, she sighed. "Write the address down then. I don't know how you stay in business if you won't give tattoos to people who want them."

"Good point." Some days it seemed like Nikki turned down more clients than she tattooed. But she had standards and she would not budge. She sent Le-Linda off with the address and some advice. "Look before you leap, tell your boyfriend to lighten up and your brother to back off." But the girl just rolled her eyes and said, "You don't know my brother."

After Le-linda left, Nikki sketched some new designs that had been rattling around in her brain, but she had trouble concentrating because of the conversation with Mariah, so she decided to take a lunch break. She turned the sign to "back in an hour" and headed into her home—the other half of the duplex that held her shop—to make a tofu salad she could hardly taste.

Her friend knew her too well. The news about Brian Collier had kicked up her pulse. The long-ago heartbreak still hurt. She'd thought Brian had really gotten into her—liked her style and her ideas. But in the end, she'd been too much for him, and he'd galloped over to Heather the minute she crooked a candy-apple-red-tipped finger at him, dumping Nikki like so much funky laundry.

That was her first twinge of insecurity. She'd never said anything to Mariah, who'd been defiant and fierce about their differentness, but she'd begun to wonder if "living an authentic life free of convention" wasn't always what it was cracked up to be. For her anyway.

Part of her would love to go to the reunion—strut through Copper Corners acting outrageous and shock the town out of its complacent parochialism. But that was a childish wish, and it would embarrass her parents.

When she'd left at seventeen, fueled by anger, resentment and pride, she hadn't cared about her parents' disappointment. She'd plunged into her future with a vengeance.

But over the years, she'd realized how difficult she'd made life for them. Sure, they hadn't understood her, they'd been too strict and too inflexible, but they'd acted out of love. So she'd made up for it the best way she knew how—by convincing them she'd found a life they'd want for her. She'd made up a husband and a business they'd like.

One day she'd have the life she really wanted— True To You Tattoo would make a profit and she wouldn't be living hand to mouth anymore. More importantly, she'd find a real husband. He'd be as dependable and successful as Warren—the fake doctor husband she'd made up to reassure her family— but with an emotional intensity that matched her own. And he'd love her for who she was in all her quirky glory.

Then maybe she'd go back to Copper Corners— the prodigal daughter returneth. She'd still have to pretend True To You Tattoo was a boutique, of course. Profitable or not, a tattoo parlor was too bizarre for the folks at home. But with her success evident and a man in tow, she'd prove to her parents and the whole town she'd turned her life around.

For a second, she entertained the thought of faking her successful life for the reunion. She'd love to see the look on Brian's face when he saw what he'd passed up.

The phone rang, interrupting her reverie.

"You have to come home." It was her sister Donna at her blunt best. Her family only had her home number and wrote to her at a P.O. box, so that Nikki never had worry about either how she answered the phone or having her parents show up at the shop out of the blue.

"Hello to you, too." She and her older sister only spoke when Nikki called on holidays and birthdays. Since she'd had kids, Donna didn't seem capable of a conversation that wasn't punctuated by kiddie sidebars.

"Oh, right," Donna said, humbled into using her manners. "I'm sorry. Hello. How are you?"

"I'm fine. How are you?"

"You have to come home."

"Did Mariah put you up to this?"

"Mariah?"

"About the reunion?"

"God no. This is about Daddy."

"Daddy? What about Daddy?"

"Brace yourself, Nikki. He's had a heart attack."

"A heart attack? Oh, no." Her throat constricted until she could hardly breathe. "How bad?"

"Very." Donna paused for effect. "They're not even sure he will make it."

"Oh, no." Nikki sank into the closest chair, her mind reeling. "But he's only fifty-five."

"I know." Donna's voice cracked. "So young." There was some commotion in the background—her niece Shelley shrieking something about a Popsicle.

"Give your sister the purple one, Byron," Donna snapped in a tone that was awfully fierce for someone who'd been overcome by grief a second ago.

"But *I* want the purple one," Byron whined.

"If you ever want to see Dimples again, do it!" Donna snapped. Though the threat was worthy of a kidnapper, Nikki figured Donna meant the green dinosaur video she'd sent her nephew for Christmas. He was wild about it, she knew.

Donna returned to the phone. "Anyway, Daddy's having one of those heart balloon thingies put in tomorrow. He's asking for you and Warren."

"He's asking for me...?"

"And Warren. Because he's a doctor. He wants to consult with him about his condition. But he'd kill me if he knew I was telling you this. Mom, too. They don't want you worrying. So, don't let on you know.''

"Sure. I understand.'' Oh, God. She floundered for something to say, while she figured out what to do. Her father was sick, maybe dying. And asking for her. Of course she'd come. "I'll have to work some things out—find someone to take care of the, um, boutique for me.'' She swallowed hard. "But I doubt that Warren will be able to make it. He's, uh, very busy at the hospital.''

"Your father may be dying, Nikki. How can you deny him this chance to meet the man you married? I'm warning you....''

"There's no need to threaten, Donna.''

"Not you, Nikki. I'm talking to Shelley. Tick-tick, young lady, the time-out clock is ticking. Get that Popsicle out of your nose. I can't talk any more right now, Nikki. Will a Popsicle melt before a person can suffocate?''

"But, Donna, I—''

"Just do it, Nikki.... Byron, don't do it.... Shelley, if you do that, I'll—oh, hell! Gotta go. Just come home.'' Click.

Nikki hung up the buzzing phone. She didn't want to think about her stern, competent father having a heart attack. Or worse, dying. Donna tended to exaggerate, but her family usually ducked talking about infirmities and she'd never make up surgery. This was definitely real.

Nikki covered her face with her hands and tried to think what to do. She'd have to go home for a few days at least. She'd say Warren was on call. She'd already used the mercy mission to South America.

Fake Warren had been a mistake. News of a rash of robberies in her Phoenix neighborhood had made the state-wide papers and her father had been so worried, Nikki had created a boyfriend, naming him after the brand of ink she was using at the moment, so her father would think she was safe.

After a year, her parents started asking how serious things were. Exasperated by all the phone calls, she'd said they were engaged. Then her mother had called early one morning while she was in the shower. The man she was sleeping with at the time picked up the phone, so Nikki'd had to say they were married. Made up an elopement story. It sounded stupid, but the delight and relief in her mother's voice was a powerful reassurance that a happy white lie was the way to go.

The thought of the disappointment, sadness and worry her parents would feel if they knew the truth made her heart ache.

She headed back into the shop, still worrying about her father and making up buyable excuses for her devoted husband's absence from his father-in-law's sick bed.

Customers kept her mind occupied the rest of the afternoon. She tattooed an eagle, a rising sun and a peace sign, and talked a couple who were clearly temporary out of putting their names on each other permanently. At 6:00 p.m., she turned her sign to "closed," locked up and went back to her home.

In the kitchen, she started water for chamomile tea and put a tiny bowl of lavender essential oil under her diffuser candle for some soothing aromatherapy. She added an extra dose of lavender for good measure. Her poor father. She had to see him. But she dreaded it, too. Manufacturing a life over the phone was a lot easier than faking one in person. If only there was a Warren in her world.

Bam. Bam. Bam. Someone was pounding so hard on the tattoo shop door the windows in her side of the duplex were rattling. Nikki frowned. True To You Tattoo was closed. Couldn't they read the sign? She'd been known to tattoo late-night lovers just for the romance of it, but she wasn't in the mood tonight, no matter what anyone's aura said.

2

HOLLISTER MARX BANGED on the shop door again. What kind of maniac put a tattoo on a nineteen-year-old girl? He'd make the guy pay to have it removed, by God. Of course, Leslie wouldn't want it removed. Not until she'd settled down and realized how stupid a tattoo was. Then she'd have to scrounge up five grand for the painful laser procedure to remove it and this guy would be long gone.

The idea made him even angrier. Bam. Bam. Come on. It was only six-thirty. Somebody had to still be there. He cupped his hands around his face so he could see through the glass of the door. The place looked clean at least—lots of hanging plants and candles. Odd for a place frequented by lowlifes, delinquents and ex-cons. And his poor confused sister.

Damn. He wished Leslie would just grow up. By the time he was her age, he was already on a career path. At a certain point you had to give up some options and just do the right thing. On top of that, he didn't have enough time to keep bailing her out of irresponsible jams.

He had enough on his hands dealing with the new office and now the new wrinkle with Rachel. He couldn't believe she'd bought the rings. Rings? They'd barely talked about taking their relationship to *the next level* and she'd gone and bought a "trio."

God. *I couldn't resist. The price was perfect.* Sometimes Rachel's practicality irked him. Besides, ever since the "M" word had come up, he'd felt dead inside. When he'd told her he needed time to figure this out, Rachel had been furious.

The door at the back of the shop opened. Good. But, instead of the big-bellied bruiser he'd expected, a petite woman strode toward the door. He caught a blaze of black leather, a multitude of earrings, an irritated expression and nice cleavage.

She opened the door an inch. "We're closed."

"I need to talk to you about a tattoo."

She opened the door wider. "*You* want a tattoo?" Amusement shadowed the annoyance in her voice. She'd pegged him as a yuppie. He shouldn't care, but he felt self-conscious in his Dockers, golf shirt and styled hair.

"It's not for me. It's my sister."

She frowned, but let him enter, crossing her arms as she waited for his explanation. Even as he steamed, he couldn't ignore how good she looked. She was pretty, despite the thick makeup, earrings everywhere and pink-tipped hair. Her leather halter top cupped great breasts and exposed a flat stomach above a skin-tight animal-spotted miniskirt. She'd look great on a motorcycle. Like the one he had in mind to rent for his make-sense-of-it-all getaway. *Focus, Hollis.*

"You gave my sister a tattoo," he said, getting to the point.

"And?"

"*And*…the thing is outrageous—this Amazon woman on her shoulder."

"What's your sister's name?"

"Leslie Marx. She was in here this afternoon."

Leslie's friend Jeannie had told him this was the shop she'd gone to.

The tattooist considered the name, a smile flickered, then faded. She shook her head. "I don't remember a *Leslie*."

"She's probably not your usual customer. She's a college student."

"Oh, really?" She was offended, he could see. Her eyes lasered in on him, a remarkably bright green. "Be that as it may, I did not give your sister a tattoo."

Calling the woman a liar wouldn't help things. "Then maybe your assistant did it."

"I don't have an assistant. And, anyway, since when is it your business what your sister does with her body?"

He'd better calm down. He needed her help here. "You have every right to run your business the way you want, as long as your clients aren't underage and you have a license." His gaze flew around the room, but all he saw were fancy photos of elaborate tattoos and some modernist paintings.

"The state doesn't require a license to tattoo."

"You're kidding." Great. The state required licenses for dog catchers and egg inspectors, but not crazy people with needles.

"Relax. The needles are single use and I have an autoclave for sterilization."

"Oh. Well. Great." That was a relief. That meant Leslie couldn't have picked up some blood-borne ailment in addition to a permanent scar. "Look, I'm not trying to give you a hard time. I just want to help my sister."

"Did she *ask* for your help?"

"She *needs* my help. And let's you and I just stick with the subject at hand."

"All right." She tilted her face at him, challenging him. "Did the design have a brown tint to it?"

"What? I don't know. I guess it was brownish. And huge. It goes clear up her neck. Turtlenecks are the only thing she'll be able to wear. She'll never survive a summer."

"Henna." She pronounced the word like it should mean something to him. "Was it Xena?"

"Henna? Xena? I don't know. It was a woman with armbands."

"That's Xena," she said confidently. "I didn't give your sister that tattoo. And even if I had, what would you want me to do about it now?"

"She's coming back," he said. "When she does, I want you to refuse to do another one."

"You want me to turn down a customer?" She seemed to be enjoying his distress.

"Yes, I do. Look, I'll pay you."

"No thanks." Her eyes flashed angry green sparks like Emerald City glittering in the distance. "Look, Mr. um—with all the accusations flying, I don't think I caught your name...."

"Sorry. Hollister Marx."

"Hollister? That's a mouthful. Listen, Hal, I don't give tattoos to people who don't really want them. Your sister came in, I think, except she gave the name Linda, not Leslie. Her aura wasn't right, so I—"

"Her what?"

"Her aura. I get a sense of each client to see whether they really want a tattoo and which design would be right for them."

"You're kidding." The woman was a complete

nutcase. He was suddenly grateful for Rachel, who, even when he disagreed with her at least made sense most of the time.

"No. And don't judge things you don't understand, Hal."

"I prefer Hollis."

"Okay, *Hollis.* Don't judge things you don't understand."

"So, go on…. Her aura wasn't right, so you…"

"So I suggested she get a temporary tattoo—it's painted on—no needles, okay? Did you even give her a chance to tell you it was temporary?"

"She didn't try to explain."

"I don't blame her—with your attitude, I wouldn't, either."

"So, you're saying it will wear off?"

"Yeah. In three weeks. Four, if she's careful with it."

Relief washed through him. "And you refused to give her a tattoo?"

She just looked at him. More Emerald-City sparks. The woman was kooky, but she had principles, at least. She was intriguing. And intense. Very intense.

And he'd been a jerk. "I guess I owe you an apology," he said. "I didn't catch your name."

"I didn't give it. It's Nikki. And you owe me more than an apology, Hal. I was having a quiet cup of tea on my own time when you dragged me out here."

"I'm sorry. I just worry about my sister. She's going through a phase."

Hollister Marx was an overbearing ass, Nikki could see, but his concern for his sister made her decide to go easy on him. "She says you're driving her nuts."

"She told you that?"

"Oh, yeah. She's nineteen, she says, and she can live her own life without you looking over her shoulder. That's where she wanted Xena, by the way. On her shoulder."

"I see." He sighed. "My sister can be difficult." A pain in the ass, more like. "I apologize for jumping to conclusions and interrupting your evening. Can I pay you for your time at least?" He reached for his wallet.

It figured. Money solved every problem for guys like him.

"Just give your sister a break. It's her life, after all."

"I'll consider that," he said with a smile. "I appreciate your not giving Leslie that tattoo. I really do." His gaze held hers for a second. She felt a little jolt of connection. Under all that mousse and designer clothes, this guy was handsome—nice cheekbones, thick hair. Honest eyes.

A nice traditional guy. Like Warren, as she'd imagined him.

He cleared his throat, then dropped his gaze. "Well, I'll let you get back to your evening."

He turned to go, then turned back. "Just to be clear, though. When she comes back, you won't give her a tattoo, correct?"

No, she wouldn't. But the way he said that—like she couldn't be trusted—hit her wrong. Plus, it was fun to bug him. "Depends on her aura. If she's ready, I won't deny her the right to illustrate her body."

"What? Come on. This is just a phase."

"Then her aura will tell me that."

"Oh, for God's sake." He was getting mad. He was the kind who did a slow burn. She couldn't wait to see what he'd say next. But he just sounded calm.

"Look, I'll give you my number. If she comes in, call me, okay?"

"Like I said, it's her body."

"I just want to talk to her before you start injecting permanent ink under her skin. Would you allow that?"

"We'll see," she said, goading him.

But he wouldn't rise to the bait. "Got a pen?" he asked calmly. She handed him one of her fine-point sketching pens. He took a business card out of his wallet, turned it over and began writing.

"The number on the front is old. I'm moving into a new office. Here's my home number." He started to hand the card to her, then he frowned and took it back. "Actually, I'll be out of town most of next week, so I'd better give you my cell phone." He wrote down another number, then handed it to her.

Their eyes met. Another peculiar jolt shot through her. "Where you headed?" she asked, just to keep him talking.

"Not really sure. I just need to get away."

"From what?"

He sighed. "My life."

"Your life's tough?" Interesting.

"Not really. I just need to do some thinking."

"About what?" Why was she poking at him? Curiosity. What kind of problems could Mr. Perfect have?

"You don't want to know my story. Just call me."

Just call me. The words hung in the air. He hesitated, as if considering their implications.

"I will." She wanted to. For all the wrong reasons.

"If my sister comes in."

"Right. If your sister comes in."

The moment stretched until Hollis seemed to realize how odd it was that they were still staring at each other. "Well, then, thanks." He turned to go.

"Good luck with your thinking."

She watched him walk out the door, tapping the business card on her lip. All in all, a nice package. Then she looked at his card. *Dr. Hollister Marx, General Dentistry.*

Doctor? Doctor Hollister Marx? God. He *could* be Warren. He was a dentist, but they still called him "doctor." Wouldn't it be cool if she could get him to come to Copper Corners with her as Warren?

He'd never do it. But what fun to try to talk him into it. He'd be perfect. Think how happy her parents would be if she arrived with him. He could even give her father the medical advice Donna said he'd been asking for. Well, dental advice, anyway. Medicine was medicine. And he *did* owe her a favor....

He was getting away. She rushed to the door and called to him. "Wait a minute."

"Yes?" He stopped on the sidewalk beside his car.

"I've got the perfect place for you to do your thinking."

"You do?" He was interested, but he thought she was joking.

"Yeah." She went close. Very close. "Come with me to my high-school reunion."

"Right." He laughed, then headed around the front of his car, still watching her.

"I'm serious. I need a date for the weekend."

"You're kidding."

"I just told you I was serious."

"I couldn't do that."

"You just said you didn't have any plans." She followed him to the driver's side.

"But we don't know each other and it would be, well, odd." He stepped back, as if she'd overwhelmed him. She tended to do that with men.

"No, it wouldn't. It would be fun."

"I'm flattered, but I don't think so." He unlocked his door and opened it. He'd turned her down just like that. Impossible. She'd felt the attraction vibe throbbing in the air between them. Did he think he was too good for her? Oooh, that did it.

She slipped her body between him and the interior of the car. "Let's cut to the chase," she said. "If you come with me to my reunion, I promise I won't give your sister a tattoo."

He stared at her, his brows high. "You're blackmailing me?"

She was bluffing. Leslie wouldn't be back for a tattoo, but he didn't need to know that.

"Not at all. You offered to pay me for my inconvenience. Consider this my fee." She folded her arms.

"But, I don't think…I mean… This is ridiculous."

But she could see he liked the idea. Good. She hadn't completely lost her touch. "Come on, Hal. It'll be fun. It'll be a great getaway. And you can think about your life to your heart's content."

"I can, huh?" A brief smile flickered onto his face. Good.

"Unless you find something better to do." That made his *eyes* flicker. Even better.

"I don't know…"

"Come on. What's the worst that could happen?"

3

HOLLIS PULLED UP in front of the tattoo parlor on
Friday afternoon to pick up Nikki, not quite sure how
this had happened. Something to do with saving Les-
lie from a tattoo and Rachel's ultimatum—*in or out?
Make up your mind on that stupid motorcycle trip.*
He didn't do well with ultimatums.

Then there was Nikki. Something about her was
tough to resist. Or refuse.

He'd be back Sunday night from this reunion in-
sanity he'd agreed to, so he'd still have a few days
for his motorcycle trip. And he wanted that, damn it.
That had been the plan before Rachel bought the
rings—enjoy his last few days of freedom before he
took over the practice. Rent a bike for old times' sake
and just drive, camp by the side of the road, stretch
his legs and his mind. Now he had to think about the
"M" word.

Maybe away from Rachel, he'd remember his feelings for her, and the cold tightness he'd carried
around since their fight would ease. Rachel was a
good person. She'd been hurt by his hesitancy, and
she'd covered it up with bossy demands. He hated
ultimatums, but she went nuts over uncertainty.

He'd told her he needed time. She said they didn't
have any. Her biological clock was ticking and after
the kids were in school, what about her career and
the glass ceiling? He'd said something about they

hadn't even moved in together and she was looking for a retirement home. From there, it was downhill.

All he'd wanted was a motorcycle ride, damn it. And now here he was, pulling in front of True To You Tattoo precisely at the agreed-upon time, locked into three days at a strange woman's reunion. Uneasily, he realized the prospect should be more unpleasant than it was.

What's the worst that could happen? That's what Nikki'd said with that wicked grin that promised she could think of a million things—and he'd hate them all.

It was only a weekend, he reminded himself, though Nikki'd been a little vague about the schedule. There would be separate hotel rooms, though, so it was completely on the up and up.

Then why hadn't he told Rachel about this detour from his plans? That bothered him. On the other hand, Rachel would never believe he was succumbing to a blackmail demand from a tattoo artist. He hardly believed it himself. He had the sinking feeling this wasn't the last surprise Nikki had for him.

He looked around. Where the hell was she? Late. Not an auspicious beginning to the weekend. That added to the sinking feeling in his gut. She was slippery, all right.

It wasn't until he'd agreed to her reunion blackmail that she'd told him her home town, Copper Corners, was a four-hour car trip, and before he knew it he'd agreed to drive. Somehow, she'd bulldozed him. Worse, he hadn't exactly struggled. One shot of those emerald eyes and he'd thrown himself under the giant tires of her will.

Something about the woman made him want to step back. She was so *there,* practically glowing with energy. Even though she dressed like a rebellious college kid, she looked his age. There was more to her than met the eye. And there was plenty that did. Meet the eye, that is.

She'd told him he looked like he could use some fun in his life. She was right about that. Work had been his world for so long he didn't know what fun was. Something told him Nikki knew all about fun. All kinds of fun. The prospect made him tighten up all over. *Get a grip.* He might be almost an engaged man.

He was doing this for Leslie, remember? And this was the last time he was bailing his sister out. He'd had enough of negotiating incompletes when she blew off her finals and covering her MasterCard bills. Now because of her—sort of—he was spending a weekend with a wild woman in leather and weird hair…and great cleavage.

Think about the bike trip. He closed his eyes and imagined getting on a motorcycle again and taking off. Except right away Nikki appeared in his mind's eye riding with him, gripping him around the waist, her body pressed against his back.

What's the worst that could happen? Plenty.

Through his open window, Hollis saw a woman heading his way with a grocery sack and a large duffel over her shoulder. The height was right, but this woman was the girl-next-door type—floral dress, chestnut hair in a soft under-curl. She shifted the sack and he got a load of her breasts. Perky, high. And familiar. Uh-oh.

A few steps closer and he could see her eyes. Emerald-City green. "Nikki?" He couldn't keep the amazement out of his voice.

"You like?" she asked, turning so he could look her over.

"You look so…"

"Normal? Ordinary?"

"Different." Never ordinary. But he had to admit he was disappointed. For some stupid reason, he'd been looking forward to leather and leopard skin.

"I'm going for the Miss Copper Corners look."

"You nailed it."

With a triumphant grin, she threw her grocery sack—provisions, she called them—into the back seat, tossed her duffel into his trunk and sank into the seat beside him, bringing in a blast of that spicy musk. At least she hadn't changed her scent.

"Why the new look?" he asked.

"For the comfort of the folks at home. They can't handle the real Nikki Winfield."

"I see." He probably couldn't either, he thought, pulling away from the curb. Unfortunately, the softer look didn't dampen her sexiness one iota.

Nikki leaned over the seat and rummaged in the sack, brushing his arm as she moved. Nice. He frowned. She plopped back into her seat with several items. "Road snacks," she said, shoving a plastic sack under his nose. "Cheese poofies dipped in sour cream. And Tecate. The best. I'll serve you poofies, not beer, since you're driving."

"It's barely noon and you're drinking beer?"

"What? You think I should get some Scotch?"

"God."

"Come on. Noon schmoon. Road trips are time-less—like Vegas. Ever notice there are no clocks in casinos? Same deal. When you're on a road trip, it's always a party." She fumbled in her purse, then pulled out a CD, which she slid into his player. "Road trip music. You like this group?"

He paused to listen. "Yeah. I do. A lot."

"Terrific. Something in common." She grinned and began to dance in her seat. He tried not to watch.

"Cheese poofie?" She waved an orange puff slathered in sour cream in front of his face. When he shook his head, she said, "You don't know what you're missing," and popped it in her mouth.

"I'll take my chances." Out of the corner of his eye he watched her mouth work over the thing.

"Mm, mm, mm," she said, the sound so orgasmic he felt a twinge below decks. He'd have to focus on what annoyed him about her and not get distracted by her natural sexiness. "You were late, you know."

"You can't be late for a road trip. They're timeless, like I said. Road Trip Law."

Road Trip Law. That was probably the only kind of law she obeyed—the ones she made up.

Nikki sucked down a poofie and pondered her position. Judging from the serious set of his jaw and his slight frown, Hollister Marx, D.D.S., wasn't ready for the real story on this trip. She wanted to break it to him gently. If all went well, he'd stay for the reunion. If she was going to be in town anyway, she'd decided to try for it. It would be fun to show off a little. Live out her fantasy of impressing the home towners. Plus, she wanted to pick up the attraction vibe from Brian.

Of course, she couldn't let anything happen with Brian. She'd be there with her "husband," and adultery was way more scandalous than painting nudes on a high-school mural. Still, the personal satisfaction would be enormous. *See what you gave up?* A childish impulse, maybe, but she had a right to gloat a little, didn't she? And high-school reunions were all about remembering when and proving things.

If she ever hoped to get there, though, she had to get Hollis into the spirit of the thing. Once they were too far to turn back, she'd tell him his whole role in her homecoming trip.

This just had to work. If she'd had any doubts about her plan, her mother's excitement when she'd told her she and "Warren" were coming had zapped them. Her mother's voice had been shaky with emotion, and the fact that Warren was coming had positively thrilled her. Nikki hadn't positively thrilled her mother since she'd won the eighth-grade art contest.

So, she had to get cracking on Hollis. She looked at the Tecate in her hand. Drinking. That would loosen him up. She'd offer to drive so he could throw back a brew or two, then she'd deal with his beer breath before they got to her folks' house.

"So, you're a dentist, huh?" she said to get him talking. "Where's your office?"

"Until last week, it was at the mercy clinic in St. Mary's Hospital," he said, pulling onto a major street. "We take care of low-income people—mostly kids—for free."

"Charity work. I'm impressed."

"Don't be. They paid me a salary. Not a great one, but still money. And last week was my last."

"So you just quit?"

"Not exactly. I bought a practice."

"You *bought* one? How does that work?"

"Dentists who quit or retire get their practices appraised and then sell them—equipment and patient records."

"Kind of instant office, huh?"

"Pretty much. Instant debt, too."

"Hmm." She dipped another poofie into the cream and ate it. She loved this treat. She leaned back and just tasted it, chewing slowly, licking her lips slowly. "Mmm." So good.

"Do you have any idea what that's doing to your arteries?" Hollis asked crossly.

She stopped chewing and stared at him. What was his problem? "The AMA changes its tune on cholesterol every time another study comes out. Why deny yourself pleasure on the off chance they're right? What happens, happens. We could get hit by a truck any minute."

"Not while I'm driving, we won't." He gripped the wheel with renewed determination. Kind of sweet, she thought, to be so committed to safety. Sweet in a boring kind of way.

"It's not you I'm worried about," she said. "It's the universe."

"That's pretty fatalistic, don't you think?" he said, braking for a red light.

She shrugged. Acting on impulse, she dipped another poofie into the cream and thrust it between his lips. He resisted, though, and sour cream smeared onto his mouth.

She ate the rejected treat, then caught sight of Hollis licking the cream from his lips. Mesmerized, she stopped chewing. She liked the color of his tongue—pink, not grossly red like some, or too pale. And he was good with it, too. Again that zing went through her.

He glanced at her, caught her staring and stopped licking. Their eyes locked. Uh-oh. Energy careened between them like steel balls in a pachinko machine. The stoplight went green. Hollis slid his gaze forward and accelerated, squeezing the wheel so hard his knuckles whitened.

Nikki sunk deeper in her seat and stared out the windshield. Uh-oh. She didn't even like the guy, but she was attracted to him. Weird. He wore Dockers, for God's sake. *Starched* Dockers.

The silence stretched.

Nikki tried to focus on her goal. "So, didn't you like working on poor people?"

"No, I loved it," he said, sounding relieved at the easing of sexual tension. "The patients were great and I was needed."

"So, why quit?"

"It was time." He shrugged. "I needed to buckle down and get serious about my practice."

"Poor people with toothaches are pretty serious."

"I always planned to open my own practice. I'm twenty-seven, so it's about time I got going. There were plenty of dentists ready to take my place at the clinic."

She heard the clear ring of regret in his voice. "But you miss the clinic already."

He jerked his head to look at her, startled by her words. She'd seen it many times. People were surprised when she seemed to read their minds. She wasn't clairvoyant, just supersensitive to people and the clues their gestures, eyes and breathing patterns gave her about what was in their heads.

"I'll love my practice, too, once I get into it."

"Sure you will." But he had doubts. She didn't need second sight to tell that.

"What about you? When did you decide to become a tattoo person?"

"You mean, between being a stripper and peddling pot at the elementary school?"

"You have to admit it's an offbeat line of work."

"I guess so. I've always been into art. When I left home with my best friend, I designed us both tattoos as symbols of our new lives. When I watched the woman put them on us I realized how amazing it was to bring a design to life on someone's body—like a human canvas, a traveling art show sharing my work with the world. Or, if the tattoo was in a personal area, a more private showing. So, I got trained. Got good. Opened up a shop."

"But you don't tattoo people who shouldn't have them?"

"A tattoo is an expression of a person's soul. I don't take that responsibility lightly. So, I don't tattoo anyone who's been drinking, who's acting on a dare or being pressured by friends or lovers. Anyone I get a no-no vibe from."

"That aura business?"

"It's a gift."

"Sure," he said.

But he thought it was an act. That irked her. "Scoff if you want, but it's real…. Like I know things about you already."

"Oh, yeah?" He glanced at her. "Like what?"

"Okay." She turned in her seat and looked him. "To do a real reading, I'd need to hold your hands and look straight into your eyes."

"Sorry." He lifted his hands from the wheel for a second to show her they were occupied, but she could tell he was as relieved as she was they couldn't link fingers and connect gazes.

"So, this will have to be a limited reading." She considered his profile—straight nose, clean lines, firm jaw. That and what his sister had told her about him made this easy. "Let's see… Hollister Marx follows the rules. As a kid, you kept your room picked up, your pencils sharp and your homework done. You wore a watch probably from age nine and never needed an alarm clock to wake up in the morning. As and Bs all through school, magna cum laude in college, and you only partied after finals and never to excess. Top marks in dental school, too.''

''I'm impressed, though I *did* need an alarm clock. And I don't *always* follow the rules.'' He frowned, though, as if annoyed that she'd nailed him.

''If you say so.''

''Keep going.''

''Okay.'' She looked a little closer. He had a solidity and predictability about him that, though boring to her, she knew most women found attractive. ''You've always had a steady girlfriend. A few breakups, but nothing devastating. No wild flings.'' Then a realization hit her with a strange disappointment. ''In fact, you have a girlfriend now.''

His sharp intake of air told her she'd been correct. That explained why he acted so jumpy around her and how relieved he'd sounded when she'd promised separate rooms at the Days Inn. But why hadn't he actually mentioned his girlfriend yet? ''What's her name?''

''Um, Rachel, actually.''

''Is it serious with Rachel Actually?''

''We've been seeing each other for quite awhile.'' She noticed his ears went pink at the edges. He wasn't sure about Rachel Actually. Double hmm.

''So, are you finished with the reading?'' he prompted, probably to distract her from more questions about his girlfriend.

''Almost. Let's see… You're careful with your money. Already you've got savings. You make New

Year's resolutions and keep them. You don't believe in luck and you've never swum naked.''

"Not bad," he said, nodding slowly. "Except you make me sound pretty dull."

"Well, if the perfectly polished wingtip fits…"

"Don't be so sure. I could surprise you," he said.

"Come on, Hal. You've never colored outside the lines in your life."

"What if I told you I dropped out of dental school, bought a motorcycle and rode through the Southwest for three months."

"I'd be surprised."

"It's true. It was a café racer. I loved that bike."

"Now I'm impressed. What happened?"

"I went back to dental school the next semester."

"Figures." So much for the Rebel without a MasterCard.

"I had some good times, but I needed to finish school. I'd invested time and effort. My parents had spent a lot of money."

"You still have the bike?"

"I sold it. Too dangerous."

"But you loved it. Hell, life is dangerous. Why not go down doing something you love?"

"It was time to move on."

"My point exactly. You're so by-the-book. You even rebel on schedule. Now you've got your practice. Next, let me guess, you'll marry Rachel Actually, buy a house and get a dog—a golden retriever, since they're good with kids and you need the practice before you have children—a boy and a girl if you can manage it. And there you have it—a perfect by-the-book life."

"What's wrong with that?" He frowned.

"Nothing, I guess." Here was a chance to get in

a plug for the little adventure she was dragging him into. "But how will you know unless you try something different?"

"I don't have to try something to know it's not for me."

"Come on. When was the last time you did anything spontaneous?"

"I do spontaneous things. This trip, for example."

"I blackmailed you, remember?" And she was afraid it would take kidnapping—a bigger crime—to keep him for ten days as a fake husband. Her courage flagged for a second. She went for more food.

They pulled up to the light before they reached the freeway access. "Poofie?" she asked. She waved the cheesy squiggle under his nose. "Come on, Hal. Live dangerously. Laugh in the face of heart disease."

He surprised her by grabbing it with his teeth, then taking it into his mouth with a slow, sexy move. He held her gaze while he chewed, his jaw muscle sliding, his eyes gleaming in a very not-by-the-book way.

Major zing. Under all that khaki and calm, Dr. Hollister Marx could be hot. Maybe there was hope for him yet. She definitely had to get him drinking. "Can I drive?"

"What?"

"I always wanted to drive a…a…um…" She located the name on the dash. "A Celica."

"I don't know…"

"Come on. Be spontaneous."

He blew out a breath—*what next?*—but pulled to the curb and let her take over. She carried her unopened beer with her and as soon as she'd sat in the driver's seat, she popped it and thrust it at him.

"What are you doing?"

"Giving you the beer. Drivers drive; navigators drink. Road Trip Law. Come on. Walk on the wild side."

"A warm beer is going to put me on the wild side?"

"You gotta start somewhere."

She managed to browbeat him through a fast Tecate by questioning his manhood. He actually sang along to some Primus tunes, then she got him talking about his old motorcycle and his blink of rebellion on it.

"Your problem is you don't have enough surprise in your life," she said. "Surprise sharpens your wits, keeps things fresh."

"The problem with surprises is you can't prepare for them."

Oh, God. "I bet you study for your eye exams. Drink up."

Halfway through the second beer, Hollister's speech got a tad looser, but his attitude was still stick-in-the-mud-ish. She wasn't sure how far they were from Copper Corners. She'd guess halfway. She'd have to tell him about Warren soon.

"Have you ever been in a play, Hal? Done any acting?"

"What makes you ask that?"

"Just thinking about surprises."

"No, no acting. Can't stand the fakery. I dated a theater major once. Everything was a performance with her. Whenever we argued, she was always looking around like she expected applause." He belched. "God, no more of those cheesie deals."

"Acting can be therapeutic, you know. It opens you up to new experiences. You should try it."

He turned his body to face her as she drove and narrowed his eyes. "What's going on here?"

"What?"

"Are you on some kind of mission? Was it something Leslie said? Because she's absolutely wrong." He hiccupped. "I'm very happy with my life. Running off getting tattoos is no answer to life's problems."

"Your sister wouldn't be running off getting tattoos if you'd given her space to be herself."

"You two must have had some talk."

"I just know that people rebel when they feel like they're not accepted or trusted."

Hollister was silent. "From personal experience?"

"Kind of." She really didn't want to get into true confession. She wanted him to help her for the fun of it, not because he felt sorry for her. But he was so Warren, she wasn't making much headway. If worse came to worst, she'd tell him the whole saga, explain about her father's illness and throw herself on his mercy. Yuck.

Luckily, just then, she spotted a diner up ahead. A perfect chance to try out Hollis' acting ability. That decided, Nikki careened off the highway onto the dirt road to the café.

4

HOLLIS GRABBED the overhead handhold as they swerved into the gravel parking lot of the diner. "What are you doing?"

"I'm hungry."

"You just ate half a bag of cheese whizzies."

"Poofies. Cheese poofies. And road snacks don't count."

"Don't tell me, let me guess—Road Trip Law."

"Exactly. There's hope for you yet, Hal."

She parked in the diner lot, and they pushed through the glass doors. A big-haired waitress in a frilly uniform told them to sit anywhere.

Nikki chose a booth at the back. She loved these kinds of places. Brown Naugahyde banquettes, cream pies rotating in a lighted tower, waitresses who called you "sugar," and a regular clientele who came for the bad coffee and stayed for the gossip.

"Ladies room," Nikki said and headed up front to start her plan.

Hollis watched Nikki sway away—oozing sex even in that modest dress—and wondered what she was cooking up. Why was she picking on his life? There was nothing wrong with having a plan, for God's sake.

He knew damn well her bravura covered up insecurity. Some of what she'd said bothered him, though. He *had* slipped his motorcycle phase neatly between semesters—hardly a speed bump on the highway of his life. Everything by the book, like she'd said.

Maybe that was partly why he'd allowed himself to be bamboozled into this trip. He wanted to do something different to mark his career switch. And spending a weekend with Nikki was nothing if not different. He didn't know what would come out of her mouth next. She was the kind of woman you could only take in small doses. Thank God this was just a weekend. After three days he'd be desperate to escape her lunacy for the safe dependability of Rachel.

Rachel knew what she wanted and went about getting it. He liked her complete assurance, even if she sometimes got pushy about it. He'd get through this rough patch with her, remember how much he cared for her, and settle down with the engagement idea. She'd just zoomed ahead of him, that was all. He needed time to catch up. He loved her. He was just a little angry right now.

The waitress delivered him a beer Nikki had obviously ordered. More Road Trip Law, he assumed, or more of her attempt to convert him to her way of thinking. Had Leslie put her up to it?

Nikki emerged from the rest room area, paused at the jukebox, where she inserted several coins, then headed his way. God, she was well put together. Squinting, he could envision her in that spotted miniskirt and leather halter. Two-and-a-half beers on an empty stomach had that effect.

She grinned at him, as if she'd read his mind. Her ability to do that—that aura nonsense—unnerved him. Of course, she was making assumptions and lucky guesses. If she *could* read his mind, he was in trouble because that was where he kept dressing her in leather and then undressing her. It was normal to have fantasies before you settled down for good, right?

Nikki slid onto the bench across from him, grinning from ear to ear. What was she up to? He realized he was looking forward to finding out.

The waitress returned and gave him an oddly gentle look, full of compassion. "Have you had a chance to decide?" She spoke to him like he was a child or seriously ill. Or both.

"Ladies first," he said. The waitress scribbled down Nikki's artery-clogging order of a burger and fries, then turned to him, all patient smile. "And for you, sir? Though there's no need to rush. Take all the time you need."

"I'll have a turkey sandwich. No mayo, please."

"I'll get that right out for you, sir. Just relax and enjoy yourself. Take deep breaths. You're doing great." She turned to Nikki and mouthed, *He's doing great.*

As the waitress left, Nikki called out, "Oh, and another beer for the gentleman."

"I don't need another—" Too late. The waitress was gone.

Hollis turned to Nikki. "What's that supposed to mean? *I'm doing great?* Why was she looking at me that way?"

"What way?"

"Like I'm feebleminded or something."

"Who knows?" She shrugged and sucked on her chocolate shake. "Drink your brew before the next one comes."

"What did you tell her, Nikki?"

Music started up—an old swing tune.

"That's my song. Come on." She jumped to her feet, grabbed his hands, and tugged him to his feet.

"There's no dance floor."

"Come on. The world is our dance floor." She began to dance around him, holding both his hands, leaning back, then rocking forward, moving her feet in a swing step.

He felt stupid standing there like a post, so he took charge, swung her out with one hand, then back around and into his chest, then reversed the move.

"You can dance," she whispered.

"Don't sound so surprised. Dancing appeals to my orderly nature." He performed a two-handed move—the eggbeater. He was just starting to enjoy it when rhythmic clapping started up. He turned to see a counterful of customers applauding them on. The women were giving him the look usually reserved for newborns.

"What did you tell these people?" Now he was getting annoyed.

"Just dance," she said.

He did—until the song ended, and a slow one started up. He turned to sit down—the beers had made him lightheaded—but Nikki thrust herself into his arms, pressing her fingers into his back so he wouldn't pull away. God knows his body thought that was a great idea, so rather than fight it *and* her, he pulled her into his arms.

She tucked herself neatly against him—a perfect fit, he couldn't help noticing. "Isn't this fun?" she murmured.

Fun? A game of squash was fun. This was... dangerous. He tried to ignore the heat of her skin and the slide of her muscles, which he could feel through her thin dress. Her face was soft against his neck, and she smelled so good.

Her stomach brushed his groin area. She tensed—noticing his arousal, he was chagrined to realize—then melted against him in a way that felt so good his mind went on hold. He kept turning with her, inhaling her scent, feeling her muscles beneath his fingers, the easy way her hips swayed against him. It was just a dance. It didn't mean anything.

He was about to close his eyes and really get into it when he caught sight of a weathered old guy in a sweat-stained cowboy hat winking at him, his coffee mug lifted in salute. What the hell was going on? The joke was on him, but what was the joke?

He broke away and yanked Nikki back to their booth. The watching diners applauded heartily.

"The song's not over," she said, sounding dazed.

"For us it is," he said. He leaned across the table and whispered, "Tell me what's going on. Now."

"Okay, okay. I told the waitress you're in therapy for agoraphobia—fear of open spaces—and this is your first field trip."

"Oh, for God's sake!"

"Relax. Get into the part. Have some fun."

"You call this fun?"

"Here you go," the waitress said, setting his turkey sandwich in front of him. "Take your time now." She patted him on the shoulder. "I had a cousin with the same problem."

While they ate, Hollis glared at Nikki, who kept telling him to relax and go with the flow. Someone sent another beer over, which Nikki urged him to drink to be polite.

Just as they were finishing up and he could escape, he looked up to see the waitress heading their way

with a piece of cake and a lit candle, trailed by two
people in cook's aprons.

"Oh, no," he said wearily. "You told them it was
my birthday."

"WHAT ARE YOU complaining about? We got lunch
free," Nikki said, trying to cheer Hollister up after
he'd stomped out of the diner. "I was surprised how
good the cake was, weren't you? The pies in the
tower looked shellacked."

"It was a lie. Possibly a criminal act," he said
grumpily. "At the very least we took advantage of
those people."

"It made everybody feel good about themselves.
Where's the harm in that?"

"Give me the keys," he said to her.

"Uh-uh. You've been drinking."

He misjudged the distance to the car door and
thumped into it. "Okay, you drive, but no more
stunts."

"I can't believe you're going to be such a poop
about this," she said, unlocking the doors.

"I mean it. One more trick, and I'm going home."

"God, you're uptight."

Well, that had backfired, Nikki thought as they
rolled down the highway. Now he was too cranky
for her to explain about Warren. She heard a little
snort, and looked over at him. His head lolled against
the headrest and his eyes were closed. Even the beer
idea had gone wrong. Instead of releasing his inhi-
bitions, it had put him to sleep. He looked cute,
though, with his hair loosely flopped over his forehead. He snored softly.

Now what? She had to jolly him up before they
got to her folks' house. She scanned the high-

way ahead looking for something spontaneous she could plan.

A half hour later, she saw it. A roadside attraction—Cactus People. Saguaros had been dressed to look like people in various postures—playing tennis, embracing, directing traffic. There was a gift shop and a snack bar. Three tourists were taking pictures of each other with their faces peeking through holes in plaster cacti with cowboy clothes painted on. This might be fun. Plus, she had to buy Hollis some mints so he wouldn't smell like a brewery when they got to her parents' house.

"Wake up, Hal, honey. Come on. I'll buy you…" she scanned the sign "…a world-famous prickly pear cactus smoothie and some ostrich jerky."

"Uh, what?" He sat up sleepily. "Are we there?"

"Not yet. Just a rest stop. Come on."

"Forget it," he said, resting his head against the door. "Keep going. You can drop me at the hotel for a nap, then pick me up when the reunion starts."

"Come on. Please."

"Oh, God. All right." He dragged himself out of the car looking disoriented, a sleep crease in his cheek, his hair mussed. While they waited for their smoothies, she found a rack of sunglasses and a variety of hats. She picked out one of each. "How about a new look?" she said to him.

He frowned, but let her set an Australian outback hat on his head and slide the glasses onto his face.

He looked great. With his eyes mysteriously hidden by the wraparound frames, she could focus on his mouth, which was sensuous, his cheekbones, high and classic, and his nose, straight and strong. She could visualize him in motorcycle leathers, his hair a little longer. Mmm. Ditch the Dockers and the man had possibilities.

He reached up to adjust the glasses. Nice fingers. Long, clean, dexterous. Trained to do precise work in tight places, too. She'd bet he knew how to use them other places. She felt a little wobbly in the knees.

"How do I look?" he asked softly, clearly feeling the same tension she was.

She swallowed the knot in her throat. "Good... um, quite good. Very *not* Hollister Marx." Or Warren, for that matter.

"Now you," he said. He moved away and returned to set a black beret on her head and slid a pair of gaudy, rhinestone-studded shades on her face, his fingers gentle at her temples, his breath warm and sweet.

He examined her so closely she felt herself blush. She couldn't even ask how she looked.

"Very *you*," Hollis said. Then his voice went low and serious. "You shouldn't have changed for this trip. There's nothing wrong with the way you are."

She tried to laugh, but his expression was too serious, almost disappointed in her. "It's a costume," she said, repeating what Mariah had said about her own business suit. "Protective coloration in an alien world."

He looked at her, his eyes searching out truth.

"Don't get all serious on me. This is make-believe. Just for fun." Embarrassed, she whipped the glasses and beret off and handed them to him. "I've got to make a pit stop. I'll meet you in the car."

But when she climbed into the driver's seat, she saw that Hollister was wearing the outback hat and wraparound shades, looking for all the world like an Australian outlaw.

He plopped the beret on her head and slid the rhinestone glasses on her face. "Who says I don't know how to be spontaneous?" She felt the heat of his fingers for miles.

Taken aback by how hot Hollis could be, Nikki didn't speak for a while, except to offer him a fistful of breath mints to cover up the beer breath. Then she caught sight of the sign for a town she knew was close to Copper Corners. She'd thought they had more time, but they were nearly there and she hadn't told Hollister about his secret identity.

She took the exit, dread in her heart. She had to come clean. Now. "There are a couple of things I need to tell you."

"Like what?"

You're my husband and your name's Warren. No, too abrupt. "I ran away from home when I was seventeen."

"Okay." He sounded puzzled.

"Because my parents and I were a mismatch. As in from different planets."

"Oh, really?"

"Really." How to tell him all of it without embarrassing herself... "Except for when my best friend got married, I haven't been back for ten years."

"That's a long time. They must miss you."

"If they think I'm doing well, they're happy. They have my perfect sister to fuss over."

"Perfect sister?"

"Yeah. She's a lot like you—always did her homework, never missed curfew, married a banker and has two darling children—a boy and a girl,

Byron and Shelley—whom she stayed home to mother.''

''By the book?''

''Exactly.''

''And you're not.''

''No. I never fit in. My parents are very serious people. Conservative…careful…and worrywarts. My father is principal of the high school. My mother teaches English. I caused them a lot of pain when I was growing up.''

''You weren't a good student?''

''That's putting it mildly. Let's say I once painted a mural on the cafeteria wall featuring the school as a prison with students holding protest signs that said 'Free Your Mind' and 'Learning Without Shackles.'''

''But you've grown up.''

''Not the way they'd recognize. My life is just too strange.''

''Hence the fake look.''

''Yeah. To protect them.'' She paused. *Here goes.* ''That's why your coming with me is so helpful…. I told them I'd be bringing…someone special.''

''Someone special? I'm just your date, right?''

''Remember what I said about how fun it would be to act out a role? The truth is I'm hoping you could pretend to be, um, close to me.''

Hollister turned to stare at her. ''Like a boyfriend? Now you want me to be your boyfriend?''

''Kind of. See, it's not just my reunion I'm coming home for. My father's had a severe heart attack. And I want to make sure he's okay. So, if you're with me and he knows we're together, he'll stop worrying about me.''

Hollister stared straight ahead, frowning. ''I

should have known there was more to this. So that's
what all the role-playing nonsense was about. You
want me to act like your *boyfriend.*''

He was silent. Very silent.

Nikki couldn't stand it. "So, will you do it? We're
almost there.'' *Hurry up. I have to tell you we're
married and your name is Warren.*

Silence.

"It'll be fun. Like wearing that hat. Wasn't that
fun?'' She was desperate now.

He frowned, took the Outback hat off his head,
peeled the sunglasses off and tossed them both into
the back seat. "Being your boyfriend is a lot more
than being your date, Nikki. Your family will ask
questions. We'll have to be…affectionate. We'll
have to put on an act.…''

"My father might be dying. Please.''

More silence. Finally, he spoke. "I think you
should tell your parents the truth. You've grown up.
They'll love you no matter what you do.''

"You don't know my family. Look, this is really
important to me. Could you just give it a try?''

"I don't see how. No.''

And then they were driving through town. And
then her house appeared. She had to slam on the
brakes, throwing them both forward, then back.
"This is it,'' she said.

Her heart tightened at the sight of the familiar
white clapboard—carefully painted with yellow trim.
As a kid, she'd felt so trapped in its compact space.
Now it looked familiar and comforting. Tears filled
her eyes and she couldn't speak. What was she going
to do now? She couldn't face her family without
Warren.

She pushed on the accelerator.

"What are you doing?"

"I can't go in," she said.

"Stop the car."

She did—in front of their next-door neighbor's house. "What?"

Hollister looked at her for a slow moment. Then he blew out a long-suffering breath. "Okay. I'll do it. It's against my better judgment, but—"

"You will? That's great." Now she had to finish the story. "Because actually, the truth is that—"

Bang. Bang. Bang.

Two children were pounding on her window. Her niece and nephew, whom she recognized from the video Donna mailed each Christmas.

"Let me guess. Byron and Shelley?" Hollis said.

"Yeah. Hollis, listen—"

But before she could explain, the kids pulled her door open and tugged her out of the car. She threw off the beret and sunglasses and staggered to her feet. "Aunt Nikki, Aunt Nikki, Aunt Nikki," Byron said and leapt into her arms, wrapping himself around her torso like a starfish. Sweet, since he hadn't even met her, just spoken to her on the phone when Donna put him on.

Evidently irritated that Byron had beat her to the punch, Shelley headed around the car for Hollis. "Uncle Warren, Uncle Warren, Uncle Warren," she chanted, tugging him out of the car.

"Uncle Warren?" Hollis asked Nikki over the top of the car.

"Here's the deal," Nikki said, talking fast and low. "Your name's Warren Langley. We've been married a year. And you're a doctor."

"But I'm a dentist," was all he managed to say before Shelley yanked him away.

"Just fake it," she called, struggling forward with her nephew. He was so heavy he felt like two boys were crammed into one skin. Then she saw that her mother was standing at the end of the walk to her house, wearing a familiar apron. Nikki's heart throbbed.

"We're going to play house, Uncle Warren," Shelley said. "You'll be the daddy, I'll be the mommy and Byron can be the baby."

"But *I* want to be the daddy," Byron whined.

"You must be Warren," her mother said, holding out her hand. "So nice to meet you. I'm Nadine Winfield."

Hollis stopped to shake her hand.

Shelley quit yanking him, folding her arms in that deeply impatient gesture Nikki remembered in her sister at that age.

"Nice to meet you, too," Hollis said dazedly.

Nikki reached them just as her mother said, "We were so disappointed when Nikki told us you'd eloped. Of course we understood the urgency, with you leaving for South America and all."

"South A—?"

"You did such wonderful work on that mercy mission," Nikki said, begging him with her eyes to go along.

"Right," he said faintly. "The mercy mission."

She put Byron down to accept her mother's hug.

"Nicolette," her mother said and held her tightly, smelling of lemon and lavender like always. Love and regret washed over Nikki. She'd missed her mother.

"But you're here now, and that's all that matters," her mother said, her eyes shiny with tears.

"Yeah," she said. "We're here now.... Aren't we, Warren?" She turned to him, blinking back wetness.

"Right," he said, managing a thin smile. "We're here, all right."

"Come in and we'll get your bags later," her mother said.

"That's okay, Mother. We'll just take them to the Days Inn."

"The Days Inn? Nonsense. You're staying in the guest room."

"But you don't have a guest room. You turned our bedroom into your sewing room and library, right?"

"With a fold-out sofa, silly. When your father snores, I sleep there."

"We can't put you out, Mrs. Winfield," Hollister said, shooting Nikki a desperate look.

"Nonsense. You're staying here and that's the end of it. And call me Mother." Nikki knew that tone. No argument. No exceptions. No extra credit. As a teen, it had inspired her to rebel. Now, despite how much it upset Hollis, it made her feel loved.

Her mother started up the walk. Nikki and Hollis fell in behind. "I'll explain it all," Nikki whispered to Hollis, who had a child tugging each arm.

"It better be good."

She'd explain it all, all right. In her childhood bedroom. All alone with her *husband*. She just hoped the door still had a lock, so she could keep him there long enough to convince him to stay.

After that, they'd have to deal with the fold-out bed.

5

INSIDE THE HOUSE, Nikki felt another rush of nostalgia. The same smell of apple pie and roses that had seemed so old-fashioned and cloying when she was young now smelled cozy and welcoming. There was the flowered sofa—a little more worn, but neat and placed just so. Everything was familiar—the maple cocktail and end tables, the curio cabinet, the tall bookshelves with books arranged by height, along with archives of the *New Republic* and *Atlantic Monthly,* and the magazine rack that held the current editions.

Family photographs from childhood hung around the room. Then she saw it on the wall above the sofa—one of her paintings. It was an impressionist picture of horses running, their eyes wild, their legs ragged slashes, and it clashed violently with the traditional look of the room. "You kept this?" she asked her mother.

"Of course, dear. It's your art."

She felt warm all over. "Where's Daddy?" she asked, eager to see him, but nervous, too. And scared to see how ill he was. "I want you to meet my father," she said to Hollis, hoping this would convince him that the charade would be worthwhile.

"I think he's napping, dear," her mother said. "He had a little procedure. I'm sure Donna told you. He's taking some painkillers that make him sleepy."

Her mother called a balloon angioplasty a "little procedure"? As if it were a bunion removal. She was being brave for Nikki's benefit. Nikki's heart swelled with pain and love.

They heard the clang of a hand bell.

"That's him," her mother said with a weary smile. "He's really milking this thing. Coming, dear." She headed across the room toward the sound. Nikki and a reluctant Hollister followed.

As they walked, her mother turned to whisper, "Don't ask him about the surgery. He's touchy about the details, as you can imagine."

"Oh, okay," she said, her heart aching for her father.

"I'd like a nice big bowl of vanilla cherry chip, please," her father said before they even got into the room.

"For heaven's sake, Harvey. You didn't get your tonsils out. Look who's here." She turned and Nikki stepped forward.

"Hello, Daddy," she said.

"Nicolette!" He beamed and held out his arms. "My dear girl."

She went to his bedside and put her arms around him for a careful hug. He felt quite solid, not frail at all. Overweight, actually, which she was sure was part of his heart trouble. It felt so good to be in his arms. There'd been lots of hugs when she was a child, but once adolescence hit, they rarely had a pleasant conversation. Why had she been so angry at him? Why had she gotten into so much trouble?

He released her. "I'm glad you could make it home," he said.

"Of course we had to come." She stopped. He

wasn't to know she was here because of his condition. "It was time we came for a visit."

"What did you do about your boutique?"

"I, um, just closed it up for a few days."

"I don't know why you would need to work," her mother said. "I mean, with a doctor in the house." She turned to Hollis.

"So this is the man who stole my daughter's heart," her father said, holding out a hand.

Hollis shook it.

"Harvey Winfield."

"I'm, um, Warren, I guess," he said.

"You sure about that, son?"

Nikki's heart skipped a beat thinking her father was on to them already, until he gave a hearty chuckle. "Relax, son. I'm not as fierce as Nicolette probably told you. Glad to meet you."

"Hey, there."

Nikki turned to see Donna in the doorway. She wore a tailored pantsuit and her hair was perfect. Her sister hadn't changed a bit.

Donna hugged her, then leaned back. "Wow. I expected you to be dressed all in black with tattoos and a hoop in your nose."

"Don't harass your sister," their mother said. "Nicolette has grown up. Those days are long behind her. Thank goodness."

"So, say, Son," her father said to Hollis. "Later on I'd like a consult with you."

"Um, oh, I don't… I mean, I can't… My specialty is…" Hollis widened his eyes at Nikki. *What* is *my specialty?*

"We need Uncle Warren now." Shelley had pushed past her mother and stood in the doorway with her hands on her hips.

Everyone smiled.

"Would you mind going along for a bit?" Donna asked Hollis.

"I'd be delighted." From the look on his face, Nikki knew that if Donna'd asked him to kill a chicken with his bare hands, he'd have jumped at the chance just to leave the room.

"How was work today, darling?"

"Just fine," Hollis said, accepting the tiny teacup from Shelley, his instant niece, with a sigh. He couldn't feel his butt anymore, it was squeezed so tightly into this puny chair. Somehow, he'd ended up in a kiddie tea party from hell.

He caught sight of Nikki's gauzy dress as she breezed into the dining room holding a stack of plates. He hardly recognized her now. The Nikki who'd carried on about auras and Xena tattoos and danced him around a diner just on a lark had been transformed into an obedient daughter meekly following her mother around the table, acting like what baked goods to make for the reunion was the most fascinating topic in the world. Completely surreal.

And she had him posing as her husband. Her husband! Playing a mental patient in a diner had been one thing. Pretending to be her boyfriend was worse, but her *husband?* That was off the charts. Her father's words ran through his head. *So, this is the man who stole my little girl's heart.*

He would not do it. No way.

"Why don't you hold the baby?" Shelley said, calling his attention back to her. She staggered under the weight of her younger brother—nearly her size— then dumped him onto Hollis' lap.

The kid let out a pretend wail that made Hollis's ears go dead for a second.

"There, there," he said, patting the kid on the back.

"Rock him," Shelley said, her hands on her hips, judging his father behavior. Her frown told him he'd come up short. Everywhere he went in this house people were asking him to playact—loving husband, physician son-in-law, doting uncle—and he wasn't any good at any of it.

"Now sing," Shelley commanded.

"Sing?"

"Do you know, 'Great green gobs of greasy, grimy gopher guts'? That's his favorite."

He swallowed. "Sorry."

"Want gopher guts! Gopher gu-u-u-ts!" the kid shrieked, overacting his role of spoiled infant.

"How about 'The worms crawl in, the worms crawl out'?" Shelley offered.

Hollis shook his head again. More wails. "Okay, okay." He had to sing something. He launched into, "Rock-a-bye, Baby," humming through the blanks in his memory of the lyrics.

"After this, I get to be the daddy," Byron said when he'd finished, eyeing Hollis like he expected an argument.

"No problem," Hollis said. Except then he realized he might have to be the baby. Or, worse, the mommy. At this point, in this family, nothing would surprise him. You'd think it couldn't get much worse, but somehow he knew it would.

"NOW, ISN'T THAT CUTE?" Donna said to Nikki. They were watching Hollis play with Shelley and

Byron through the archway to the play alcove. "Warren is really getting into it."

Donna was wishfully thinking. Hollis looked shell-shocked. Cute, though, crammed into the little white slatted chair, his knees up to his shoulders, pretending to sip tea under Shelley's watchful eye.

For a second, she flashed on how he'd be as a father. He'd give the child total attention, read lots of childcare books so he knew exactly how to do everything. Such a careful, cautious man. She felt a stab of guilt. She should have prepared him for this before they arrived, but she hadn't had time. She'd have to make it up to him somehow.

"Looks like you picked a good one," Donna said. Then she frowned. "He doesn't have a drinking problem, does he? I smelled beer and it's barely three o'clock."

"I made him drink a couple of brews so he'd be calm about meeting everybody. Why do you expect the worst?"

"Sorry, Sis. I'm glad you've gotten your life together." Donna hugged her around the shoulder. "It's hard to stop worrying, I guess."

She understood completely. She'd given her family plenty to worry about in the past. "Daddy doesn't seem as sick as I expected," she said to change the subject.

"He's hiding it from you. You know how he is—gotta be the Rock of Gibraltar. You're making him feel better just being here. Trust me." There was something about Donna's tone she wanted to explore, but the doorbell rang before she could say anything.

"Would you get that, sweetie?" her mother called. "Donna, can you help me get the silver down?"

"Oooh, you get the good utensils. I'm jealous," Donna said, clearly teasing.

Nikki headed for the door. Hollis caught her eye in passing. *Help me.*

"Dinner's soon," she said to give him hope.

He just rolled his eyes.

"Time to go inside," Shelley caroled, indicating her plastic playhouse. With a sigh, Hollis got onto his knees and crawled inside the pink shelter, giving Nikki a shot of his tight butt. He'd been working at the gym, too, besides the dental clinic.

With a last wistful look, she went to the front door.

"Nikki!" Mariah threw her arms around Nikki, nearly bowling her over.

She laughed with the joy of seeing her best friend again after nearly two years. They separated long enough to do their old Rebel Girls Forever handshake, then hugged again and laughed into each other's faces.

"Look at you," Mariah said. "You look so, so…"

"Miss Copper Corners?"

"Absolutely. God. I can't believe it's you." Then she leaned in conspiratorially. "Where is he and how's it going? Does he know?" Nikki'd filled Mariah in on her plan right after talking Hollis into it.

"Barely. I didn't get a chance to explain much. He seems to be in shock. Maybe you can reassure him."

As they passed the kitchen, Mariah stuck her head in. "Hi, Mrs. W."

"Mariah Goodman," her mother said. "Don't you get my little girl in any trouble now." She wagged a finger in pretend annoyance. Her mother used to blame Mariah for their bad behavior, but they'd been completely in sync.

"Our rebel days are over, I'm sad to say." She sounded absolutely wistful. One day Nikki hoped to look back with nostalgia on the rebel years. For the time being, by her mother's standards, she was still living them.

As soon as Nikki and Mariah entered the alcove, Hollis's face appeared in the small pink window of the playhouse. "Tell me you need me," he pleaded.

"I need you." That sounded strange. "I mean, let me introduce you to my best friend."

"Great." He crawled out of the house and stood, brushing his knees.

Shelley came around the corner with an armload of mangled dolls. "What are you doing?"

"We have to take Uncle Warren back for a while," Nikki said.

"Oh." She frowned, paused, then shrugged. "He takes up too much room anyway." She threw the dolls in the house, then headed down the hall. "Byron, come he-re...." Nikki hoped her nephew was well hidden, if he knew what was good for him.

"Oh, God, you *do* look exactly like Warren," Mariah said, briskly shaking Hollis's hand. "I'm Mariah Goodman and I know the whole story. God, just wait until Brian Collier gets a load of you."

"Brian Collier?" He looked at Nikki.

"Her old boyfriend," Mariah chimed in before she could respond. "He dumped her for Heather Haver, head cheerleader, but now he's divorced and pining for Nikki."

"I see..." Hollis said slowly. "So, besides impressing your family, you want me to be your successful and devoted husband and make your old boyfriend jealous?"

Nikki shrugged sheepishly.

"Nail on the head," Mariah said. She turned to Nikki. "I thought you said he wasn't into it."

"I'm not," Hollis said. "This is insane."

"No, it's not. You'll have a blast. Reunions are a big, big deal in this town. Copper Corners is like a pep squad on steroids. We're always having reunions and everyone comes. This is the biggie for *our* class. Also, you'll get to meet my husband Nathan. You'll like him. He used to be a lot like you—uptight, straight-and-narrow, boring—until I got hold of him."

"Look," Hollis said, "This isn't what I—"

"But the most important thing is that you'll be doing a good deed for Nikki. This means a lot to her."

"Maybe, but I still—"

"Oh, there you are!" Nikki's mother said to Hollis, popping out of the kitchen. "Can I get you to help us with the leaf in the table? It's so nice to have another man around the house." Her mother beamed at him.

"See what I mean?" Mariah said.

Hollis rolled his eyes, but he followed Nikki's mother into the dining room.

"He'll come around," Mariah said.

Nikki hoped so. Maybe the after-dinner games and sing-along would do the trick.

Then her mother's voice carried to her. "So, Warren, did you learn any Spanish while you were in South America?"

"SHELLEY NICOLETTE WILSON, get your elbow off that slice of bread," Donna said to her daughter after they'd said the blessing and started eating.

"I'm just flattening it," Shelley said innocently.

"Then I roll it in a ball"—she did that—"and pop it in my mouth"—she did that, too. "Mmm. Tastes like dough."

"Kids change your life, Warren," Donna's husband Dave said to Hollister. "Take your time deciding to have them."

"Better to have them while you have the energy," Nikki's mother countered firmly. She looked straight at Nikki in that "homework first, TV later" way that used to demoralize her.

Luckily, Donna changed the subject. "So, Warren, why don't you tell us the story of how you two met?"

Hollis choked on his milk.

Nikki patted his back. "I'll tell them, dear. See, Warren came into my shop for something for his sister, right, dear?"

He nodded, still coughing.

"We got to talking and...well, the rest is history."

"I never knew what hit me," he said through a cough.

The cowbell clanged, a welcome interruption.

"Oh, my, I've forgotten to take your father his dinner," her mother said.

"Let me do it," Nikki said. She made up a plate, careful to remove the skin from the chicken and pile on lots of salad. She added one bun, no butter, then carried it to her father's room, where she found him engrossed in television.

He looked up. "Why, thank you, dear. What a treat to be served by my daughter."

"I'm glad to do it," she said, putting the plate on the bed tray and placing it on his lap. She sat beside him. "How are you feeling, Daddy?"

"A little iffy down there, but let's not dwell," he

said, digging into the meal as if he weren't in any danger of dying at all.

Her throat tightened at his bravery. "What are you watching?" she asked him, indicating the TV.

"The history of bridge-building," he said, pointing his fork at the screen. "Fascinating stuff. Amazing engineering feats. I always thought you would have made a terrific engineer. With your artist's eye, you know." He looked at her for a moment. There it was, that disappointment. He'd had high hopes for her. If he knew what she really did, he'd be devastated. The closest she came to a bridge was drawing one for a tattoo.

"Doesn't matter." He waved his fork, chasing away his letdown. "You found a nice man, it looks like." He took another bite of chicken. "You want to watch the drinking, though."

"He doesn't drink, Dad. It was a special occasion." She thought about explaining Road Trip Law, but her father would not be amused.

"Where are the mashed potatoes?" he asked, frowning at his plate. "And the butter?"

"I thought you'd want to be careful. I mean, in your condition." Potatoes and butter were the last thing his clogged heart needed.

He gave her that look. "We'll not be talking about my condition."

"Okay, but really, you shouldn't—"

"Butter, please. On the double." There was no use arguing with him when he got like this. She fetched potatoes and butter, feeling like she was putting nails of cholesterol into his coffin.

"Down by the oooold...mill...stream," they sang. The after-dinner sing-along was going just as it used to when Nikki was little. Her mother doggedly pounded out the melody on the piano, and everyone bellowed out the words. Everyone except Hollis.

He mouthed the words, a faint smile on his face, and spoke only when spoken to. He looked like a spy expecting his cover to be blown any second. Nikki sat close to him so they looked like a loving couple, and shot him encouraging smiles, but he was rigid with tension.

Finishing the song, her mother turned the piano stool to face them. "How about some charades?"

"Wonderful," Nikki said.

Hollis stepped on her foot.

"Ouch."

"Maybe we should get some sleep," he whispered. Except the room had fallen silent so that everyone heard him.

"Sleep? Riiiiight," Dave said with a theatrical wink.

"It's early, dear," Nikki said. She did not want to be alone with him in her bedroom. They wouldn't be doing what Dave was leering about, either. There probably would be yelling involved.

"I'll write up the slips then," her mother said and headed into the kitchen.

"I know you're on vacation, Bro-in-law," Dave said to Hollis, "but I've got this little bump on my back and I wonder if you'd mind taking a look?"

"Oh, I don't think—"

But Dave had already lifted his shirt and thrust his bare back under Hollister's nose.

Hollis shot Nikki a look before he leaned in to study the spot. "I'd have your GP take a look at it," he said.

"But do *you* think it's anything? As a doctor."

"Talk to your GP."

"Okay," he said, putting down his shirt, still worried.

"I'm sorry, Dave," Nikki said. "His malpractice insurance company is very strict about not diagnosing stuff outside the office."

"Oh, right. That makes sense."

Hollis gave her a grateful look.

"Choose a slip," her mother called gaily, wiggling the bowl in front of Hollis.

He smiled up at her. "I think we'll call it a night, Mrs. Winfield."

He stood, pulling Nikki with him.

"But we haven't played Boggle or Scrabble yet," Nikki said, not ready for the confrontation. "And Pictionary is my specialty."

He turned his fake smile to her. "But, darling, we want to be rested for the reunion tomorrow, don't we?"

"Tomorrow?" her mother said. "Oh, no, dear. The reunion's *next* weekend. Lord, I've still got baking to do and the decorations to arrange. There's tons to be done."

"Next week?" Hollis repeated, blanching.

"Know anything about fly fishing?" Dave asked.

"Fly fishing?" He stared at Nikki, color draining from his face.

"I was thinking you and me could go out in the morning and try my new flies. After breakfast. Sound good?"

"I don't know," he said faintly, looking like he thought he'd just slipped into an episode of *The Twilight Zone*.

After fifteen minutes of discourse on the art and

frustration of fly tying, Hollis dragged Nikki to the guest room and descended on her. "I don't believe this, Nikki—"

"Me, either," she said, pushing away from the door to pretend to explore the room. Anything to delay the quarrel. "This is so different." She crossed the colorful throw rug. "Our beds were here," she said, indicating the space on the saltillo tile floor. "We divided the room along this line." She walked the grout they'd used as the line of demarcation.

"And I had my paintings all over here." She indicated two walls that now were lined with built-in bookshelves. "Our desks were there." She pointed to the opposite wall where her mother's sewing machine shared space with the notorious sofa-bed.

"Donna couldn't stand how messy I was and I thought she was neurotic about neatness. Sometimes I would drop a scarf over the line just to see her go nuts. Or I'd rearrange her pillows, and—"

Hollis grabbed her arm as she moved past. "This is impossible."

"Not really. You can take the bed. I'll sleep on the floor on the cushions. Unless you want to sleep in shifts?"

"I don't mean the sleeping arrangements."

She sighed. "I know. I should have given you more details before we got here, but—"

"Details? You didn't tell me a damn thing until your niece and nephew started banging on the car window. When were you going to fill me in? When you mother asked to see our wedding pictures? And what is this about the reunion being *next* weekend?"

"I thought you might get into being here and stay for the reunion, too." Considering the expression on his face, that was the longest shot of all.

"You're nuts, you know that?" Then he dropped his anger for something worse—deadly seriousness. "I can't pretend to be your husband, Nikki. It's a lie. Your family keeps giving me these looks like I've saved you or something."

"That's the point," she said, searching his face. "See how relieved they are that you're with me? And you saw my dad—he's very ill."

"He doesn't seem that sick to me."

"He's just being brave. This means a lot to them. And to me."

"I can't do it." He shook his head, his hands on his hips.

"I know it's a shock, but think about it, okay?"

"I don't need to think about it."

"Sleep on it and see how you feel in the morning. There's nothing you can do about it tonight anyway." She rushed to the sofa and began yanking off the sofa cushions, figuring if she made the bed quickly, he might be convinced. She lifted the mattress up and out.

Then, there it was, all open and ready for them. A bed. Where you slept, made love, spooned all night. Nikki looked up at Hollis. Their eyes snagged. Heat like a softball plowed into her stomach.

Something crossed Hollis' face—a matching reaction—then he frowned. "I'll leave in the morning."

"Leave? How can you leave?"

"In my car."

"What about me? I can't leave."

"Then stay here. Borrow a car and go back later. That isn't my problem."

"But you agreed to come."

"And you tricked me."

Good point. "What will my family think if we leave?"

"I don't know. You tell me. You're the one who reads auras."

"Not when it comes to me or the people I love. With anyone close to me, I'm blind as a bat."

"Then make up a story. Say I have to go to Africa on a mission to cure smallpox. I don't care. You're the storyteller. I can't spend another day deceiving these people."

"But I'll help you."

"I can't."

She looked into his eyes. He wouldn't budge. "I guess I can't really make you stay," she wheedled.

He held her gaze, not backing down. "No, you can't."

"And I suppose the reunion's definitely out?"

"Nikki."

"Okay." She briefly considered a full-blown tantrum, but the noise would attract her family. She blew out a breath. "You win. In the morning, I'll tell them we have to rush back because of an emergency with one of your patients. Are you happy?"

"No. I'm not happy. But I will be once we get out of here."

Nikki stomped over to her suitcase and opened it.

"What are you doing?"

"I'm getting ready for bed, what else?" She snatched up her nightie, robe and toiletry kit and marched into the bathroom, fuming. He was right, but why'd he have to be such a poop about it? She changed clothes angrily, swearing under her breath, then fiercely scrubbed her teeth. Foaming paste flew onto the mirror in big drops.

When she came out of the bathroom, Hollis was

standing in the middle of the room in blue-striped pajamas straight from a fifties Sears catalogue. Charmingly old-fashioned, just like the guy. Except that old-fashionedness was why her plan had crashed and burned.

He seemed taken aback by what she was wearing.

"What?" She looked down. Nothing unusual. Black silk kimono with red dragon design, modest neckline. Then she saw that a little bit of her tattoo peeked out from the top of her robe. She wasn't about to show that to him, not with his attitude.

She lifted her lapel over it, tightened her sash and went to the closet, where she found pillows for both of them and an extra blanket she could use to make a bed on the sofa cushions. Silently, she tucked the blanket under the edges of the puffy cushions. She felt Hollis's eyes on her, so she jerked up. "What now?"

He flushed, and she realized he hadn't been waiting to say something, he'd been staring at her behind. He turned his wistful gawk into a frown. "You're not sleeping on the floor," he said. "I'll sleep on the cushions."

"Forget it. I promised you a hotel room when I got you into this. You should at least get a bed." She kept adjusting the blanket.

She was aware of him moving behind her. She stood and found herself in his arms. He smelled good and felt so warm. She remembered that dance at the diner that had made her want to melt to the floor and dribble away.

His eyes flared and he gripped her upper arms. For an impossible second, she thought he might pull her into a kiss. Then he lifted her up effortlessly, and set her firmly to the side—a temptation conquered. "I'll sleep on the floor,'' he said, then crawled onto the cushion bed and yanked the blanket up and over him. His feet stuck out impossibly far past the blanket and the cushions.

"If you insist," she said, and flopped onto the bed. She considered arguing, but she wasn't about to get into a wrestling match with him. Hmm. On the other hand, wrestling could lead to sex. And sex could lead to Hollis deciding to stay. No. Too blatant. Too complicated. Still, the idea of getting pinned by Hollis had delicious possibilities. Not to mention all those wrestling holds....

There was a tap at the door.

"Oh, God," she said. "Someone's coming to say good night. Get off the floor and up here." She struggled to tug Hollis up on the bed and called to the visitor, "Just a sec!"

When the door opened, revealing her mother, Hollis was halfway on her body, his mouth at breast level.

"Oh, my!" Her mother colored, yanked the door shut, then shouted through it, "I thought you said, 'Come in!' I'm so sorry."

Nikki scrambled out from under Hollis and lunged for the door. "It's okay, Mother. We were just horsing around."

Her mother's eyes were wide, her face red. "I just wanted to tell you that breakfast is at seven." Then she whispered, "I'm so sorry."

"It's okay. Truly." She went back into the bedroom, shut the door and leaned on it.

"See what I mean?" Hollis said. "This would just get more and more complicated."

"Okay, okay. You won. Stop trying to convince me." She clicked the light switch by the door and lay down on the bed again. For a few minutes, she listened to Hollis rustle and fidget and mutter under his breath. "Do you want the bed?" she finally asked.

"No, I'm fine." He paused, then sighed in resignation. "You meant well, I guess." He wasn't even mad any more. He was such a civilized guy. Part of her wanted him to yell and argue so she'd feel justified in tricking him.

"Good night, then." She pulled the sheets up to her chin and let feelings swamp her. Disappointment. Embarrassment. Nostalgia. Regret. Worry about her father.

And awareness. Pricking awareness that Hollis lay in the dark just a few feet away in those incredibly sexy pajamas. She could practically hear him breathing. She could roll over and be in his arms in a couple of racing heartbeats.

It had been nice pretending to be married to him that afternoon—even if he'd mostly looked stunned. If she'd had more time, she could have gotten him into the spirit of things, she was sure.

Oh, well. They were leaving tomorrow. She hoped her family would understand their early departure.

That made her heart sink. She didn't *want* to leave yet. She wanted to spend more time with her father—soak up his wisdom, his ideas, his love. Make sure he would recover all right. She wanted to get recipes from her mother—not that she ever cooked, really, but still, that's what mothers and daughters did, exchange recipes. And pick strawberries and look through photo albums and play Pictionary. And even play house with her steamroller niece and pudgy nephew. But that was all over.

In the meantime, she'd have to endure hours and

hours lying next to Hollis in the dark while he fidgeted and groaned, reminding her constantly how close he was. This was shaping up to be a very long night.

THUMP. Hollis's butt slid between two of the incredibly uncomfortable cushions—were they stuffed with squirrel carcasses?—and hit the cold tile floor. Damn. As if things weren't bad enough, he wouldn't get any sleep tonight. He turned on his side and his pillow fell off the back of the cushion.

Might as well go to the bathroom. If he ever did find a comfortable position, he wouldn't want to get up again. He looked up and saw a curvy mass of covers. Nikki, sleeping like a baby. She should be feeling too guilty to sleep.

After meeting her family, he did understand a little of why she'd wanted to pull this stunt. Her parents had definite ideas about things and they clearly loved her and worried about her. Her intentions were admirable....

Forget it. The woman had tricked and manipulated him from the minute he first walked into her tattoo parlor. He pushed open the bathroom door, flipped on the light and found Nikki sitting on the edge of the tub, tears streaming down her cheeks.

6

"I'M IN HERE!" Nikki yelped.

"I'm sorry," Hollis said, startled and embarrassed to see her weeping.

"I had a scary dream, okay?" She jumped to her feet, grabbed a tissue and brushed past him.

He closed the door and used the toilet, feeling ashamed. He'd made her cry. She acted so cool and breezy, but she must be a marshmallow inside. He should have known. Why else would she cook up such an elaborate scheme to please her family? He turned off the light and walked into the darkened bedroom. He could hear her trying not to sniffle. Maybe he needed to understand more. Rethink things a bit. He sat on the side of the bed near her head. "Nikki? You okay?"

She rolled away from him. "Sometimes I just cry. It relieves te-e-ension."

"Talk to me about all this. Why this whole charade?"

She collected herself for a few seconds, and when she spoke, her voice was soft. "I was just such a screwup as a kid. I guess I was mad because Donna was so damned perfect. I don't know. I'm no shrink. I just kept doing things to be acknowledged. I was wild just to be wild. And so mean. Once, I made my mother burst into tears right in the middle of teaching

Hamlet! I hurt my parents. So now I want to make up for that."

She spoke haltingly and he was touched by the honesty in her voice. Her flashy, let-me-shock-you style was gone.

"I made up a life that would make them happy. And when my sister told me Dad was sick I had to come and prove to them I'm okay. With my dad's condition, I don't want him worrying about me living alone behind a tattoo shop."

"But your neighborhood's decent, isn't it?" Maybe her dad had reason for concern. "And you always lock up, right? What do you do if someone dangerous comes into the shop?"

"For crying out loud, Hollis. Don't *you* start worrying about me. I can read people, remember? I know when they're dangerous. I have a brown belt in martial arts."

"That's good." He relaxed a little.

"A black belt and full-body armor wouldn't be enough for my father, though. He feels responsible for me until I am safe with a man. That's out-of-date and chauvinistic as hell, but that's my dad. That's his way. I've had my way all my life and I'll have it again when I'm home. For now I do things his way."

Yeah. He understood that. Completely. And he would help her. The fact came to him as clear as a headline. He hated pretending, he hated lying, but in her misguided way, Nikki was trying to do the right thing. He had the time, after all. He could give up the weekend at least and still take his motorcycle trip. "I'll help you," he said softly.

"What?!" She looked up at him. "You will?" The moonlight glistened on her damp cheeks, making her skin look silvery. She looked like an elf lying there, glimmering in the dark.

"I will," he said. "Just for the weekend. Monday, I'm taking off on the motorcycle trip I had planned."

"You're staying! I can't believe it!" In a burst of enthusiasm, she sat up, threw her arms around him and kissed him square on the mouth.

He felt like a needle had struck a nerve—alive with electricity. Stunned, he pulled away. "Well. Good, um, that's settled then."

"Thank you so much. You won't regret this. You'll have fun, too. I promise."

"It's just the weekend. Long enough for you to make your parents feel better." His lips still tingled from that kiss.

"Sure. Unless you like it so much you decide to stay the week, check out the reunion and all."

"No way. I couldn't fake this for that long. In fact, we'd better talk this through a bit," he said in as businesslike a tone as he could manage after that kiss.

"What do you mean?"

"I mean I'll need some help if I'm going to be able to play the part of Warren. I need some background to be realistic."

"Oh, I see what you mean. Like what's your motivation? What's Warren like? What are we like together? That kind of thing?" She kept holding his gaze, making him uncomfortable.

"Something like that," he said. He lay down on the bed to keep from having to look into her bewitching face. Except now he was lying beside her. In bed. Sheesh. He forced himself to stare at the ceiling, but his awareness didn't change. Even his peripheral vision was working overtime. Nothing about Nikki felt safe to him.

"Great idea," she said, turning onto her side to look down at him, bracing her chin with her palm. Too close. One tiny movement and she'd be on top of him.

"Okay, I'll start," she said. "We know how we met—in my store—the boutique, of course, not the tattoo shop. Okay, what next?" She paused. "We became inseparable."

"Yeah?" He swallowed hard.

Her bubbly tone turned sultry. "Yeah. We couldn't keep our hands off each other."

"Really?" He cleared his throat.

"Oh, yeah. It was sex, sex, sex. We didn't eat, barely came up for air. We—"

He made a choked sound. "Move on to something else."

"Okay." She chuckled softly, enjoying teasing him, he could tell. "Then you got the call to go to South America. You couldn't turn it down, and I couldn't go with you, so to ease our grief while we were apart those three months, we decided to strengthen our bond by tying the knot."

"Okay," he said, sucked into the seductiveness of the moment. Nikki's whiskey voice came softly to him in the dark, intimate as pillow talk. He kept staring at the ceiling, but out of the corner of his eye he saw how the moonlight lit her curves, making them magically erotic. He could almost imagine that robe slipping away....

"Where did we get married?" Nikki continued. "Hmm. I've got it. At the Grand Canyon on one of those bluffs. I've always wanted to do that."

"You mean on the way to Bright Angel?"

"You've been there?"

"Yeah. It's very scenic. Beautiful colors—red, purple and brown with pine trees and scrub here and there."

"Perfect, then. We chose that because...we were making a huge *leap* into the future.... Yeah. And because...it's a wonder of nature. Like our love."

"Right." He grinned at the corny romance of it.

"The ceremony was brief," she continued. "We wrote our own vows on the way—memorized them, too—and as soon as we'd signed the papers, we zipped right to our suite overlooking the Canyon for the honeymoon."

"The honeymoon?" He gulped.

They both thought about that for a long, tense moment. Here they were in a bed together, just like the honeymoon. Except for the view of the Grand Canyon, of course. And who needed that when they had each other?

Hollis caught himself. "And then we went home," he said matter-of-factly. "To our ordinary workaday world. Where do we live?"

She chuckled softly—a low, sexy sound that he wanted to taste. "Okay. Let's see. My place is too funky. What about yours? Where do you live?"

"Montgomery Place—Twenty-Fourth Street south of Lincoln."

"Oh, I know those. Nice apartments. On the mountain. What number?"

"Four-three-two."

"Okay. We can live at Four-three-two Montgomery Place for now. We have a lot of money, of course, since you're a fabulously successful physician, but we live modestly—every piece of furniture or piece of art lovingly chosen together...or—I

know—purchased as a gift to surprise the other...
followed by long, thank-you lovemaking.''

"Nikki..." he warned, but his voice had a hitch
in it. "Could you not talk so much about—"

"Sex? Okay. I'm just trying to get into this. A
great marriage has lots of sex, and of course we have
a great marriage, right?"

"Right." He sighed. She was so indomitable.

"So, a typical day. Even though we've made love
several times the night before, you wake up early—
all the sex rejuvenates you—so you kiss me awake
and we—"

"Nikki..."

"Okay, okay. Moving on to breakfast. Can you
cook?"

"Omelets are my specialty," he said, relieved to
get into something as ordinary as food.

"Great. I don't really cook, but in this case, let's
say I make great waffles. And while I'm mixing the
batter, you come up behind me and slip off my lacy
black apron, and I can't move because my hands are
covered in batter, but that doesn't stop you—"

"Pleeeeze," he groaned.

"Sorry," she whispered. "Guess I got carried
away. It's just that food is so sensual, you know.
Texture and taste and smell, licking and moving
around in your mouth...with your tongue so..."

A shudder went through him. "Okay, so I make
the omelet and you make the waffles and we eat
breakfast."

"Off the same plate, feeding each other bite after
bite, staring into each others' eyes...watching our
lips move moistly, our tongues swirl tantalizingly,
darting out to lick a crumb from the corner of..."

"Don't do this."

She lowered her voice. "Come on, Hollis, get into the spirit of things. You want us to be believable tomorrow, don't you?"

He groaned.

"In fact," she continued, "food is so sensuous, that we sometimes knock everything off the table and make love right there...or on the counter...or against the refrigerator...."

Her words were like fingers on his body, stroking him, bringing him more and more into the fantasy. It seemed so natural, really. Ridiculous to fight it. They'd been playing husband and wife all afternoon and evening, after all, and now she was mesmerizing him with her voice, which dripped with sex. He just had to get closer, to hear her better.

"Nikki," he breathed. And then he turned his body toward her, moved over her and their mouths were together. He wasn't sure how it happened—it was like they were dreaming the same dream and just found each other in the dark.

"Hollis," she said, the word a surrender. She was so soft in his arms, perfectly molded to his body like she belonged there. And she was sweet. Giving, but with strength and mischief. Her mouth felt just like he'd imagined while watching her suck down those cheese dippies—teasing and playful. Her tongue darted, hard to catch. His hands slid under her arm, felt her ribs, moved forward to cup her perfect breasts.

She was swept away, too, he could tell by the way she trembled and her breath rasped. She reached to hold him through his pajamas.

God. His vision faded as all his blood—and most of his mind—dropped below his waist. Any minute now, he'd shove the robe off her shoulders, take her breast into his mouth, reach between her legs and then he'd be a goner.

What was he doing? What about Rachel, his almost fiancée?

"I can't." He released her and rolled onto his back.

Just like that the bubble burst for Nikki. It had felt so right. They were husband and wife. And the story had been so perfect. She hadn't even gotten to the part where they came home at the end of the day and went at each other like crazed minks or bunnies or guinea pigs—some creature that considered sex a way of life.

"Why not?" she asked, knowing the answer already. "Your girlfriend, right?"

"Yes." His chest rose and fell unevenly. "We're almost engaged."

"What?" She sat up. "You're almost engaged? You said she was your girlfriend. And you don't kiss like a man with a fiancée."

"I can't help that. You were so…so very…all over me."

"I was all over you? Oh, that's rich. What about you? Your hands and your mouth? You were pretty all over me, don't you think? Unless you lost your keys or something."

"Come on. You were deliberately seducing me."

"I was just getting into the story. And maybe letting nature take its course. *You* kissed *me*, not the other way around, buster."

"How could I help it? You kept talking about sex, sex, sex. You pushed things too far."

"What?" She jerked to a sit and stared at him. "You're *blaming* me? I don't believe this!" She stood up and stomped around the bed to flop down on the awful cushions.

"What are you doing?"

"I'm going to sleep. Ouch." A button had stabbed her hip.

"Don't play martyr. You can sleep up here, too. I won't bother you."

"Oh, *no*. I wouldn't want to tempt you with my sluttish ways. I might snore seductively and you'd be forced to have your way with me. What would Rachel Actually say?"

"Stop calling her that. Her name's—"

"And, anyway, if you were so sold on her, why did you come on this trip with me in the first place?"

"You blackmailed me?" But the question was weak.

"Baloney. I saw that look in your eye. You wanted to come."

He was silent, so she knew she'd gotten him.

"I think you should think long and hard about your intentions toward Rachel Actually, Hal. You have a hell of a lot of free-floating sexual ions for a guy who's supposedly bonded. A house and one-point-two children will not cut it if you don't get a zing from the woman you're married to. I don't care whether it's by the book or not."

"If this is more aura nonsense, I don't want to hear it."

"I don't need to read your aura to know an unsatisfied man when I kiss one." She jerked to the side and fell right off the cushions. Ice-cold tile. She shrieked.

"Oh, for God's sake. Get up here where you can sleep."

"Forget it." She wouldn't give him the satisfaction. She climbed back onto the cushions, but they shifted under her and her bare thigh hit the cold tile.

"Ah!"

"Get up or I'll haul you up," he said through gritted teeth. "I'm not listening to you squeal all night."

"I'm staying right here. I'll be quiet."

But after fifteen minutes of buttons poking her, her pillow falling off, and the blanket failing to cover her, the bed sounded awfully nice. Maybe just a nap.

As soon Hollis's breathing slowed to a sleep level, Nikki tiptoed around to the other side of the bed and slipped carefully onto the very edge of the mattress. She'd pop back down onto the cushions before Hollis woke up and realized what she'd done.

Hollis snorted, rolled over and flung his arm across her body. His fingers slapped her cheek, then dangled over her nose, blocking her airway. She shifted slightly. He dragged his hand lower, clutching her upper arm. Now she was trapped. She'd slide out the instant he relaxed his grip, she told herself, snuggling deeper into the mattress, loving the steady, comforting sound of his breathing. Too bad he was such a pain when he was awake.

STILL HALF ASLEEP, Hollis cozied up to the warm body in his bed. Mmm. Rachel'd gotten less angular somehow. His arousal brought him more awake. He was just reaching around to grab a breast when he realized the warm body he was spooned around wasn't Rachel's, it was Nikki's. His lusty haze evaporated instantly. Had he dreamed the woman into his bed?

She gave a sweet little moan in her sleep, then moved her bottom against his—uh-oh. God, that felt good. This was insane. What was he doing? He'd never last the night with Nikki this close. Careful not to wake her, he slipped out of bed and crawled onto the cushions, almost grateful for the cold, since it distracted him from all that warm, sexy woman just a mattress away.

What a rat he was. He deserved the cold floor and lumpy cushions. Poor trusting Rachel believed he was whipping along the highway on a motorcycle. Instead, he'd been sliding up and down Nikki's curves, longing for more. Rachel's last admonition to him had been, "Don't pick up any hitchhikers. Remember *Easy Rider*." Hitchhikers? No problem. How about roommates? He'd certainly picked up one of those. And she was a doozy.

He settled in and made himself imagine doing a difficult root canal, or, even worse, making that first loan payment on his new practice. But it was no use. He couldn't get Nikki out of his mind. Or what she'd said about him. He did have a lot of "free-floating sexual ions" for someone who was almost engaged. The truth was he didn't want to get married. Not right now.

Worse, he was a little worried about how he felt about Rachel. He'd never reacted to Rachel the way he was reacting to Nikki. Her scent and kiss and touch, even the sexy rasp of her voice, were intensely arousing. He considered himself a man with a normal range of passion. But right now he fairly surged with it. A tremendous tidal wave of lust sloshed through him at just the thought of Nikki.

Maybe it was just a subconscious urge for freedom. Just like his longed-for motorcycle escape. Maybe Rachel represented a life with boundaries and Nikki one without limits. Maybe he wasn't ready to

be locked down. Maybe that's what his intense reaction to Nikki was about.

No matter what, he owed Rachel another chance.
If he was having some weird pre-engagement crisis,
he couldn't let it get the best of him. No matter that
Nikki lay inches away in the slinkiest, most remov-
able nightgown he'd ever seen....

Damn. He forced himself to face the wall and
squeezed his eyes shut. Thump. His hip hit icy tile.
Served him right for getting into a car with a
stranger. A stranger with Emerald-City eyes. Nikki
Winfield gave a whole new meaning to the phrase
Stranger Danger.

NIKKI WOKE UP with a jolt. Early light lit the room.
Oops. She'd stayed on the bed longer than she'd
meant to. She rolled carefully off the mattress and
tiptoed around the bed. Except there was Hollis on
the makeshift bed, the middle of his body on the floor
between the two cushions, one leg sprawled out,
touching the floor, the other dangling off the end of
the cushion. His arm was flung under his head. His
pillow lay against the wall.

God, he looked delicious. Big and manly and sexy
in his old-fashioned pajamas. Kissing him had been
better than she'd imagined. She'd thought he'd be a
tight-lipped, controlling tongue-withholder. Instead,
he'd been sensuous and giving, but going for what
he wanted in her mouth, too. And his body had felt
so natural against hers. She'd forgotten they were
strangers. Incompatible strangers, at that. She'd just
wanted him.

But he'd wimped out, claiming to be nearly engaged. Bull. It was an excuse to keep her at arms'
length. She overwhelmed men. She knew that. Es-

pecially Normal Norman guys like Hollis. She was too *there*. Too eager, too talkative, too emotional, too lively. Too sexual, really.

You're too much. That was what Brian Collier had told her when she'd demanded an explanation for their breakup back in high school. *You're too intense. You've got, like, X-ray vision. You make me tired. Too many questions. Too much about feelings.*

The few men she'd tried to get serious with had said similar things. As a result, she'd learned to keep things light. She had men who were just friends— many of them musicians and former tattoo clients— and men she counted on for friendly sex. But the real deal—melding with a soul mate—was somewhere in the future. Some day she'd find someone as intense as she was and it would be fireworks 24/7. In the meantime, she kept busy.

She lay on the bed, crosswise, her head hanging over the edge to watch Hollis sleep. He was so serious, even asleep. But he had a streak of humor she'd just begun to tap into. She wished she hadn't created that fantasy of their life together. It made her want it, as impossible as it was.

Now that she'd kissed him and knew the potential for mind-blowing sex, it wouldn't be easy for her to sleep in the same room with him and not get carried away again. Even for just two more days. She'd hoped he'd stay for the reunion, but that might be too much closeness for both of them.

Hollister rolled over and opened his eyes. He blinked up at her in confusion. "Morning," he said, his voice thick with sleep.

"Morning," she said, realizing she was in kissing range. "I didn't mean to steal the bed. Was I crowding you?"

"No. I just needed to, um, move." He reddened strangely.

She scooted back and sat up.

He sat up, too. "Look, Nikki, last night—"

"Was not my fault," she said firmly. She would not take the blame for his wimping out. "Don't try to say I—"

"Let me finish. Last night I got carried away. It was being there with you, so close, talking about…you know… It just…"

"Happened," she whispered.

"Right." His eyes searched her face. She could see he still wanted her, but he hated himself for it.

"I know you said you'd stay, but I don't want you to feel obligated, Hollis. I tricked you, after all. And you do have a girlfriend. Or should I say fiancée?"

"I said I'd help you," he said. "And I will."

He was such a stand-up guy. "Are you sure?"

"We can be sensible about this. We're adults, right? We can exercise some self-control."

"You think so?" she asked. She loved his eyes—so sincere, so kind. And when they flared with lust, like they were doing right now, they made her melt.

"We have to."

"Then we'd better make the bed," she said. "Remove temptation."

"Great." He went to the door side of the sofa and they straightened the sheets together. She went to the end to lift the mattress, while Hollis leaned forward and pushed at the middle of the bed.

"Hold it!" He grimaced and hunched over.

"What?"

"My pants are, um, caught in the hinge here."

"Oh, Lord." She put down her side and crawled across the bed. Yep. The crotch area of Hollis's pajamas was twisted between the folding metal pieces of the sofa. "You're not actually...?"

"Caught in there? God no." He flushed.

"Let me look." She tugged at the fabric, then the hinge.

This was the strangest way she'd ever gotten close to a man's penis. She tried to ignore the fact that as she worked the back of her hand kept bumping into...

He didn't seem to mind, though.

She straightened the fabric with both hands, careful not to grab him, too. "It's the button. It's really caught. I'm going to have to rip off the threads." Her hands were full, so she bent down to tear the button threads with her teeth.

There was a tap on the door, then it burst open.

"Shelley, don't disturb—" Her mother's shocked face appeared behind Shelley.

"What are you doing, Aunt Nikki?" Shelley asked.

Nikki jerked her head up from Hollis' crotch. Oh, God. Not what it looked like, that was for sure.

"Oh, my!" Her mother clutched Shelley, backed away and pulled the door shut. "Shelley wanted to tell you breakfast is nearly ready," she called through the door. "But take all the time you need."

Hollis burst out laughing.

"It's not funny," she said. "My mother thinks we go at each other like sex fiends."

"If only."

Startled by his wistful tone, she looked straight at him.

He shrugged. "I mean in theory." He looked away, but not before she got another zing.

"Let me get this." She resumed her efforts at his

pjs, then tugged the button loose and stood. "Ta-da," she said, sticking out her tongue with the button on it.

He took it from her tongue. "Great work." There was a little sizzle at the intimacy of the moment, then they both laughed, looking into each other's eyes. It felt good. Like they were a team, united in their effort to impress her family. And fight their urges.

"You get dressed," she told him, "and I'll go make sure I haven't scarred my niece for life."

She found her mother nervously setting the table, her face blotched with red. The forks were crooked and the napkins weren't folded perfectly.

"It wasn't what you thought, Mother. Warren's pajamas got stuck in the hinge and—"

"Don't say another word," her mother said. "What goes on behind the bedroom door between a man and his wife is no one's business."

"Really, though…"

"I told Shelley you were, um, doing your exercises."

Right. Sadly, the only thing they'd be exercising would be self-control.

HOLLIS HAD NO CLUE what to do. He was intensely attracted to Nikki. So much so he had a hard time thinking about anything else. Should he call Rachel? Tell her he was attracted to another woman and let the chips fall where they may? But this whole episode—from agreeing to Nikki's blackmail to drooling over sexual fantasies of being married to her could just be a manifestation of his desire to break away, do something different, abandon "the book" for a while.

This weird reaction to Nikki could very well be

temporary and his life would resume its predictable path when he got back to Phoenix—or even just away from Nikki. If he told Rachel what was going on now, he would have scared her for nothing.

No, he'd get through this weekend somehow, then do some serious thinking on his bike trip. By the end of that he should have his head on straight.

Or not.

7

HOLLIS ENTERED THE DINING ROOM looking thoughtful, just as Shelley bounced out of the kitchen carrying a sloshing pitcher of orange juice bigger than her head.

"After breakfast, we can play dress-up, Uncle Warren," she said, then pranced back into the kitchen.

Hollis leaned near Nikki's ear. "Save me."

"I'll try," she said.

She turned to her mother. "Don't the kids ever leave?"

"We think of this as their second home." Her mother sighed, but she sounded proud, which surprised Nikki because her niece and nephew seemed chaos incarnate and she remembered her mother being very strict. No mess, no eating anywhere but the kitchen, inside voices in the house and absolutely no running.

"We love having them. When you two have children," her mother continued, "plan on having them come out and stay with us for as long as you want."

"That would be nice, Mom," she said faintly. Children. This was the second time her mother had mentioned the idea. She was upping the ante on her. Faking pregnancy would be impossible. Maybe she could borrow a baby.... Despair washed through her.

Her gaze dashed to Hollis. His long frame bent

gracefully over the table, putting the water glasses precisely in place—exactly where her mother would have. He fit right in here.

Look at those fingers, efficient, careful, gentle....

Stop it. He's not for you. He'd bore you. You'd make him crazy. She tuned back into what her mother was saying.

"That's what grandparents are for, dear. We won't spoil them though. We didn't spoil you, did we?"

"Oh, no." God forbid.

"Between you and me," her mother said, leaning close to whisper, "Donna indulges them too much. She doesn't seem able to say no."

Nikki was shocked. Her mother was criticizing Donna? Unheard of. "Where is Donna, anyway?" she asked.

"Getting ready probably. I didn't raise you girls to be so appearance-minded. Pretty is as pretty does, in my book."

Ooooh, more disapproval. This was great. Perfect Donna wasn't quite so perfect. Nikki felt a rush of sympathy and affection for her sister. It had been hard to love her when she was held up as the perfect example—completely out of Nikki's reach. Donna seemed more human all of a sudden, and Nikki had the urge to hug her.

"I don't know why the children bother her so much," her mother mused.

Because Donna's a perfectionist like you, she wanted to say. But her mother didn't seem as tense and critical as she'd remembered her being.

"Ta-da. Grandma's cinnamon rolls," Shelley announced, holding the tray over her head above a leaping Byron.

"I want to carry it. Me, me!"

"You're too little. You'll drop them," she said, swerving the tray away from him. The top layer of rolls tumbled to the floor, frosting side down.

"Look what you did!" Shelley glared at Byron.

Byron looked devastated, then he rallied. "You did it."

"Nuh-huh."

"Uh-huh."

"It was an accident," Nikki's mother said in that no-nonsense voice Nikki remembered so well.

Mollified, Byron picked up two of the fallen rolls, which he held against his chest. "Look, boobies." He began to prance around the table, his chest outthrust. "I've go-ot boobies and you-ou don't," he sing-songed.

"That is so gross," Shelley said. "You are such a baby."

"You are."

At that moment, Donna and Dave came through the front door. Her brother-in-law was decked out in full fishing regalia—pocketed vest over a flannel shirt, khaki hat dotted with flies.

"We've got to get out there, Bro-in-law," he said to Hollis, slapping him on the back. Hollis look startled. "We should have left at the crack, but I wanted to leave you time for a little..." he leaned in to mutter "...vacation nookie."

Hollister smiled uneasily. "Sure."

"Look, Mommy, I've got boobies like you," Byron said.

"Oh, God. What now?" Donna sank into a chair. She wore a linen sheath with full makeup, her hair perfect.

"It's all right, dear. I've handled it," her mother said.

Shelley was setting a cinnamon roll on each plate, licking her fingers of frosting after each deposit.

"Sorry about the kids," Donna whispered to her. "Sometimes they just get to me. If Mother didn't take them, I don't know what I'd do. I need some peace. I go home and put something in alphabetical order to relax."

"I imagine it could be tiring."

"Just wait until you have kids. It's not how you picture it—adoring babes you can dress up and show off, who play quiet games together and let you teach them things."

Tiring of the boob game, Byron had put the cinnamon rolls over his eyes. "I'm a bug-eyed monster," he said, sticking his head in front of Shelley, who promptly pushed a finger into the middle of each monster eye and removed the center rings.

"Mommy," Byron wailed. "Shelley poked out my eyes."

"Cut it out," Donna said tiredly.

"Never mind. Come and sit," Nikki's mother said, helping Byron into the chair beside her.

Donna confided softly to Nikki. "Shelley bullies Byron, I'm sorry to say. Then he acts out to get attention."

"Kind of like you and me used to be, huh?"

Her sister looked puzzled. "We weren't like that…were we?"

"Remember the time you tied me to the sandbox canopy pole?"

"You were supposed to be Prince Charming in the dungeon. I told you I was coming to rescue you. I was Merriweather the fairy. I would have, too, but you wouldn't wait. You bashed down the pole with a baseball bat."

"I didn't want to be tied up. You were always so bossy."

"I was helping you. Besides, you were a tagalong."

Nikki smiled at her. "Kind of like Byron?"

Before Donna could answer, Shelley announced, "I'll say grace," then launched in. "Thank you, O Lord, for our food."

"Thank you, O Lord," Byron echoed, "for our—*ouch*. She kicked me!"

"Don't kick, Shelley."

"Bless that it will nourish us," Shelley continued. Byron repeated. "Stop copying me," Shelley hissed.

"Stop copying me," Byron said. "Ouch. She kicked me again."

"Cut it out," Donna said. "Let Shelley finish the prayer, Byron, and you can say it at dinner." Then she muttered to Nikki, "I think I see your point."

When the prayer was over, Nikki asked about her father.

"He's already eaten," her mother said. "He's living like a king in there. I'm cutting him off the pain meds today. He should be up and around."

"But we don't want to take any chances, do we? I mean we don't want to strain his...you know."

"His you-know needs to get moving."

She was shocked at her mother's words and tone. "Don't you think we should be careful...."

"Your father's fine."

Wasn't her mother taking this stoicism about illness too far? Maybe she was in denial about her husband's condition. Nikki cast a worried look at Donna, who mouthed, *it's okay.*

"Listen, sweetheart," her mother said to Nikki, "I was wondering if you could help me. I'm doing some appliquéd aprons for the church bazaar and I thought maybe you could draw the design.''

"Sure, I'd love to,'' she said, touched by the invitation.

"She's so creative, our Nicolette,'' her mother said to Hollis. "We thought she'd go into commercial design, you know.'' She gave Nikki a regretful look. "But she made a different choice.''

"I think Nikki's very creative in her work,'' Hollis said, putting his arm around her shoulder and hugging her to him.

"Oh, I'm sure you're right,'' her mother said, reddening at her poor manners.

Nikki felt a foolish tickle of grateful tears at his gesture of support. When the conversation shifted, she caught Hollis's eye. *Thank you.*

He squeezed her hand. The warmth went right through her.

They were halfway through the meal when her father's cowbell rang out.

"What?'' her mother yelled, then caught the startled looks around the table, and said calmly, "Excuse me, won't you?'' She daintily wiped the corners of her mouth, then left the table.

She returned in a moment. "Warren, your father-in-law would like a brief consultation before you leave to go fishing.''

Hollis shot Nikki a look. *What'll I say?*

She shot one back. *Fake it.*

HOLLIS WENT into the bedroom, desperately wracking his brain for what he knew about the heart. He knew cranial anatomy like the back of his hand, but he hadn't studied the heart since undergraduate physiology. *Let's see. Ventricular, arterial...*

"Have a seat, son," Mr. Winfield said, patting the chair beside his bed. His color and energy were good for someone with heart disease.

"How are you feeling, sir?"

"Fine. Fine. And call me Harvey."

"Great. Harvey it is. I'm sorry to say I'm not a specialist in your condition."

"God, I hope not," he said heartily. "That's not why I wanted to talk to you. I just wanted to tell you how glad I am to put a face to a name." He gripped Hollis by the forearm. "To tell the truth, Nadine and I thought she was making you up."

Hollis tried to laugh, but it came out a choked sound.

"We were planning to come up to Phoenix to make sure she was all right—after I got over this, uh, condition. Then Donna told us she was coming for the reunion and bringing you. So, I just wanted to thank you for what you've done for our Nicolette."

Now he felt like a complete heel.

"When she left home ten years ago, she was so wild, so angry." He paused, turned away and blinked, then cleared his throat. "Sorry about that. Anyway, her mother and I did our best to help her see the world as it was. We tried to teach her that the rules had purpose—that the rules led to the freedom she said she wanted. But she wouldn't listen. We had some tough times." He paused, shook his head. "But that's all over. I can see she's come into her own, become sure of herself, thanks to you."

"Actually, Mr. Winfield—"

"Harvey. Or Dad, if you prefer."

"Harvey," he said firmly. Calling him Dad would be too awful. "Nikki's not a bit different today than she was the day I met her.'' Completely true, since they'd only met five days ago. ''She's been her own woman for a long time.''

''You're being modest, son. The most important thing, though, is how you feel about each other. I can see she adores *you*.''

Hardly. She thought he was a boring nerd who considered not wearing seat belts an act of rebellion.

Harvey was staring at him, and Hollis realized he was waiting for him to say *I adore her, too.* But he couldn't use those words without meaning them. He felt sweat break out on his forehead. What to say, what to say...

Finally it came to him. ''I can assure you, Mr. Winfield—I mean, Harvey—Nikki and I feel exactly the same way about each other.'' Brilliant. The truth delivered in a way Harvey could interpret the way he needed to.

''Glad to hear it, son.'' He reached for Hollis's hand and gave it a somber shake. ''We're counting on you to watch out for our little girl. I know you won't let us down.'' He had the same intense green eyes as Nikki's and they locked on. That principal look. That no nonsense, no retakes, if-you-blow-it-you're-suspended look. Harvey held his gaze a little longer. There was a hint of doubt there—as if he suspected something wasn't right—so Hollis excused himself right away, before the man could ask him something he'd have to lie about.

As it was, Hollis had the terrible feeling that after they'd returned to Phoenix, he'd be checking on Nikki monthly just to fulfill this duty her father had practically knighted him with. What had Nikki gotten him into?

AFTER BREAKFAST, Nikki went with her mother into the sewing room, where they set to work on the appliqués. She created a spring design that was traditional enough to please her mother, but original enough for her to be happy with it. In fact, she decided to add it to her tattoo design collection. If only she could tell her mother about that.

By noon, they were busy baking for the class reunion picnic. Her mother was in charge of the picnic desserts, decorations for the dance and the entertainment. Practically the whole town got involved in the reunions, which were held every two years, with the official reunion class playing the starring roles.

Her mother was in the basement loading goodies into the freezer and Nikki had just removed the very first apple pie she'd ever made on her own from the oven, when Hollister and Dave returned from their fishing trip.

"Look what I caught." Hollis held out a length of fishing line from which dangled a fish not much bigger than a sardine. He was so proud, standing there holding out his tiny trophy for her to admire, that Nikki had to grin.

She hardly recognized him. In place of the spotlessly groomed dentist she'd first met was a sunburned outdoorsman with mussed hair, mud-streaked clothes and dirt around his fingernails. When he got closer, she saw that his hand had several blood-streaked cuts and he smelled of beer.

"It must have put up a hell of a fight," she said. "I didn't think fish teeth could break the skin."

"The hook caught me a couple of times." He shrugged.

"But he did great," Dave said, slapping him on the back. Dave was quite the back slapper—more like an insurance agent than a banker. "He wouldn't have got snagged except I made him chug a couple beers with me to get in the mood.''

''We'll cook these with dinner,'' she said. She took the fish from Hollis, along with the four decent-sized trout Dave had caught.

Dave headed home to clean up, and they were alone. Immediately, the electricity between them crackled.

''That was fun. You may be right about doing new things.''

''You look completely outdoorsy,'' she said.

''Probably smell that way, too.''

''No, you smell great.'' Energy sparked and zinged between them.

''You, too.'' Crackle. Zip. Zing.

''It's just cinnamon and vanilla—scientifically proven to turn men on.'' It got suddenly hot in the already warm kitchen.

''Well, it's working,'' he said, shifting his position so they were close enough to embrace. She felt herself sway closer.

''What are you cooking?''

''My first pie.''

''Your first, huh?'' he said. ''Mmm. You know food is very sensual.'' Instantly, they were back in that midnight fantasy about making love atop or against any kitchen surface.

''Oh, yeah,'' she said. ''Especially when you feed it to each other.''

''Actually, you look good enough to eat,'' he said, brushing something—probably flour—off her cheek with a sensuous stroke of the back of his hand.

''You've had too many beers in the sun.''

''Probably,'' he said. ''But you're not helping

matters wearing an apron like the one you were talking about last night.''

She was actually wearing a gingham monstrosity of her mother's. "This old thing?" She tried to sound sassy, but she felt overheated, so it came out wobbly. She reached behind her waist and slowly untied it, sliding the cheery fabric away from her body like she was doing a striptease.

''Yeah. That old thing. Now, how about you feed me a bite of your first pie?'' His voice was rough with desire. So what if that was due to too many beers in the sun. She'd never been so gratified by a man's reaction to her.

''You want some?'' she asked, teasing.

''Oh, yeah.'' He nodded, his smile wicked. "I want some.''

Holding his gaze, she slapped at the drawers, yanked one open and grabbed a fork. She stabbed the center of her pie, trying to dig out a bite. The crust resisted, but she managed to get a morsel on the tines. ''Open up.''

He opened his mouth slightly, his terrific tongue reaching out to accept the pie. Her knees went rubbery. She wanted to be that bit of crust and apples sliding between his lips.

He closed his mouth and started to chew. He paused, his eyes widened in distress. Then he chewed more, trying to smile. Obviously, something was wrong with the pie. The sensuous mood evaporated.

''What is it?'' She forked a bite for herself. *Blech.* The crust was the texture of cardboard and tasted like Play-Doh. She'd done something to the filling, too. The apple chunks were salty and sour—almost pickled. She spit the bite into her hand, then rushed to toss it in the trash. "That is nasty," she said, trying to get the taste off her tongue.

"It's not that bad."

"I can't cook." Her mother had demonstrated for her, but Nikki'd insisted on doing the whole thing on her own. She'd obviously blown it. She felt stupid and disappointed.

"It's okay," he said softly. "You have other talents."

"Yeah, but I want to be able to cook."

"Oh, you're cooking, all right. On high." He looked at her, his gaze hotter than he was declaring her cooking to be.

"Oh, hell," he muttered and yanked her to him for a kiss that was slow and sweet and more delicious than any pie anywhere.

She kissed him back, her hands sliding into his hair. He made a sound and deepened the kiss.

"Mmm," she said into his mouth. He began to walk backward with her, his hands sliding along her back, lowering to cup her bottom, to tug her to him. Then there she was against the refrigerator door, just like the fantasy, except her head bumped into the freezer handle, but who cared?

"Hollis," she said into his ear. She was going for his mouth when she heard a gasp that hadn't come from either of them and looked past his head to see her mother standing there, looking shocked, holding out a stack of empty baking pans. She'd returned from the basement.

"Mother," Nikki said and slid away from Hollis and the fridge.

"Who's Hollis?" her mother asked, looking from one to the other of them.

"Hollis?" they both said, trying to collect themselves.

"Um, that's Warren's middle name," Nikki said, amazed at how quickly she came up with that. "Sometimes I call him that. When—"

"Say no more," her mother said, taking the trays to the table. She brushed at her hair, cleared her throat. "Why don't you two take some time to rest up before dinner. A nice private nap can relieve tension."

"Oh, but we shouldn't…"

"Oh, yes, you should. I want your full attention tonight when we play bridge. We can't have a lot of distracting footsie going on under the table. I expect to clean up." Her mother gave her a mischievous smile.

She stared at her mother. Pretty racy talk. And pretty understanding. This was a side of her mother she'd never seen before. Hollis took her hand, warm and tight, and led her down the hall.

What the hell are you doing? Hollis's rational side demanded. *Taking Nikki to bed* the rest of him answered. Hell, he'd never be able to wait long enough to fold out the bed. The sofa would do. Or maybe the floor. Or the back of the door. He wanted Nikki like he'd never wanted a woman before.

He'd never get over this in two days. He'd need more time. He'd have to stay. Forget the motorcycle trip. He could do that later. Right now he needed this. He'd call Rachel and tell her he wasn't ready to get married, that he needed to see other people.

Other people, hell. He needed to see Nikki. She was all he could think of, all he wanted to see and touch. She was in his blood, which was rushing through him like a flood, making it impossible to think.

Hollis was serious about this, Nikki realized when he yanked her into the bedroom and started kissing her as he walked her backward toward the couch.

"What's happening?" she managed to murmur between kisses.

"I'm staying," he said. He kissed her mouth, then moved down her neck.

Wow. So good. Go lower. Then she realized what he'd said. "You're staying? You mean for the reunion?"

He lifted his face. "For the reunion, for us, for this thing between us," he whispered, his voice rough with emotion. "I don't know what it is about you, but I can't keep my hands off you."

She felt a rush of gratification and arousal. She could only say, "Oh," before his mouth was on her again. Somehow, his fingers magically found their way under both her blouse and her bra. God bless dentistry for making him so dexterous. He held her breasts the way she loved—firm and delicate at the same time. Lust spun along her nerves to her brain, making her dizzy. Had she ever felt this with a man before? Not that she could remember at the moment. This was different.

Why? Because Hollis was different? Because he'd been resisting her and now he couldn't? Did it matter? It was only sex, right?

A bolt of alarm shot through her. Since when could sex be "only sex" with a guy like Hollis? And he was supposedly nearly engaged. Something else bothered her, something about how she was beginning to feel, but forget that now. She mustered what remained of her self-control and broke off the kiss. "What about Rachel Actually?"

"Rachel Actually—I mean Rachel?" He looked at her with lust-bleary eyes, then blinked, trying to think, she could see. "I'll talk to her," he said. "I'll simply explain what happened, and…and tell her that I'm not ready to be engaged. That I need some time to, um, see other people." As he talked she could see the worry come into his eyes.

This wasn't right. She did not want to be responsible for breaking up Hollis and his girlfriend. Maybe he didn't want to marry the woman—her instincts told her that for sure—but she would not be his excuse for deciding that. He had to discover he wasn't in love with Rachel Actually on his own, not because Nikki had tempted him just by being who she was.

"We can't do this," she said. "You can't do this to Rachel. Not over the phone."

Hollis looked desperate and confused. For a second, she thought maybe he'd just go for it, overwhelm her, storm her barriers, which were so flimsy that one kiss, one word, one touch and she'd fold like a bad poker hand.

But Hollis was a stand-up guy who did the right thing. Even when it hurt. "You're right. It's not fair to Rachel. It's not fair to you. I don't know what came over me." He frowned in bewilderment.

Lust, you idiot. Wild-eyed, breathless, panting lust. He obviously didn't have much passion with Rachel Actually. Not like he was feeling for her. That wasn't unusual. Nikki was a sensual person and men were drawn to that. If she stayed interested in them and got too intense about it, they backed off. And if ever there was a man she'd be too much for, it was straight-arrow Hollis Marx.

So cooling it was for the best really. "Will you still stay for the reunion, though? It will mean a lot to me." At least she could still impress her classmates, the town and Brian Collier. They'd come this far.

"Sure," he said, trying to smile. "I have to be certain this Brian Collier fellow is good enough for you."

"Thank you," she said, warmed by the affection in his gaze. He was such a sweet man. If only he were hers. No, no. He wasn't her kind of man at all. It was only in Copper Corners, when she was pretending to fit in, wrapped in the approving embrace of her family, that he seemed so perfect. Once she got home and could be herself again, she wouldn't be interested in him at all.

"I'm walking down the hall!" Her mother was shouting to them. "I'm a few feet away from your door! Just telling you dinner's ready. Don't want to surprise you!"

They smiled wistfully at each other, then Nikki opened the door. "You don't have to shout, Mom. You aren't interrupting a thing."

8

THE NEXT EVENING, Nikki placed plates around the table and tried not to think about how much she wanted Hollis. They'd both been busy all day. Hollis was filling in for her father with yard work, and she was doing decorations for the reunion dance.

She'd had fun and been blessedly distracted from hot thoughts of Hollis. The dance theme was "The Magic of Memory," so she'd sketched fairies in the woods with mystical castles in the background that she would paint on butcher paper and hang on the gym walls. Tomorrow Hollis would cut small plywood displays in her dad's workshop.

She'd designed centerpieces for the tables they would scatter around the room that included magic wands, ribbons and pink-and-orchid silk flowers. Cactus Confections had supplied the ingredients for the party favors—a selection of cactus candy jellies and lollipops tied to tiny containers of soap bubbles. Nikki had kept Shelley busy that afternoon assembling them, until she'd eaten too much candy and wanted to quit. Her mother had pointed out more than once that Donna hadn't turned out to be the best of mothers and she had high hopes for Nikki's mothering skills. Sigh.

Then Nikki had stopped painting and she and Hollis had played hide-and-go-seek with the kids. Now Nikki was setting the table for dinner, happy to keep moving. Despite how busy she was, she felt irritable and jumpy being home. It wasn't just Hollis. She was glad to see her family, to feel like a normal woman for a change, but the daily activities bored her.

So domestic. Half the day was spent setting up, cooking and cleaning up after meals, with a little sewing, reading and television in between. The only excitement came from Donna's children.

Nikki liked visiting with her father though. He'd moved out to the couch in the living room, where he coerced people into bringing him unhealthy snacks and magazines. His color did seem better, so he might be pulling out of it. She could only hope. She kept trying to have a heart-to-heart with Donna about him, but her sister had been elusive, leaving the kids with them and heading off for a facial, promising eternal gratitude for the sitting.

To tell the truth, Nikki was homesick. She missed her shop and her kooky friends—musicians and artists most of them—and the unusual people who came in for tattoos. She'd even opened her suitcase and looked over the travel tattoo kit she'd brought as a reassurance about who she was.

Oh, well. Only a week more. At least Hollis would be with her at the reunion. Hollis. Whenever she thought of him, she got a tight feeling inside. To distract herself, she started folding a napkin into a bird shape. *Forget Hollis. He'd bore you.*

Fold, fold, fold. *His idea of a night out would be reading dental magazines at a Starbucks.* Fold, twist, fold. *Dullsville, Daddy-O.*

Except for the sex. That would be far from dull. Nikki's whole body throbbed with the desire to sleep with Hollis. But not like this. He wouldn't admit it even to himself, probably, but Nikki was just a vacation fling for him—like that motorcycle rebellion between semesters. She looked at the bird napkin she'd made. It was one big knot. Like her stomach.

Nikki heard voices—Shelley had absconded with Hollis earlier—so she set off to tell them dinner was ready.

Back home, Hollis would be all wrong—a mismatch in her life like an oak tree in a tropical garden. She rounded the corner to the guest bath where Hollis and Shelley must be. She needed someone with imagination and flexibility, someone interested in new ideas, open to new experiences. That was not Hollis.

She looked into the room and boggled. Hollis was seated on the edge of the tub, wearing lipstick and two huge circles of rouge, with his hair in a series of miniscule ponytails. Shelley was busy painting his fingernails.

"Oh, my God," she said. Talk about being open to new experiences!

"Shelley's getting me ready to go out tonight," he said, winking at her. "We thought candy-apple-red polish was the right color for my complexion," he said. "Don't you agree?"

"Perfect!" Her heart just ached. Okay, maybe he wasn't as limited as she'd thought. And pretty confident of his masculinity, too.

She needed to talk to Mariah about this. She and Hollis were headed to Mariah and Nathan's house after dinner. She was looking forward to the chance to be who they really were.

As soon as everyone started eating, Nikki fixed a plate for her father and carried it into him.

"Sure is nice to have you home, baby girl," he said, smiling at her affectionately. He looked at the

plate she'd set before him. "I'll need more ham."
He frowned. "And you keep forgetting the potatoes."

"Maybe later."

Clearly disappointed, her father took a bite of his
less-than-satisfactory meal, then looked at her
thoughtfully. "Your husband is a serious man, isn't
he?"

"Yes. He is serious."

He looked down to cut another bite. "Awfully nervous, though." He didn't look at her, but she could
tell he was intent on her answer.

"Oh, you know, Daddy. He wants to impress
you."

His eyes shot to hers. "The only person he needs
to impress, Nicolette, is you." He pointed the fork
at her. Then he gave her that I-know-you-ditched
look. "You seem nervous, too. Is this man up to our
standards?"

"Of course, Daddy. Why would you say that?"

"Maybe I'm wrong," he said. He took a thoughtful bite of ham. "You know you can always talk to
me."

"Sure. I know that, Daddy. And I would." *Not in
a million years.* She had the uneasy realization that
her gift for reading people had come from her father.

"Didn't your mother make any gravy for this
ham?"

"She did, but I didn't think—"

"When you bring me the potatoes, get extra gravy,
please."

After her death-dealing errand for her father, she
went back to the dining room where everyone was
eating dessert, each with a different grimace on
their face.

"Do I have to eat this?" Shelley whined.

"Yes," Donna hissed. "It's Nikki's first pie."

Oh, God. She'd forgotten to throw it away!

"Nasty," Byron said, spitting his bite onto his plate. "Sorry, Aunt Nikki."

"It's okay. Please everybody don't eat that," Nikki said. "It's terrible."

Her mother smiled at her. "Don't feel bad, dear. My first pie tasted like plywood and pickles."

"Really?"

"Oh, yes. Baking is a skill. I didn't learn to bake until I had you girls. You'll learn then, too. When you start baking cookies for your babies."

"Right," she said. She glanced over at Hollis. His eyes were wide with alarm and he mouthed *babies?*

NATHAN AND MARIAH'S home was an impressive upper-income house that gave Nikki a flicker of worry that Mariah had lost all her flair. But the minute Nathan let them in, she saw she needn't have worried. The riot of color and design inside proved Mariah had made Nathan's house her own. Funky artwork, including a couple of Nikki's paintings, tons of flowers and bizarre furniture filled the place. Her eye snagged on a settee shaped like a chunky high heel in leopard skin.

Nathan hugged Nikki, then released her. "Nice to see you again. We hardly got a chance to talk at the wedding."

That was because the man wouldn't let his bride out of his sight. He'd had reasons to be nervous, though, since Mariah had run out on him the first time.

"And you're the man of the hour, I hear," Nathan said, giving Hollis's hand a hearty pump. "Nice to meet you. Good of you to help out our Nikki this way.''

A dog—a huge beagle-St. Bernard looking thing—galloped over to them, sniffed at both their crotches, then ran away.

"Wow! Big dog," Nikki said.

"Yeah," Nathan said. "That's Maynard. Mariah decided I was lonely. He worships her, though." Mariah rushed toward them from the back of the house, Maynard at her heels. "I worship her, too," Nathan said on a happy sigh.

"You're early," Mariah said, hugging Nikki carefully, a mascara tube in one hand, the wand in the other. Only half her hair was curled.

"We're not early. You're late, as always. I'm so glad. I was afraid you'd changed."

"Very funny. Nice to see you again, Hollis," Mariah said. She reached to shake his hand with three fingers. "Wow. Is that nail polish? Candy apple red, I'd say. Hmm."

Hollis blushed charmingly. "Nikki's niece did it."

"How sweet." She gave Nikki a look—*Keep him.* "Now don't anybody say anything interesting until I get back." She scampered back to finish her makeup.

Nathan headed to the bar to fix them drinks and Hollis and Nikki sat on the leather sofa in the living room. She was careful to leave plenty of space between them. Since the close call, each time their eyes met, things got hot. Trying to resist was making her tired.

Nathan trundled over holding a tray with a martini shaker decorated with pink elephants and small glasses to match. He poured pink liquid into the glasses and handed them each one.

"Just in time," Mariah said, sailing into the room and sitting on the loveseat next to her husband. Maynard parked on her feet and Nathan put her drink on the table.

"Cranberry martinis," Nathan said. "Mariah couldn't leave a perfectly respectable cocktail alone." He shook his head affectionately at her. "I refuse to put umbrellas in them, though. Leave the drink some dignity, for God's sake."

Nathan lifted his glass in a toast, tapping Hollis's glass last. "Here's to you for joining me in a Rebel Girl's snare. Worse things can happen to a guy." Nathan watched his wife as he sipped his drink, his expression so intimate, so full of worship that Nikki felt the ache of longing. She wanted a man who adored her, too.

She glanced at Hollis, but he'd looked away, probably embarrassed.

"How are you holding up?" Nathan asked Hollis.

"So far, so good, I guess," he said.

"He's doing great," Nikki said. "Everyone's very impressed. Except for that drinking problem." She laughed.

"What drinking problem?" Hollis asked.

"All those beers I made you drink on the way down here. The mints didn't cover it."

"Oh, Lord," he said, sipping his martini and shaking his head. "And Dave made me drink more on the lake."

"And my dad thinks we're too nervous." She frowned.

"We *are* nervous."

"But I think I smoothed that over."

"Your parents worry too much," Hollis said.

"You should have seen them in high school," Mariah said. "They cut her no slack."

"Yeah, but we were pretty outrageous. When we weren't ditching we were pure trouble."

"I'll say. Remember when you rigged up Pink Floyd on the loudspeaker for the opening exercises?"

Nikki grimaced.

"It was fabulous. Everyone standing there with their hands on the hearts and suddenly we hear, 'We don't need no education' screaming out across the campus. Everyone went wild."

"So did my parents."

"Come on. You made a good point."

"They were rebels, all right," Nathan said. "I met Mariah right in the middle of all that." Another affectionate look.

"I was so busy trying to not fit in, I didn't realize Nate really loved me," Mariah said. "So Nikki and I just took off—"

"Stranding me at the altar," Nathan said.

"After *you* stranded *me*."

"My car broke down."

"Yeah." She reached over and brushed at his hair. "Those were the days." Then she turned to Hollis. "Anyway, as soon as we got to Phoenix, we declared our independence with tattoos." She slid the shoulder of her scooped blouse off to reveal her butterfly tattoo. "Isn't it gorgeous?" she asked. "Nikki designed it."

"Very nice." Hollis cleared his throat, embarrassed to be admiring another woman's bare shoulder, Nikki assumed. He was such an old-fashioned guy.

"Nikki has a gift. The tattoos had meaning for us. A butterfly was me because—"

"It's dazzling, but elusive, and leaves you breathless with memories when it flies away," Nathan finished.

"You remembered!" Mariah beamed at her husband, then continued. "And Nikki's... Have you seen Nikki's tattoo?"

"Um, no, um, not really." Hollis reddened.

"Well, show him, girl."

"I don't think so." Nikki shot Mariah a warning look. Her tattoo was too personal to share with Hollis, especially considering how muddled she was about him.

"Okay, but I hope you're not turning all modest on us. Speaking of which, what are you wearing to the dance?"

"I have a nice black cocktail dress. Very simple."

"That's no good. I have just what you need. Hang on." She ran into the back of the house and returned a moment later bearing a hanger that contained a black-lace bustier, a black leather skirt, dangling fishnets and a feather boa. Her Madonna-the-early-years outfit.

"No way, Mariah."

"It's perfect. Don't you think so, Hollis?"

"Um, I don't know." But he couldn't take his eyes off the outfit.

"I'm not wearing that," she said firmly.

"Don't say no, say maybe." Mariah laid the clothes on the leopard-skin lounger. "It's good to remind folks there are other ways to live."

"If you're so hot on going back to the old days, why don't you wear it?"

"I just might. Would you like me in that, Nathan?"

"Mmm, sure, baby love." He nuzzled her neck.

Hollis and Nikki looked at each other, then away. This was making Nikki feel lonelier than lonely.

Coming back to them, Mariah blushed. "Sorry. We'll stop all this lovey-dovey stuff. We're just feeling kind of emotional lately. You two can just go ahead and make out if you want." She waggled her fingers at them.

"Of course we can't *make out*," Nikki said, messaging her friend with her eyes. "Hollis is almost engaged, you know."

"No!" Mariah exclaimed, looking from one to the other of them. "You can't be engaged," she said to him. "You can't take your eyes off Nikki. No, this is unacceptable." She shook her head. "You'll have to rethink this. I mean—"

"Mariah, stop it," Nikki said through gritted teeth. "You're embarrassing the man." Hollis had gone bright red. "Hollis is doing me a tremendous favor to stay for the reunion. That's all it is—a favor. He's giving up a motorcycle trip he planned just to help me out."

Nathan perked up. "You like bikes?"

"Yes, as a matter of fact, I do," Hollis said, sounding relieved at the change of subject. "I haven't been on one in a while."

"We can fix that. Mariah and I have a bike. You can borrow it. While you're here. We're so busy at the factory, Mariah and I hardly have time to use it. And we're going to be busier than ever pretty soon." More affectionate looks.

"Maybe we could go for a spin now," Hollis said to Nathan. "If you wouldn't mind."

"I can't, I'm not dressed for it," Nikki said, knowing that riding behind Hollis on a motorcycle, the engine hot and humming beneath them, would be an near-irresistible invitation to lust.

"I'm sure Mariah has something she could loan you," Hollis said, gripping Nikki's thigh, giving her a no-nonsense look, the first she'd ever seen from him. She lost interest in arguing and took a big gulp of the cranberry martini.

"Here's to bikes," Nathan said, holding out his glass to click with hers. Hollis joined in. So did Mariah. They all took a drink, except Nikki noticed that Mariah didn't swallow a drop. "Okay, what's going on?" she said. "You're not drinking."

Mariah grinned.

Abruptly, she figured it out. "You're pregnant!"

"Eight weeks! I just found out." She looked lovingly at Nathan. "We haven't even told our parents."

"I'm so happy for you," Nikki said, hugging Mariah and laughing.

"Congratulations," Hollis said, gravely shaking Nathan's hands. "Family is a wonderful thing."

"It was time," Nathan said, hugging Mariah to him.

Hollis looked straight into Nikki's eyes. "By the book, huh?" He had a point. Sometimes the book was pretty damn good.

Twenty minutes later, Nikki headed out to meet Hollis in the driveway wearing a leather jacket decorated with studs, leather pants and black studded boots Mariah had loaned her. She felt good dressed this way—like herself again. She looked forward to this ride, too, even though it was against her better judgment. She loved motorcycles—the freedom, the risk, the sense of flying. The only down side was having to tuck herself tight against Hollis.

Hollis waited for her on the growling bike. He'd borrowed a leather jacket from Nathan, but wore his jeans. He looked absolutely hot. When he saw her, the helmet he'd been holding slipped out of his hand and hit the driveway. "Wow." He swallowed.

"I'll take that as a compliment," she said, smiling. She started to climb behind him, but he stopped her.

"Helmet."

She wanted to object, but he had that dogged look, so she put on Mariah's helmet. He was such a stick-in-the-mud. But sweet about it. She climbed aboard the bike. Her thighs slid along his warm and strong ones.

Hollis made the engine roar, popped it into gear and steered it expertly onto the street. She wrapped her arms around his chest and held on tight. God, it felt good to be plastered against Hollis's back. She could feel his heartbeat in her forearms locked onto his rib cage.

"You okay?" he called over his shoulder.

"Fine," she whispered in his ear.

"Then hang on," he said. They tore off.

For awhile she soaked in the sensations of the ride—Hollis's firm control of the big engine between his legs, the way he moved like he was part of the machine, cornering with smooth grace. They were flying and it was wonderful. She never wanted to stop. She wanted to pretend they were a couple, free, moving where they wanted, only stopping to make love, explore the countryside and towns along the way, experiencing it all. She wished she'd not worn the helmet so she could feel the wind in her hair. She opened her mouth to let the wind snatch her breath away.

After they'd ridden for a half hour, Hollis slowed down at a lookout point, pulled off the road and stopped the bike. "Want to take a look?" he asked.

She nodded, removed her helmet and walked beside him to the guard rail. The full moon had brushed the landscape with silver and turned the river into a shining ribbon winding among low hills.

Hollis sat on a boulder and patted a place beside him for her. She joined him. "This is great," he said, looking out over the scene, sighing as if he'd been holding his breath until now. He sounded different—relaxed and comfortable for the first time since she'd known him. She realized every moment with her until now had been a strain for him—he'd been playacting and on edge since they arrived. Guilt washed through her.

What a good man he was. He'd agreed to help her even though it meant pretending and lying and faking it—things he hated. "I'm sorry I'm putting you through this," she said.

He shrugged. "It's okay, Nikki. I'm glad to help. I like being with you."

"But it's hard, I know, having to fake things with my family."

He shrugged. "But other things are nice." He looked at her for a long moment.

"Yeah. Nice." She dragged her gaze away.

"It feels good to be on a bike again," he said.

"Maybe you should buy one. When you get back."

He started to shake his head, then he said, "Maybe I will." He turned to her. "You make me want to, Nikki."

"Really?" She leaned closer—she couldn't help it....

He cupped her face in his hands. "You make me consider...possibilities."

Her heart began to pound. This wasn't good, but she loved it.

His eyes searched her face. "Will you do me a favor? Show me your tattoo?"

The request startled her. She laughed.

"And tell me what it means." His expression and what he'd said about her effect on him eased her doubts.

With trembling fingers, she unsnapped the leather jacket. Pulling it open, she felt more naked than she would have if they'd made love the day before. She felt like she was baring her soul. The sensation intensified when she unbuttoned the top two buttons of her blouse and slid it off her shoulder, revealing the whimsical sprite just above her heart. She felt vulnerable and shaky.

Hollis touched the tattoo. She trembled under his fingers. "What does it mean?" he asked.

She met his gaze. "Magic and miracles."

"And surprise?"

She could only nod.

"Do you have any others?"

"No."

"You don't need any others. This one says it all." He dragged his gaze from the tattoo to her face.

She shrugged her blouse closed.

"What about me?" he asked. "Do I need a tattoo?"

His voice was so serious, his question so intense that she felt compelled to find out. "Give me your hands."

He held them out, steady and sure. Her own, which she placed under his, trembled like aspen leaves. She closed her eyes and waited for the orange swirl. Everything was gray and hazy. Nothing. She focused harder. Maybe the heat of his hands and the sound of his breathing were distracting her. She could practically hear his heartbeat, racing like hers.

Still nothing. She closed her eyes more tightly. Nothing.

The she realized what had happened. Of course she couldn't read him. She was falling in love with him, might be already there. And that made her blind to his aura, as she was with everyone she cared for.

She shook her head, pulled her hands away. "I can't see anything."

"You can't? Keep trying. I want to know what tattoo would be right for me, if I ever wanted to get one." He reached for her hands.

She pulled them away, looked out over the landscape. "I can't. When I feel…when I get close to someone, I can't read their aura any more."

He absorbed her words. "And you feel close to me?"

She looked at him. "I don't want to talk about this."

"It's okay, Nikki…because I feel close to you, too." He smiled, but his eyes were serious. "I think I can read you."

"You can't," she said.

"Sure, I can. Let me try."

She let him take her hands, but instead of balancing them on his palms, he gripped them tight and looked into her eyes. "You're an artist, with an artist's desire to give beauty to the world, an artist's quest for perfection, an artist's sensitivity and restlessness. And you're a sprite, too. You make magic in the lives of people around you."

"That's lovely," she said, trying to pull her hands away, needing him to stop.

"I'm not finished," he said with that no-nonsense look that sent a thrill through her. "The only problem is that you're not quite sure that's what you really want, what will make you truly happy. Being an artist free of the rules has its price."

"That's enough," she said, yanking her hands back. He was way too close. She didn't like the judgmental tone he'd begun to take. "You're just guessing. And what about you? Are you so certain of your life? If you like living by the book so much, why are you here with me on a motorcycle in the moonlight?"

He gave her a wry smile. "I'm asking myself that same question. I didn't exactly start out to become a dentist, you know. I liked biology, wanted to go into research, maybe teach. But my father was a plumber—he had his own business—and he wanted more for me. He knew I was good with my hands and he saw how much dentists made and encouraged me to apply to dental school. Dentistry turned out to be interesting."

"But you'd rather be a biology teacher. With summers off for motorcycle trips. Why not quit and do what you want?"

"That's just a fantasy."

"Yeah. I'm having those, too." The words were out before she realized it.

"You're having fantasies? About what?" His gaze heated.

"About you," she said, too overwhelmed to lie.

"Me, too," he said softly. "Lots of fantasies."

It started again, that twisting desire that made everything hot inside her. She had to stop it. "I just mean us pretending to be husband and wife. Now that's a fantasy." She tried to laugh, but made a mess of it.

"That's not what I meant," he said low and sure. "You're so different from any woman I've ever known. You are so full of surprises, so fresh, so…"

"So crazy and wild and intense," she said, citing the litany that described her. "So *not* what you want, Hollis. I'd make you crazy." She held her breath, begging him to contradict her.

His eyes went flat and he dropped his hand. "Maybe. And I owe it to Rachel to see how I feel when I get back."

"Right." She jerked her face away, her eyes filled with sudden tears. So stupid.

"Are you okay?"

She gathered herself. "Of course. You'd make me crazy, too. I bet all your socks match and you always know where your toothbrush is."

He looked puzzled, as if everyone did that.

"Never mind. The point is we're from different planets."

He shrugged, giving in, but his expression was full of yearning. "We would be something together, though, wouldn't we?"

"Yeah," she said. "We would be something." She rubbed her arms, cold even in the leather jacket. "A big mistake." She stood. "Let's get back."

As they roared away, she tried to keep space between their bodies, but Hollis reached back with one hand and tugged her close to him. He wasn't making it a bit easier on her. She gave up and just rested her cheek on his sturdy back, listened to his heart beat, and felt the wind dry her tears before they even touched the leather of his jacket.

9

THAT NIGHT THEY SLEPT back to back, so far apart Nikki kept banging her knee on the metal hinge at the edge of the mattress. Once she awoke to find Hollis spooned around her. Mustering all her self-control, she pushed him away. Two hours later, she found herself wrapped around him. After that, she slept on the cushions on the floor. Occasional contact with cold tile was better than risking sex with someone so wrong for her.

By mutual agreement, they kept busy and apart the next five days.

She spent time helping her mother sew, working in the garden, picking strawberries, making jam, learning more about baking for her "babies," and finishing up the decorations and details for the reunion dance on Saturday and the picnic Sunday afternoon.

Hollis borrowed Nathan's motorcycle for long afternoon drives—more to escape the attraction between them than out of love for the bike, she knew.

Holding hands and exchanging loving looks for the benefit of her family became more and more painful. The fakery made her feel hollowed out and sad. She couldn't wait for the reunion to happen, so this torture would be over, and they could go home. When she'd cooked up the plan, she'd had no idea how hard it would be.

She could tell Hollis felt the same way. When they held hands, his fingers tightened on hers like a vise and she felt the sexual tension in his body like wire.

She forced herself spend time talking with her father, though it made her nervous—both because of how ill he was, and how many secrets she was keeping from him. She kept him away from questions about her life, so he talked about how the school had changed, and about how much more badly behaved students were today than when she'd gone to Copper Corners High. He didn't seem to remember how miserable she'd made him back then. During one talk, he told her he was considering early retirement so he could take up photography and dig into genealogy.

Her heart caught in her throat. Did he think his time was short? Was it? "Dad, be careful," she said. "Take it slow."

"Stop worrying, Nicolette. I'm fine. Would you warm me up one of your mother's brownies out of the freezer?"

With a heavy heart, she brought him the killer dessert, though she peeled off the frosting, giving him a bit more life.

Finally, Saturday came. Nikki spent the day putting up the murals and displays for the dance and helping her mother with last-minute details—calling the district electrician when they blew a fuse testing the disco ball, and confirming the people who would staff the refreshment stand and registration.

Before she knew it, it was seven. She barely had time to dress before the dance was to begin at seven-thirty. She rushed into the bedroom to get dressed for the dance and was met by a breathtaking sight.

Hollis stood naked to the waist in the middle of the room. She caught her breath.

"What's wrong?" he asked.

"You're half naked."

"I'm half dressed."

"That's splitting hairs." Chest hairs. His were nice—a dusting of straight brown strands that narrowed to a vee, then disappeared beneath his waistband. He had nice chest muscles—delineated, but not showy. And he wore the tailored slacks that were half of the suit he'd wear to the dance. He'd borrowed clothes from Nathan, but he'd brought the suit for the reunion.

"Just hurry up," she said crossly.

"I laid out your clothes for you. In the bathroom." He grinned.

"You did?" How odd.

She went into the bathroom. There was the bustier outfit. Mariah must have given it to him during one of his forays with the motorcycle. She yanked it from the hook. "I can't wear this."

"I think you should," he said, leaning into the doorjamb. "For old times' sake, like Mariah said. Don't you want to feel like yourself for once?" All the while he was talking about her getting dressed, his eyes were busily undressing her.

She looked at the outfit. It was just outrageous enough to give her a rush of satisfaction. Then she thought of her parents, who were so proud about this chance to show her off. One look at her in the fishnets, come-get-me pumps, miniskirt and bustier, and her father would have the big one for sure.

She shook her head. "Nope. I can't."

"It's for your own good," he said, giving the outfit an appreciative look.

"For *my* own good?"

"Not that I wouldn't enjoy it, of course. I'm no

saint.'' He moved close to her, all half-naked male animal of him.

She couldn't keep from looking at his upper body. She longed to touch his skin, feel the heat of him. She wondered if his muscles would slide under her fingers or remain tense....

''Well?'' he asked. ''Are you going to do it?''

''Huh?'' For a second, she thought he'd read her mind, but then she realized he was asking about the wild outfit. ''No way,'' she said and pushed past him headed for the closet.

Despite his disappointment about her Madonna outfit, Hollis looked pretty impressed when she came out in her black cocktail dress. A rhinestone neck piece was a splash of elegance that looked almost regal. ''No doubt about it. You'll definitely take 'Evening Wear' in the Miss Copper Corners pageant,'' he said.

''You look great, too. Very GQ.'' He wore an olive green suit with a subtle weave and jewel-toned tie. Very classy. She didn't realize shirts could get that white—or that crisp.

''One more thing.'' Hollis picked a box off the bureau and she saw it was a corsage—a delicate miniature white orchid with two tiny white rosebuds and a narrow green sprig as accent. Very elegant.

''It's perfect,'' she said.

''Let me pin it on.'' He got close, his fingers slipped under her neckline. She watched the pulse-point in his neck, smelled his spicy cologne, the starch of his shirt.

This was like high school, only a million times better. Or worse, if you considered how much she wanted to make love with him but didn't dare. At least in high school, she'd gotten laid.

She covered Mariah's Madonna outfit in an opaque plastic bag so she could give it back to Mariah at the dance.

Her parents oohed and aahed at how they looked—her father from the sofa. Since he'd be welcoming the guests at the dance, his first night out, he was preserving his energy. And Shelley asked for their autographs. It was all just as she'd imagined it.

Once they reached the dance, though, her fantasy broke down. She'd wanted Hollis at her side so she could catch the amazed looks of her classmates when they saw the transformed Nikki with her fabulously successful doctor husband—kind of like a reception line tableau. Unfortunately, the minute they arrived she got dragged away to handle detail after detail.

Finally free for a moment, Nikki spotted Hollis talking to a woman by the punch bowl. As she got closer, she recognized the woman as her nemesis, Heather Haver. The former cheerleader looked like she was just about to eat Hollis up. Whole.

Just as Nikki reached them, Heather said, "Surely, you're not here by your lonesome. Who do you belong to?"

"Me," Nikki said, linking arms with Hollis. "Heather Haver, meet my husband, Dr. Holl-um-Warren Langley."

Heather's forehead creased while she tried to place Nikki. "God, it's Nikki Winfield!"

"The one and only."

"You're so...different." She looked Nikki up and down. There was surprise and pleasure in her face. No superiority. No resentment.

Caught off guard, Nikki blushed. "People change."

"And you're married." Heather gave Hollis an appreciative once-over. "And did you say *Doctor* Langley?"

She nodded.

"Oh, girl. You did it. Married a doctor. Talk about coming a long way, baby. Your parents must be so proud."

"Yes, they are." But the pretense of it all made her feel hollow inside.

"You look great, too," Nikki said to her. Though she'd thickened through the face and hips, Heather was still gorgeous. Just a bit more lush.

"Let's not do that fake thing," Heather said, scrunching up her nose. "I slapped on some weight. Kids'll do that to you." She shrugged.

"You're married?" Nikki said.

"Divorced." She shook her head. "Marriage was a mistake, but my kids are great—boy and a girl, four and five. I'm a real-estate agent in Tucson. How about you? Let me guess. Actress or artist?"

"Oh, um." She wanted to say artist so bad she ached. "I, um, own a boutique."

"Really? That's different." Disappointment flickered in Heather's face, then she blinked. "So, have you seen Brian yet?"

"I don't think he's arrived." She'd been keeping an eye out for him, too.

"Remember when you and I fought over him?"

Fought over him? Hardly. Brian had run straight into Heather's arms.

"God, high school," Heather continued, shaking her head. "We made such a big deal out of the dumbest things." She smiled at Hollis, then turned to Nikki. "Whenever Brian talked about you, I would get so mad." She took a swallow of her punch, then frowned. "They call this punch? There's no kick."

"Really?"

"Yeah. No booze whatsoever."

"No. I mean Brian talked about me?"

"Yeah." She shrugged. "Like I said, so high school. Now look at you, a doctor's wife…wow."

"Yeah," she said. *Look at me. Lying through my teeth.* She couldn't get over it. Heather Haver, the perfect cheerleader who'd stolen Brian Collier, turned out to be a down-to-earth woman, who seemed honestly happy for her. Suddenly, she wanted to take her aside and tell her everything, even that she was falling in love with Hollis.

"You got anything racy planned?" Heather asked. "This looks like a dull show so far. People are barely sipping wine and there's way too much club soda going around."

"Not really. I did the decorations."

Heather looked around. "Nice. But kind of tame. Hell, I don't see a single bared breast."

"That was high school," she said.

"Come on, I was counting on you to do something crazy." She shook her head fondly. "When you did that thing at the talent show about free expression and faked those swear words, I was so shocked I almost swallowed my gum. What a rush. I always wished I had the nerve to be like you. Hanging it out there, saying, 'This is me, take me or go screw yourself.' I was so worried about being popular. What a waste."

"Really?"

"Oh, yeah. It sounds dumb, but being hot stuff in high school can make the rest of life seem sad. That's what my divorce counselor told me."

"I didn't realize…"

But Heather had moved on. "Well, if you're not going to do it, I've gotta see if I can stir up some trouble—find Collier and see if I can still get his motor running. We've gotta make some memories here." She waggled her fingers and swayed away.

Hollis squeezed her hand. "So that was the notorious boyfriend snatcher."

"The very one."

"You're much prettier than she is. Smarter, too."

She laughed and punched his arm. "You're just saying that to make me happy."

"Yes, as a matter of fact I am. It's still true, but I do want you to be happy. That's why I'm here, right?" Their gazes locked. Heat rose. "So, what would make you happy, Nikki?" he asked softy.

You. In bed. "I am happy," she said. "You're doing great. This is just harder than I thought it would be. I feel kind of like a ghost."

"I'm sorry," he said and pulled her into his arms for a gentle hug.

"It's all right," she said, stepping back, not wanting to get distracted from her purpose by Hollis's kindness and her growing feelings for him. "We won't stay late."

"Be sure to point out Brian, so we can put on a good show."

"He's not here yet. Maybe he isn't coming." That would be a disappointment. He was the main reason she'd kept Hollis here so long.

"Anyone else you want to show me off to? I met those folks." He pointed at a clump of people—the class president, three football players and some from the drama club she'd hung with a little. She could go over and accept their compliments and amazement, but she just didn't feel like it. Her conversation with Heather had her rethinking things like mad. Hollis had been right. She should have been herself tonight.

She had the urge to run out to the car and change into that Madonna outfit she'd forgotten to give to Mariah, go home to grab her tattoo kit and offer free tattoos to everyone to commemorate the evening. Now that would make a statement. She looked into Hollis's face and knew he'd support her—even help her.

Then she saw her mother and father heading toward the stage. Her mother had her father on her arm, bent over, hobbling a little. She couldn't embarrass them, even to redeem herself in her own eyes. She didn't dare risk her father's health.

Except... There was one thing she could do that would help everyone relax. And it would be like old times.... She could spike the punch.

"I'll be right back," she told Hollis.

She rushed out the door behind the stage and practically ran head-on into two guys carrying a huge speaker toward the door. The band had arrived.

"Let me get the door," she said, and held it open for them. As they passed, one of them said, "Hey, I know you."

She remembered him instantly as a tattoo client. "Flaming guitar, right? A year ago?"

"That's the one." He set down the speaker with a clunk.

His band mate groaned. "Come on, Paul. We gotta set up."

"Take a look." He turned so Nikki could see the large tattoo on his right arm, exposed by his muscle shirt. She studied the bright tattoo of an electric guitar alive with fire. She'd sketched it after reading his aura. "You've taken good care of it," she said.

"You bet. I keep it covered in daylight or slap on sun-screen—SPF 45—like you said. This baby changed my life." He tapped it lovingly.

"Really?"

"Oh, yeah. Soon as I got this, I started playing better, got a band together. We got some gigs, did a little touring. We cut a CD last month."

"That's wonderful," she said.

"Yeah. Means a lot." He held her gaze.

"Could we set up now?" The other guy said.

"You should get one, J.J."

"I have a tattoo." He shrugged.

"Not like this, you don't. This lady reads you, like, gets inside your head, and tells you what you need. It's spooky. Kinda spiritual."

His friend paused to consider. "Maybe...."

"Give me your hands," she said to him, the words out before she could stop herself. She was so hungry to remember who she was, she itched to read the guy's aura, prescribe a tattoo, fetch her supplies and put it on.

"What are you...?" He stepped away from her like he thought she was nuts.

"I want to read your energy, that's all."

"Maybe later," he said. "We gotta set up."

"Sure, sure," she said. They picked up the speaker and went inside. She followed after them, talking as she went. "When you're in Phoenix, come to my shop. I'm at the same place, Paul. Third and Mc-Dowell, remember?"

"You bet," he said. "Got it. We'll come in."

She stopped herself, realizing she was chasing them like a puppy. The strain was getting to her.

By the time she'd slipped a quart of vodka into the punch, her father was at the microphone. "Be sure all you new reunionites have one of the printed programs," he said, "Take a moment to vote for your classmates—who do you believe is the most changed? The least changed? And find out who's got the biggest family and who's traveled the farthest. We'll announce the answers—and name the winners—at the picnic tomorrow."

He paused and beamed out at the crowd. Her father was in his element. He'd always loved the assemblies, where he could act like the patriarch of a giant dysfunctional family. "With that out of the way, I'd like to say a few words before the band starts destroying what's left of your hearing."

Nikki felt arms come around her body and leaned to the side to see that it was Hollis. Right where she needed him. As if he had second sight. For a moment, she let herself feel safe in his arms.

"I want to congratulate you all for coming," her father said. "I don't think there's a town anywhere in the U.S. that honors its graduates so well." He proceeded to list the accomplishments and careers of numerous Copper Corners High alumni from the last ten years.

"You make me proud to have been part of your lives. I've had the pleasure of watching many of you settle down and start your families right here in Copper Corners. Those of you who're visiting from other places—Flagstaff and Phoenix and Tucson and California, and even Lyle Wood all the way from Vancouver, Canada—that's a hint on who's traveled the farthest...."

"Vote for me, eh!" Lyle yelled up. Everyone applauded.

"I thank you all for returning to us," her father continued. "No matter how old we get, the memories of high school live on inside us. It's good to remember the people who knew you as you truly were when you first discovered yourselves. I want you to think of Copper Corners High as your home. You're always a part of this place."

A quiet murmur of warm assent traveled in a wave across the room.

"This reunion class is especially important to me," her father said, blinking for a second. "As most of you know, my daughter Nicolette is part of this class. She hasn't been home in ten years. And this week she's returned to us with her wonderful husband. Be sure and say hello to them."

She listened to her father, glad to make him happy, wanting to feel proud of herself, but instead, she felt like bursting into tears and running from the room. She felt lonely, confused and so lost she was afraid she was disappearing altogether.

Her father finished, her classmates applauded, and the taped music began to play while the band tuned up.

Hollis murmured into her hair above her ear. "I'm glad I could help you do this, Nikki."

She tried to smile up at him, blinking water from her eyes.

"What's the matter?" He turned her to face him, holding her upper arms.

She blurted the truth. "I don't know who I am any more."

"I do," he said, looking at her steadily. "I know who you are. You're Nikki Winfield. You make your own way in life, but you're willing to sacrifice a bit to make those you love feel better. And this is you," he said. He patted her above her heart—at the spot where her sprite tattoo lay.

He was so dear. "Oh, Hollis," she said, and threw her arms around his neck and kissed him. She didn't care that this might make things worse.

A hum of titillation passed through the crowd. A bright light glowed around them. At first she thought her imagination had created a heavenly beam—the kiss *was* glorious—but then she realized a spotlight was shining on them and everyone was staring. "Get a room!" someone shouted out cheerfully.

She pulled out of Hollis's embrace, but he held her at his side, accepting the crowd's attention with a prom king wave.

After a few more seconds, the spotlight left them in warm darkness. She turned to him. "Sorry about that."

"Don't be. I've wanted to kiss you all night. What husband in his right mind could resist a wife like you?"

They looked into each other's eyes for entirely too long. If only Brian Collier would get here and she could show off Hollis and get out of there.

The taped music stopped and the band began to play, opening with a great dance song.

"Shall we?" Hollis asked. "I hope Warren can dance, because Hollis can."

"Why not?" At least a fast dance would distract her, if she could keep from watching Hollis's hips and imagining other moves....

Whap. A flailing arm hit her across the back. "Sorry," its owner said. Soon another couple stumbled into them, then staggered away. Nikki stopped moving to look more closely at the crowd.

Nearby, two men were giving each other bea

hugs, sloppily slapping each other's backs. Someone else was doing a terrible break dance. That would hurt in the morning. What was going on?

Then she remembered the punch. She wasn't drinking, since she wanted to be clearheaded for her big charade, but the liquor had loosened people up, all right. Maybe too much. She watched a couple who seemed to be relying on each other to stay upright—not very successfully. Another group of men were laughing too loudly. A quart of liquor shouldn't have done that much damage to the room's equilibrium.

The three-song medley ended and Paul went up to the microphone. "Hello, Copper Corners!"

The answering cheer went on waaay too long.

When he could shout over the crowd, he said, "I'm Paul Preston, and this is Beat Down."

More overlong applause.

"Sounds like you guys are having fun," he said. "I want to dedicate this next song to someone special in the audience. If it wasn't for her this band would still be playing in my garage."

The drummer did a riff.

"Oh, God," Nikki said, grabbing Hollis's arm. "He's talking about me. I gave him a tattoo. What if he tells everyone? I've got to get him away from the mike!" She set off running, while Paul talked about how hard it was to get started as a band, building momentum before he announced her name, she knew. She rushed past tipsy classmates, several of whom spoke to her.

At the steps to the stage, Carl Adams, a football teammate of Brian's, blocked her path. "Nikki Winfield. You were sooooo hot in high school," he said.

He'd clearly had a good slug of the punch. "Brian was a dick."

"Thanks. Glad to hear it." She slid past him and up the stairs.

She'd just entered the stage when Paul said, "Then I went into this tattoo shop and—" God, she was too late.

Except his next words came out unamplified, impossible to hear beyond the stage. Paul tapped his mike, frowned stage left.

She looked where he was looking and saw Hollis standing by a breaker box. He grinned at her, and gave her a thumbs-up. He'd flipped off the microphone, rescuing her.

She hurried across the stage, pretending she was there to help Paul with the mike. She explained the problem in a fast mutter, after which he nodded and Hollis flipped the breaker back on.

"Anyway, like I was saying," Paul said, "I went into this tattoo shop and, um, there was an, um, *painting* on the wall that made me decide I could make it big. And the person who'd painted that painting was Nikki Winfield."

Everyone cheered and she smiled and accepted a hug from him, promising a twenty-percent discount to his band mates on all their tattoos, then hurried to Hollis, her partner in crime. "Thank you," she said. "You saved me."

"That's why I'm 'ere," he said, his words smearing together. He was swaying, too.

"Are you drunk?"

"Maybe a little," he said with a crooked smile, his fingers indicating an inch. "Heather must have put in too much vodka."

"Heather?"

"Yeah, she spiked the punch."

"Oh, God. So did I." They looked out at the crowd from the stage. People were hanging all over each other. "They're all stumbly wumbly," she said.

They headed back to the dance floor and met Mariah and Nathan heading their way. "Man, these people are lightweights," Mariah said. "One quart of rum and they're slobbering drunk. 'Course maybe I notice it more since I'm not drinking."

"One quart of rum?" Nikki asked.

"Yeah. I dosed the punch."

"That makes three of us," Nikki said. "Heather did, too. Triple spike!"

"Wow. Just like old times," Mariah said, hugging her friend. "The whole town will be one giant hangover." The two gave each other the Rebel Girls Forever handshake, then showed Hollis and Nathan how to do it, though Hollis's inebriation made it difficult for him to get the rhythm of it.

It was the first time Nikki'd really laughed since she'd been here. It felt so good to share this moment with three people who knew what was really going on. And really knew her, too. There in the middle of the reunion, they were an island of comfort in a sea of strangers.

"Well, it's about time," Mariah said, looking over Nikki's shoulder.

"What?" she said. Then strong arms grabbed her from behind, lifted her off her feet, then set her down.

She whirled to see what drunken idiot had grabbed her. Brian Collier. As handsome as ever. What little weight he'd gained made him look even better.

He looked at her like he wasn't sure who she was. "Nikki?"

"That's me."

"You look so different. Let me see if you feel the same." He grabbed her in a bear hug—an unnaturally tight one that involved a pelvic grind—and she was overpowered by the scent of whiskey.

He released her. "Yep. That's Nikki in there." He gave her an admiring once-over. "Have I missed *you*." He seemed unaware that anyone else was present, a fact that would have been flattering if he weren't so obviously smashed.

"Where have you been?" she asked.

"Getting fortified at the Cue and Brew. Tell me I missed the 'whatever happened to...?' bullsh—"

"I want you to meet my—"

"So I put on a little weight and my marriage broke up. What of it? High school's over."

"I know, Brian. Listen, this is my husband." She tugged Hollis forward, forcing Brian to acknowledge him.

"Right. I heard you were married." He held out a hand. "Brian Collier, First Place Fidelity Insurance."

"Warren Langley," Hollis said, giving him a firm shake.

"A doctor, right? I heard that," Brian said, frowning.

"Nice to meet you," Hollis said, deepening his voice to hide how loaded he was. "Nikki told me a lot about you."

"She did, huh?" He looked at her again—his longing obvious. "Did she tell you I was so stupid I let her go?"

"Not exactly, but..."

"You're a lucky man, Warner," he said, still looking at Nikki.

"That's Warren," Hollis said edgily.

Nikki felt the attraction vibe shimmering her way from Brian. He still wanted her and he envied her husband. He'd said it right out loud. She'd gotten what she'd wanted out of the reunion, but there was no satisfaction in the accomplishment. It was like an overcooked eggplant, dry and tasteless in her mouth.

She found herself saying the strangest thing. "There's no point in regretting things, Brian. You did the best you could at the time. We were kids."

He stared at her, oblivious to her words. Beyond his shoulder, Nikki could see that Heather was practically trotting toward him. "Here's someone you'll be glad to see, too," she said.

"Bri!" Heather called, her eyes bright. For the first time, Nikki saw what a good match the two were—a sadder but wiser pair of dethroned high-school royals.

Reluctantly, Brian turned from Nikki to Heather.

Nikki tugged at Hollis, wanting to get away.

When they were out of earshot, he said, "Did I do good?"

"Perfect."

"He really wanted you," he said softly.

"Yeah," she said, trying hard to find satisfaction in that fact.

Hollis stared past her at Brian, an odd expression on his face.

"What's wrong?" She tugged at his arm.

Reluctantly, he brought his gaze back to her. "Nothing. I just didn't like his attitude."

"Forget it. He's drunk."

Hollis sighed. "I guess you're right. I'm not so steady on my feet myself."

"We can go now," she said, smiling up at him.

"I've done what I wanted to. Thanks to you." She touched his cheek. "I'm thinking we should skip the picnic. Everyone will be hung over and any more conversations will just be rehashing stuff. I'm tired of the whole thing."

"I never thought I'd hear you say that," he said, hiccupping.

"Me, neither."

"Let me hit the john and we can go."

"I'll meet you outside." Her parents had gone home an hour ago, and Nikki didn't want to make the round of goodbyes.

She watched Hollis head across the room. He was so handsome that women couldn't help following him with their eyes. She felt proud. *He's mine.* But of course he wasn't. He might not be Rachel Actually's, but he wasn't hers either.

At the reception table on the way out, she snatched a sheet of blank name tags and a thin-line marker to sketch some new tattoo designs while she waited for Hollis.

It was nice outside. She found a picnic table a few feet from Hollis's car and sat on it, resting her feet on the bench. The air was muggy with a pending monsoon, but a light breeze kept it from being oppressive. She started a sketch for Paul's band mate featuring a drum, but the muffled sounds of a slow song being played in the gym made her mind drift to memories of dancing with Hollis. She looked down at what she'd been doodling and saw she'd sketched a playful, lace-bordered heart with the word "Hollis" fancifully drawn within its borders. Like scribbling a boy's name in your history binder. *So high school. Would she ever grow up?*

"Whatcha doin'?"

She looked up with a start to see Brian Collier standing in front of her.

"Come here," he said, easily lifting her from her perch and setting her onto the ground very close to him. "I need another hug." He mashed her against him with unpleasant suggestiveness. "The only reason I dragged my sorry ass to this freak show was to see you," he said urgently in her ear.

"It was nice to see you, too," she said, pushing out of his arms.

"I was an ass to break up with you. I've been thinking about that lately. A lot."

He continued to hold her shoulders.

She leaned her body away, embarrassed by his confession, startled to realize how unwanted it was. All these years when she'd longed to have Brian look at her this way and now it just made her feel ill—sorry for him, but annoyed at the same time. Didn't the man have any dignity?

"I was just led around by my dick in those days, you know?"

"Wasn't it nice to see Heather?" she asked hopefully. "She's divorced, too. You have a lot in common."

"That's the problem. I don't want to look at somebody who reminds me of me...." He looked her over, his eyes gleaming. "So, where's the hubster?"

"He'll be out in a minute."

"The marriage working out for you? You happy and all?"

"Uh, yeah, um…sure."

"Hmm. Trouble in paradise? He a jerk?"

"No, he's a great guy."

"Gotta say I'm sorry to hear that." He squeezed her shoulders, then shook her gently. "You look so different.'' He leaned in, staring into her eyes with his bloodshot ones. ''But I can still see that wild woman in there.''

''Brian, I—''

''You ever let her out to play? Like for special occasions? When no one's looking?''

He was harmless. Too drunk to realize his sloppy grip was inappropriate. She was just about to pull away when...

''What the hell do you think you're doing?'' Hollis's words ran together tipsily, but with an undercurrent of solid anger. He was striding purposefully toward them with a little wobble in each step. ''You wanna take your hands off my wife?''

''Sorry, pal.'' Brian released her shoulders and held up his hands. ''Just remembering old times, that's all.''

''Are you okay, sweetheart?'' Hollis said, pulling her close to him by her waist.

''I'm fine. It's okay.''

''You don't have to be pawed by this fathead,'' he said.

''Hey, hey, my friend,'' Brian said warningly. ''Nikki and I go way back. No need for you to go insulting anybody.''

''That was then. This is now.'' Hollis's eyes glittered with anger. She felt a little shiver at the primitive possessiveness in his tone.

''Would you tell this guy to relax?'' Brian said to her.

''Don't ask her to fight your battles. You treated her like crap in high school. You didn't have a clue about what you had, you...you...'' he hiccupped, then leaned forward and finished ''...you ass.''

''You're calling me an ass?''

"You want to make something of it?"

"Hollis, stop this," Nikki said. "You're drunk."

"I'm not drunk. I'm defending your honor. *He's* drunk."

"Tell your husband to lay off or I'll have to lay him out," Brian slurred.

"Oh, yeah? Just try it," Hollis said.

Nikki moved between them, leaning back to restrain Hollis.

"How about a kiss, Nikki?" Brian said, deliberately baiting Hollis. "For old times' sake?" He took her by her upper arms.

"I don't think so," she said.

"Take your hands off her," Hollis said, sounding remarkably sober for someone so drunk.

Brian didn't move.

Hollis escaped Nikki and shoved Brian hard. Brian shoved back. Hollis lunged and they hit the dirt, struggling, straining, rolling over on the ground, trying to get in punches, but both missing.

"You broke her heart," Hollis said, swinging and missing.

"Yeah, well, you don't own her," Brian replied, missing.

"Stop it, stop it," she said, trying to grab a limb as it flailed within reach.

Finally, Brian pulled away and got to his feet, panting. "When you're done with this lame-ass, I'm in the book," he said to her, pushing down his jacket, stretching his neck. "You deserve better than him." He looked down at Hollis, who was leaning back on his elbows, trying to catch his breath.

No, she didn't, she realized. They didn't come any better than Hollister Marx.

10

HOLLIS LET HIMSELF FALL back to the ground and watched the stars spin and blur, feeling like he was on a merry-go-round. All that was missing was the calliope and the way his mind was whirling, he'd hear that any minute.

What the hell is wrong with you? He'd just tried to punch a guy who could clock him in a heartbeat—and would have if he hadn't been absolutely faced. Why had he done that?

Pure jealousy. He'd seen that clod with his hands on Nikki and he'd wanted to shove the guy into the trash can and roll it down the hill. It was stupid. But he knew that Nikki had once been in love with the creep and might be again. And that was all it had taken to turn him into Neanderthal Man defending his Woman. She hadn't been in any danger. He was a fool.

"Are you okay?" Nikki kneeled beside him, her hair falling in his face, her scent washing over him. Even if the guy had clocked him, it would have been worth every minute, he realized because looking up into her face it dawned on him exactly what was wrong with him.

This wasn't a rebellious phase he'd get over. Maybe he was drunk, but he was just drunk enough to know the truth. He was in love with Nikki—for better or worse, with cheese poofies or without, with chestnut hair or pink spikes. He wanted her, how-ever—or whoever—she was.

"Now that was acting!" Nikki said, in wonder-ment and confusion. "I can't believe you actually picked a fight with Brian. You looked really mad. I thought you said you couldn't do make-believe."

He pushed himself up on his elbows, light-headed and aching. "That wasn't acting."

"It wasn't?" She swallowed hard.

"No." Then he grabbed her into his arms and kissed her.

"Stop it. You don't mean this." She panted the words and her eyes filled with the same yearning he'd struggled with all week.

He pushed himself to his feet, grabbed her by the hand and yanked her forward. "Come on."

"Where are we going?"

"To the closest place we can get naked," he said, pulling his keys from his pocket as they reached the passenger side of his car. He opened the door. "Get in," he said.

Nikki got into the car, stunned. *Get naked?*

Hollis got in beside her and reached for her.

"What are you doing?"

"This is the closest place," he said. "I'm too drunk to drive anywhere."

"No, that's not what I mean. What's going on here?"

"What's going on? What's going on is I'm mak-ing love to my wife," he said fiercely. Then he kissed her—hard—while his hands went around her neck. He unzipped her dress, shoved her sleeves and bra straps off her shoulders, trapping her arms, kiss-ing her all the while.

She wanted to stop him, to think this through, but

she was so mixed up, so confused, so upset about who she was and what she wanted that she just went with her feeling.

They were going to do it. In a car. A small car. The old high-school thrill of doing the forbidden filled her. Maybe this was what they needed. Maybe this would tell them once and for all what they meant to each other.

Whatever it was, she was in. She would allow herself to have what she'd wanted since they'd arrived—sex with Hollis. She pulled away long enough to get her arms out of her sleeves, then started in on the buttons of Hollis's crisp white shirt, while he kissed her wherever he could reach. She shoved his shirt and jacket off his shoulders, but then he couldn't use his arms.

He moved to the side to get at his sleeves.

Her head banged the armrest of the passenger seat. "Ow."

"Sorry. Ow." He'd clunked his own head on the mirror. He shifted her around, shook his hand to get the sleeve loose, but it had become a straitjacket.

Shifting to give him room to maneuver, she found her face mashed into the dash, the Celica emblem digging into her cheek. Something really hard and knobby poked her in the butt. God, was it Hollis? No. Gearshift knob, she realized in relief.

Hollis shook his hands, still trapped by sleeves.

"Let me get the buttons." She slid to the side, bracing herself against the steering wheel. She managed to unbutton one sleeve, and Hollis got the other, then shoved off the jacket and shirt.

Thump. Her hip hit the gearshift. That would leave a bruise. "I don't remember making out in a car being so difficult before," she said.

"Hold it." Hollis clicked something and the passenger car seat flopped back under her, opening up space. He did the same to the driver's seat. "Just like a dental chair," he said, kissing her neck, his hands clicking her bra and whisking it away. God, he was good with his hands. "They teach you that in dental school?" she asked.

"This I already knew," he said.

Then they were naked to the waist except for her rhinestone neck piece, Hollis's chest hair a soft friction on her nipples, their abdomens meeting, muscles straining. She put her hand on him through his pants. He was there for her, solid and ready. And she was ready for him, desire tight as a knot, so aroused she couldn't think. Hot inside and out. The night was warm, but the new heat they were generating had turned the car into a sauna.

He moaned into her mouth at her touch, then slid his clever fingers under her panties and touched her just so. Electricity shot through her. She'd never been so aroused. She was afraid she might spontaneously combust.

She needed him inside her. Now. For that, she needed him naked. He still had on his pants and her dress was bunched at her waist. Even with the seats down the car was crowded.

Then there was some noise. Tap. Tap. Tap.

She ignored it, reached for Hollis's belt.

Tap. Tap.

Hollis froze.

She stopped kissing him, looked past him. Through the steam on the window, she could just make out Mariah and Nathan standing outside the driver's window, arm in arm, grinning from ear to ear, both holding their thumbs up.

Oh, God. They couldn't see any body parts through the steamed windows, plus Hollis's back covered her, but they knew what was going on. Hollis turned to look, and Nikki covered herself with the top of her dress.

Nathan and Mariah motioned at them not to get up. Then they were gone.

Nikki and Hollis stared at each other, panting. She could practically hear Hollis's heart beat in time with hers. Gradually, she became aware of the way her head and cheek throbbed from where she'd bumped into the dash and her butt ached from the gearshift knob. She started to think. They'd been caught like teens at a make-out spot. They should be sensible about this.

Hollis opened his mouth to speak. Here it came. *I don't know what came over me.* "You'll have to drive," he said softly. "I'm drunk."

She nodded, her heart aching. Damn. Why did he have to be so rational? She slipped her dress back on. Hollis pulled on his shirt. They both climbed out of the car, and switched sides.

"I guess we got carried away," she said as she reached for the keys.

Instead Hollis kissed her, slow and sweet, then looked into her eyes, his expression making her tingle from her scalp to her toes. "Uh-uh. We just need a bed and a door that locks."

Joy rushed through her in a wave. She started the car and roared out of there. As she drove, Hollis caressed her, his tongue tickling her ear, his fingers tickling her *there,* until she had to make him stop him before she lost consciousness and drove them into a tree.

She'd never wanted to be home so much in her

life. Familiar scenery flashed by and her ricocheting mind touched on the old feelings—loneliness, anger at being misunderstood, gratitude for Mariah's friendship—and new regrets—the longing to be herself, to live a life she wanted without disappointing anyone.

She glanced at Hollis, who, though obediently not stroking her mindless, was looking at her in a way that made her feel like he as might well be. Maybe it was just the rush of being desired, of making him so hot he couldn't resist her, but somehow being with Hollis made her feel better about herself. He knew who she was—more or less—and wanted her anyway.

He's drunk. He's mixed up. But she pushed away the thought. They had tonight. They were going to take it.

And then they were home. Giggling like teenagers, they tiptoed down the hall so as not to wake her parents.

Inside their room, Hollis locked the door. Then Nikki thought of something wonderful. "You get naked. I'll be right back."

She dashed out to the car, glad she'd forgotten to give Mariah the Madonna outfit. She scooped up the sack, along with the decoration supplies she'd used in the gym—the roll of duct tape, scissors and yardstick.

She changed clothes in the entryway so she could walk through the bedroom door and watch Hollis go crazy. She felt good—like the old Nikki, and she knew the old Nikki was what really turned Hollis on. She threw her cocktail dress in the sack, put the duct tape roll on her wrist and picked up the yardstick and scissors to throw them into the hall closet on her way to the room. She tiptoed down the hall.

"Nikki! You scared me to death!" Her mother stood in a long robe, her face pale with surprise. "I heard all that clunking and banging. Good lord…" She gave her a long look.

Nikki's face flamed. She looked like a member of the *Rocky Horror Picture Show* cast. Even worse, she was wielding a yardstick and a roll of tape. "This is just a joke, Mother. I—"

"Don't tell me." She started to put her hands over her ears, then stopped. "You don't, um, hurt each other, do you?"

"No. Of course not. This is just an outfit that Mariah—"

"Say no more." Her mother walked away, shaking her head in bewilderment.

Nikki hurried to the bedroom, slammed the bedroom door with her body, barely aware that Hollis lay naked and aroused on the opened-up sofa.

"Whoa," Hollis said. "You walked straight out of my fantasy."

"And into my mother's nightmare," she said. The encounter had blown her mood.

"God. Don't tell me. Nadine strikes again."

"Yeah. I was waving this—" she held up the ruler and the tape "—so now she thinks we're kinky."

"Mmm, sounds good." He smiled a slow, predatory smile, climbed out of the bed and came toward her. "Maybe I'm all wrong, though," he said, reaching her, "and you'll have to punish me, O, Mistress of the Night," he pulled her away from the door, "by making me fulfill your every desire."

She dropped the dress, the ruler and the duct tape.

The blaze of desire in Hollis's face—I want you. I'll have you—turned her to liquid want.

All games stopped. They were so hungry for each other, they shoved, dragged and kicked clothes off as fast as they could and fell into bed.

It felt so good to be naked together on a roomy bed. She couldn't believe how much she wanted this. Hollis felt the same, she could tell, and they were both trembling like crazy.

He looked at her with such amazement and worship, it was as if he'd never made love to a woman before. As they kissed, slow and sweet, and the heat built, she couldn't believe the aching sounds that came out of her mouth—muffled, though, so her mother wouldn't be any more scandalized.

He kept saying her name. She'd never heard it sound so beautiful. She felt all woman—innocent, sweet, sexy and raw all in one. All because of the way he touched her, the way her name sounded on his lips. The way his mouth found her—worshipful and aggressive, gentle and rough, changing just when she needed a new sensation.

Then he was easing inside her, gently, making sure it was okay. Lust must have burned away the effects of the alcohol because he was steady and sure. And soon they were rocking together, moving as one, as natural as breathing. The orgasm was a wave of joy she never wanted to end.

And when they'd stopped moving and were panting into each others' faces, Hollis's eyes were so filled with feeling that she knew what he was going to say before he said it. "I love you, Nikki."

"Me, too." And she knew it was true, though it made her uneasy to have said it out loud. She snuggled against his chest, damp with their shared sweat, and tried not to scare herself. *This is temporary. He's just infatuated.* She banished the thought. She would not ruin this moment.

"Give me a tattoo," Hollis said sleepily. "I want you to give me a tattoo." Without the adrenaline of sex, he sounded intoxicated again.

"What kind of tattoo?" she murmured, humoring him.

"You choose. Something symbolic... Whatever you think..."

"We'll see how you feel in the morning."

"Mmm." He was already half asleep.

Soon, his breathing slowed into sleep, but she was still awake enough for mischief to zip through her brain. She knew exactly what to do.

OH, MY GOD, Hollis thought the next morning. Furry animals had taken up residence in his head—running around in his mouth and building nests of cotton balls in his brain. The act of opening his eyes felt like tectonic plates shifting within the earth.

He'd been drunk. Very drunk. And he'd...had he? He sat up. There was Nikki in his bed. Yep, he had. Then he remembered it all. The fistfight—rather, roll in the dirt with Brian Collier—then crashing around in his car with Nikki trying to get naked. Nathan and Mariah cheering them on through the window. Nikki in that bustier...

What had happened to him? He had sudden empathy for Nikki's confusion. He was beginning to wonder what had become of rational, responsible Hollister Marx, D.D.S. He'd become a stranger who attacked women in cars and picked fights and suggested tattoos. Where had that come from?

Maybe he *was* having some kind of midlife crisis.

Then he looked at Nikki's sleeping face, softly snuggled into the pillow. So pretty, so tender. No, he wasn't having a life crisis. He was just in love.

He was filled with a rush of affection and lust so confusing, his aching head began to spin—and those squirrels started dashing around, some even barreling down to his stomach, and...uh, oh.

He was going to be sick. He pushed himself to his feet, the room seemed to dip, and he stumbled into the bathroom.

When he'd finished throwing up, he pushed himself up to the sink, where he rinsed out his mouth. He looked at himself in the mirror. He looked like a seasick sailor—gray-faced and grim, with dark circles under his eyes...and a tattoo on his chest.

A tattoo on his chest? He touched it. A heart with some Russian word—IKKIN... No, it was "Nikki" backwards in the mirror, inside a heart—a bright red goofy heart, with lace around the edges. "Nooo!" he said softly.

There was a flicker of movement behind him and he saw Nikki reflected in the mirror. She'd come to the door grinning, but now the grin emptied out, leaving her face sad.

NIKKI WOKE to a terrible sound. The love of her life was throwing up his guts. She rushed to the bathroom to hold his head. She loved him so much. She would help him with everything. She'd show him how to loosen up, help him pick out a motorcycle. Maybe he'd sell his practice and become the biology teacher he wanted to be.

But when she got to the bathroom, Hollis was staring at the joke tattoo, horror on his face. An icy feeling moved up her body. "Don't look so shocked,'' she said more harshly than she meant to. ''You told me to do it. Don't you like it?''

''Sure. It's nice,'' he said faintly, running his fingers over the surface of the heart.

''Oh, for heaven's sake, Hollis, relax. It's painted on. If I'd tattooed you, believe me, you'd know it. I'm good, but you'd never be able to sleep through a thousand needle pricks.''

''Oh, right.''

She avoided his attempt to kiss her by turning to grab her robe. She wasn't about to show him the matching ''Hollis'' she'd painted on the inside of her thigh.

''It was a shock, okay?'' he said, knowing he'd hurt her.

She was more that hurt. She was stunned, slapped in the face with reality. Last night, Hollis had been drunk and swept away by the whole reunion, old boyfriend dynamic.

Today was reality. He might not even really be in love with her. Maybe he didn't feel right about having sex unless there was love involved. He was an old-fashioned guy, after all.

Before she could voice any of these doubts, she heard someone shouting, ''I'm coming down the hall.'' Her mother—probably giving them time to undo the handcuffs. ''I'm at your door… I'm going to knock now.''

''Just a minute!'' she called back.

Hollis grabbed his pajama bottoms off the hook in the bathroom and yanked them on.

She went to the door. ''It's all right, Mother,'' she said, trying not to think about what she'd just realized. She opened the door.

''I wouldn't disturb you—believe me—but Warren's phone kept ringing..." Her mother extended the cell phone to Hollis, looking worried. "I put it on hold."

Wordlessly, Hollis accepted the device. "It must have fallen out of my jacket last night when we came in."

"Every ten minutes it started up again. Like on a timer. So I finally answered it. It's a woman," she said. "She called you Hollis? Your middle name?" Fingers of blush had moved up her mother's neck. "She says she's your *girlfriend*." Her voice cracked on the last word.

"Thanks," he said. "I'll take care of it." He was waiting for her to leave, but her mother just stood there.

"We'll be down in a minute," Nikki said, moving out of her stunned state to hold the door for her mother.

"Oh, certainly, sure. I'm sure it's a mistake?"

Nikki shut the door on her mother's questioning face.

Nikki and Hollis looked at each other in stunned silence for several heartbeats. "It's okay," he said to her softly. "She's calling to see when I'll be home today. And to find out what I've decided."

"What are you going to tell her?"

"The truth." He blew out a breath. "It would be better in person, but looks like now's the time. We have to start telling everyone the truth. I guess I'm first." He looked so grim and so unhappy her heart just sank.

He pushed the green button on the phone. "Hello, Rachel. Yes, I know. I'll be back tonight, but I need to tell you something now."

Nikki couldn't listen to this. She didn't want to

hear what he would say. She went into the bathroom and shut the door, sitting on the edge of the tub with her fingers in her ears. She felt terrible. Even though Hollis wasn't in love with the woman, it was Nikki's fault he was breaking up with her now. Hollis was such a great guy. How would Rachel ever get over him? Nikki ached with guilt and sympathy.

After a few minutes, Hollis opened the bathroom door.

She looked up and took her fingers out of her ears.

"I did it," he said, flushed. "I told her."

"Everything? You told her about us?"

"Yeah. She's upset. She yelled. Said I was undependable and irresponsible. She's angry that I didn't tell her about this trip. She's right about that. We'll talk more when I get back, but it's over. She agrees."

"Wow. You did it."

"Yeah. She's a good person. She said if I was going to act like a kid she's glad I didn't wait until we were engaged and humiliate her with her friends and family."

"That sounds pretty rational." Not at all like Nikki. Nikki would have gone crazy at having lost Hollis.

"That's Rachel. Practical to the core."

Like Hollis, Nikki couldn't help thinking. The real Hollis. Not the guy pretending to be her husband and asking for a tattoo he freaked about afterward.

He lifted her up from the edge of the bathtub. "Don't look so stricken. This is good. Now I'm free."

"Yes," she said. "You're free."

"It's like a weight is off me." He kissed her, but

she barely felt it. "Now, it's your turn. Let's go down and tell your parents the truth."

"My parents?" she repeated, holding back. She wasn't ready for that. "Don't you think that's a little much all at once? Can't we wait until we get home and see how things go?"

"Uh-uh, Nikki," he scolded. "Truth time." He took her by the elbow and led her to the door.

Truth time, huh? And what was the truth, she wondered as they clumped down the stairs—entirely too quickly, to her way of thinking. She loved Hollis. That was true. But did he love her? She wasn't so sure. He *wanted* to love her, she knew. Maybe because he didn't love Rachel and wanted out he thought this was love.

"I need to think about this, Hollis. I can't do this right now."

"Sure, you can. I'll support you every step of the way." He gave her a loving look, but there was resignation in it, too. *He was doing the right thing.*

She never wanted to be *the right thing* for the man she loved. This whole situation was make-believe for Hollis. He was in some zone of infatuation.

The real Hollister Marx didn't get drunk and pick fights and get tattoos. The real Hollister Marx wore those little starched dentist uniforms from the fifties and never raised his voice. The real Hollister Marx couldn't love her any more than her parents could understand her.

"I won't change, you know," she said, stopping halfway down the stairs. "I'm not Miss Copper Corners. I stay up all night just for the hell of it. I swim naked. My house is always a mess. I have kooky friends. I let musicians practice at my place all hours of the night. I owe back taxes."

"You owe back taxes?"

"Yeah. See what I mean? You don't even know me."

"Nikki, what are you trying to do? Talk me out of loving you? It doesn't work that way. Besides, you're not that bad."

"Yes, I am. I'm worse."

"You're scared to tell your parents. It'll be okay. They love you. They love me. They love us together. They'll love the real us, too. Come on." He pushed her forward.

And then they were at the ground floor. Her father and mother sat at the dining room table. Donna stood above her father, who was pale and frowning, deeply disappointed. Even Shelley and Byron looked at Hollis with accusing eyes.

"I can't," she whispered, but he'd stepped forward and was addressing her family.

"You're probably wondering who that was on the phone and what the call was all about," Hollis said, trying to sound hearty.

Silence.

"We'll explain it all. Nikki, why don't you start?" He squeezed her hand in encouragement.

But she couldn't speak.

"Nikki?" he asked again.

"Okay, you see, Hollis and I…" *Have been lying to you since we drove up a week ago.*

Her family looked at her expectantly, waiting for her to make it all right. *But now we're in love. Or at least I am. And this isn't Warren Langley, by the way. This is Hollister Marx. He's not a doctor, he's a dentist. And we just met. At my tattoo parlor. You see, I don't own a boutique. I'm a tattoo artist.*

She couldn't do it. Not now. Maybe not ever.

"Who was that woman?" Donna demanded. "And why did she say she was your girlfriend?"

"She *was* my girlfriend," Hollis started. "In fact, until I came on this trip…" He was going to tell the whole sordid story. She couldn't let him. Not when it could all crumble to nothing once they returned to Phoenix.

"She's been stalking him," Nikki blurted. "She's an old girlfriend who can't let go."

Hollis went stiff beside her. She glanced at him—he looked stunned.

"Stalking him?" Donna said. Her mother gasped.

"He changed his phone number," Nikki said, "but she knows a P.I. and somehow gets the new one every time."

"What's stalking?" Byron asked.

"Oh, well, that explains it," her mother said, breathless with relief. "Whew!" She caught herself. "I mean that's terrible. Would she hurt you?"

"Is it like at Christmas? Christmas stalking?"

Before Hollis could answer, Nikki jumped in. "She's harmless. She just calls him and talks to him like they're still together."

"So, get a restraining order," Donna said, sounding skeptical.

"We might," she said. She glanced at Hollis. His expression devastated her. For a second, she wanted to tell the truth just to erase that look of wounded disappointment. It was almost worse than how she'd imagined her father would react to knowing about her real life. "It's okay, really," she said. "We'll work it out."

"Well, I hope so," her mother said. "That's so stressful."

Everyone nodded sympathetically, but there was

definite awkwardness. The tension between her and the silent Hollis was thick as smoke.

"Can I help with breakfast?" she asked, "We'll be needing to get on the road fairly soon."

"You're not coming to the picnic?" her mother asked, startled.

"We need to be getting back, don't we, Warren?"

"Yes," he said. "We're done here."

"Sure…okay," her mother said, flustered and confused. "Let me take the frittatas out of the oven."

"Ow!" her father said and grabbed his chest.

"What is it, Daddy?" Nikki said, rushing to him. "Is it your heart?"

"My heart? God, no," he said. "I sampled some of the eggs. Onions tend to back up on me."

She ached at his bravery, but she couldn't stand it any more. "Please don't pretend with me," she said, dropping to her knees beside him. "It's too dangerous. You had a heart attack, Daddy. And I've been so scared.…" Her voice broke.

"Good lord, Nikki, I had hemorrhoids," he muttered. "Where did you get the idea I had a heart attack?"

"I don't know." She glared at Donna, who shrugged sheepishly. "Where *did* I get that idea?"

"You needed a reason to come down here," Donna said. Nikki wasn't the only Winfield who could make up a story when she needed to, she guessed.

Never mind. The important thing was that her father wasn't dying. "I'm so glad you're okay." She hugged him. Tears of relief filled her eyes, intensified by her distress about Hollis. "I was so scared we'd lose you."

"Of course not," he said, patting her. "I have too

many things to do before I die. I've got to see Shelley and Byron grow up. And your kids, too. When you have them.''

She felt so relieved she couldn't even be angry about the fact that Donna had tricked her to get her down here and she'd performed this elaborate masquerade, dragging Hollis along, over a simple case of hemorrhoids.

Hollis was grim all through breakfast. He answered questions, but each word fell flat on the air. It was clear everyone was just making conversation to ease the tension.

Nikki and Hollis packed silently and said goodbye to her family. At the door Shelley threw her arms around Hollis's knees, nearly tumbling him. ''Next time, we can act out fairy tales, okay?''

He squatted down to shake her hand with a sober look. ''It was a pleasure playing with you, Shelley. I suggest you let Byron choose the game now and then.''

''But he's a doofus,'' she whispered.

''Maybe. But he's a doofus who's around. And he'll get better if you help him.''

Shelley just looked at him like he'd lost his mind. Hollis, bless his heart, thought people could change.

Hollis thanked her parents for their hospitality. Nikki hugged everyone, promising to call and to return soon. They drove off, with everyone standing in the driveway waving. She watched them, barely able to see for the water in her eyes.

At the corner of Main Street and Cholla, a red Mustang came honking up behind them, Mariah waving frantically out the window.

Hollis braked, and Mariah jumped out and ran up to Nikki's side of the car.

"Where do you think you're going?" Mariah yelled.

"Home," she said softly. "We're skipping the picnic."

"That stinks," Mariah said. "I was thinking we'd start a water balloon fight, throw some cream pies, that kind of thing."

"It's time to go." Nikki fought tears.

"What's wrong? Did you two fight?" She looked past Nikki at Hollis, who was staring stonily ahead. That said it all. "Oh, no."

"I'll get your outfit dry-cleaned and send it to you," Nikki said, her voice wobbling.

"Don't give up so easy, girl," Mariah whispered.

"I'll call you when I get home."

Her friend studied her face, her expression full of love. "I didn't realize how much I missed you until you were here."

"Me, too," she said. Tears filled her eyes and pain filled her heart. "I'll call," she said.

Reluctantly, Mariah backed up and waved goodbye, and they drove off.

Nikki asked Hollis stop at the Circle K for some Tecate and cheese poofies, but she didn't have the heart to pull them out of the bag. So much for Road Trip Law.

Nikki glanced at Hollis's grim profile as he drove. A muscle in his cheek twitched. She felt sick inside. Coming to see her family had been the right thing to do, hadn't it? Even if her father wasn't even sick? At least now they knew she was okay.

She decided to try to lighten the tension between them. They could still see each other, couldn't they? "Don't be so glum, Hollis," she said. "It's not the end of the world."

Silence.

When they drove past the Cactus People, she remembered something that might help. She dug
around in her bag and pulled out the outback hat and
beret they'd picked out for each other. She slid her
beret on, then tried to put the hat on Hollis's head.

He pushed it off, but the wind caught it and it
tipped out the window and blew away.

He didn't even stop the car.

"Aren't you going to go back for the hat?" She
watched it bounce across the highway.

"What's the point?"

"I had to do it, Hollis. Don't you see? It's too
soon to dump all this on my parents. We have to see
how we feel about each other after we get back to
our real lives."

"I know how I feel," he said, looking straight
ahead.

"Don't be so sure. Let me remind you that ten
days ago you thought you loved Rachel Actually."

"Stop calling her that."

"Sorry. It's a habit. A bad one. Being sarcastic
when I'm hurt. I have lots of bad habits you don't
even know about. I bite my nails, I eat pork rinds in
bed. I watch TV on Mute while playing old Rolling
Stones albums full blast."

"We're not in high school, Nikki. Adults adjust to
each other's idiosyncrasies."

"Adults who are at least from the same planet,
maybe. But not us. You'd always be on my case. I'd
always be on yours."

"What are you afraid of?"

"I'm not afraid. I'm being honest."

"Bull. You had the chance to be honest back
there, and you wouldn't do it. You have someone

who loves you, who's willing to share his life with you...." He hesitated.

She jumped on it. "You're not so sure about being together, are you? Be honest."

"We have some things to work out, no question. I like a certain amount of calm in my life. We're different. But we love each other."

Her heart aching, Nikki knew she had to make things clear to him. "It's a fantasy, Hollis. Just like that picture I painted of our imaginary life together. Remember? You kissing me awake, omelets in the morning, making love on the kitchen table?"

"I remember."

"Well, here's how it would really be. First of all, you wake up to the alarm, exhausted because my friends and I kept you awake half the night. I have friends in a band and sometimes they hang out with me and jam until two in the morning."

"You're exaggerating."

"Not a bit. So, the manager would finally break us up at 2:00 a.m. I jump into bed ready for sex, but you need your sleep so you can do a root canal in the morning."

"I refer out most root canals."

"Whatever. The point is that now I'm mad at you and sexually frustrated on top of that. In the morning, you drag yourself out of bed, while I roll over to sleep longer. I don't open the shop until eleven. You need breakfast, but there's no food because I forgot to go to the store."

"Everybody forgets now and then."

"*Every* time? So, you can't have your oatmeal and o.j. and—"

"How'd you know I have oatmeal and orange juice for breakfast?"

"A hunch, Hollis. I'm good at that, remember? So, now you have to settle for leftover miso soup and some margarita mix for the vitamin C, but you're steaming."

She could see it now as clear as day, like a movie rolling on her orange screen. "So, after a long, long day of drill, fill and bill, you have to stop at the store because your lazy wife is so lame, but you decide to be positive. You pick up some nice steaks to fix for dinner, thinking you'll surprise me and we'd have a nice romantic evening. But when you get home at six-thirty, I'm not home and the place is a mess. I'm still at the tattoo shop, probably hanging with my friends—the ones you think are too unsavory to bring to our apartment. And when I do come home and the steaks are burned, I say, 'Forget it, I don't eat beef.'"

"Stop it, Nikki. You're trying to make this sound bad."

"I don't have to try. It *is* bad."

"Why did I ever think you'd be honest with your family? You can't even be honest with yourself."

That made her angry. Hollis was a self-righteous jerk. She'd known that the minute he walked into her shop and looked at her like she was some lowlife with dirty needles. She'd been so attracted to him, she'd ignored that fact. A rush of relief washed through her. Anger was much better than sadness.

"What's so almighty holy about how you approach the world? You claim to be into truth and honesty, but if I hadn't come along, you would have let Rachel Actually drag you into marriage when you weren't even in love with the woman."

"That's not fair."

"You bet it is. You didn't even want to be a dentist. You wanted to be a biology teacher, with summers off to ride around on a motorcycle.''

"It's not that simple."

"Oh, yes it is. The only difference between you and me is that you pretended you wanted what your parents wanted. At least I made the life I wanted. I'm not whining about what I gave up like you are."

"You're wrong."

"No, you're wrong."

There was a long pause. *Fight me. Stand up to me. Pull over and kiss me senseless.* But he didn't. Sensible, rational, reasonable Hollister Marx just gave up. "Maybe you're right," he said, and the fight went right out of him.

She didn't want him to know she was crying, so she pretended to be asleep, leaning her head against the door. She heard the gentle click as he pushed the button to lock the door, ensuring she wouldn't fall out.

She was right about Hollis, though. He was acting all free and easy now, but he'd turn back into a boring stick and then where would they be? Stuck with each other and miserable. She'd be too much for him. She'd overwhelm him. And he'd bore her senseless.

As they pulled up to True To You Tattoo, Nikki felt her heart lift with joy at seeing it—the ornate lettering on the window, the green plants showing through the glass. This was her place and her life. She was so glad to be back.

She did owe Hollis a lot, though. He'd allowed her to make her family happy. "I do appreciate your coming with me, and sticking with it even when it was tough," she said. "You'll find a woman who's right for you. Someone better for you than Rachel Actually. Someone better for you than me. But you have to go for what you want, Hollis, not just do the right thing all the time.''

"You're wrong, Nikki, but I can't fight you," he said.

For one bleak moment, she hoped he would, but he didn't, so she climbed out of his car and ran home where she belonged.

11

HOLLIS DROVE HOME feeling empty inside. Of all the times for Nikki to make sense. She *would* drive him crazy. She'd been right about that. Not because of her idiosyncrasies, though they would be annoying, but because she'd always be pushing him, wanting him to change. She'd want him to swim naked and other things he'd never done before or didn't want to do again. She thought he didn't approve of her. The truth was *she* didn't approve of *him.*

He didn't want to question his life. He just wanted to live it. Right now, he had a practice to build. He should concentrate on that, not have every bit of his heart, mind and soul tied up with Nikki and how impossible she could be.

SLEEP DID NOT COME to Nikki that night. She drank an entire pot of chamomile tea, throwing in some St. John's Wort for its calming effect, but it was no use. The bed felt empty, and her cozy home felt so hollow it seemed to echo.

She missed Hollis. She missed her family. She felt lost and uncomfortable in her own home. And it was all Hollis's fault. Sort of.

She should be happy. She'd done everything she set out to do. So why did she feel like she'd completely blown it?

Hollis again. Damn him.

At three in the morning, she realized she couldn't remember where she'd put Hollis's business card with his phone number on it. She tore out of bed and ran to the front of her shop to paw through the drawers near the phone. She finally found it—on the floor under her chair. *Dr. Hollister Marx, General Dentistry.*

She flipped over the card. There it was. His home and cell numbers. Like an "in case of emergency, break glass" firebox, she could reach him if she had to—if for no other reason than to remind herself why they could never be happy together. She woke up the next morning with the card stuck to her cheek.

Somehow, Nikki got through two weeks without calling Hollis. The one good thing about the breakup was that her creative urge went into overdrive. It became an outlet for her sadness and sexual frustration. She purchased a used sewing machine and began to design patches incorporating her tattoo designs—an alternative for people not quite ready for tattoos.

She created a new series of romantic tattoos featuring hearts and lace and fairy tales. Her favorite was the heart she'd designed for her and Hollis. Before it faded, she copied the one she'd put on her thigh—the mate to Hollis's.

Her tattoo work had never been better, and her psychic instincts seemed as keenly sharp as one of her needles. She focused intently on each tattoo, as if her life depended on it. Sometimes it seemed to. It was all she had.

She was at the drafting table late one afternoon two weeks after returning from Copper Corners when the door clanged. She jerked her head up, her heart pounding. Stupidly, she kept thinking Hollis would come back.

But the customer wasn't Hollis. It was his sister Leslie.

"Hey!" Nikki said, pushing up from the stool.

"What did you do to my brother?"

"Excuse me?" Had Hollis told his sister about the trip?

"When he came in here to talk to you about the tattoo that day," she said, walking closer. "What did you tell him? He's, like, a new man."

"Is that, um, better?"

"Tons. He says to me, 'Leslie,'" she lowered her voice in an imitation of Hollis's serious tone, "'I've realized your life is your own to live. You've got to be true to yourself.' It's like super weird. He got all wise. Like a priest or something."

"Amazing."

"I asked him what happened to him, and he said I should thank you. So, here I am. Thanks. Now what did you tell him?"

"I told him that your life was your own."

"Come on. It was more than that. Hollis is too stubborn to buy that."

"I can be very convincing." She did not want to tell Leslie what had really happened.

"Whatever it was, it worked. Kinda takes all the fun out of breaking the rules, though." Leslie sighed, then smiled. "No one picks up the pieces of whatever I drop anymore. It's good though. Kind of a relief. And you were right about a tattoo. I didn't need that."

"I'm glad I could help you," she said. At least this was something good that had come from the misadventure.

"Yeah. Now I wish you could help Hollis."

"Really?"

"Yeah. His girlfriend broke up with him—this really uptight control queen that I never liked anyway—and now he's moping around like his life is over. I didn't think he had it that bad for her."

"I'm sorry to hear that," she said, though it was some comfort to know Hollis was as sad as she was. "How about if you give Hollis a message for me?" she said, struggling to keep her voice steady.

"Okay."

"Tell him that he's not alone in his pain and that time will heal both of, um, the people involved."

"Okay." She shrugged, then grinned. She had an idea. "Hey. How about if you go out with him? He's cute, right? You could cheer him up, maybe show him there are other women in the world."

"I don't think so."

"He's not your type, I know. Not at first glance, but he might surprise you. When I went to his place he was playing loud oldies rock-and-roll and kind of dancing by himself with these Blues Brothers sunglasses on and a Crocodile Dundee hat. Weird, but kinda hot, too. At least he can dance."

"Thanks anyway, Leslie. I'm a little tied up emotionally right now. But do give him that message, okay? Maybe that will help."

"I guess." She shrugged.

Her private phone rang. "Excuse me," she said and answered, grateful for the reprieve.

"Nicolette, honey, it's your mother."

"Hi, Mom." She cleared her throat.

"I'm calling to let you know we'll be in Phoenix on Friday. Your father's seeing a specialist for a follow-up check on his little, um, problem, so we thought we'd stop by—see your house, maybe have supper with you and Warren."

"Oh, uh, well. Friday, you say?" She panicked.

"Yes. We'll see you about five, after the doctor's appointment. You'll have to give us your address and tell us how to get there."

"My address?" She used her P.O. box to communicate with her family. "Oh, uh." Address, address. She couldn't tell them to come here. Hollis's address popped into her mind. Four Three Two, Montgomery Place—the place they lived in that fantasy.

Could she convince Hollis to play her husband one more time? Give her parents that address? "Traffic is terrible at that time of day," she said finally. "How about we meet you at Vincent's for dinner?"

"Home-cooked would be fine, dear. Maybe you could bake us a pie, get some practice in."

"I insist." She gave them the directions and hung up the phone, in full panic.

"What's wrong?" Leslie asked.

"My parents. They want to come see me. They don't exactly know about my tattoo shop."

"What's the big deal?"

"You'd have to know my parents." Damn. She thought she'd gotten away with her happy white lie. Now, what? She could never tell Hollis. She wouldn't want to hear his lecture about integrity and honesty. She had to figure out something. Say Warren was out of town and they had to fumigate their apartment, maybe? She had three days to decide.

HOLLIS DROVE like a lunatic to Vincent's, fighting his analytical instincts all the way. He'd missed Nikki at the shop. Now he had to hope he'd make it in time. All he knew was that Nikki needed his help and he had to give it to her. Leslie had given him

Nikki's cryptic message about pain and time healing them, and he'd felt such an ache of longing that he knew he had to see her again. Even if it led to nothing more than another argument about how crazy they'd make each other.

Leslie had mentioned in passing that Nikki was meeting her parents for dinner at Vincent's on Friday. She hadn't called him, so that must mean she was going to tell them the truth. At least he hoped that was what it meant.

What if it was another lie?

No. She wouldn't do that again. He locked his jaw. He'd be there to support her, to take her into his arms and tell her that he loved her right in front of her parents.

He pulled into the parking lot and dashed inside. There they were—at the far end of the restaurant at a window table. No one was crying yet. Good. He could still help. He took a deep breath and headed their way.

"Hollis!" The word was out of her mouth before Nikki realized it. For a second, she thought she might have hallucinated the man out of pure longing. Leslie must have told him about her parents coming. He was here to help her, bless his heart. She jumped up to meet his hug.

He squeezed her so hard she could barely breathe and she never wanted him to let go. But she had to clue him in. "What are you doing here?" she asked, making up the story as she went. "Was your flight to San Francisco canceled?" She signaled him to go along.

His face just dropped. He'd looked so eager to see her. Now he looked dead. What, did he think she was going to tell her parents the truth? Now? When it was all over between them?

"Oh," he said so sadly her heart just broke. "I canceled my trip," he said. "I didn't see a need to...um, do what I was going to do...."

"Present your research on the spleen," she finished for him.

"Precisely," he said, hanging in there. "Hello, Nadine and Harvey," he said, shaking her father's hand and kissing her mother's cheek. "So nice to see you again."

Nikki wanted to cry. All she'd done since she'd sat at the table was make up stories and she was feeling so sick. Now here was Hollis, even as disappointed as he was, willing to pick up his lines for their little charade.

"Dad had to see a specialist in Phoenix, remember?" she said to Hollis so he knew why her parents were in town.

"And it's just one great pain in the you-know-what, let me tell you," her father said.

"Harvey, not over a meal, please," her mother said. "Nikki was just telling us how the water damage in your apartment has forced you into a hotel. That's so awful. It will be nice when you build your house so you can get away from thoughtless neighbors who leave their bathtubs running."

"Build our...?" He looked at Nikki for guidance.

Miserable about her storytelling and sinking deeper and deeper into the mire by the second, she didn't answer.

"You'll need something bigger soon, anyway," her mother continued, "for when the babies come."

"The babies?" he repeated faintly.

"Of course it's none of our business, but yo

know if there's a problem, they have wonderful fertility treatments these days, and—''

"Mother, please," Nikki said tightly. "We'll handle that on our own."

"Of course, dear." Her mother colored. "I just
mean…''

"I know what you mean." She had to get away,
if only for a moment, to collect herself, to calm
down, to cry a little. "I need to use the rest room."

"I'll come with you," Hollis said, jumping up. "I
have to make a call." He took her elbow. As soon
as they had rounded the corner out of sight of her
parents, they both spoke at once.

"I can't do this."

"You don't have to do this."

"Making up lies…." Hollis added.

"About babies and fertility treatments, I know. It's
too much. I understand completely. Believe me."

"I thought you were telling them the truth."

"I couldn't." She felt sick inside, confused and
sad. But there was also a growing anger. At her family for their expectations of her and herself for going
along with them. "I'll tell them you had to leave.
Thanks for trying to help me. You're a good man,
Hollis."

"You're a good woman, too. You just have to
realize it."

And then he was gone. She stood there watching
him. She could see her parents talking at the table,
looking worried. Again. But they loved her. They
wanted the best for her. They were concerned about
her. She had to keep that in mind. That was why
she'd done all this.

She returned slowly to the table, then slid into the

seat. "Holl—Warren got paged to an emergency," she said.

Her mother and father looked at each other, then at her. "It's all right, sweetheart," her mother said, patting her hand. "We know you're trying to be brave."

"What?"

"It's that woman, isn't it?" her mother said. "We knew something was wrong the morning he got that call. You don't need to cover for him anymore."

"I'd like to give him a piece of my mind for hurting my little girl," her father said gruffly. "Not to mention the drinking."

"You think Hollis is seeing another woman?"

"Honey, you don't need to pretend," her mother said.

"How could you think that?" she demanded.

"All that stalking business," he mother said. "Sounded pretty fishy to me."

"Your mother and I just want you to know that your happiness is all that matters to us," her father said. "We'll support you however you need us to. Testify in the divorce, if that helps you. And if you do decide to work things out—though I don't see how you could, there being infidelity and all—but if you do, why, we'll just stand by you. However, if he doesn't—"

"Stop it!" She pounded the table with both fists. She couldn't take this any more. "Enough."

"What's wrong, dear?"

"Everything. The man who just walked out that door is the best man I've ever known. Shame on you for doubting him. Worse, shame on me for giving you reason to."

She knew then that she had to tell the truth. Fo

Hollis. And for herself. She'd never stop her family from worrying about her, so they'd just have to love her the way she was. Or not.

"Let's order a bottle of wine," she said. "Maybe two. I have something to tell you."

"You do? Are you pregnant? You shouldn't have wine."

"No. I'm not pregnant, Mother. I'm not a lot of things you think I am."

HER PARENTS WERE SHOCKED, then angry, then hurt, then worried. It was just as she'd always dreaded. But, strangely enough, it was okay. Every word of truth about herself she shared with them made her feel more solidly grounded. This was who she was. She was happy this way. They had to accept that and share her happiness wherever she found it. If she'd ever find it without Hollis. But maybe now they had a chance. If Hollis still wanted to work things out.

Her parents drove off, pale and uncertain, headed for home. She refused to feel guilty. She'd call later and reassure them further, but the worst was over. She'd done the right thing. Hollis had a point about that. Sometimes the right thing *was* the right thing to do.

Back at her place, she went straight for the phone to call Hollis and tell him what she'd done. He wasn't home. She didn't leave a message, wanting to tell him in person. She couldn't wait to see how proud he'd be of her. And if maybe, just maybe, he wanted to try again.

She'd just hung up when she heard pounding on the shop door. It was after-hours, but she headed for the door. In the dim light, she made out a man in a leather jacket, a motorcycle helmet under his arm. A biker wanting to prove his manhood with a tattoo, probably something involving a skull.

Then the man lifted his face into the light and she saw it was no biker. It was Hollis.

She threw open the door. "What are you doing here?" She felt abruptly shy.

"I came to take you for a ride on my new motorcycle."

"You bought a bike?"

"Yep. Right after I left the restaurant. You were right about me. I have been going by the book, doing what I *should* do, whether that was what I really wanted or not. I've decided that if I don't like my practice, I'll go back to the clinic or be a biology teacher."

"That's great, Hollis. I'm glad to hear that you're doing what you truly want." She paused, trying to read on his face how he felt about her. "You were right about me, too. They thought you were seeing another woman. It was so terrible and so wrong. I couldn't stand the fact that I'd let them suspect you of that, when you're the best man I know." Tears came into her eyes and she could barely speak. "I had to tell them the truth about you. And I realized it was time they knew the real me. They have to love me the way I am."

"That's the way I love you, Nikki."

"You do?" Hope rose inside her.

"I can't live without you."

Her heart surged with joy at his words, and then dropped to her stomach with doubt. "But I'm afraid I'll overwhelm you. I'm scared I'll be too much for you."

"Me, too," he said, laughing softly. "But it doesn't matter. We'll work it out. I love you just the way you are—with weird hair and scary musician friends and a pathological inability to remember groceries.''

''But I can be so intense....''

''Bring it on. Maybe you'll be too much, maybe you'll overwhelm me, but that's what I need. You keep me alive. You keep me honest—doing what I want—which is to love you for the rest of my life.''

And she believed him with all her heart. Maybe because for the first time in her life she believed in herself. ''Oh, Hollis.'' She threw her arms around him and held on tight.

Hollis squeezed back, the leather of his coat squeaking. ''Except we have to do something about your back taxes.''

''I don't owe taxes. I lied to scare you off. And I like oatmeal and orange juice for breakfast, too,'' she said. ''And I promise not to laugh about the *Wall Street Journal* and—''

''Wait,'' he said, releasing her. ''There's one other thing I want—besides you forever and ever. A tattoo.''

''A tattoo? Hollis, you're not the type. I don't think—''

''Now, now. If you didn't love me, you could read my aura and then you'd know this is right.'' He reached into his pocket and pulled out a piece of paper. On it was a decent sketch of the heart she'd painted on his chest, only it held both their names.

''Hollis! You sweet man. This isn't half bad.''

''I was thinking a tattoo for two?''

Her heart swelled with love and joy. ''Perfect,'' she whispered.

''And I'm thinking Grand Canyon for the ceremony,'' he said, ''since we are a wonder of nature.''

And when she kissed him she was already making up her wedding vow to love him forever, for richer or poorer, for uptight or open, serious or silly, with Dockers or without. He was her Hollis and she was his Nikki. And they loved each other just the way they were.

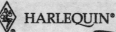

HARLEQUIN® *Blaze*™

From: **Erin Thatcher**
To: **Samantha Tyler;**
           Tess Norton
Subject: **Men To Do**

Ladies, I'm talking about a hot fling with
the type of man no girl in her right mind
would settle down with. You know, a man to
do before we say "I do." What do you think?
Couldn't we use an uncomplicated sexfest?
Why let men corner the market on fun when
we girls have the same urges and needs?
I've already picked mine out….

Don't miss the steamy new Men To Do miniseries
from bestselling Blaze authors!

THE SWEETEST TABOO by Alison Kent
December 2002

A DASH OF TEMPTATION by Jo Leigh
January 2003

A TASTE OF FANTASY by Isabel Sharpe
February 2003

Available wherever Harlequin books are sold.

HARLEQUIN®
Makes any time special ®

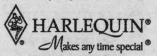

**When Suzanne, Nicole and Taylor vow to stay
single, they don't count on meeting these sexy
bachelors!**

ROUGHING IT WITH RYAN
January 2003

TANGLING WITH TY
February 2003

MESSING WITH MAC
March 2003

Don't miss this sexy new miniseries by Jill Shalvis–
one of Temptation's hottest authors!

Available at your favorite retail outlet.

HTS

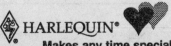

There's something for everyone...

Behind the
Red Doors

From favorite authors

Vicki Lewis Thompson

Stephanie Bond

Leslie Kelly

A fun and sexy collection about the romantic encounters
that take place at The Red Doors lingerie shop.

**Behind the Red Doors—
you'll never guess which one leads to love...**

Look for it in January 2003.

HARLEQUIN®
Makes any time special®